The Wrong Briefcase

Ian Cummins

Prologue - The Tale of Peter the Carpenter

Peter was a carpenter. A very good carpenter. Skilled at his craft, diligent in its execution and proud of the results he produced, Peter worked his whole life for the local builder in the small town where he lived. Often, the working days were long, and there were many of them. Sometimes the tasks were small and routine – repairs and additions to people's houses, replacing windows and doors that were broken or worn out, or adding shelves and such. Sometimes he worked on bigger projects, such as the building of a whole house, where not only windows and doors had to be crafted, but beams, skirting boards, cupboards, shelves, picture rails. These jobs would often take many months. Much of the furniture which would be placed in a new house was the result of many hours of the application of his skills.

And such was the quality of the items he made that they would last as long as the house, and often last longer than its occupants. Peter would always make whatever he was making as well as it could be made. Often, he would work past his supposed finishing time, just to ensure that the task of the day was completed properly.

He was well respected by the local townspeople and very well regarded by his employer.

As his life progressed and his family grew and spread, Peter found himself looking forward more and more to his retirement. As might be expected of such a skilled and careful man, he had made sure to regularly save a little money and deposit it in the bank, so that when retirement came, he and his wife would have a little extra above their pension. Whilst never aspiring to luxury, they could live in comfort, sharing simple pleasures and all the time in the world.

As retirement day moved closer, he anticipated that there would be a small party on his last day, and – as he had seen for fellow workers who had retired before him – a small presentation of some suitable gift. Maybe a clock or some decorative item for his home. So, when the owner of the

3

building company called him into his office one Monday morning, Peter expected this to be the subject of their conversation. But to his disappointment, his boss told him that he had to ask for a favour. He needed to build a house for a very special customer in the town. Not a big house, but it needed to be finished as soon as possible. He wanted to have it built by his best men, and he wanted Peter to work on the house – even though he would need to postpone his retirement by three months.

The house was to be built to the highest possible standard. Each bedroom was to be fitted with wardrobes; the kitchen was to be fitted with storage cupboards and equipped with modern appliances. In the living room, the alcoves to each side of the fireplace were to house wooden shelves for the storage of books or the display of ornaments and nick-nacks. Every window in the building was to have a curtain rail fitted, and suitable curtains were to be hung. A handrail would be fixed to the wall on one side of the staircase and a banister on the other. The finest materials were to be used throughout, and the bedrooms, halls, stairs, and living room were all to be carpeted.

Peter could choose whether he worked just the normal working week or worked weekends in addition so that the job would be completed all the sooner, in which case he would be paid the appropriate full overtime rates.

Of course, he agreed to his boss's request and began work on the house the next week. But he could not hide his disappointment, nor could he avoid it turning into resentment. For the first time in his life, he set lower standards for himself. If the window didn't quite fit and there was a small draught – what the hell. If the skirting boards didn't form a neat right angle in the corner – who cared? And if the shelves were not quite level – surely nobody would notice. The house would be finished on time for his boss's precious customer, and Peter could make a belated start to his retirement.

True enough, the house was finished within the three-month deadline, and Peter's retirement party was planned and announced. A huge crowd gathered, and his boss, as expected, asked for everyone to be quiet when he came to say farewell to Peter and to give him his retirement gift. He also promised another announcement – the name of the special customer for the new house – the mystery which had been a source of much speculation in the town for the last three months.

Having spoken of Peter's long, loyal, and skilful service, his boss went on to say that such a lifetime of dedication deserved a special retirement gift – and that accordingly, he would be receiving a gift that no other worker had ever received. The owner of the new house which they had just completed would be none other than Peter himself!

His boss thought that Peter would love the comfort of this brand-new house which had been built with all the latest features – and that he could sell his own house and have more money to live in greater comfort for his remaining years.

Peter was overcome. This was a total and utter surprise for him, and he was both surprised by, and very grateful for, his boss's generous gesture.

But he knew that his final years would be lived in a house where some of the windows had draughts; where some of the doors did not quite fit properly; where the corners of skirting boards and picture rails were not quite perfect right angles; and where some of the shelves were not completely level. His punishment for his sloppy application in the last three months of his working life would stay with him forevermore.

The moral of the story is that we all live in a world that we have helped to build. While very few of us have built the physical surroundings we live in, we have all contributed to the building of the situation of our life and the relationships which form such an important part of that life.

We need to remember this throughout our life, as we build those relationships. We should never cut corners, set low standards for ourselves, or include faulty materials in what we build. The only people who will suffer from faulty workmanship in this important area of the life we fashion is ourselves.

The Opening
April 2005

Mark turned the key in the front door, pushed it open and entered his house. Stepping over the few letters lying on the floor, he entered the kitchen and laid the briefcase carefully on the small table.

The kitchen could have been a display unit in the local showroom – where it would have been labelled as 'Compact'. In other words, it was small. The worksurfaces were almost empty. Only an electric kettle, a bread bin and a microwave cooker were permanently kept on show. And the room had no smell of cooking. Both Mark and Charlotte worked full time, and neither was a dab hand at the culinary arts, so their evening fare was usually either a takeaway or a ping meal – so-called since it was a meal that they unwrapped, placed in the microwave, set the controls, and waited until the 'ping'.

Mark decided his first job was to perform a sanity check. He went into the dining room, fetched his briefcase, and placed it on the kitchen table next to the one he had just put there. They were identical. Mark was reassured that although he had made a stupid mistake, he was not completely mad. He had picked up a briefcase that was identical to his own. Much heavier – but identical. A large briefcase, dark grey, made of moulded plastic with a dimpled finish and a robust look and feel. The handle was a lighter shade of heavy-duty plastic, and on each side, the clasps were protected by a three-digit lock.

Returning his briefcase to the dining room, he stopped in the hall and picked up the letters, two for him two for Charlotte, none of them looking important. He would read his later. Charlotte was in Newcastle for the half-term break visiting her mother, so her letters would have to wait for a few days.

He put them on the work surface and turned on the light. Even though it was only late afternoon, it was already getting dark in the kitchen. With only a small window, it was always a little gloomy, which was why they had chosen light pine for the cupboard doors and pale grey stone for the work surfaces when it was fitted a couple of years ago. The small round table and two chairs were in matching light pine.

Mark removed his jacket and hung it over the back of the chair, loosened his tie, and took a can of beer out of the fridge. This was unusual behaviour – normally when he got home, he would immediately go up to the bedroom, remove his suit and tie, place them on hangers and change into jeans and a sweater. Less time spent wearing the suit meant it would look that bit better when next worn, and Mark always tried to look his best. He was blessed with genes that allowed him to stay thin, no matter what he ate - and making the best of his appearance had always been important. But those same genes that kept his body thin were also responsible for his hair being thinner than it should be for a man not yet in his forties. There were occasional grey hairs amidst the light brown and his hairline was just beginning to recede. Or as Mark would put it, one part of his body was still growing – his forehead.

The envelopes, briefcase, and jacket, plus Mark and his can of beer made the kitchen look distinctly untidy.

Untidiness normally bothered Mark but now he had more important matters on his mind. He opened the can, took a swig, and examined the briefcase. The combination had been set, as neither clasp button would move when pressed, and there was absolutely no way to identify its rightful owner.

It certainly was not empty. It was even heavier than Mark's case had been when he'd carried all those papers to the meeting the previous day. He somehow felt that this briefcase also had paper in it. It just somehow felt like it.

"Well, Reynolds, we're going to have to eat that frog," he said aloud.

Mark had recently read a book on time management with the title: Eat That Frog. It was one of those self-help books that takes a simple idea, puts a new spin on it, and spreads it out over two hundred pages. Each chapter starting with an introduction that tells you what you are going to learn in this chapter and ending with a summary that tells you what you have learned in this chapter. In 'Eat That Frog', the message was that if you had a difficult task to complete - a frog to eat - and a deadline for its completion, then the best strategy is to tackle the task (eat the frog) as soon as possible. So much better than spending the whole day dreading and being distracted by the task hanging over your head.

7

The particular frog he had to eat was to discover the combination of the briefcase. After that, he could hopefully find the owner and start the process of explaining why it was sitting in Mark's kitchen and working out how owner and briefcase could be reunited as soon as possible.

He used his mobile phone to take a photo of the combination as it was currently set. 763 on the left and 829 on the right. This might not be important, but he would take every precaution, just in case.

He set the left lock to 000 and pressed the catch. No movement. He turned the dial to 001, pressed the catch again, and began to build up a rhythm.

The first part of the frog was eaten in less than five minutes. 260 turned out to be the magic number, and the left-hand clasp was released. But it offered no additional clue to the contents of the case nor any assistance in the identification of its owner. Mark took another swig of the beer, flexed and rubbed his slightly cramped fingers, and adjusted his chair so he was now in line with the right-hand clasp. He turned the dial to 000 and pressed the catch. No movement. 001. His pulse rate increased slightly, and he grew ever closer to the edge of his seat as he progressed, digit by careful digit.

He was not so lucky the second time around. Dusk was beginning to fall when 730 was reached and the right-hand clasp opened. Mark took one last swig of the beer and lifted the lid.

He let out a loud expletive. The briefcase certainly did contain paper, just as he had suspected. Underneath two sheets of plastic bubble wrap were lots of pieces of paper, each about fifteen centimetres by eight centimetres, printed mostly in red ink with a picture of Queen Elizabeth and the numbers five and zero. A helluva lot of money in fifty-pound notes. Not in flat piles like you see in every good heist film, the notes were stacked on edge in three columns from the front of the case to the back. With the briefcase flat on the table, it was like the world's most beautiful card index system. Three columns of fifties. The small space that was left at the side was packed with rolls of twenty-pound notes. 'Now there's a novel way of safely packing your parcel contents,' thought Mark. 'Don't use environmentally unfriendly bubble-wrap or polystyrene, go for bundles of recyclable twenty-pound notes.'

There was nothing to give any clue to the owner of the case. The filing separators that could be clipped into the top section of the case (as they were in Mark's) had been removed, and there was nothing other than the money inside. Just to make sure, Mark took out a chunk of the money and gradually moved the rest around until he had looked at every square inch of the floor of the briefcase. Nothing.

When confronted with a shock - and the discovery of such a huge amount of money on your kitchen table certainly qualified as a shock - the human mind tends to do one of two things. It either goes into stasis and is incapable of thought – or it races immediately in several different directions. Mark's mind fell into the second category. The first of these many thoughts was 'What am I going to do with all this money?'

It was worth noting that Mark's first thought had not been 'I wonder who owns all this money,' nor had it been 'How the hell am I going to get this money back to whoever owns it?' Although these thoughts were amongst the myriad of thoughts that followed his initial reaction – that important first thought had been 'What am I going to do with it?' And if having that thought implied that he had already assumed some ownership of the money, so be it.

Considering the matter of handing it back, he assumed the money was probably "hot" in some way or other. Whilst it is not unknown for people to collect quantities of cash under the mattress for all types of reasons, he thought this was highly unlikely to explain the origins of so large a sum. It was much more likely that this amount of money had to be the result of illicit activities, probably drug-related he guessed.

How to return it? And where? And to whom?

Should he go to the police? He considered this briefly but decided the idea was a definite non-starter. He just knew that the original owner would be very unlikely to want the forces of law and order to be involved in tracing its ownership, and Mark was concerned that some element of the 'dirt' that surely had to be attached to the money would metaphorically rub off on him. His background and upbringing had certainly given him due respect for authority and the rule of law. But it also bred in him a belief that you avoided all unnecessary involvement with the boys in blue if you possibly could.

What the hell could he do with it? He could lock the briefcase and take it to wherever you were supposed to take items that were lost and found in a taxi. This might be the same place as stuff lost on London Transport buses and trains – he could certainly find out. But then what would the receiving person do?

"Can you tell us what's in it, sir? Oh, hundreds of thousands of pounds, you say. I'll just make a note of that." Not going to happen. There would be security implications after all. They would open it. And if he did go to a lost property office he would certainly be caught on CCTV and would either need to give his full name and address or arouse immediate suspicion by giving false details.

Could he post something on the internet detailing where it had been found? Then thousands of people would know – and his anonymity would not last the week. Bad idea. There seemed to be no safe way of giving it back. Maybe take out an advert in a newspaper? It might have been easier if he had found it locally – a local paper would give a much better chance of tracing its true owner – but it had been in a taxi in the middle of London. The owner could have come from anywhere on the planet. How about an advert in the classified section of the Times? Would the owner read that paper? And does the Sun even have a classified advertisement section?

Interspersed with these thoughts, questions were forming in his mind about how you go about spending such a large sum. You could not just put it in the bank, he was sure of that. He seemed to remember that the banks carried out checks on any amount over ten thousand pounds. And who is to say that the bank teller who processed the transaction would not say something to his mates, or even worse, chatter about it online. And then there was the Inland Revenue. Would they get involved?

Maybe you could open two or three accounts and put ten grand in each without causing too many ripples. And then you could use some of it to pay your regular bills. Filling up the car, eating out more often, paying for hotel bills on his business trips, and the weekly supermarket shop. That would use up a few hundred every month. But that way would take forever to spend it.

He thought of a TV programme that he had seen recently where some people had gone into a casino and used forged notes to buy betting chips and then cashed them in to get real money. No, that would not help him – he needed to convert cash into a bank balance. What about buying some stuff at auction and then selling it on eBay? Yes, that would work, but that would take a helluva long time to move the amount that was sitting in front of him.

His thoughts were not entirely selfish. He would give some of the money to the good causes he believed in. Whenever he went shopping with Charlotte, he always bought one of the largest items in the food section of the supermarket – a mega box of cereal, a giant bag of pasta or a multi-pack of tins of baked beans, whatever – and then put it in the collection box for the foodbank, hoping that by being more visible in his actions he might remind others to do likewise. He strongly believed that in a country that was as economically successful as Britain, it was a national disgrace that foodbanks still existed halfway through the first decade of the twenty-first century. But if he were to donate cash to a good cause, he would have to be careful. Someone out there was missing this money and a news story of a charity suddenly receiving a huge donation would be just the sort of story they would be looking for.

Thinking of the supermarket made him realise another problem. What to tell Charlotte? She would certainly not be happy, and she would need some heavy persuasion for them to keep it, even though she would benefit considerably. He still remembered the huge row they had when he opened a bank account in the USA during one of their Florida holidays. She had not accepted his explanation that he had only done it to make it easier for them to withdraw cash on their future holidays – she had seen through him immediately and forced him to admit that he had really done it to help 'minimise his tax exposure'. She was sure (probably correctly) that it was not entirely legal. And being not entirely legal was, as she had so succinctly put it, a lot like being slightly pregnant.

He would have to give this some thought. She would not be back for a few days, so he postponed that part of his problem for the time being.

Without taking any decisions, Mark determined there were a few actions that needed to be taken immediately. Find out exactly how much was in the briefcase, make sure the money was genuine, and find somewhere safe to put it until he decided what to do with it. That would be as far as he would go tonight.

He opened the right-hand drawer of the kitchen units - the drawer that exists in every household, crammed full of batteries, pens, spare phone chargers, keys, curtain hooks and a hundred and one other items, thankfully including what he was looking for – a measuring tape.

He measured a four-centimetre wedge of money and counted it. The money certainly looked and felt real. There was no sign of any duplicate serial numbers. He counted two hundred and twenty notes.

The briefcase had three columns of notes and measured thirty-six centimetres from front to back.

Mark was reasonably confident of his mental arithmetic but checked his figures several times to make sure. One hundred and eight centimetres of money was roughly six thousand notes, or in more important terms, the content of the case was damned close to three hundred thousand pounds.

He got up, threw the empty beer can into the waste bin, went into the dining room, took a large envelope from the filing cabinet, and returned to the kitchen.

He counted out a thousand pounds and put it into the envelope, took it upstairs and put it into his bedside drawer. This would be his test sample. He would spend it in a few different places to make sure that it was genuine. And spend it immediately so that if there was any trace on the numbers or anything like that then they (whoever 'they' were) would be in contact with him before too much of it was gone. And he would keep it out of sight of anyone, including Charlotte, at least until he had formed a plan as to what to do about his problem – or what to do with his newfound wealth.

He returned to the kitchen, closed the briefcase, photographed the new lock settings, and reset the combinations to the original ones. Then he carried the briefcase upstairs, pulled down the loft ladder and deposited it in the loft.

He would now celebrate with another beer and a Domino's pizza - and think long and hard about what his next actions would be.

Harry Lavinsky

April 2005

James Lavinsky was furious. Seething. Livid. He would not want to be described as mad – not out of any misplaced feelings of political correctness for use of an unacceptable term, but because that word would imply some form of active rage. His anger was the quiet type. The type that is brought on by a close friend or relative - in this case, his father - doing something so unutterably stupid that it could never have been predicted. Steps could have been taken to prevent it. Steps that he, himself had recommended but his father had brushed aside. And now he would have to try and resolve the problem and deal with the consequences.

James and his father, Harry, had met as agreed, at noon in Solly's office. The venue had been chosen out of necessity for what needed to be done, and the time had been chosen for the convenience of a pleasant lunch together at the end of the meeting, which should have taken less than an hour.

When James arrived, it was immediately obvious that something was wrong with his father. Despite his advanced age, Harry had always been robust, even appearing young for his age. When James entered the reception area, he found him slumped in a chair, ashen grey and muttering quietly.

"I've lost it", he repeated several times. Whether this remark was directed to himself, to James or anyone else, it was hard to determine, but the meeting would obviously have to be postponed, so James apologised to Solly and took his dad outside into a taxi to start the journey home.

Harry was not ready to talk, so their taxi ride to London Bridge Station was silent. Once there, James steered them to a café and ordered a flat white for himself and a strong cup of tea for his father. Only after a few mouthfuls of the strong tea was he finally able to tell his son that he had lost his briefcase, containing the money he had brought to Solly's office. The money that was the whole reason for the meeting.

Harry Lavinsky would best be described as a rogue. Perhaps even a loveable old rogue. Not a gangster, nor, at least in his own eyes, even a criminal. But he would accept the label of rogue.

He'd grown up in the war-ravaged area of southeast London around the Old Kent Road, spending the duration of the war there because his parents never got around to having him evacuated. School was very intermittent during the war years, and afterwards, as a young teenager (even though the term had not yet been invented) in the aftermath of the war, any hope of a proper education was a case of too little too late. So, instead, he began to help his father re-establish his tailoring and haberdashery business after his demobilisation. There was no shortage of people wanting new things to wear, but there were plenty of shortages of both materials with which to make them - and money to pay for them.

Having spent the previous five years running errands and making small deliveries for the street entrepreneurs of southeast London, Harry used the information and contacts he had gathered to find his father some bits and pieces of material. Harry's one blot on his copybook had occurred when he sourced some materials in all too direct a manner, which resulted in him spending a year in a Borstal young offenders centre. This taught him an important lesson and he vowed never again to spend any time behind bars – making sure throughout the rest of his life that if something was to go wrong, he would not be the one left holding the baby (or the barrow load of stolen cloth).

Unlike his father, Harry had no special skill, and didn't have any great wish to acquire any – but was not afraid of hard work. His father was unable to provide enough work to fill all the hours in a day and certainly could not pay him anything like a proper wage - even the lowly rate for a young apprentice. So, he found work at the local pub – collecting empties, washing glasses, emptying ashtrays and sweeping floors – whatever was going to get him a few bob. Big for his age, he was serving behind the bar well before his eighteenth birthday. But even with the hours he was putting in, he still had time to spare and plenty of restless energy unused.

One evening he realised that some of the customers from the saloon bar of the pub were moving on at closing time to continue their drinking elsewhere. These were people willing to pay an extra penny on each drink to enjoy it in a separate bar of the public house, with more comfortable seats and a threadbare carpet on the floor instead of sawdust. They were the nearest that he would know as rich or posh people for a long time yet to come, and he realised that his best chance of making money would come from people like this – not from the customers who did not have enough money to rub two ha'pennies together.

One night after the pub closed, Harry discretely followed them to a local club, anonymously located behind a door between two shops on the Old Kent Road. He hung around for an hour but did not see anyone emerge. He reckoned that there must be some money being spent somehow behind this door and decided to return the following day to see if they needed any work done.

Before starting his evening shift at the pub the next day, he retraced his steps of the previous night, knocked at the anonymous door, and was allowed in. The drinking club was owned by Wally Goodman, a local entrepreneur who had reached the age when he wanted to spend his hours in front of the bar talking to his friends and customers, rather than behind it serving them drinks and smokes. So, the possibility of hiring a young man who had experience in serving drinks and seemed to be smart (in every sense of the word), polite, enthusiastic, and best of all, cheap, appealed strongly to Wally, so he offered him a job. Harry quit the pub that night and started full-time work at the club the following day.

His world suddenly had new horizons. Not only were the customers at the club occasionally kind enough to give him a tip – especially if he ferried their drinks to one of the tables in the back room where card games for varying sums of money took place almost every night – but also as his familiarity with the clientele grew, he found other ways to increase the amount of money he took home.

He noticed that some of the 'ladies' who entered the club would often make their drinks last a very long time and would refuse more than one offer of a refill from gentlemen customers – irrespective of whether they were in that gentleman's company for many minutes or just a few. So, one by one, he informed them that there was a bottle of gin at the far end of the bar that contained ninety per cent water and ten per cent gin – for the flavour and smell – and if their companions offered to buy them a drink, he would make sure they were served from this bottle, charge their companion for a full measure of gin, and split the profit with them.

This proved to be very popular. On the occasions when they did not leave the bar in the company of a gentleman, they did not have to leave empty-handed - and when they did leave with a gentleman, they sometimes were not able to collect their share immediately from Harry, and perhaps even forgot all about it. All the more for Harry!

Over the next few years, Wally spent less and less time running the club, handing over more responsibility to his young apprentice. And, most important of all, Harry was also very popular with Wally's wife, Beryl. He was wise enough to know that the real power in a marriage often did not rest in the obvious place, and, despite Beryl not knowing everything that went on at the club, she was nonetheless very influential in every decision Wally made. Harry often joined the two of them for a late lunch on Sunday (one of the few times when the club followed the national licensing laws and closed at 2 pm) and in many ways, became the son that they never had.

Harry noticed some of the many changes that were occurring in peacetime. One that was significant for the club was that police were beginning to crack down on places that allowed unlicensed gambling. The law in this area was somewhat unclear and they were taking a direct approach in stopping any and every occurrence of gambling that they found. He suggested to Wally that the games in his backroom should no longer have money on the table. He should make his customers buy tokens (or chips they were called in the American movies) and use them for all betting. Not only would this make it more difficult for anyone of an official nature to walk into the club and immediately see that gambling was taking place – there being no cash on the table - but it would also enable Wally to charge a 10% premium for the chips. Wally jumped at the chance of this extra income, bought some chips, and gave Harry a pay rise.

Eventually, Wally's love of drink and cigars, and his sedentary lifestyle caught up with him, and, after a few weeks of nursing him at home and a few days of visiting him in hospital, Beryl (and Harry) said their last farewells to him.

Harry allowed Beryl to pass a few weeks of mourning – making sure to visit her once a week and deliver the takings from the business (or to be more precise, half the takings - since this is what he knew Wally had delivered to her over the years) before discussing the future with her. Then over the Sunday lunch that they still shared, he broached the subject

16

of the ownership of the business. He obviously did not have the money to buy it but suggested that if she transferred the business to him, he would continue to deliver the same amount of money that she currently received every week for the rest of her life, and she wouldn't even have to lift finger for it. As he expected, this suited her just fine and, at his insistence, she got the family solicitor to draw up a document that legalised it.

He knew that she never visited the club and felt free to start running the place as his own as soon as the ink was dry on the agreement. He was careful not to make too many changes to the business immediately - it was a place where people came because it was comfortable. Change was uncomfortable and had to be slow and stealthy. But he did start a few new ways of generating a little more cash. He had no objection to the ladies making their living from their assignations at his club (he loved thinking of it as his club) but made sure that they now paid a small entrance fee for any evening they attended 'on business'. He also made sure that his regular customers knew that they did not need to come into the club if they wanted the company of one of the ladies for the evening – they had only to give him a call and he would make the necessary arrangements – for a small fee, of course.

And he wanted to take advantage of the new craze of 'buy now pay later' that was beginning to sweep the country. So, he let all his customers know that if anyone found that a Friday night game of cards at his club left them unable to make their wage packet stretch to the next payday, they need only to ask, and an advance could be arranged – with a 10% charge being added for the week's delay in repayment, of course.

A business study would probably describe his other change as diversifying his sources of supply. Once in a while, he would buy a crate of scotch, or a couple of thousand cigarettes from a different supplier – one that wasn't listed in any directory – not knowing, asking or caring where they had come from and enjoying the significantly reduced price at which they were offered. Not every week – and not repeatedly from the same person. Not often enough to be called a regular buyer – just often enough to have a healthy impact on his business's bottom line.

Harry also made an important hiring decision.

Ivan provided 'security' to the club and Harry appreciated his importance to the business and had given him a pay rise as soon as he had taken over from Wally to help further cement his loyalty. He was pretty sure that his name was not actually Ivan – and that he probably was not Russian (which is where the nickname had come from) but he was large, quiet and reliable. His presence was enough to act as an encouragement to certain types of desirable behaviour, and a deterrent to other types of undesirable behaviour by customers. But Ivan was not getting any younger, and Harry knew that some of his expansion plans might create additional needs for security resources. He decided to have a quiet chat with Ivan one midweek evening.

Happily, Ivan realised that he was not as fit as he once was and welcomed the chance to share the load. He asked if his son, Dmitri, could be considered for the position. He brought Dmitri in the next day, and as soon as they met, Harry had no hesitation in adding him to the payroll. Dmitri was tall, well-muscled, and fit. Quiet, just like his father, Harry was sure that Dmitri would carry just the right amount of polished menace in any difficult situation.

Over time, and in response to customer demand, he extended his financial dealings to offer longer-term loans – never more than a year in duration - and with the assistance of his security personnel in ensuring timely repayment schedules, grew this part of his business steadily.

The business prospered, and when Beryl followed Wally to the afterlife a few years later, ending the need to pay her a weekly dividend, Harry began to accumulate a healthy cash balance.

But some of his customers were beginning to drift away. Post-war prosperity and the want for better surroundings was driving the younger and wealthier sections of the Old Kent Road population into the suburbs. Harry decided to accompany them and took out the lease on a modest location close to the shopping centre in Bexleyheath, a place which never made up its mind whether it was the southeasternmost suburb of London or the westernmost point of the county of Kent.

Over the next few years, he followed the population drift and opened clubs in Dartford and Chatham, small towns in Kent that were attracting people from the dirty London city into the countryside.

While looking for a suitable venue for his business in Dartford, he was shown around a few properties by a new employee at the local estate agency.

Rose Everson was completely swept off her feet by Harry. He had style, energy, and charisma, and was not short of money either. Respecting the older generation as he always had done, Harry asked Rose's father for permission to marry his daughter, which was granted without hesitation – Rose's father could see that there was a good chance that this young man, although slightly older than he would have chosen, would keep her in the style she aspired to.

They married within a year of his first property guided tour, and a year later along came young James, followed a couple of years later by baby Elizabeth.

Harry split his time equally between his four businesses. It was in the Chatham club that he heard of an additional business opening. Ever keen to help his customers with their problems (when there was something in it for him) he heard some of his customers expressing difficulty in hiring unskilled labour, mostly for building and agricultural work. Harry asked Dmitri if he had any cousins who might be able to help, and so was introduced to Dragan. Soon, a few of the local business owners found that their hiring problems were solved – and Dragan, Harry (and a couple of retired bus drivers who ferried crews of eastern European labourers from south London into Kent every day) all made money.

These, then, were the activities that formed the business that Harry had built up over the last fifty years, all the time maintaining his total distrust of anything to do with banks. He had carefully hoarded all his cash all these years, keeping it in safes in each of his offices and at his home. All this cash was in the briefcase that he had lost.

-

Harry still did not seem to want to talk very much while they were on the train home, so James took the opportunity to gather his thoughts. What to do first? He would have to find out where you called when you left something in a taxi. There must be hundreds of things left in taxis, so there was bound to be a place where they get handed in – and there was a chance that was where the briefcase was. But only a chance. If the taxi driver had discovered it immediately, would he have remembered where he had dropped the old man? Maybe Harry had given him the exact address of Solly's office. But even if he had, would the cabbie have remembered it? And weren't there several different companies at that address? He would call Solly just in case the briefcase did show up there.

But if it didn't, and if it wasn't handed into the lost property office, then he needed to face the probability that someone had found it. And if they did not hand it in, then that would mean only one thing. They had opened it and discovered its contents. And once that happened there was as much chance of them handing it in as there was of Harry becoming a monk. He would have to find someone to help, and as soon as they got home, he would make that the number one priority.

At the end of the forty-minute train journey, it was a short cab ride from Abbeywood Station to Harry's home. James paid the taxi and went in with his father. Rose was working in her garden when they arrived but, coming into the house, she was immediately very concerned. Even though Harry had recovered a little from the initial shock, she had never seen her husband as quiet as this. James asked if she could get them something to eat – it was now mid-afternoon, and they had not had anything for lunch. Food would help restore his dad, and anyway it would help his mum to have something useful to do and not to worry so much. Meanwhile, he took out his Blackberry and found out what to do if you lose something in a London taxi. Bypassing the option to call the police, he took a note of the number for lost property. He would call them tomorrow.

Rose brought in a round of sandwiches. This, and another strong cup of tea, further restored Harry.

"Dad, I need to try to find this briefcase. Can you remember anything about the taxi you left it in?" he asked.

"The driver had blond hair – he was a Londoner", Harry paused for thought. "His taxi had my initials in its number plate. I remember that".

"Anything else? Did you pick it up at the rank at the station?"

"Yep. London Bridge – straight to Baker Street"

"And did you give him Solly's address?"

"No, I just asked him to drop me on the corner by Baker Street tube – I wanted to walk for two minutes to stretch my legs."

James realised that any chance of the taxi driver knowing where he was heading and thus any chance of him coming back and handing the briefcase into Solly's office has gone out the window.

"If it's not returned, we'll need to have someone help us look for it. Can you think of anyone who could help?" James asked.

"Ron's the guy. He'll find it if anyone can."

James was pleased to see that his dad was beginning to re-engage.

"Who's Ron, and how do I get hold of him?"

"He's in this line of work. Used to be a copper. A detective. I've got his number here - I'll give him a ring". Harry took a small black notebook out of his jacket pocket.

James suggested he make the call himself. He was a little concerned that his dad might not give a fully coherent account of what had happened and what needed to be done. He also wondered if it might be a good idea for his dad to take a couple of days off work to recover.

Harry passed the number over to James. He was pleased to see it was a mobile number, so there was a good chance of getting through immediately. There was no time to waste. He also wanted to meet Ron face to face – this man had a very important task, and James wanted to make sure that they had a good mutual understanding.

Ron agreed to meet them the following morning at the house.

Having made sure that his dad was OK, and that he would not do anything or call anyone before they met again the next morning, James called a taxi. Before leaving, he decided, while his mum was not in the room, to make one attempt at the sixty-four-thousand-dollar question (even though he knew it would be worth even more than that).

"Dad, do you know how much was in the briefcase?"

"No, son, I'm afraid I don't. I knew I could trust Solly to count it. I can only say that it was bloody near full. And it was everything I've put together for my whole life".

"Dad, I promise you I'll do everything I can to help you find it."

James thought the chances of finding it were not good. And he was pretty sure his dad would agree as soon as he had recovered.

He told the taxi driver that he needed to be taken to Sevenoaks, but before that, to the parade of shops next to Abbeywood station as there was a couple of things he needed to do.

He made two stops. Firstly, at a bank branch to withdraw five hundred pounds. He was not sure how much Ron would want, and he might even need to advance his father some money. He was entering his father's domain where cash was always king.

Secondly, he went into the local post office and bought a pocket-size notebook. He was certain to need to take a lot of notes in the next few days. His leather-bound A4 notebook and folder were sat safely on his office desk, and anyway, he did not want to intimidate his dad. Using a notebook like the one that Harry himself used might help him divulge some of his business secrets.

During the taxi ride home, he called his boss, Alex, and let him know that he needed a couple of days off for a family emergency.

"Not a problem, James. I'm sure you're owed some time. Let us know if there's anything, and I mean *anything* we can do to help," was Alex's immediate response. James knew the offer was genuine. He made so much money for Libera that nothing would be too much trouble if it ensured that any distraction he suffered would be minimised.

He also called his wife to let her know he would be arriving home before eight and would not be leaving until nine the next morning. He needed to prepare her for the shock of him spending so many consecutive hours at home in the working week.

Unwrapping and opening his new notebook, he took out his Mont Blanc pen and began to make a list of what needed doing.

Mark Reynolds
April 2005

Mark pushed the loft ladder back and went downstairs to phone for a pizza. 'This will definitely be cash on delivery, not credit card' he thought to himself and smiled.

He saw the envelope on the kitchen table for the first time. (He had not noticed it when putting the briefcase on top of it earlier - after all, there was a major excuse for being distracted). His name was handwritten on it, so he opened it and discovered, with some surprise, that Charlotte had left him. She had indeed gone to see her mother, but the letter told him that she had taken a couple of suitcases of clothes with her, and she would not be returning other than to collect the rest of her stuff. She would arrange for the two of them to meet so that they could settle up financially.

He knew that things had not been at their best recently and that the comments she had been making about turning their living together relationship into something more committed were getting more and more barbed, but he was not aware that it had gone this far.

They had been together for over five years - since meeting on a double date when she had originally been with Brian, Mark's friend since school days - a good bloke but never the brightest jewel on the necklace. Mark could not even remember the girl he had been paired with on the date – all he could remember was being struck by how beautifully slim and pretty Charlotte was. For him, the only memorable part of the evening was when he had been left alone with her for a few minutes and persuaded her to give him her phone number. The next date they went on was not a double.

Most of Mark's friends were surprised when he got together with Charlotte. A primary school teacher, very reserved, some might even say prim and proper, she was the opposite of the girls that he usually dated. Always known as Charlotte (pronounced with a soft 'sh' at the start, and with an ending to rhyme with scarlet or starlet, neither of which she was) and never to be called Charlie, she had a good influence on Mark and helped him to settle down. They began living together shortly after they

23

met - and had bought the house not long afterwards. How much of his decision to settle down was a response to the nagging he was getting from his mother and older sister, Susan, he was never sure. Thankfully there had not been any more pressure from them afterwards.

Mark remembered that this had all happened just before Susan quit her high-flying job in some government ministry to move to Colchester where her husband, Hugh, had joined some exciting technology start-up company working with Essex University. Susan had taken a part-time job in the local museum – a move which Mark found hard to understand. All she would say is that it was the ideal town for a history buff like her to move to. If you put a spade in the ground, you were sure to dig up something from the Romans or the English Civil War. The decision to move was explained a year later when she announced her pregnancy. And when she delivered twins – a boy and a girl – Mark was off the hook with his mother in the producing grandchildren stakes.

It was not that he was unhappy with Charlotte. They had had five good years together and there would always be a host of good memories. He owed her a lot. She had made him quit smoking as a condition of going out with him – and it had stuck. He had been smoke-free ever since and would never regress. And he was very pleased that she had helped him 'settle down' into the nice new-build house that they had bought together four years ago. He had needed to, and almost certainly would not have done it without her. But he always had a feeling that this was not the way the rest of his life would pan out, and this inner restlessness continued to make her uneasy and unhappy.

'I guess I don't have to worry about how to tell her about the briefcase,' he thought. 'And no doubt a few thousand of its contents will have to go her way to pay for her half of the house.' He realised that these thoughts should not be the first things to cross his mind on learning of the abrupt end of a five-year relationship – but having three hundred grand in front of you was likely to slightly disturb one's normal thought process.

He read the letter again – realising that he had not taken in much of the detail the first time. She had thought things through and was very firm in her decision. She did not want to conduct a blaming session and asked him to please send her a text message, so she knew he had read the letter – but to wait for her to contact him in a few days. If he wanted to talk it over, she would agree – but if he just wanted her to make the practical arrangements, that would be her preference.

He sent her a text saying he had read her letter and was very sad to do so. He would do what she asked and would wait to hear from her as she had requested.

He returned to his other problem and continued to run through the possibilities in his mind and firm up his opinions. He would do nothing for a while – other than spend the thousand pounds taken from the case. This would make sure that there was no trace on the notes and that they were genuine. He would withdraw the same amount from his bank account ready to substitute in the briefcase if needed - and do his best to check the press and social media. He would also sweat a little, in case an unexpected knock came on his door. But he could not think of any way to actively return the cash. He remained firm in his opinion that if the money was kosher, then somebody would be sure to publicise its loss.

If he was s superstitious man, he might have considered that the arrival of the briefcase and the departure of Charlotte were uncannily linked. Not only that the first thing it had touched was her farewell letter, but that the letter had been placed on the table at almost the same instant that he had first picked up his new find.

But he was not at all superstitious and consumed the second beer while waiting for his pizza to arrive.

-

Mark and his sister, Susan, had had a normal upbringing. Susan was the intelligent one – excelling at school and going on to a history degree at university – the first in the family to get that far. Not that he was not clever – he just could never see the point in schoolwork, studying and all that. There were far more enjoyable things to do – and the only part of the school that he had any fond memories of was the proverbial bike sheds.

Leaving school with no idea what to do next, he accepted his father's suggestion of going to Technical College to learn some practical skills. His father probably envisaged him following in his footsteps and making a decent living as a skilled tradesman. He worked hard enough to pass all the tests in the two-year course but had long since noticed that the people who had the nice cars, nice clothes and nice watches seemed to have jobs that involved wearing a suit and tie - rather than jeans, a hard hat, and Doc Martens boots.

At the end of his course, he reached a compromise with his dad and took a job at Reede's, the large builders' merchants where his father was a regular customer. The job entailed wearing a collar and tie and dealing with people - which was always his strong point. The job was OK, and he was very successful in handling the customers and getting them to buy. Eddie Reede, the owner, was delighted with his latest recruit and made sure that Mark was rewarded with the occasional bonus.

Mark had always been, somewhat surprisingly, an avid reader. It provided him with an escape throughout his childhood, through adolescence and into adulthood. Initially, it had been Science Fiction that engrossed him – he devoured the works of Isaac Asimov, Arthur C. Clarke, Ray Bradbury and anything else he could lay his hands on. He then moved on to war books, thrillers, and the spy genre. Frederick Forsyth, Len Deighton, John Le Carre and, his favourite, Robert Ludlum, helped him dream his dreams. Almost anything that he could source from charity shops and boot-fairs would help him pass his spare time since his pay packet didn't yet support a lifestyle of going out more than once a week.

It's often been said that a book can change a life – and this happened to Mark a couple of years after starting work. He'd been browsing through a pile of books at a local charity shop and had picked up a book on Sales Skills and Techniques. Mark had never thought about the techniques of the sales job that he did every day of the week – he just did it. But the thought that there might be some skills involved in it intrigued him, and he bought the book – having negotiated a lower price from the shop since the book was not a novel.

It was to become the first of many books about sales techniques and business management that Mark bought, although it was the last that he bought from a charity shop. The rest were mostly bought from bookstalls at motorway service stations, and, eventually, airports.

He read it avidly, learning about structuring a sale using the AIDA principle (Attention Interest Desire Action), techniques of overcoming customers' objections, methods for closing a sale like the Alternate Close (where the customer is offered two choices, both of which are favourable to the salesman – 'Would you prefer it in red or blue?', 'Will you be paying cash or using our easy credit option?'), the Second Question Close (where the customer is asked two questions, and by answering the second commits to the first ('All you need to decide is whether to go ahead and where you are going to put it?'), and so much more.

Mark's response to the various chapters alternated between "Yes, of course, I do that!" to "Wow, I've never thought of that!" The book supplied him with the ingredient he did not even know he had been missing, the one that would enable him to take the next step - from the shop floor to a job as one of the suppliers' reps who came into Reede's every week, wearing nice suits and driving company cars. Armed with this formal selling knowledge, his college diploma, and two years of shop experience Mark was sure he could get one of their jobs.

He was right. Eddie knew he would not be able to keep him for long – and had no problem in giving an excellent reference to his next employer. He would have a significant consolation in having a good contact when Mark became a sales rep in one of his big suppliers, which could be beneficial to his business. A couple of months later, Mark started as a sales rep covering Essex for one of the larger building materials companies, traded in his second-hand car for a new company car, and never looked back.

Eddie was correct – Mark was always grateful to him and made sure that Eddie's business got first-class treatment, the very best terms, a hotline to resolve any problems, and the inside track on any offers – not only in his first job but also the second and third jobs - as he moved to better positions in more established companies. And Eddie was able to keep the contacts and terms with the suppliers that Mark had given him, long after he had moved on.

He also supplied Eddie with regular updates of local market intelligence - information about nearby companies in the same line of business as Eddie. This information, the improved buying terms, and Eddie's skills combined to allow Reede's to go from strength to strength. Eddie was able to buy out a couple of nearby companies and build a business with multiple branches.

And the favours went both ways – Eddie was always there to place the right order at the right time when Mark needed to achieve a target or win a sales competition. Mark was a good and hard-working salesman. But this special relationship was the icing on the cake and contributed to Mark's successful and rewarding sales career.

Eventually, Mark was recruited into his current job. A small company making power tools, American Power, was entering the UK market for the first time, setting up a small office. Mark was one of a handful of applicants for the crucial role of Sales Manager interviewed by the founder and president, Martin Johnson, on his visit to the UK.

Mark and Martin connected immediately. Both were of a similar age and had similar backgrounds; most aspects of their experience and personality were either very similar or healthily complementary. Mark's broad experience of the industry and the territory was just what Martin was looking for, and if his technical background was lacking, his sales skills and obvious energy more than made up for it.

Mark was fascinated by Martin's view of the UK. "Do you think we are the fifty-first state?" he'd asked Martin when it came to that part of the interview where the candidate gets to ask some questions. Mark wanted to understand his prospective new boss's attitudes because he quite rightly guessed it would play a crucial part in his business life if he got the job.

"Not the fifty-first state. No, I've never heard that expression before, but I'll certainly remember it. Not the fifty-first state - the fourth sales territory," was Martin's answer.

Mark did not understand and asked him to explain.

"In the US there are three sales territories. The West Coast, which is just another way of saying California. Unless you're doing business with Boeing or Microsoft, there's only California on the West Coast. Then there's the East Coast – New York and a whole bunch of other cities – Boston, Pittsburgh, Washington for the government business, Atlanta and so on. And then there's the huge bit in between – what we call the Mid-West. Lots of land with little islands of people. Those three territories are each roughly a third of business in the US, and any other split is just a breakdown of those. Then over here you've got the UK. Sixty million people, reasonably civilized, and speaking a very similar language."

Mark was pleased to see a smile on Martin's face as he delivered these last remarks and was beginning to understand his dry humour.

"It's not as big a territory as one of the US ones – they have about a hundred million in each and we do split some of them into sub-territories, like Texas. And there are complications 'cos you guys have different electricity and different safety standards, but we can overcome that. But if we do well here, we can go to the fifth territory – Europe and then maybe, one day, even Asia."

Mark asked a couple more questions to understand what was being looked for, and the interview ended with a promise from Martin that Mark would know the outcome within the week. He thought it had gone well and was very soon proved right. A month later, Mark became American Power's UK Sales Manager (and, at the same time, their entire UK sales force) and joined Pat and Cheryl to form their UK office in a business centre in southwest Essex, just east of London, close to the Dartford Tunnel.

Pat handled all the logistics. The physical aspects of warehousing and delivery were subcontracted to outside agencies, but Pat's experience and skills in processing every aspect of logistics paperwork: imports, customs, haulage, and delivery, was invaluable. He was a rather dour Scotsman, but his very different personality from Mark's contributed to the successful functioning of the business

Cheryl was an Essex girl in every accepted sense of the phrase. Blonde, buxom, and outgoing, she dealt with customer relations and admin – and her cheerful and cheeky nature charmed everyone.

Mark loved his job. He travelled the length and breadth of the UK – and even enjoyed staying in Premier Inns and eating at Harvester restaurants. Hard work had never daunted him – and his long days of breaking new customer ground were well rewarded. He ordered a top-of-the-range company car. Nothing too flash – the wrong outward appearance could have a negative impact on some customers – but inside it was equipped with the best sound system and all the gadgets that Mark loved.

Life was good for young Mr Reynolds.

James Lavinsky
April 2005

Harry kept his business and family life separate. He appreciated that many people considered what he did to be grubby, but never saw it that way himself – he was supplying men with some of the small pleasures of life – a drink, a smoke, a bet, and maybe access to a bit of the other. He never told Rose everything he did for a living – as far as she knew, he simply managed four clubs. The rest of his business was never a part of their conversations.

He had been fortunate to amass his retirement pot and knowing how close to the wind he had sailed all his life wanted to make sure that James, their only son, had nothing to do with the business. He wanted his son to make his way in the world without making the compromises that he had.

He made sure that James had every chance at an education. He was immensely proud when his son entered Grammar School and was delighted that the boy seemed to want to study. His ability with numbers and his joy at spending time manipulating them meant he was almost predetermined for a career in accountancy, which is where he landed. And Harry was able to keep his world to himself and never involve James in any of his dealings.

Although not involved in the business in any way, by the time he reached adulthood, James was smart enough to know what was going on – and in recent years had begun to grow concerned about his father's ability to keep afloat in the shark-infested waters in which he was swimming. He eventually persuaded Harry that it was time to retire and to cash in his nest egg. Hence the visit to Solly's office with the briefcase full of cash. Harry agreed to gather all his spare cash and take it there. He hoped to make one last impact in his business life by presenting Solly with the largest challenge of his life in terms of sanitising a very large pile of very unclean cash. Having always been careful about letting anyone know how much money he was making, he insisted on gathering the money himself and refused any assistance in a secure delivery. After all, what could possibly go wrong with one old man carrying a briefcase?

-

James called the number for Lost Property and had received confirmation that any taxi driver finding customers' possessions in his cab had a legal responsibility to hand it into a police station, and that the police would inform TfL in due course. He left his details and was told that he would be contacted if anything showed up.

There was not much else he could do until he'd spoken to Ron. Meanwhile he updated the list of actions to be taken concerning his father's business, splitting them into two categories: short term actions – assuming his dad would take a few days' rest - and longer-term actions assuming Harry would now proceed to retirement in the near term.

Dreading what he might find, he set out for his parents' house.

-

James had always loved numbers. Although he got good school grades in most subjects, Maths was his passion. In his final year, he had applied for, and got, a bursary with one of the 'Big Five' accountancy firms. Throughout his time at university, he not only had all his tuition fees paid but also received an allowance during term time and a guarantee of paid employment during each of the holidays. He was proud of the fact that he had never asked his parents for a penny – and, truth be told, had always had a worry that if he had asked, he might not have been happy with the answer.

So, when he left university (to work for his sponsoring company, of course) he was not encumbered with the debt that so many of his contemporaries were. Quite the contrary, he had already got some money in the bank, and this, together with the decent salary that his employers were paying him, meant that he was soon able to move out of the family home into a flat of his own in the burgeoning new dockland development where the new financial centre of London was developing.

He progressed in the corporate taxation division of the company, where he stayed for the next five years. Not only working as hard as was possible – but also finding time to meet, court, and marry a fellow employee, Sarah, along the way. It was somewhat inevitable that he would wed a fellow accountant since he spent so much of his time in the office.

James was headhunted by Libera, one of the Private Equity companies that sprouted up in London at the turn of the century. These companies organised and financed business buyouts and takeovers. Deals worth billions of dollars hinged on their input, and the company's employees made substantial profits. James, like the other hundred or so employees at all levels in Libera, worked exceptionally hard. The 05:40 train from Sevenoaks (where he had moved when becoming a family man) deposited him at London's Charing Cross Station at twenty minutes past six, five mornings a week. From the station it was a short walk to his office building, where he spent an hour in the well-appointed private gym in the office basement, showered and changed, and was at his desk with a cup of strong black coffee from the expensive in-house coffee machine, before eight a.m. The earliest departure he made would be the 18:30 train back to Sevenoaks.

Like many of the newcomers to the thriving financial market in London, his employers had shunned the traditions of the established financial institutions. Their offices were not located in either the old financial centre close to the Bank of England or the newer financial centre at Canary Wharf. To differentiate themselves from the pack they located close to Covent Garden, one of the more cosmopolitan areas of London. The offices were spacious and comfortable to work in – and the whole company culture was one of hard work, high reward, and personal comfort for all employees. Lunch was delivered, paid for by the company, from a range of quality caterers, and an informal dress code for all employees was the rule.

James loved his job. He was involved at the heart of huge deals. His speciality was reading company financial statements and establishing the real worth of businesses and, more importantly, highlighting where financial restructuring could produce better returns. And he was well rewarded for it. A generous salary plus a share in the considerable profits that were generated by a successful deal – typically a merger, acquisition, or buyout – meant that the first digit of his six-figure annual earnings was no longer a one, and in good years was not a two either.

The long and the short of it was that despite being in his early forties, he had a nest egg that was sufficient for retirement, but not the interpersonal skills vital for managing his father's business. He knew this was going to be a new challenge – one for which he was feeling decidedly ill-prepared.

A Lucky Find?

April 2005

While waiting for the pizza to arrive, Mark mused on the set of events that had led to him picking up the briefcase in the first place, thinking that in some ways it was all because of the 'spring clean' that the office company had done.

The office he shared with Pat and Cheryl was a managed facility and the owners of the complex had notified tenants that a new company would be taking ownership of the building and the management of the facility. They reassured everyone that there would be no reduction in the superb levels of service, and to reinforce this, they would enjoy a one-off 'super clean' of their offices when the takeover was complete.

The cleaners reached the parts that no others did. Whilst conducting the super clean, they scoured every nook and cranny of Mark's (and everyone else's) office. In one of the nooks (or possibly in one of the crannies) they had found his old briefcase – where it had been stowed a couple of years ago and completely forgotten about.

The briefcase was a sturdy animal, large and deep. Once upon a time, it had been a necessary tool for Mark, back in the day when he had to carry product samples and loads of brochures and paperwork to every sales call. Nowadays almost everything he needed to show to a prospective customer, and just about all the paperwork he needed on his calls, could be contained on a laptop computer. Accordingly, he'd migrated from using a briefcase to a laptop shoulder bag several years since.

But the reappearance of his old friend could not have been more timely. He had a big presentation to give at the head office of one of the major UK DIY chains and had been briefed that there would be ten people at the meeting. Each person would want a paper copy of the proposed distribution contract and the business plan. When these were assembled into individual plastic folders, together with his laptop and one or two other items, he knew that his laptop bag would not be sufficient to carry it all, and his large briefcase – thankfully having been dusted and polished as part of the super-clean - would be ideal. So, it made a re-appearance for the day.

The day after the meeting he was scheduled to meet a customer from Scotland who was making a rare visit to London. To fit the client's crowded schedule, Mark agreed to meet him for breakfast at the customer's hotel near Kings Cross rail terminal and had decided to call in on Gina before returning to the office. He'd left Gina's apartment with his usual feeling of slight euphoria and decided to hail a taxi rather than take the seven-stop tube journey to Liverpool Street Station. He called Cheryl from the taxi to let her know when he would be in the office and to ask if there were any messages and discovered that Darren Palmer had asked him to call back.

Darren was Mark's contact for the major contract he was working on, the one which had caused him to take the briefcase full of papers the previous day – and Mark thought that a call from him was important enough for him to return the call as soon as possible. He had high hopes for this deal. The size of the organisation would transform his sales figures, not only giving him the promise of significantly more money in his pay packet but creating the possibility he had discussed with Martin of taking on more people and opening the European market. Whenever this company asked him to jump, his reply would be "How high?"

As soon as the cab dropped him at the station – the driver had asked if it was OK to drop him at the Bishopsgate entry as it would make it easier for him to pick up his next fare and Mark was happy to oblige – he made sure to call Darren. There were some benches around the back of the station entrance which always had a few spare seats, so, having paid the taxi driver he went there to make the call, which was quickly dealt with, Darren wanted an extra set of documentation and Mark promised to send it that afternoon.

He picked up the briefcase and took the downward escalator into the station. Placing the case on the step behind him, he was surprised at how heavy it felt. 'It should be lighter,' he thought, 'now that I've removed those papers.' It was then the realisation dawned. He picked it up at the foot of the escalator and realised that the meeting for which he'd needed the briefcase was the previous day. He had not taken a briefcase with him today.

He could not just stand there amongst the milling crowd in the station concourse while he worked out what to do, so he turned left into Starbucks, bought a flat white and took it to an empty table to think things over. He put the briefcase on the table and looked at it. It looked the same as his case. 'Exactly the same,' he thought (and hoped, for the sake of his sanity). He tried the clasps, neither would move.

'What the fuck do I do now?' he thought to himself. 'I must have picked it up in the taxi. That's long gone – and the driver probably doesn't even know I've got it – presumably doesn't even know someone left it there, or else he would surely have put it in his luggage rack, not just left it in the back of the cab.'

There was no way to see who it belonged to – and any thought of returning to Baker Street to see if some poor soul was standing there wondering where his case was - just seemed crazy. 'I'll take it home and see what's in it – that's bound to help identify its owner. Yes, that's what I'll do'

-

He managed to keep a reasonable focus for the month following his lucky find. Charlotte called him after she returned from Newcastle, and they set a time and place for a meeting a week later.

When they met at six in the evening at the local pub – a venue chosen as neutral territory and at a time when they could be sure of a quiet table to talk - she was very business-like. She wanted a whole day alone in the house to gather her possessions and would give him a list of any items that she felt were in their joint ownership so he could select half of them. He offered to take all the boxes down from the attic so she could go through them, knowing that some of her stuff was up there. Not only had she never liked climbing up there, but Mark had another important reason for not wanting her to do so now. He also offered to bring some empty boxes home from work in case she needed them. She thanked him for this kindness and told him she would be accompanied by a girlfriend when she cleared her stuff, and some extra boxes would be very useful. His only other contribution to the meeting was to remind her that they had booked tickets to a couple of gigs, and they agreed that each of them would have one set of tickets.

They set a date for her to collect her stuff and Mark promised faithfully to be out of the house by nine and not return before five. On his return, the boxes had all gone, as had all Charlotte's possessions. This time the note on the kitchen table gave him a list of things she had taken that he might think of as joint possessions. There was also a list of the things left behind that she thought came into this category that she was willing for him to keep. 'Efficient as ever,' he thought. She said in the note that she was confident that the split was fair – but he should let her know if he disagreed. He did not.

At their second meeting, they had been apart for a month, and the following day was his self-appointed day for deciding what to do with the contents of the briefcase.

They met again in the same pub and Charlotte told him she believed he owed her some money from the house. She realised they had made very little impact on repaying the mortgage, but she was sure that the house had increased in value by about £40,000 and she was entitled to half of it. Mark silently cursed Zoopla for how easy it had made the task of valuing a house but reluctantly agreed. He explained that he did not have that much in his bank account but could raise half of it by selling his ISAs and asked her if he could pay the other half in cash. In a roundabout way, this helped him crystalise his decision to keep the money from the briefcase. She would be the first recipient of some of it.

For some reason he failed to understand, his suggestion of how he wanted to pay her came the closest to causing her to lose her cool and break into tears. She accused him of being always on the make – the cash had to originate from somewhere suspicious - and he was being far too business-like and not showing any emotion, which he found strange in the light of her coming to the meeting with a carefully prepared list of demands, but he let it pass. She accepted his offer and he agreed to bring the money to one last meeting a week hence.

Until that point, Mark made no withdrawals from the briefcase. He had paid cash for every personal and business expense in the month since the discovery – including more than his normal number of takeaways and a single visit to Gina - and the envelope he'd put in his draw was now empty. He'd also looked everywhere he could think of – local news, social media, chatrooms, and mainstream news - to see if there had been any mention of the lost briefcase. As he'd expected, there was nothing. Now he had to decide what to do, and then execute his decision.

"It's not like one of your spill-sheets"

April 2005

James arrived at his parents' home just before nine a.m. He had found it impossible to re-set his body clock from his normal daily routine, and so he had already been up for over three hours, enjoyed a decent breakfast and had written several pages of notes in his new notebook. His mum opened the front door. Even though he had a key, he visited so seldom over the years that he still did not feel comfortable using it.

"Your dad's in the garden. Would you like a cup of tea?"

Years of supplying Harry with an eternally refilled cup of tea led her to assume that everyone would want the same. Despite his strong preference for coffee, James remembered that only basic instant coffee was ever available in his parents' house. He asked if she could just get him a glass of water.

He found his dad sitting at the table in the garden, which was looking as lovely as ever, thanks to it being the subject of his mother's obsession for her entire adult life.

On the table, his dad had a cup of tea, his ancient mobile 'phone and his trusty little black book.

Rose brought out his glass of water, asked after Sarah and the children, and then showing her skills for diplomacy, left them alone.

James opened the conversation carefully. He knew that the subject of his dad's advancing years was a minefield.

"Dad, Ron will be here in an hour, and we'll talk about the briefcase then, but can we talk about your other plans for a while before he gets here?"

"Well, that's what it's all about isn't it?" Harry replied.

"You're coming up to seventy and when we last talked, you were planning to wind down. I just want to make sure that is still your plan"

"Seventy-five" was Harry's reply

"What?"

"I'm coming up to seventy-five. I've always taken a few years off my age. Never wanted to be sixty, let alone this age."

James had a brief memory of the joke his father had told at his last birthday party, which had been entirely inappropriate as many of his father's jokes were. It relied totally on the punchline that he would be sixty-nine years old a few days later.

"Have you told anyone else?" he asked his father.

"No, and I'll thank you not to either".

"OK. So, you're still planning to wind down."

When they had last discussed the issue, Harry had agreed to take things a bit easier, and when he'd talked about taking his pension pot to Solly's office, James had strongly suggested he take someone with him, but his father had refused.

By the time Ron arrived, they had got as far as agreeing that Harry was still planning to wind down – but no specific plans had been made. James knew he had to strike while the iron was hot – and they agreed to continue the discussion when Ron had left.

-

Ron Jenkins had retired from the police after serving his thirty years and was still too young to join the pipe and slippers brigade. He wanted to fill the hours more productively and be ready when his wife finally grew tired of being a supervisor at Marks & Spencer so they could travel outside Europe for the first time.

Ron had everything a thirty-year police veteran is expected to have: a couple of commendations, a tendency to drink too much, a couple of visible scars where he had come off badly confronting armed assailants (and several more invisible mental scars he did not intend to enumerate), one divorce, a good understanding of human nature, a jaded opinion of large sections of it, and several good, trustworthy friends on both sides of the law.

Ron's current employment had been neatly described by his brother-in-law when they first met.

"I believe we have a lot in common," had been his opening remark. Ron wondered what he could possibly have in common with a man who ran a dry-cleaning business in Aylesford and asked what it might be.

"We both make a living out of other people's dirt."

Ron chuckled politely and the conversation moved on. But the more he thought about it, the more he tended to agree. A lot of his job involved other people's dirty linen.

The mainstay of the business was uncovering infidelity by husband or wife; and the newest, and fastest-growing segment of the business - infidelity by civil partner. Ron was sure that if he decided to expand his business, he would take on a gay assistant. He had no prejudice in that area, but for some of the work he now did, particularly surveillance, he tended to stick out like a … well, better not to go there.

Not that he was successful enough yet to consider expansion. He had just enough work to fill the number of hours he intended to devote to his trade, and that suited him just fine. He earned a decent living exposing philanderers, finding the occasional fugitive, and tackling the occasional unusual request. Such as now. Find a missing briefcase with a lot of money in it. A job which, like so many others he performed, was something that the client could probably do on his own but did not have the time or connections to do, but still wanted a solution just short of the waving of a magic wand.

He had known of Harry through his time in the force, and since his retirement had come to know the man behind the image. He knew that Harry lived his life in that grey area just the wrong side of the line, but close enough to that line to stay out of the crime statistics.

It was obvious why he had not engaged the police in the search, and why he wanted to make sure that they would not be officially involved in any way. A large sum of money in cash was never, in Ron's experience, the result of honest labour and prudent saving. But that was not his problem. His problem was finding the bloody thing. He knew that the task was highly unlikely to be successful, and only took it on because he was sure that his clients (at least the younger one) knew this.

He established what was known. Harry had taken a taxi from the rank at London Bridge Station. The cab had the letters H and R in its number plate; the driver, a Londoner with blonde hair, had dropped him on the crossroads by Baker Street Tube Station just before noon the previous day, and a briefcase containing an unspecified but large amount of cash had been left in the back of the taxi. Not a lot to go on. He asked Harry to describe the briefcase.

"Where did you get the briefcase?" James interrupted.

"From Tony" Harry replied

They established that Tony, surname unknown, was a regular customer in the Bexleyheath club, and his contact details would be on his membership card in the club office. Harry also did not know how much it cost. All he knew was that Tony sold luggage in his shop and had asked him if he had a large briefcase. Tony had left one behind the bar the next time he was in the club, and Harry made sure the club steward took care of Tony's bar bill that day and gave him a bottle of his favourite tipple to take home. James realised that if he was going to get involved in his father's business, this was the kind of record-keeping that he was going to have to get used to.

After half an hour, Ron reckoned he had all the information there was. James promised to let him know Tony's contact details and that he would continue to check with the Lost Property office. Ron promised to get back to them in forty-eight hours with a progress report. As James walked him to the front door, he asked "How much is this going to cost me?"

"Harry's been very good to me over the years. I'll only charge you expenses."

"There's not much chance of finding it is there?" James ventured.

"If the taxi driver didn't pick it up, I don't reckon there's much chance of ever seeing it again – but I'll do what I can."

"I don't want to tell you your job – but just in case the lucky bugger who found it does something stupid, is there any way we can keep our eyes open to see if there's any news coverage of someone splurging out?"

"I'll speak to a mate who runs a press cuttings agency and ask them to look out for anyone – including a charity - getting a sudden windfall. You know he might be a really decent guy."

"Or someone who wants to ease his conscience".

They shook hands and James returned to his father in the garden. Rose reappeared and refreshed Harry's cup of tea, and they moved on to the subject of what to do next. James thought he might try a different tack.

"Do you know anyone who might be interested in buying the business off you?" James ventured.

"Look son, this business isn't one that you're used to dealing with. It's all in here and here," Harry indicated his notebook and his head. "It's not like one of your spill-sheets or whatever, you know".

James suppressed a smile at his father's attempt at computer terminology, then steered the conversation to the plan he had worked out that morning. He suggested that Harry let him know all that was going on in the business, and he would then try to find out how to sell it, to whom and for how much. Harry had no problem in agreeing, and James noticed with some surprise that the morning session had taken a lot out of his father. They agreed to make a start on their plan the following morning, and James drove home to an empty house. The children were, of course, at school and Sarah would no doubt be out running some part of the vital committee infrastructure that kept the social fabric of their village going.

-

James loved his wife, Sarah. Of course, it was no longer that passionate frantic love that they had shared in his apartment in Docklands when they had first begun going out together – or, more often, staying in together – in the early days of their relationship.

Now it was a warmer gentler, more mature love which he was confident his wife shared. But in his case, it was also mixed with the slight sense of awe which he felt for his wife, which probably was not shared.

They were a well-matched pair. Like many married couples, there was the look of brother and sister about them. After meeting Sarah, many would remember her energy and liveliness and her pleasant conversation skills. Some might remember how well her short brown hair was cut, or her beautiful nails. But describing her appearance would be difficult.

After they had married and spent a couple of years working together and sharing the same tiny apartment, they had moved out to the countryside when they were able to afford the family that they both desired. He could not ever remember them discussing what would happen when Sarah became pregnant. It was just automatic. She gave up her job and became a full-time mum. He had moved to Libera, and they were able to live comfortably on his pay. And when Ashleigh arrived to join Joshua and complete their family three years later, their comfortable lifestyle had become firmly fixed.

To say his wife was a full-time mum was a totally inaccurate description of her life. She not only managed to keep house (with the assistance of the indomitable Tanya who cleaned their house twice a week) and bring up the children with the inevitable round of deliveries to and from school, gymnastics and ballet classes (Ashleigh), swimming and either football or cricket according to season (Joshua) and scouts (both Ashleigh and Joshua), but she also did committee work for the PTA and the Scouts and had recently been co-opted onto the Parish Council. Her ability to manage all these different and diverse activities, exercise the kind of people skills which James knew he sorely lacked, and remember every childhood birthday, event, playdate, and sleepover, was a constant source of amazement to him.

They chose rural Kent as a suitable environment to bring up their family, settling in a small village just outside Sevenoaks, a town which combined the advantages of being a rural location and a railway station with frequent trains to the centre of London and a thirty-minute journey time. Rural location plus fast access to London made it one of the most expensive areas of the UK to live in. James's salary permitted this, just as it permitted Sarah to patronise many local businesses. She bought meat at the local butcher, bread and cakes at the local bakery, and fruit and vegetables at the local greengrocer. When she needed to visit a supermarket, it was either Marks & Spencer or Waitrose. Her patronage also extended to local wine merchants, hairdressers, and nail bars at least once a month.

They had a good life, and when James let her know of the change in his circumstances caused by his father's demise, he was quick to reassure her that their lifestyle would not need to change.

-

Driving home, he realised that getting to grips with his father's business, assessing the value, finding a likely buyer, and negotiating a price was going to take more time than he originally thought. He also wondered if today was going to be typical and that he would only be able to rely on his dad's full attention to last a few hours at a time. But it had to be done, there was nobody else who could do it, and it needed to be done as well as possible to make sure that there was something in it for Harry – since his life's pension was now in a briefcase in somebody else's possession.

James thought the discussion with his employers was going to be difficult, but it proved to be easier than expected. They did not want to lose him – so after only a few minutes on the phone to Alex, his boss, they reached a compromise. He would continue to work two days a week, with a proportionate salary, until the family problem was resolved. Fortunately, even forty per cent of his pay would more than keep the wolf from the door – and he thought that three days a week should give him enough time to sort the family business out in a month or two.

Later he would realise it was going to take a lot longer than that. And he smiled quietly to himself, knowing that he was always going to refer to spreadsheets as spill-sheets from now on.

Trains and ..

April 2005

Ron went into action as soon as he left Harry's house. He called a long-time friend in the Met and asked if he could look at some CCTV images. He explained that he was trying to trace someone who was dropped off by a taxi close to Baker Street tube station at around noon the previous day and waited for a call back. Meanwhile, James had given him the contact details for Tony, which enabled Ron to visit and purchase a briefcase identical to the one Harry had lost. The receipt was the first of his expenses.

Later that day he got a call confirming that he could look at the CCTV footage the following morning. The crossroads of Baker Street and Marylebone Road was well covered – there were plenty of views to choose from.

By lunchtime the following day, he had identified the registration number of the taxi that Harry had used and noted that immediately after dropping Harry, it had turned left into Baker Street. About a hundred yards later it had been hailed by a man wearing a grey suit and had then continued its journey south along Baker Street. It was impossible for Ron, acting on his own, to trace the remainder of the journey. Given a full team and enough time, no problem. But this was a private enquiry, not a major terrorist incident. Nevertheless, Ron was sure that tracing this passenger and the cab driver represented the best chances of recovering the briefcase.

It took only a few steps to identify the name and address of the taxi driver – albeit that in taking those few steps Ron trampled over several laws protecting data privacy. The driver was Lee Austin, aged 29, living in Stevenage. That evening, he called James and let him know what he'd discovered so far.

"My suggestion is that you contact Lee and ask nicely to come and see him with your dad to prompt his memory. You can be all friendly. Then, depending on how things turn out, I can make a second visit a few days later and maybe be a little less friendly."

"You mean good cop, bad cop?" said James.

Ron agreed without sharing any of James's apparent amusement. James called Lee and explained what had happened, telling him that the briefcase had some important family papers in it ('one way of describing them', James thought) and that his elderly father was quite upset at losing them. Lee agreed that they could come and see him – but was not sure how he could help – he certainly hadn't seen the briefcase. "I'm just hoping that if you see my father, it might prompt your memory," was James's closing remark.

-

Lee's house showed plenty of evidence of a family with two small children – photos on display, toys to trip over, and finger marks all over the walls and furniture. Lee's wife offered them a cup of tea – Harry accepted but James didn't. She left them with Lee while she bathed and bedded the two children. Lee vaguely remembered Harry, they had spoken little on his ride, but he remembered dropping him where Harry had asked – so he could take a short walk to his destination. Lee had absolutely no memory of any briefcase.

Lee started a diatribe about what a pain in the neck it was when people left stuff in his cab – which they did all the time. James let him ramble for a few minutes in the hope that something useful might emerge. But all he heard was how most people left mobile phones behind and then called him a few minutes later and how he would charge them the fare from wherever he was to wherever they wanted the phone dropping off.

"Only once did I go through the full lost property palaver," he continued.

"Someone left a laptop in the back. Right royal pain. Had to go to the police station, and they didn't want the hassle. Fill in loads of paperwork and wait three months to see if it's claimed. Must have been claimed because I got something – a tenner I think - sent to me."

James interrupted to pose the crucial question

"Do you remember who your next passenger was after you dropped my dad?"

He didn't prompt him by saying that he already knew that Lee had turned left into Baker Street and picked up someone there – it might not be helpful if he thought that he was already being watched.

Lee could usually remember his fares for the previous couple of days, and he thought aloud.

"If I dropped him on Marylebone Road, I would have wanted to turn off quickly, that's a lousy road to pick up fares. So, I'd have turned left to go south on Baker Street. Yes, I picked up someone a couple of hundred yards later. Just before the junction with Paddington Street. Took him to Liverpool Street."

"Can you remember anything about him?"

"He was a business guy. Wearing a grey suit. I'd put his age, I don't know, thirty to forty."

"And you took him to the station?"

"Yeah. I asked him if it was alright to drop him at the Bishopsgate entrance because it makes it easier for me to pick up my next fare and he said OK. Then I picked up a couple of Australians – I hate Aussies, you know they never tip."

James interrupted him again and asked some more about the businessman he had dropped at the station.

"Did you talk to him at all?"

"No, he made a call on his mobile phone that took up almost the whole journey – sounded like he was calling his office. Not that I listen you understand, but when you hear as many calls as I do in a day you kinda get to know the rhythm of the call. His was definitely a 'I'll be in the office later' type of call."

"Anything else you can remember?"

"Rounded the fare up to twenty-five quid so I got a bit of a tip and asked for a receipt, I remember that."

"Did you notice if he had a briefcase?"

"Maybe – can't really say, sorry."

After trying a few angles to see if there was anything else that he could pull out of Lee's memory, James thanked him and gave him his business card just in case there was anything else he could remember.

"We could come up with a reward if you remember anything that helped us get it back," was his parting statement.

On his way home, he called Ron and let him know what they had found out. He reported that Lee did not show any signs of guilt. There were no new appliances visible in the house, nor any new vehicles on the driveway and he seemed completely relaxed about talking to them. Ron said he would do a bit more digging and keep his eye on him from time to time, just in case.

Ron pulled one last favour and got a look at the CCTV of the taxi drop-off area at the Bishopsgate entrance to Liverpool Street Station and achieved a breakthrough. The passenger picked up from Baker Street, a businessman, probably mid-thirties, slim and above-average height, wearing a grey suit, was carrying a briefcase when he got out of the taxi and had headed towards the main platforms of the station. But that was as far as he got. His connection could not get him access to the CCTV of the station itself - not without official approval, which, of course, Ron was unable to supply.

Ron worked on the reasonable assumption that his man boarded a train with a commuter destination. He was travelling without luggage, so he must have come into London that morning. If he'd been from further away, there would have been an overnight bag. Besides, he had called his office to say he would be in later – so it was not going to be too far away.

So, when he arrived at Liverpool Street Station at noon the next day, he checked the departure board to see which trains would have been available for his mystery man. He ruled out the three that were going to very local stations – it would have made no sense for his man to travel from Baker Street to Liverpool Street to catch one of those, he could have made much easier connections. He also ruled out the train to Norwich – that would be too long a journey. Which left him a choice of three destinations: Colchester, Cambridge, and Southend. Plus, the half dozen or so intermediate stops on each of these three routes.

Ron travelled on every one of the equivalent trains on the next three Thursdays and once on each train on another day, carrying his briefcase and a sketch of the man he was looking for – recreated from the small blurry CCTV images of him getting into and out of the taxi - asking the passengers if they had seen anyone looking like this and carrying such a briefcase on the day in question. All to no avail.

He also contacted a couple of ex-colleagues in Essex Police – he had worked on some joint operations over the years and had quite a few contacts there. One was still active in the force and the other was now in a similar line of work to himself. Both promised to keep their eyes and ears open – but so far, no results had come his way.

He reluctantly reported his total lack of progress to Harry and James – they did not seem too surprised at his lack of progress. They seemed to be two people who had reconciled themselves to their loss – even though he suspected it was quite considerable.

Investing
May 2005

Having decided to use the money, the question facing Mark was how to invest it. Like many men, he had always believed he could make money as well as the next man – and that those around him often had achieved great things only because they had access to capital that he did not. Now was his chance to show it. He had certain skills, and a strong drive to make money – in occasional rows with Charlotte, she had more than once accused him of having a stronger drive to make money than any other drive. Hitting below the belt, perhaps – but not entirely inaccurate. For him, money was certainly a more constant drive than any other.

He had often thought of buying and selling property – he loved the saying 'Buy land, God isn't making any more,' and in the course of his work, had spoken with several builders who had made some very healthy profits by buying, renovating, and then selling houses. He could put down a deposit, raise a mortgage based on his current salary, buy a property, do it up and sell it. And what builder would not agree to do the work in return for cash? The proceeds from the sale of the property could then appear as a legitimate amount in his bank – and he would get a copy of all the receipts for materials (and possibly even for some of the labour) for tax purposes.

His first thought was to work with his father. He had a wide range of skills, and for those that he did not possess himself, always knew a reliable person, be it electrician, plasterer or whatever. But surprisingly his dad was not able to help. He told Mark that his order book was full, and he would be 'chocka' for several months. But he had no hesitation in recommending Howard Turnbull.

Mark met Howard a few days later and outlined his planned partnership. Put simply, he would buy a property that needed work doing on it, Howard would do the work for an agreed price, and then get a bonus of ten per cent of the profit on the final sale. Mark knew the notorious reputation of builders for not completing work and thought that by offering him a percentage of profit on the sale he would encourage him to complete more quickly. The deal suited Howard well – and he certainly liked the proposal that everything would be paid in cash.

Mark had prepared for the meeting by printing out details of a couple of properties from the catalogue of an upcoming property auction in Chelmsford, and Howard agreed that either one of them would fit the bill, and they would visit them together before the auction. After their visit confirmed their first impression, Mark went to the auction and bought one of them for only slightly above the auctioneer's estimated price, Howard and his team completed the work in six weeks, and a month later it was sold. Mark was delighted at his first success in converting his 'cash mountain' into real money. 'Now all I need to do is Rinse and Repeat!' he thought to himself.

The next few months were some of the busiest of Mark's life. He continued his normal job and spent evenings and weekends working to build his property empire, arranging mortgages, checking on building progress, contacting estate agents, and so on. And he was also able to conduct a bit of business diversification in a way that was not planned.

Halfway through their second project, Howard called and asked him if they could have a chat over a drink after work one evening. As he had never asked this before, Mark was quick to agree and worried what the cause could be, but Howard quickly put his mind to rest by telling him that the reason for the meeting was that Craig, a reliable young guy working for him had got into a bit of trouble.

It was clear that Howard was struggling to carry out a conversation that was not concerned with work, so Mark patiently let him slowly tell the tale. Craig had got way too deep into online gambling, and if that was not daft enough, had also borrowed some money from a very dubious source to pay his credit card. Being young and having no credit history, he had nowhere to borrow the money. Although Howard wanted to help him, he had no way of accessing the kind of sums needed. Craig was a very reliable worker so he promised to ask if Mark could help.

Mark agreed to meet Craig the next day when he came to the rapid conclusion that this was a solid young guy who had made a couple of very foolish mistakes, so he would help him if possible. But he also needed to make sure that this help did not encourage him to make the same mistake again.

Mark established that Craig owed ten thousand pounds, including 'interest'.

"How much can you pay off?" he asked.

Of course, Craig had zero funds – but reckoned that by working overtime and cutting back he could pay back a hundred a week.

"So, if you're good with numbers, you'll be able to tell me how long it would take you to pay off ten grand at the rate of a hundred a week?" Mark asked and got the expected answer of a couple of years.

"Here's what I'm prepared to do", Mark offered.

"I'll pay this guy off, and you'll pay me off at a hundred a week. Howard will take it right out of your wages, and you'll pay every week for the next two years, and then you'll pay every week for another year to pay my interest. If you don't pay, you'll be screwing me and Howard – and probably the other people that work with you because I might not put so much work your way. How does that grab you?"

Craig was bright enough to know he had no alternative and was pleased to accept.

"Who do you owe it to?" asked Mark.

"I've only got this 'phone number," Craig replied, handing him a piece of paper. Mark asked for the guy's name, but Craig told him he didn't have a name – he'd just been introduced by a mate in a pub. 'Some mate', thought Mark and pocketed the piece of paper.

He made the call as soon as got home. As expected, the phone was answered with a rough "Who's this?"

"My cousin Craig gave me your number. He owes you a bit of money," said Mark. He thought the assumed family connection would easily explain his involvement.

"That's right. Are you gonna pay me, then?" was the answer.

"I want to sort it out", said Mark "Can we meet?"

"You know the big transport caff on the A12 near Witham?"

Anyone who travelled around Essex knew the place he referred to.

"Meet me there at eight tomorrow morning."

"OK. How will I know who you are?"

"You won't, but I'll know who you are," and he hung up.

-

Mark arrived just before eight the next morning and treated himself to a bacon sandwich and a cup of strong tea. He sat at a corner table and surveyed the clientele. He reckoned that every customer was either a truck driver, a motorbike rider, or a criminal – and some could well be members of multiple groups. One of them who could have belonged to any of the three categories left his table and came to sit with Mark. 'Do I stand out that much?' thought Mark, and then realised he almost certainly did. The dialogue was brief and to the point.

"Have you got my money?"

"How much does he owe you?"

"Ten grand."

"And this includes *interest*?" said Mark, giving the last word emphasis, which was not missed.

"Yeah – it includes *interest*"

"And when have you told him he has to pay it back?"

"I've given him till the end of next week – and if I don't have it by then, I know where he lives and I'll be visiting him, along with my business associate".

He obviously had a sense of humour (of sorts) as the term 'business associate' would not normally be applied to the large chunk of human flesh that he pointed to on a nearby table. Mark thought he was far too big to be either a bike rider or a lorry driver, which, based on his earlier categorisation of the clientele of the café, left only one possibility.

"Look, I'd like to save you the trouble of waiting another week and a half for your money, and not have to bother your business associate. So - what if I give you eight grand now and call it quits."

"I like your style. Nine."

Mark assumed that despite the earlier display of a sense of humour, he was unlikely to be receiving a refusal in German – it was a counter-offer.

"Deal," he replied, and reached into the inside pocket of the bulky leather jacket he had worn especially for the meeting, took out two brown envelopes and put them on the table. One contained eight thousand pounds (prepared in the hope that his first offer had been accepted) and the other was one of two envelopes each containing a thousand pounds, prepared in case the meeting had not gone too well.

The two envelopes were picked up and pocketed. Mark realised that this was a man who never even considered the possibility that someone would not pay him every penny he promised.

"Pleasure doing business with you," he said, got up and left the café with his business associate in tow. Mark took a deep breath and finished off his bacon sandwich and his cup of tea. He was pleasantly surprised at how quickly and easily the meeting had gone. He also had a wry smile when he thought that the business had been completely concluded as a verbal contract between two people who did not even know each other's names.

'I guess I'm now in the private finance business' he thought to himself - and felt pretty good about it too. He might have felt even better if he realised that his first venture into this business would achieve a return on investment of around 49% APR.

A True and Fair Picture of the Business
May 2005

James arrived at Solly's office just after eight a.m. and was pleased to be welcomed with a freshly brewed cup of coffee. Solly was alone in the office, and they sat in a pair of easy chairs in his private office.

Solly's real name was David Stone. His father, Isaac, known to everyone as Jack, had until recently run a successful scrap metal business in the east end of London.

David's nickname had been given to him soon after he was born. His grandparents, who had come to England from Germany in the nineteen-thirties, had changed the family name, for obvious reasons, from Spegelstein to Stone. When Isaac had told them that their first grandson was to be called David, they remarked "That's a lovely Jewish name," and Isaac had quipped, "Well I was thinking of calling him Solly but decided against it". At the next family gathering, one of Jack's brothers had asked, "How's Solly?" and the name had stuck. Solly he was from then on.

At first, he had hated it, and while at college had made sure that everyone knew him as David. But when he finished his accountancy exams and his father helped him open his own practice, introducing him to some of his business acquaintances, the nickname returned.

He noticed when he tried to prepare the accounts for the companies owned by his father's friends, that several shared a similar pattern. There was a significant lack of information about certain financial transactions, and, on the face of it, the business was hugely unprofitable. Of course, he knew the reason – the cash that had disappeared from the company. Some would be in their pockets, but much more was housed in safes and strongboxes in their homes and offices.

He had to persuade them that filing accounts showing their business was continuously losing large amounts of money was not a good idea, especially when the taxman came to look at them. Yes, he would explain to them, if they reported figures that were closer to reality, they would need to pay a little more tax – and he reassured them that it was only *very* little more tax – but they would be safe from Inland Revenue concerns, and there would be no need to worry about someone coming to their office, or worse, to their home, to take the cash by force. This last argument was always the telling one – and Solly became the magician they always wanted – one who could turn illicit cash into safe money in the bank. After all, money in the bank also earned interest.

David thought that the nickname gave him a little further insulation between the real world and the fantasy world he began to create, and so used it more and more in his business dealings. A fantasy world of ghost companies began to emerge, some of them registered in David's name and at his firm's address, others in the name of his customers and their family members. A world of circular transactions – all totally legal, of course – that earned him the reputation of champion cash cleanser.

-

The entrance to Solly's office – suitably located in a nondescript building in Baker Street (after all, who wouldn't trust someone located in the same street as Sherlock Holmes) displayed respectable-looking brass plaques for several anonymous companies registered there. He was particularly pleased with his printing company that traded extensively with all his clients (all businesses need something printing, don't they) and generated a considerable income - without ever having printed a single item.

If anyone had investigated the situation in more detail (and thankfully nobody ever had), they would have been surprised to see that Solly and many of his clients owned several pieces of derelict property around the East End of London. They would have been surprised because these properties on the books appeared to generate good rental income and appeared to be sites of thriving businesses. Businesses that were usually cash-generating and free from requirements for official inspection (hairdressers were a particular favourite).

Harry Lavinsky, through his association with a scrap metal dealer in South London, was one of the early customers of the newly established accountancy practice. Solly prepared the books for Harry's business and minimised (sorry, optimised) his tax exposure. However, Harry had never availed himself of Solly's expertise in dealing with excess cash. Harry had long ago decided to keep that in safes in his home and his offices.

Ever since the early days of taking a weekly envelope to Beryl, Harry had hoarded cash. First in the safe in his office in the club, and later in safes in each of his other offices, and his home. Originally, they were blue fivers, then tenners, then twenties, and latterly fifties. Inflation over the years, and the extremely annoying habit of the Bank of England in updating the currency every few years, meant that he had to recycle the cash – in with the new and out with the old – which was a tiresome but necessary task.

Harry's world was a world of cash. His wife received her housekeeping in cash, and any supplier – business or domestic – was always paid the same way whenever possible.

When he finally bowed to the inevitable march of time and the subtle pressure from his son and started to prepare for retirement, it was to Solly that Harry had arranged to come. Solly would be tasked with 'handling' the accumulated cash, investing it wisely and discretely.

-

"Can you give me your overview of my dad's business?" James asked, adding as an afterthought, "I suppose there's no point in asking for a set of accounts?"

"Well, James, I could let you see a set of accounts, but I don't believe it would be helpful. You see it might not accurately represent a true and fair picture of the business." James stayed silent and adopted a quizzical look, hoping Solly would be more forthcoming.

"It might show a higher level of activity than you might expect."

James understood. "You mean there might be many more cash deposits into the accounts than I might expect. And several payments to suppliers that I might not recognise."

"Exactly," said Solly. He hoped that this was all the information about the accounting that James was going to need.

"You see your father and I have known each other a very long time. He trusted me to pay his suppliers and his staff, and even to send out reminders for his members to renew their membership. And I've never taken a penny from him in all these years."

'I'll bet you haven't,' thought James, 'you're laundering thousands through the business in a way that would be very difficult to trace.' But he knew there was no point in pursuing this thread - there was other information he wanted more pressingly.

"I understand, Solly, and I don't need to do anything to change that right now. But can you answer me honestly? What is the real state of the business?'

Solly thought for a moment. "I'll do my best – but you probably know that your father is rather backward in coming forward, so there's a lot I don't know."

He then went on to cover the basics – there were four clubs, and a total of six employees on the payroll – the club steward for each club, Peter, who covered each of the steward's days off, and Zlatan who helped Harry on what he had always euphemistically referred to as 'security matters.' (James later discovered that Zlatan was Dmitri's son, and so was the third-generation holder of this role in Harry's business.) Both Harry and Rose had a monthly draw against profits paid into their account. But this was only a minimal amount, structured for tax efficiency. All the usual recurring bills – rent, rates, utilities, and so on were paid on direct debit and cheques to pay suppliers were done by Solly's firm.

"What about the other income?" James asked.

"I know that your dad collects rent from a couple of properties. But like all his other activities, it's purely cash – and I don't see any of that."

"And what about investments, do you handle those for him?"

James was surprised to learn that as far as Solly knew, his father had no investments. Despite Solly having suggested to him several times over the years that he could help him 'process' the cash, Harry had kept it all to himself.

"Jesus Christ! There must have been a helluva lot of money in that briefcase." James very seldom swore, and it felt and sounded, strange. "For forty years he's been squirrelling it away. And now it's all gone."

"Is there any chance of finding it?" Solly asked with genuine interest.

"We've got a private detective looking into it – but I reckon there are two chances we'll find it. A slim chance and a fat chance. So, tell me, what is the true state of the business?"

"I've been trying to tell your father for the last couple of years. James. It's a good job that he has other business interests because the one that I am dealing with – the clubs themselves - is in trouble. I was going to have to tell him that it was no longer possible for him to pay even the small salary he pays himself and Rose. Maybe one of them, but not both. I'm very sorry."

James asked a few more questions to fill in the details, before thanking Solly and leaving. He had made very few notes and did not feel that he had made much progress in understanding where and how his father really earned his money. But the first conclusion was that something would have to be done to change the business - because it was losing money. And he knew only too well that trying to persuade his father to make the sort of changes that were needed was not going to be easy.

The Festival of the Envelopes

May 2005

Harry was grateful for the large garden that had been the pride and joy of his wife for so many years. There had been very little time to enjoy it until recently, and he had always been happy that it had consumed so much of his wife's time and given her so much pleasure. Their marriage had lasted all these years and had been blessed with two children of whom they were so proud. Rose had devoted her life, her time, and her energy to raising the children, doing the occasional good works, and tending to the large peaceful oasis in which he was now beginning to spend more of his time.

He remembered buying the property, a large three-bedroomed end of terrace property in Plumstead, in the south-eastern suburbs of London, all those years ago.

One of his best customers at the time was Jim Hooper, a local builder and developer. He had approached Harry for some assistance in one of his projects to buy and develop some land as part of the government's post-war slum clearance programme. He had arranged for Jim and himself to enjoy a few nights out with a couple of the local council development team. Never-to-be-forgotten nights of wine, women, and song - although the stuff they drank was considerably stronger than wine, and there was not much singing!

The nights were certainly not to be forgotten as Jim was able to remind the two council employees, and show them photographic evidence, at a key juncture in the process of the council awarding development contracts. Jim was able to purchase the land he wanted at a very favourable price and to secure very rapid progress through the planning process.

To thank Harry for his assistance, Jim had allowed him to purchase one of the properties in the development at a very low price, even for those times. It was hard to believe that a house could be built for such a low price – but Jim was very generous to those who helped him.

Such a good business deal was not the sort of thing you could repeat too often – and he and Jim were only able to repeat it two more times over the years. Staging the same play, but with different actors, you might say. Each time, Harry acquired a small property – which he then rented out (for cash, of course).

Living his life without the burden of paying a mortgage, and with the receipt of rental income (without the necessity of deductions for such matters as agents' commissions or income tax) had been one of the reasons he had been able to acquire his sizeable 'pension pot'. But when he thought of his stupidity in losing it, he once more became depressed and awaited the visit of his son, hoping against hope that he could pull something out of the ashes. Harry realised he was still not ready to get back to work and decided he would let James take up some of the strain for the next few weeks.

-

There was only one area of technology in which Harry was anywhere near up to date. A mobile phone. Not a smart 'phone. On the contrary, it was one of the oldest models you were likely to see still in current use. He continually had to put up with jibes from his colleagues: "Do you get a grant from the National Trust for keeping that 'phone?" or "Is it true that the user manual for that phone was written in Latin?"

He used his phone for two things only. Making and receiving telephone calls.

There were two reasons for Harry's early adoption of this technology. Firstly, it was enormously convenient for him to be able to be in touch with people as he moved between his home, his four different business premises and his many face-to-face meetings. And secondly, one of his customers was Freddy, who had started selling mobile 'phones when they were a new idea, and the marketplace was still open to cowboys.

So, Harry had become an early user. But he had never used any of the features that it offered – not even storing details of his many contacts. Partly this was because of his fundamental distrust of technology, and partly because of a cautionary tale he had heard from Freddy about a (nameless) mutual acquaintance.

This unfortunate fellow had made two mistakes. Firstly, he had stored his top ten contacts in his new toy. Secondly, he had let his wife get her hands on it. She had often accused him that his office was more important to him than his wife, so when the phone came into her hands she decided to find out if it was true, and which number was first on the phone. When she pressed "Recall Asterisk 1", or whatever it was, to automatically dial the first number in his phone's memory, she immediately discovered that her home phone did not ring. Moreover, the woman who answered the call did not repeat the company name of her husband's firm but instead hung up as soon as she heard that the caller was a woman.

It was obvious that there was someone – a female someone - who was more important to her husband than either his wife or his office. This had been a costly error for their mutual acquaintance, and so Harry always kept all contact details in a small black book. James knew that the handover of the business would only be complete when his father agreed to hand over the little black book.

Shortly after James arrived, they resumed their discussion on the future of the business. He was pleased to hear that his father wanted to take a few days off but was aware that with the business being in such a precarious state, this could not be allowed to continue too long. They came up with a plan for his father to ease himself back in over the next few weeks, and that this period could also be used for James to learn the ropes.

Back in the old days, before it was made to appear new, shiny, and government-approved, an apprenticeship was a straightforward procedure. The lad being apprenticed would be assigned to an experienced worker, skilled in the trade being sought by the apprentice, and told to stick with him. Initially, the tasks for the apprentice would be limited to fetching and carrying, making the tea, and watching the craftsman at work. Learning by example. Later he would graduate to being allowed to ask questions, then to assist in some of the simpler procedures before finally being allowed to conduct some small tasks on his own - under supervision, of course.

James felt that he was in the first stages of such an apprenticeship now. He would watch what Harry did, ask the occasional question, make notes, and sometimes seek out additional information on his own. Information such as copies of property leases and standard club membership terms which he thought important to his proposed new role.

His apprenticeship to Harry developed a weekly timetable. On Monday they arrived at the Old Kent Road Club– the original business and still the place where most official paperwork was sent – at about ten in the morning and Harry dealt with everything that needed doing – which at his reduced speed, and with a break for lunch, took them through until about two in the afternoon. He then spent another hour chatting with the club steward and any members who wanted to talk to him. By then, he was more than ready to go home.

Tuesday meant a visit to the Bexleyheath club for a couple of hours, followed by the Dartford club for a couple more. On Wednesday it was the Chatham club in the morning, leaving the afternoon for a random visit to one of the other clubs – which for the first two weeks turned out to be the club where Peter was working so that Harry could keep in touch with him. In this way, all four clubs got visited at least once each week, and James was able to fit them into his three-day availability.

-

As he became familiar with his father's empire, James found things much as he had expected. The main business of selling alcohol in the four clubs was just about profitable – at least in the three newer ones.

There was still regular gambling going on in all four clubs. The proliferation of casinos, and the easy access to them that was now available, meant that this source of income had diminished, but the recent rise in popularity of poker, resulting from its TV coverage and the ability for young people to play online, meant that all four clubs would now fill at least one table on their twice-weekly poker nights. And with each participant paying a five-pound entry fee, as well as buying their drinks for the duration of the session, takings were healthy.

The earnings from "the ladies" (as Harry always referred to them) had diminished from the early days. Punters now only needed to look in local newspaper small ads, newsagents' windows, or public telephone boxes, or enter keywords into a search engine on the internet, and a plethora of options would be open to them. Not much need for personal introductions anymore. Almost the only time Harry received a call for this type of service was when one of his business customers wanted to hire multiple girls for a corporate event or to provide entertainment for a special customer.

The 'finance' part of the business was producing income – the event of payday loans had made even his father's rates of interest seem reasonable, and there was still a steady flow of customers for this unofficial source of credit. And finally, the 'employment agency' was developing steadily with a growing number of customers and a seemingly endless supply of willing workers. James realised that this part of the business was heavily dependent on Dragan, and he made sure that his father set up a meeting with him as soon as possible.

Of course, the business was still run on very old-fashioned principles and practices – information on what was making how much money was hard to find – and there was, not surprisingly a lack of any modern technology anywhere. He knew this had to be put right if he was ever to have a hope of selling it as a going concern.

He organised his thoughts into a business plan. He needed his father to fill in as many of the details as possible – so much was kept between his father's ears and there was no hope of him turning round the business without understanding some of the finer points. Then each of the four areas of the operation would need to be improved. All of them would benefit from using more modern technology – he knew that information on a business and its customers was the first key to success. Then there would need to be changes made to bring the business into the new century. A wider mix of customers for the clubs and more ways to generate income would both be needed. The loan business needed to be streamlined to make it more efficient. The gambling income could be improved by making it more interesting and taking advantage of the recent relaxation in legislation that meant it did not have to be quite so secretive as in the past. The business with 'the ladies' would need either updating or abandoning. The 'employment agency' could possibly be hived off – he would have a better understanding of this possibility once he had met Dragan.

But his priority was to get his father to show him the ropes. How easy was that going to be? He feared for the worst.

-

Harry also told him that the clubs also had another important rota. Each club was managed by a steward, and each steward had a day off a week and a day off a month. The clubs operated from noon until three and from six to midnight every day except Sunday when only the lunchtime session ran. The stewards' days off were covered by the indomitable Peter, who also organised cover for annual holidays with the occasional help of Dmitri and the very occasional help of hired staff. Each club had some casual cash-paid employees who dealt with cleaning and assisted on busy sessions by collecting glasses, washing up and restocking shelves.

On their first visit to a club together, James witnessed something that he forever thought of as the festival of the envelopes. Harry greeted the club steward and assured him that he was feeling much better (all the staff had been told that he had taken a few days off unwell and that his son was helping him get back on his feet as soon as possible).

Once in his office, Harry started his normal routine. First, he opened the few letters that were on his table. Most of them went straight into the waste bin. The one that was an invoice from a supplier was put to one side. He would check it with the steward and then, if there were no problems, it would be sent to Solly for payment.

Harry then unlocked his top drawer and took out several envelopes. Turning around, he entered a combination onto the keyboard of the wall-safe behind his desk, removed a cash box, and anticipated James's obvious question.

"Twenty-six, oh seven, thirty. My date of birth. Only combination I ever use, so's I don't forget it."

Each envelope contained cash and almost all had some handwriting on them. James made sure to understand what each was, and how his dad dealt with them. The ones with no explanation were fifty-pound notes that had been taken over the counter since Harry had last been there. These were placed into the safe, and an equivalent sum was removed from the cash box and replaced into the till. James later learned that all the stewards were under instruction to put any fifty-pound notes into the top drawer so that the money in the safe could be comprised of fifties, and not take up as much space as tens and twenties would. The stewards were responsible for putting all other bar takings into the local bank night safe at the end of every day.

Some of the envelopes contained loan repayments, and these were also placed in the safe after the appropriate update had been made on the relevant individual's index card (kept in a box in another desk drawer).

One or more of the envelopes would contain the money from the weekly card games in the back room. Harry made a mental note of the amount and then placed it into the till to be banked later. Other envelopes – of which there were not many – would contain money from customers for 'favours' that had been done for them. Their contents also went into the safe – but James realised that no record was made of these transactions. Lastly, Harry made a quick count of the money in the cashbox – which was, of course, kept in several different envelopes, each containing a thousand pounds. Harry updated the latest total on a piece of paper that rested on top of the pile of cash.

As he returned the box to the safe and locked it, Harry remarked "I like to keep five to ten thousand in each club – in case someone wants a loan urgently. When it gets above that, I take some out and put it in the safe at home."

-

James learned about one other aspect of his father's business the next morning. A small, smartly dressed, middle-aged man was waiting in Harry's office when they arrived. The club steward, who was in early doing some restocking of the bar postponed from a late finish the previous night, let them know.

"Bloke by the name of George Wallace wants to see you – I've put him in your office," he called from behind the bar.

"George. Good to see you. How's things?" was his father's immediate greeting, complete with a friendly handshake.

"You know my son? He's in the process of taking over from me. None of us getting any younger, are we?"

James wondered if his father really did know this man and would have known his name if the steward hadn't told him. 'Probably not' he thought to himself. 'Doubt if I'd get a straight answer if I asked, anyway.' All that mattered was that George thought that the club owner knew him, and he was more at ease as a result.

"What can I do for you George?" Harry asked - as if he didn't have a damned good idea what it was.

"Need to borrow some money, Harry. You see, I err …." Harry interrupted him and held up his hands to bring him to a halt.

"George, there's no need to explain what you want the money for if you don't want to. As a club member, you're fully entitled to borrow some of the club's money so long as you follow the terms of repayment. You don't have to say anything if you don't want to." He said this casually while simultaneously removing a box of index cards as discretely as possible from his locked desk drawer.

Once again James saw the signs of his father looking and sounding more like his former self. It seemed that conducting club business – the stuff he knew and had been doing all his life – had started to work its restorative powers on him.

"Well let's just say I'm in a bit of bother," George continued.

"How much is it going to take to get you out of this bit of bother, George?"

"About five thousand, I think," said George. His voice, which had never been strong from the start, was getting a little quieter every minute.

"Not a problem. You've not borrowed from the club before, have you?" Harry asked, but James was certain that the combination of his father's memory, and the information on the card that he had carefully withdrawn from the box, made the question unnecessary.

"No, never needed to".

"And are you still at St. Annes Road?" he asked, reading the address on the card. George nodded.

"Well, the terms are straightforward. The money's yours as soon as you want. You'll have a year to pay it back – five hundred, once a month, any time up until the ..." Harry consulted his watch to check the date, "fifteenth of the month. Twelve payments in all. But the first one has to be made immediately, so if you need to walk out with five grand it's probably better that you borrow six – your first payment will be made, and you'll already have almost enough for the second one. That'll then be six hundred a month for the next eleven months."

He paused to let it all sink in. There was no response from George, so he continued.

"All you need to do to make a repayment is to hand an envelope with the money in it to me or to Gerry behind the bar – any time. Of course, everything will be in cash."

Harry paused again and allowed the tone in his voice to become more serious.

"Now, if you miss a payment - and let's be honest we all have those months when things can be difficult – that's not a problem – but we will have to add another payment on at the end, so you'd be making twelve more payments and not just eleven. OK?"

"But George, don't miss more than one payment, now will you. Because I have to look after the members' money and if you miss out a second time, then I'll have to get Dmitri involved – you know Dmitri don't you?" George's more animated nod carried the message that missing two payments was the furthest thing imaginable from his mind.

"Excellent. So, are we ready to proceed? Six thousand minus the first payment of six hundred is that correct?" George nodded with the enthusiasm of someone for whom a difficult encounter was coming to an end, and Harry got to his feet and opened the wall-safe behind him. He took out a cash box and unlocked it, removed six envelopes removed six hundred from one of them, and passed the remainder to George. The whole operation took only a few seconds and was conducted with the dexterity that only comes from repeated practice.

"Nothing to sign?" George asked innocently with some surprise showing in his tone.

"No – I trust you completely," Harry said. "You just remember six hundred every month for the next eleven months and everything will be fine. Now, anything else I can do for you?"

"No, no that will be all thanks," George replied. He placed the envelopes into his inside jacket pocket, shook hands with both Harry and James and got himself out of the office as fast as he politely could.

Harry tidied up the six hundred from his desk, replacing it in the cashbox and looking at the contents.

"Good piece of business," he said to his son.

"Asking for the first payment immediately – that's a bit unusual, isn't it?" James replied.

What he was thinking about was the calculation of total repayments of six thousand six hundred pounds on a loan that had effectively been for five thousand four hundred pounds – and what that meant in terms of an effective rate of interest.

"Yes – I picked up that idea from an Asian guy I used to do business with. He told me that was the way they always handled their loans. It gets the client used to the idea of making repayments straight away. And it's about forty-six per cent."

"What is?" asked James as if he didn't know.

"The APR" answered Harry with a smile that said he knew what his son was thinking.

"Only I don't make that much, because half the last payment goes to Dmitri as soon as it's made – even if he doesn't get involved in the collection. Keeps him interested, though."

-

A few days later, on one of their unplanned club visits, James was surprised when the steward told them that they couldn't immediately go into the office, as one of the members was using it. This uncovered another of his father's unique business practices. Right from the start, he had allowed any club member to use the office at any one of the club premises at any time. James thought about it and realised that it was not as crazy as it might at first seem. Any hospitality would have to be paid for, and there was no cost – the office wasn't in use anyway. He also noticed that Harry always seemed to know why the member was using the office. He knew that this was a custom that would have to continue when he took over.

-

James received his next tutorial a few days later when Harry received a phone call.

Harry's habit of frequently using someone's name when talking to them, whether on the phone or face to face, ensured that James knew that it was Jerry at the other end of the call, and although he only heard one half of the call, it was very clear what was occurring.

After friendly greetings had been exchanged, Harry spent more time than usual congratulating Jerry on his business success, including what must have been a recent major achievement.

"And how can I help you and your colleague celebrate this win?" was Harry's lead into the business element of the call.

"Of course you do. Yes, I think I can help you with this. When are you planning the celebration?"

"Oh, not much notice, but I'm sure I can find what you're looking for. What time would you plan on meeting the ladies?"

"Nice touch. Where are you planning on having the meal?"

"Is that the new hotel out on the Maidstone Road? I've heard the restaurant is really good, and the rooms are very nice too – if you have a chance to look at the room, of course." There was some shared laughter before Jerry replied.

Harry continued, "I understand, yes – all evening and a taxi home on Saturday morning. And do you have any particular requirements where the ladies are concerned?"

"Oh, he does, does he? Well, I'll make sure that at least one of the ladies is blonde."

And then, after another short burst of coarse laughter, "Of course. I'll make a couple of calls and get back to you with the results, OK?"

Harry ended the call and immediately started looking through his little black book. He didn't even acknowledge his son's presence in the room, and James noticed once again how a 'piece of business' as Harry would no doubt refer to the call, had injected life into his father.

James sat quietly and patiently listened to one half of the next call.

"Estelle? This is Harry," it began.

He relayed the requirements received from Jerry and confirmed that Estelle would be available and ready for the night's work. She also obviously had a friend called Tamsin who would be available to make up the foursome.

"And are you still blonde?"

"Good." Having established this vital fact, Harry moved on to talk prices.

"Ooh that's a bit steep," was his response to Estelle's answer on this subject,

"You used to charge three hundred a night, I'm not sure he'll go to four. I'll get him to go to three-fifty each, but you'll both have to pay your own taxi home, OK?"

"Great – I'll have the cash ready for you here on Friday. Do you want me to split it? No, one envelope's fine. I'll leave it with you to tell Tamsin - they'll be meeting you here at seven. They're hiring a limo."

"Yes, that's what I said. See you then."

After such a long period of conversation, Harry's first words to James surprised him. With a broad smile, he turned to his son and said "Gotta love a pro. She wants me to give her the money in one envelope. There's no way she'll be giving half of it to Tamsin, I bet."

Harry then immediately rang Jerry and let him know everything was fixed – they would meet at the club at seven on Friday. The price was, of course, eight hundred - and Jerry promised to drop in with the cash sometime before Friday evening.

"Nice bit of business," Harry said again when the call was over. "Made us a hundred quid – and there'll be a couple of rounds of drinks on Friday – and Jerry'll probably have a drink or two when he drops the money off."

James offered a "Well done," and appreciated the lesson he had just been given. But he also noticed that his father started to look quite tired soon after – just as he had been after arranging the loan to George a few days earlier. It was not long before they were homeward bound.

A Pleasure Doing Business
June 2005

Mark's next business diversification came from an unexpected source. His 'friend', Gina.

He first met Gina several years ago while attending a building industry exhibition at Earls Court in west London. He had taken clients out to dinner one evening during the show and, expecting a late finish, had booked an overnight stay for himself in a hotel close to the exhibition. The clients had an early start the following morning, so the evening session finished earlier than expected, and he returned to the hotel bar for a nightcap. Which is where he met her.

It was immediately obvious that she was a working girl; well dressed, very slim with more than a passing resemblance to Jennifer Aniston, exaggerated by having her hair the same colour and style as the famous actress. There was only one reason why a woman like this would be sitting alone late at night in a hotel in the West End of London. Mark was instantly attracted and started talking to her. He bought her a drink and soon decided to pay for an hour of her company in his room.

Why did he do it? I suppose Mark would use the same excuse that mountaineers always did - *because it was there*. He had never previously paid for sex. Being nearly six feet tall, slim, always well dressed and with a good line in chatter, he had never needed to. But, like many men, he had always wondered what it would be like to have sex with a prostitute. And there was the chance to find out, conveniently placed right in front of him. He had no other vices (once you excluded his addiction to West Ham United), so why not? One of Mark's faults was that when he saw an opportunity, he tended to take it first and think about the consequences afterwards. And that is what he did that night.

Did he enjoy it? You bet! Suffice it to say he enjoyed it so much that he kept the card she left and called her when he stayed overnight in London for a building industry awards event a couple of months later.

When they met for the second time, he was impressed that she remembered him. Not just his name and what he did for a job – but more to the point, she remembered what he particularly liked, and he enjoyed their second meeting even more than the first.

She told him that she was planning to rent a flat in Marylebone and share it with her friend Samantha and would therefore have a place to meet on Mondays, Wednesdays, and Fridays (the other days being worked by Samantha). Ever since then he had paid her a visit (with the use of the word 'paid' being particularly apposite) every couple of months. She obviously was doing well in her chosen profession – Mark was not at all surprised, since she was very good at her job – and after a few months she let him know that she'd now be available every day of the week as she had enough customers of her own to longer need to share the flat with Samantha.

He always left their assignations with a warm glow and a light-headed feeling, having enjoyed an hour of ecstasy. This may well have contributed to him doing something as daft as picking up a briefcase that did not belong to him soon after his most recent visit – but the less said about that the better.

On his most recent visit, they chatted for a few minutes – before and after, so to speak – and she asked if he had recently come into some money. Immediately he was a little concerned about her powers of observation (he was sure that he had not said anything relevant) and asked her why she made this remark.

"It's just that you have been visiting me more often recently", she replied.

"Not that I've got any complaints of course," she added in a flirtatious way.

He told her he was dealing with a major new customer and had meetings in London more often these days.

"If you've got all this extra money, maybe you could help me with my problem" she continued. Of course, Mark had to find out more.

Gina's problem was that her landlord had recently let her know that he was selling the property. This was going to cause Gina some problems as whoever took over the lease might not want her as a tenant, and in the period while the property was up for sale, she would have to be very careful to make it look like this was her home and not just her place of

72

work. Some landlords had moral scruples about what their premises were used for – and there was always the fact that landlords believed they could be breaking the law by letting her carry on her line of business.

Gina told him that the main reason that she was disappointed was that she had planned to make some changes to the apartment. She had bought some 'kit' from a friend and wanted to put it into the spare room.

"Kit?" he asked.

"Well, some of my customers do like me to er, kind of boss them about a bit, you know", was the explanation he got.

"Are you planning to be some sort of dominatrix?" he asked.

He always found the whole area of men needing to use whips and chains to get aroused to be somewhere between comic and ridiculous. Vanilla had always been his favourite flavour, and he was surprised that someone as 'normal' as Gina would be involved in this. When Gina replied that it was a lot easier way to make a living and joked that this was one area where it was always better to give than to receive, he began to understand.

"Just don't come any of that funny stuff with me," he told her.

"No, I know you're completely normal. *Excessively* normal," she replied and squeezed him affectionately – in the place where he most enjoyed her squeezing him affectionately. A place where she had squeezed him affectionately on many occasions – not just with her hand but also with several other parts of her body.

"Anyway", she said, many minutes later when they resumed their conversation, "it would be way better if I had a landlord who understood things and left me alone."

Mark's mind was going down the path of commercial opportunity. He told Gina that he might be able to help, but could not promise anything, and asked if she could put him in contact with her landlord, which she was more than happy to do – writing the name Johnny and a telephone number on a piece of paper and handing it to him.

Before deciding whether to ring the number which she had given him for her landlord, he considered what he knew about Gina. If he was going to enter a business relationship with her, he wanted to make sure that his decisions were driven by his brain, and not by any other organ of his body.

73

So, what did he know? She was twenty-eight years old – but was in good enough shape to easily get away with the twenty-three she claimed on her website. Her friends called her Roo (a shortening of her real name which was Ruth). She had married and had two kids - one boy, one girl - before she reached twenty-one, and had not seen their father in years. She had kept her married name for the sake of the kids, and because, as she so succinctly put it, she couldn't be arsed with all the paperwork of changing it. She lived in Hendon, close to her older sister who looked after the children whenever Gina could not get home in time, and who was the only person in her private life who knew what she did for a living.

Gina had held down an office job for a short time after leaving school but had soon started work in a club in Great Portland Street – one that did not follow the usual rules of 'no touching' with the dancers. The very opposite: they actively encouraged it. From there it was a small step to working for an escort agency – which was where she was when he had first met her – before she went self-employed.

She was successful and very good at her chosen line of work. And she was intelligent too. Her website was well put together, and she updated its content frequently and was an active blogger. He believed she was fundamentally honest, and so decided that despite the well-known maxim about mixing business with pleasure, he would see if there was an angle for him to make money out of this situation.

He called Johnny and told him that he had heard from his cousin Ruth (she always used her real name for anyone except her clients) that he might be interested in selling the property she rented from him.

'Another cousin,' he thought to himself (remembering this was how he had described Craig a few weeks earlier). 'My family is getting larger every month'.

He arranged to meet at Dirty Dick's, a well-known pub on the corner of Bishopsgate and Middlesex Street, which he was confident would be familiar to his new business contact. Mark chose the venue because it was conveniently located close to Liverpool Street Station and would be on his way home from London. It was also renowned for its dark, dingy décor, which he thought suited the nature of the business they would be discussing and, like so many before him, he just enjoyed saying "Let's meet at Dirty Dick's."

74

Mark was still 'spinning plates' trying to keep his daytime job and his new investment career going at the same time. He frequently reminded himself that this new business line must always be in addition to, and not a replacement for, his real job – which remained his best source of income in the long term. Thanks to the ongoing negotiations with the large DIY chain, he was in London more often lately, but still wanted to make sure his private meetings were not encroaching too much on his business hours. So, when he could specify the venue, he chose one that was on his way in or out of the city.

They could have had their discussions by 'phone of course, but Mark had always felt better doing business face to face, especially when, as in this case, it might involve some delicate discussions.

Johnny, whose real name turned out to be Quentin Johnstone, was in his late fifties. He had a shock of white hair above a long thin face dominated by what might be called a 'Roman' nose. His tanned complexion clearly stated: "I go to expensive places for holidays, quite often." Impeccably dressed in a dark blue blazer, grey trousers, a crisp white shirt, and a navy and claret striped tie, Mark thought he was what his mother would call 'very dapper'.

They ordered posh burgers and craft beers, and Johnny gave Mark a business card carrying the logo and name of a well-known London estate agency. The logo and name were ones normally seen where a whole block of apartments or a major office building was being sold or let. Johnny quickly explained that the property they were going to discuss had nothing to do with his employers.

"These are just my contact details. What we're talking about is nothing to do with my employers. I've acquired a few properties over the years in my private portfolio to aid my retirement," he explained.

The vowel sounds in the word portfolio, and the way that he pronounced 'years' so that it almost rhymed with 'hairs' told Mark that he was in conversation with someone who came from old money.

"I noticed the start of a steady uptick in the value of this type of property a few years ago and I've managed to acquire a few of them," he continued, "I've seen a healthy growth in their value and now is a very opportune time to realise some of my profits."

Mark had spent some time with estate agents over the last few months and reckoned that 'a healthy growth in the value' was estate agent speak for doubling his money. He also thought that if Johnny had acquired a few of them then he probably had more than one tenant in the same line of business as Gina. He must know what the apartments were being used for, and almost certainly incorporated that knowledge into the level of rent he charged.

Mark established that the lease had about seventy-five years to run. He thought that there was a distinct possibility that Johnny would be pleased to make a quick sale and might be open to suggestions that would minimise his capital gains tax situation. The period remaining on the lease meant that there was still likely to be some appreciation in the value of the property, as well as its value in rental return. Gina had told him she paid twelve hundred a month rent. and he had decided to believe this. 'Trust but verify' as Ronald Reagan used to say. The way Gina put it, she worked the first day and the last day of the month for the landlord and the rest of the month for herself.

The food plates were cleared, and they ordered coffees and started to talk serious business. Johnny said he was looking to get around two hundred and forty to two hundred and fifty thousand for the place. Mark agreed that this was about the going rate ('Thank you, internet', he thought) but hoped that Johnny might be interested in a quick sale and avoid the costs of an agent, not to mention the time and trouble it would take.

"I've bought and sold a few properties," Mark continued, "and I was wondering if it would be of any use to you if the transaction was split into two parts – the property itself, and the fixtures and fittings – with some of the transaction being conducted in cash?"

"Of course, it would be beneficial to me if the sale documentation reflected a slightly lower, but still realistic, price, so long as I wasn't out of pocket," was the cautiously positive response. Mark thought he would start with a cheeky offer of two hundred thousand – twenty-five thousand of it in cash.

"Shall we say two hundred for the property itself and thirty for the fixtures and fittings?" Johnny suggested.

Mark had seen the 'fixtures and fittings' and knew that they weren't worth a tenth of this sum but understood that this was a way of minimising tax liability. Suffice it to say that after a few more minutes of verbal fencing they agreed on a hundred and ninety-five thousand for the flat, and twenty-five thousand for the fittings.

As an afterthought, Johnny also made it clear that a rent rise to thirteen hundred and fifty per month had already been agreed with the tenant and was due to commence next month.

Mark paid the bill for lunch – they agreed that Johnny would pay when they next met, which should be at the finalisation of the deal.

'If only I could sell all my properties this easily,' Johnny thought.

Mark asked if his other properties were all like the one that they had discussed today.

"Pretty much, but Ruth is one of my longest-serving tenants, so her rent is the lowest of the lot – the rest are rather higher."

"Well, I'm not in a place to buy another right now," replied Mark, "but should you find the time is right to move another one in a year or so's time, let me know".

It was obvious that Johnny intended to sell his portfolio in stages to minimise his tax liabilities, and they both knew that there was a strong likelihood of them doing business together again in the not-too-distant future.

-

The following week Mark was back at Dirty Dick's – this time in the early evening in the company of Gina. He wanted to meet away from the flat so that it was clear that this meeting was about his line of business, not hers. He told her the good news that he was to become her new landlord, so she could get on with buying and installing the 'kit' she had bought.

"Have you thought about letting any of your friends use the room once it's ready?" he asked. Gina thought this was an excellent idea – and thanked him for the suggestion.

"Just make sure that there's only ever one of you in the place at the same time", he added. "We wouldn't want to be breaking the law now, would we?"

They then discussed the rent and Mark told her that despite her possible new income stream, the rent would stay at twelve hundred.

"You wouldn't let me pay it in cash, would you?" she asked. "Only I do have a bit of a problem with my business all being in cash and not knowing where to put it."

'If only you knew what my problem with cash was,' he thought – but said nothing.

"I might be prepared to pay a bit more for the convenience" Gina continued. Mark could not resist the temptation.

"How about…" he mused "you pay me thirteen fifty a month in cash. But when I collect it, I'll give you back a hundred and fifty towards the next month?" (A hundred and fifty being the normal rate she charged him).

"So really I only have to give you twelve hundred?"

"Plus" he paused for effect, "an hour of your time, of course".

"Yeah, yeah. I get it." She paused for a moment's thought and smiled. "OK, It's a deal."

It was a perfect result. Mark considered that he was getting thirteen fifty, and Gina understood that she would only part with twelve hundred in real money. They separated with a peck on the cheek, and he told her she would have to pay Johnny for another month or two, but he would let her know when he was going to take over. He was quite pleased with the return on his investment. He would take the cash from Gina, and deposit it in his bank account – but not all of it, of course. A reasonable return, he calculated – with the possibility of some increase in the property value. More importantly, he had made significant progress in reducing his cash mountain!

He could not help but see the wonderful irony in the situation. He was thinking that it had been a real pleasure doing business with Gina – and that this was the reverse of the previous normal. In the past, it had always been a business doing pleasure with her.

A Curious Kind of Honesty
June 2005

As he moved into retirement, there remained several habits of a lifetime that Harry could not forsake. He still got up at half-past seven every morning – leaving Rose to lie in for another hour - and shaved before doing anything else. And shaving meant wet shaving, of course. He had made a few concessions to the modern-day – he used a disposable multi-bladed razor, and his lather came from a spray can. He would have preferred to work up a lather with a badger-hair brush on a soap stick, scraping the stubble off his face with a keen-edged cutthroat, but progress was progress.

He was standing in the bathroom by the side of a sink filled with piping hot water, his face wetted and covered with a healthy layer of foam, and his hand holding the razor when the heart attack struck. It arrived so quickly and with such force that, to quote the words of the paramedic summarising the situation to the attending police officer, "he was dead before he hit the floor."

An hour after the attack, Rose discovered him and called James while still in a state of total shock. "He's lying on the bathroom floor. I can't get him to move," was all he could understand. He gently told her to call 999 and ask for an ambulance, and he would be there as soon as possible.

He left Sarah to look after the children and knocked a full ten minutes off his best time between his house and his parents', arriving just after the ambulance. He settled his mother in the sitting room with a cup of hot sweet tea in the company of her neighbour who had arrived to offer help as soon as she'd seen the ambulance. He introduced himself to the ambulance crew, and, after a brief check, they confirmed what he had suspected.

The funeral was held at the local church ten days later. Despite it being only the fourth time Harry had ever been in a church in his life – his wedding, and the christenings of his two children being the other occasions – his funeral was an exceptionally well-attended event. He was one of the few survivors of a special generation, well known and well-liked. Although the family was small, there were enough members of the clubs (which were all closed for the day out of respect), business associates, suppliers, and colleagues to fill the church on a cold, grey Tuesday morning.

It was a proper old-fashioned do – just as Harry would have wanted – with a horse-drawn carriage and plenty of flowers. None of this modern 'donate to a suitable cause' palaver. Harry had been something of a showman all his life, and it was only fitting that he went out with a bang.

His passing gave James a whole new set of problems, but also a renewed impetus to solve them. For the past few weeks, he had not been entirely clear in his purpose. He was unsure whether his father would ever really retire, or if he even wanted to – even though he had often said this was his wish. Now he was gone, James knew exactly what needed doing. He needed to ensure that his mother was financially secure, with enough money to afford the distractions needed to fill the Harry-sized hole that was now, and forever would be, part of her life.

He made sure to spend as much of his available time as possible with his mother over the next few weeks. He wanted to make sure she was alright – but also to find out how she thought his father had been in the last few months of his life. Eventually, his mother said what he wanted to hear.

Reminiscing one night over a cup of cocoa, his mum had spoken – partly to James and partly to herself.

"I miss him terribly, you know. But in a way, I am glad that he went when he did. He was …" she paused, looking for the right word, "fading, you know." Then, after another pause, "Harry hasn't been Harry for the last few months, you know. It would have been terrible if he'd had to live less of a life. I've seen so many poor souls, sitting in their chairs with their minds no longer fully there. Harry would have hated to go that way."

"In what way had he been fading, mum?" James prompted.

"Oh, you know, the usual ways. Forgetting things. Not remembering people's names, saying some silly stuff. He tried hard to cover it up – I don't think too many people noticed – even you."

James had to agree and said so. He was pleased that his mum had this solace. And to be perfectly frank, he was assuaged of some of the guilt he had been carrying. Harry losing the briefcase and all the money was a symptom of his decline, and not, as James had been worrying, a cause of it. He could stop beating himself up about leaving Harry to carry it. Now he needed to focus his energies on saving something from the business and making sure that his mum would spend the rest of her days in the home where she was so comfortable, tending and enjoying the garden she loved so much. Making sure of this would be, as one of his colleagues in the office liked to say, a non-trivial task.

Between the day that his father died and the day he was buried, James was preoccupied with the arrangements – the funeral itself, the statutory obligations of notifying the various authorities, the financial and administrative arrangements with banks and institutions which all seemed endless.

Thankfully Harry had left everything in as neat a condition as he could. His funeral had been pre-paid, his will was properly completed and straightforward – his son appointed as executor, and everything left to Rose. There were a couple of anomalies. Harry had never claimed an old-age pension for himself or his wife. James wondered whether this had been a deliberate act, deferring the pensions until he had retired from the business because the money was not yet needed and would be higher if left for a few years. He doubted this. It was much more likely that his father was showing a curious kind of honesty, acknowledging that he had avoided paying income tax for so long that he did not now feel justified in drawing from a pot to which he had never contributed.

Nonetheless, James arranged for his mother to begin receiving her pension. He declined the option of it being paid directly into a bank account because he was sure that she would feel more comfortable with a weekly cash payment, and it would ensure that she would have one face-to-face contact every week at the local post office. She would not get that from a bank ATM.

If he had not realised before, he now saw how dependant she was on Harry.

"Where am I going to get money from?" she asked him a few days after Harry's death. "He used to give me cash every week. Am I going to have to sell the house?"

James reassured her that this was not going to be needed.

"Mum, I've spoken to the people who rent the flats that Harry bought, and they'll pay their rent directly into your bank account. With that money and the income that you get from the clubs, there's more than enough to pay all your bills. The gas, electric, council tax, everything, are all taken care of automatically – and if you have any questions any time about bills or anything, you just let me know, OK."

"But what about the cash that he used to give me every week?"

James told her that he would give her money for the next few weeks, but then she would be getting a pension card and she would need to go to the post office once a week and they would give her cash.

"Will you come with me the first time?" she asked.

"Mum, you took me to school the first time, I think it's only right that I take you to get your pension the first time," he told her.

Gina

June 2005

Today had been a day of anxiety for Gina. She had been anxious about the meeting with Mark. Anxious because she was breaking one of her few golden rules.

To Gina, there were two types of men in the world: men and punters. All her punters were men - but not all men were punters. She always believed that she could tell whether a man was a potential punter or not. She could not tell you *how* she knew, she just knew. Watching for a few seconds, seeing how he looked at her and how he looked at other women was enough. Not that she needed to put her theory to the test nowadays. The skill was no longer of any value to her - but it had been very useful back in the days when she had worked in the club. Many of her colleagues often complained about the amount of time they wasted on blokes who did not want to go any further. This had never been a problem for her.

She had no difficulty relating to men in normal life. Friend, relative, business supplier, whatever, she treated them in the way that she assumed everyone else treated them. And she did not think any the less of the punters – or any more of them either. From the moment they picked up that phone and dialled her number they became a punter. And her job was to provide them with what they wanted, and to get paid as much as possible for it.

The popular saying was that men only wanted one thing. Well, most of her clients certainly did want this one thing – but they wanted other things too. Reassurance, affection, the illusion of power, or complete submission to another person's desires (within agreed and defined limits, of course), the feeling of being pampered, companionship – yes, even simple companionship - were amongst the many and complex reasons that her clients came to her and returned again and again. Many simply wanted what was known in the trade as a GFE – a girlfriend experience. Others put more of an emphasis on more carnal pleasures, each of which might have a three-letter or two-letter acronym of its own. Her job was to find out what they wanted her to be and to do. And then be it and do it. And she thought she was pretty good at it. After all, they keep coming back, don't they?

Did she enjoy her job? Does anyone really enjoy their job? Many years ago, she had a normal office job: typing, filing, answering calls, making tea and coffee. Did anyone enjoy doing that? Surely, they just did what they had to do, took satisfaction in doing it well and the rewards they got for doing it. She often thought about care workers and nurses. They had to do some pretty unpleasant tasks from time to time, she was sure. And they got paid a whole lot less for it than she got paid for whatever unpleasant tasks she had to perform. So how was she different? She even often wore a uniform (in fact many different ones) as part of her job too!

But she was anxious about Mark becoming both her landlord and a punter. She had only broken the unwritten rule about mixing business with pleasure twice before. Once with Roger, the web designer. (She smiled to herself thinking of the appropriateness of his name). It probably was not his real name - he certainly would not be the only one to use a false name when meeting her.

She had found his contact details on the foot of a webpage of one of her colleagues. She liked the way the website had been put together and at that time she had no idea how to do it herself and so she'd called, and he had quoted a price for a similar website – to be paid half up front and half on delivery – and she had accepted. After the website was up and running, he contacted her and booked an hour of her time. Normal price. Just the once. What was it he said? "Some men want to visit all the football clubs in England. I just want to fuck all the prostitutes in London. And there's a lot more than ninety-two of them!"

And then there was Christopher, her solicitor. He was the only other one to cross the line. In the brief chat that she usually had with her clients at the end of a session, she had talked about a problem she was experiencing with a neighbour, and he offered to write a letter on her behalf, explaining what his profession was. He charged the same for preparing a letter as she did for an hour of her services, and they agreed that their business together on this occasion would take the ancient form of barter.

All he needed to know was her surname, whether she was Miss, Ms. or Mrs., and the address details of the neighbour. She gave him the information; he wrote and sent the letter, and the problem disappeared.

She had also used the same barter relationship to have her will prepared. And she was still able to revert to a normal cash-based business relationship when she was his naughty little niece again. once a month.

Mark seemed to be a decent enough bloke and she thought that they could manage the changed situation going forward. Which only left the other two anxieties she was facing.

One was completely irrational: she just did not like travelling on the tube in smart clothes. She took the tube to and from work almost every day and she always dressed down. Jogging bottoms, a shapeless sweater, and scruffy trainers. Not even a tight pair of jeans was allowed. And not a shred of makeup. Not that she wore much makeup anyway, she was lucky enough to have a good complexion that did not need covering or enhancing and she wanted to keep it that way for as long as possible. There were also good practical reasons for wearing as little make-up as possible. Her clients would not welcome its appearance on their clothing, and she did not want to have to continually wash pillowcases either.

But the journey between home and work was much more than a work commute. It was a transition between the real world and a fantasy world. A world where she was a different person with a different personality and even a different name. That transition drove her need for anonymity. What Clark Kent achieved in the course of a few minutes in a phone booth, she needed a whole journey to complete. It was Gina that entered the tube station at Baker Street, but it had to be Ruth that emerged from Hendon Central half an hour later.

She had to dress better than her normal drab travel attire to meet Mark, and even though she was wearing a business-like trouser suit, she felt distinctly uncomfortable.

The final element of her travel anxiety was the more rational apprehension of carrying money. It had been a busy day, and there had been no time to get to a bank before meeting Mark. She had started the day with two hundred quid in her purse, and now there was almost a thousand - a lot more than she liked to carry.

She was very methodical (at least in her mind) with money. She had four bank accounts. A normal one to pay all the standing charges – the mortgage on her home, the rent for the flat, two lots of council tax, Sky Television, mobile phone and so on. She knew how much to put into the account every month to cover those. When that was done, some money went into the extra account which was used for unplanned expenses. The broken boiler or the new piece of furniture type of expense.

The third account was for holiday money. She made sure to have a really good fortnight away with her two children every summer. Somewhere with loads of sun for her, and plenty of activities for her children. And a separate week away on her own in the autumn or spring.

And then lastly an account for her ISAs. She knew that she would have to retire from her line of work long before normal retirement age - although she did know of one or two women who were gainfully employed in the same line of work well into their sixties, she did not see this as her future. One of her reasons for investing in the extra equipment she planned to install into the spare bedroom was that it was much easier to do the dominatrix stuff as you got older. Looks were not nearly as important in that role.

She often thought of the similarity between her money management and that of her mother, who had a plethora of jugs and jars secreted around their house, each with a nominated financial purpose. After every shopping trip it was 'Fifty pence pieces go in this one for Christmas, twenty pence pieces go in this one for birthdays, the first pound coin goes in this one for birthdays, the next pound coin goes into this for savings, and so on.' Every so often a jar would be emptied onto the kitchen table, and the contents counted into a little plastic bag which would be taken to the bank to be exchanged for notes that would then be carefully added to the roll in the proper jar or jug.

She liked to think that there was a little more method in her system. She could not possibly keep all the cash she earned lying around her home. All four accounts were in mainstream banks or building societies, so she never had to walk too far along Marylebone High Street to make a deposit. And having multiple accounts meant that there was less chance of suspicion of the multiple cash deposits. Of course, she declared the amount deposited in the main account to the taxman on her annual return – but not the cash for her shopping, her clothes, her underground season ticket, and anything else she could pay for in cash. Nobody reports all their income to the taxman – don't be silly.

She managed to survive the tube journey, even in her posh clothes, and eventually arrived home with everything – including the money – intact.

As she walked up the front path of her sister's house to collect her children, Ruth left all her anxieties behind her. Her sister noticed the improvement in her outfit and asked what the special occasion was. Gina had to disappoint her by telling her it had only been a meeting with her landlord. Did the children remark on her change of clothes from what she normally wore when she picked them up? Be serious – do any children ever pay any attention to what their parent is wearing?

Making Changes
July 2005

After Harry's funeral, James resumed the routine that he had been following during his brief apprenticeship. He knew it was important to reassure all the clubs' employees and members that he planned to keep the businesses going and that any changes would be few and all would be made with their interests in mind.

He also met Dragan at the usual venue, a transport café just off the A2, close to its intersection with the M25 near Dartford. The café could only be accessed by turning off the main road and using a side road but was nonetheless always crowded with lorry drivers. Dragan thought it served the best English breakfast in the South of England and made it his meeting venue as often as possible.

They had only spoken briefly at Harry's funeral and James wanted to reassure Dragan that it would be business as usual. He would let him know of any new customers and would continue to meet on the second Tuesday of every month as had been the pattern with Harry. He also accepted the envelope from Dragan with the monthly commission for the customers his father had introduced.

After visiting each club once to accept final condolences and dispense reassurance, James instigated the first two changes - but was careful enough to only introduce one change per club. The Old Kent Road and Bexleyheath clubs got a gaming machine, while Dartford and Chatham got a coffee machine.

James had wondered why there was not a gaming machine (or one-armed-bandit as he tended to call it) in any of the clubs. One of the advantages of having a club license was that it permitted the installation of a gaming machine with a much higher jackpot than those permitted in pubs. Asking his father just one question had furnished him with the reason. Harry did not like them.

James did not have the same prejudices and knew that these machines would provide significant additional income to the clubs. This rapidly proved to be correct - after an initial problem had been overcome (the machines proved to be so popular with some customers that the two clubs had to set up a booking system to let everyone have a turn).

Conversation between the stewards of different branches and one or two customers who visited more than one club meant that within a couple of weeks he was being asked why there were not similar machines in the other two clubs, so he swiftly bowed to customer requests and installed them.

Before he could install the coffee machines, he needed to get the agreement of the stewards of the two clubs where they were installed to change their opening time from noon to eleven a.m. – with an appropriate increase in their remuneration, of course. He knew that it would take time for people to change their habits – but this was part of his longer-term plans to open the membership to younger people - and to fully implement this change in the way he wanted, he needed to put one more vital piece into the jigsaw.

One other change that James made was to establish the office in the Chatham club as his own. The room was a small one, opening out from the doorway and was almost triangular. One wall contained the two windows that looked out onto the street. The view was hardly distracting since it consisted of a row of small, drab shops on the opposite side of the street and the traffic that passed along between. In the corner opposite the doorway were the desk and the black leather-look office chair he had inherited, with the wall-mounted safe behind it. There was barely enough room for the two visitors' chairs that made up the entirety of the rest of the furnishings.

James personalised the office - it was, after all, the first real office he had ever had. His two previous jobs had each provided him with a state-of-the-art ergonomically designed high tech workspace – but not a real office. This was a real, old-fashioned office. A battered old desk with lockable drawers stood in the corner and the wall next to it was decorated with James's roll of honour. Frames containing his university degree, accountancy qualifications, and association memberships were accompanied by a framed copy of the front page of one of the leading accountancy magazines which featured his photograph (as a much younger man) proudly displayed on the front page. His employers at that time had employed some PR consultancy to promote its investment in young talent, and they had run an article, allegedly written by him but professionally ghost-written, which led to the photoshoot. It all helped to establish his credentials. It also confirmed that he was a fish out of water in his current situation, but he refused to dwell on that aspect.

The other wall carried testaments to his two other interests. Next to his desk was a framed print of 'Going to the Match' by L. S. Lowry. James was a big fan of his work – he had several more prints at home, and his pride and joy, an original sketch by the great man, for which he had paid an extortionate sum at auction. He loved the way that Lowry painted what was there, but at the same time invested it with his commentary on both the buildings and the people. Back in the days when he was earning megabucks it was his ambition to acquire some more Lowry originals, but that plan had been placed on ice.

The print linked to his other piece of decoration further along the wall. A framed West Ham United shirt, signed by the first team. He created this as his 'football wall' (Most people, especially those from the south of England, assumed that the match shown in the Lowry painting was a football match. James, having read up on the subject, knew that it probably was a crowd going to a rugby league match, but that didn't matter) to serve two purposes – giving him something nice to look at and letting any visitors know that he was a football fan.

-

James's path to becoming a football fan was an unusual one. He had not played much, if at all, as a child. Getting muddy and sweaty with several other boys was never his idea of fun. And his dad was never a football fan either, so he did not acquire his liking for the game in the tag-along way that most football fans do. He had come to the sport later in life, attending a few corporate events held at several premier league football clubs around London. His exposure was to the highest level of the game (the English Premier League) and viewed from the best seats in the house with the accompaniment of significant creature comforts.

He would not have minded being referred to as part of the 'prawn sandwich brigade', an epithet which one of the leading TV football pundits had used to describe this type of football supporter. The description had stuck and was frequently quoted. As far as James was concerned, he was contributing the high-end money that enabled the clubs to purchase the services of the best players in the world, and anyway, he had never eaten a prawn sandwich in his life. He also had very little time for TV football pundits, thinking of them solely as men who had two characteristics – firstly a playing career at the high end of the game to establish their credentials, and secondly a complete failure to obtain a high-end management role which meant they were available for TV punditry when the games were being played.

Having watched a few games from executive suites, he had taken out a subscription to Sky TV Sport channels to continue his enjoyment of the game, and when his son had shown some interest, he immediately capitalised on this by buying two season tickets to West Ham United – in the best available seats, of course. He had chosen West Ham partly because his wife's brother had bought Joshua a West Ham top as his first football shirt, and partly because James felt that West Ham was the club most likely to provide a local team in the premier league in the longer term. Neither Gillingham nor Charlton Athletic, despite being geographically closer, inspired his confidence as being likely to sustain long-term premier league status.

James had decided that this room would be his main office – he would have to visit the other clubs at least once every week, but since the club in Chatham was the busiest, he would spend most of his time here.; and even though his stay was planned to be short he felt it important to stamp something of his personality on the place. After all, he had a very tough act to follow.

Coming to America
August 2005

For Mark, one of the best things about his job was the chance to visit the USA twice a year. Other people in similar circumstances might have found it to be onerous. It was certainly hard work and involved a long plane journey. But the key was that he loved America and almost everything about it. So, the strenuous week he was about to embark on was something he really looked forward to.

He made two visits to the States each year. One for the annual building Industry exhibition in the spring at the Jacob Javitts Center in New York, and the other for his employer's annual sales conference at the company's New Jersey headquarters in August.

This was his third such trip, and he had established a routine. The company allowed him to travel a day early so that he could adjust to the jetlag, so, after driving to Gatwick airport and parking in the long-term car park on Saturday morning, he boarded the flight to Newark International Airport and settled down in an aisle seat in the cramped economy section and began his final preparations. He read the information about the new products the company was planning to launch, made sure he understood as much as he could and made notes of the questions he needed to get answered.

He also read once again the two brief emails, one from Pat and one from Cheryl, that listed the issues they wanted him to raise when he was over there. Before going, he also always made sure to ask Cheryl what the key pieces of office gossip were. He was not very good at getting to know this kind of stuff but knew it was important and that it was very much part of Cheryl's interaction with her opposite numbers in head office. There was apparently one impending maternity leave, one new engagement and one suspected forthcoming divorce.

The sales conference – and the rest of the visit to HQ was important and he liked to be as well-prepared as possible. He had one chance per year to be face to face with people who had a significant influence on his business life and needed to maximise the opportunity. He had to continually remember that he was probably the only Englishman most of these people would ever meet, and for the whole time, he would be on trial in one way or another. Three days of hard work in unfamiliar surroundings - a form of pressure he relished.

He prepared his list of questions and topics for each of the key people in the US office. Finally, he prepared his power-point presentation for the meeting and went over it a couple of times. He was particularly looking forward to talking, maybe even boasting, about his progress towards striking a deal with a big DIY chain in the UK. This deal would produce significant extra business for the company and would do his career no harm at all – hopefully leading to an increase in people in the UK office and some expansion into mainland Europe.

In between his work activities, he ate every morsel of the meals served, watched a movie, and took full advantage of each offer of drinks – both alcoholic and non-alcoholic. He was not one of those people who complained about airline food. Quite frankly he was always amazed that they managed to prepare and serve an edible three-course meal for several hundred people from a kitchen that was the size of a large handkerchief situated thirty thousand feet above the ground. It was like the old saying about seeing a dog singing. You should not consider how well it was done - just marvel that it happened in the first place.

-

Being a single traveller, he was inevitably next to a stranger on most journeys. Sometimes there would be no communication – his neighbour placing headphones on and indicating by his body language that he had no wish to communicate. On other occasions, an interesting conversation occurred with a person he would possibly never have come across in any other situation.

On one occasion he had learned all one would ever want to learn, and a whole lot more, about steam engines. Another time an executive in the oil industry told him that, knowing what he knew, he would never buy petrol from a supermarket petrol station. Mark could not remember exactly why it was, but he followed the advice from then on.

Probably the most relevant advice he ever received from a fellow traveller came from an old IT guy he met on one of his early trips to the US. They had been talking about the differences between Americans and Brits – always a popular topic between strangers on transatlantic flights.

"You've got to understand how they think of us," his fellow-traveller opined. "Now, I have no reason whatsoever to believe you are racist, and I'd never wish to imply it. But I would ask you to consider how you think of people from India. You must come across some of them in business – you certainly would if you were in IT like me. Companies are always outsourcing their call centre or development or support to Mumbai. And we think of them as not quite as good as us Brits. Be honest – like I said, not racist at all. They speak good English – better than some of our own to be truthful – with a bit of a strange accent. They're perfectly polite and business-like – you can even talk cricket with them which puts them well ahead of the inhabitants of one other English-speaking country I could mention. But if you're honest you will never quite think of them as equals. And that is how the Yanks think of us. Not saying they're right or wrong. They just do. And if you want to be successful in dealing with them, you'll understand this, accept it – 'cos you're never going to change it. And take their money – because they've got loads of it and can be very generous if you do a good job for them."

Mark did not completely agree with the guy – but he never forgot the conversation and maybe it just influenced him a little in his dealings with his colleagues.

At Newark airport he suffered the lengthy delays that America inflicts on all foreign visitors, before getting his passport stamped, claiming his luggage, and eventually getting a taxi to his hotel.

The hotel was a run of the mill Holiday Inn Express situated on the edge of the business park where the headquarters of American Power was located. It served the needs of the business visitors to the companies on the business park, and so was almost empty on Saturday evenings, which suited Mark just fine. There was a small swimming pool, separated from the bar and lobby area by a wall of frosted glass. It was only about thirty feet long, with a small area at the far end where three pieces of exercise equipment sat unused. He would not have wanted to be there when it was crowded, but as he was entered, the only other guests using it, a mother and daughter, left, so he had exclusive use of the pool for an hour of gentle exercise,

After this, he returned to his room and tried to find something other than sport to watch on the ridiculously large TV in his room. His liking for all things American did not extend to their sports. He thought that watching basketball was like watching ping-pong in slow motion – 'the ball is at one end at it's gone in, and now it's at the other end and it's gone in again, oooh and now it's back to the other end' … ad nauseam.

Their version of football seemed to involve a few seconds of orchestrated and utterly incomprehensible mayhem, replayed umpteen times from every camera angle before an advert break. And as for baseball – that offered all the excitement and intrigue of watching paint dry.

The last five feet of the hotel reception desk was set up as a bar. Shelves behind the counter held the spirits (or the liquor as they put it) and a cool cabinet underneath where the bottled beer, soft drinks, and wine were kept. No draft beer - and even the red wine was chilled in America.

In the reception area, there were half a dozen round white plastic tables. Around each, there were a few chairs that appeared to have been designed to a specification that said "Make some chairs that have two arms and are comfortable for half an hour, but are as small as possible while still being classed as adult furniture.

It was not a drinking hole of choice for Mark – nor for that matter for anyone else – but it was a good enough place to while away an hour, have a couple of beers to unwind and peruse the Saturday newspaper.

A weekend newspaper in America is a sight to see, with more supplements than a branch of Holland and Barrett's. When he read a newspaper back home, he would always read it back to front, starting with the sports section and finishing with the boring bits on the front page. Here it was different. He had no wish to read the sports section – for reasons already stated. He was more interested in reading the national news to give him a chance to keep up with any news-related conversations his colleagues might be having in the next few days. During an earlier visit, he had been unable to contribute to a lengthy political discussion amongst his colleagues that referred extensively to 'the GOP'. He had since broadened his education to find that this was how most Americans referred to the Republican Party.

Like everything else, these discussions would be America-centric, so Mark had to update himself on the latest political shenanigans in the Land of the Free. This was not relaxation – it was the last part of his preparation for the meeting. But he did also enjoy reading the local news section. It was remarkably parochial and quite entertaining.

Sunday morning, having slept reasonably well, he was one of the first people sitting down for breakfast in the diner across the road which was also quiet on weekends, and there were a dozen four-seater booths, complete with red vinyl benches each side of a Formica-topped table, to choose from. Or at least there would have been if he was permitted a choice, but of course, he had to obey the sign and wait to be seated.

His Sunday was going to closely follow its normal pattern. A taxi from the hotel to the local suburban railway station and then a train into central New York. On a previous trip when he had told his US colleagues that he had done this, it reinforced their opinion of him as a strange person. Normal people in the USA only took a train if it was part of a compulsory commute. Nobody rode them by choice.

The ride into New York was brief and uncomfortable, with a few stops at nearly deserted suburban train stations and a view that was almost uniformly 'American Industrial Ugly'. Mark loved it.

His agenda today was to visit the Empire State Building and Times Square. His previous visits to the Big Apple had been longer. His first had been a full day riding around on the bus tour, getting off at key points to marvel at the sites and to add vital experiences such as ordering a salt beef sandwich from a genuine New York deli. His next visit was a pre-booked whole day spent climbing the Statue of Liberty and taking the full guided tour of Ellis Island. He was surprised at how moving that experience was.

But today's agenda had to be shortened. Normally he had only to return to the hotel in time for dinner with his US counterparts, who would arrive throughout the day. But today, he had to get back earlier because Ziegler had asked to meet at five. He had something he wanted to chat about.

Ziegler's full name was Stefan Ziegler, and he was the sales rep (actually, his title, in line with all American salesmen, Mark had discovered, was Regional Sales Manager - everything was always bigger in America). Ziegler was based at the company's head office and covered the East Coast.

When they had first been introduced, Mark was puzzled at him being known only by his last name – the last time Mark had known of this practice was when he was at school, and it seemed disrespectful to refer to a colleague in this way. But Ziegler was known to his friends and family as Steve, and there was already a Steve in American Power, so something had to give. Ziegler hated being called Stefan and refused to use that. There was a very popular TV show at the time in the USA, whose star was known by the one-word title - Seinfeld - so it was apparently now cool to be known by just your last name.

Ziegler and Mark got on like a house on fire from their first meeting. Ziegler also had a father who was a builder, and both he and Mark possessed a similarly high level of restless energy. Mark had always accepted criticism of his inability to sit still – both literally and figuratively - and had to work on keeping himself focussed. But he was positively serene when compared with Ziegler.

Ziegler had previously invited Mark and Charlotte to enjoy a vacation in New York, but this was never going to happen. New York was way too loud and noisy for Charlotte. 'Maybe with the next partner,' Mark thought.

Ziegler showed up in the hotel lobby right on five o'clock, accompanied by his wife Amy, and their twin daughters. Amy gave him a huge hug - in the way that American women always seem to greet anyone other than complete strangers. She was petite, slim, blonde, pretty, and very outgoing. Mark could have quite fancied her but for one thing – her voice. It was, like that of so many of the American women he met, high pitched to the borderline of being squeaky. Mark had discovered or had explained to him, most of the differences between things in America and the UK but had never been able to fathom why so many American women seemed to have a voice that was pitched an octave higher than their British counterparts.

He knew that Ziegler had married very young, and the twin girls had arrived very early in the marriage, but he was unsure whether their early arrival was a result of, or a cause of the very early marriage and was far too polite to ask. The family were on their way back from the girls' soccer game, which they told Mark they had won 'two zero' and he chatted to them briefly about 'soccer' and told them that it really should be called football and not soccer. They enjoyed the joke.

Dad shooed them out as soon as he politely could.

"Can we grab a coffee at the diner?" he asked, "Only the other guys will all be arriving about now, and we'll never get the chance to talk if we stay here". Mark was quick to consent. His tight schedule for the day had meant that he had eaten nothing since breakfast and an American-sized slice of cheesecake would go down a treat.

Once they had been seated at a table and ordered, Ziegler was straight into his pitch before the pleasantries were even complete.

"I've got the chance to buy this building. It used to be an office and storage depot," he started, pronouncing it deep-oh in the American way.

"It's close to the railroad station and due to go to auction next month, but I've been told that a bid of two hundred thousand will clinch it before the sale date. And my builder tells me it would cost about another fifty thousand to convert it into five studio apartments. Those things are selling like hotcakes right now, and each one of them would go for a hundred grand."

As he began to accelerate into his proposition and gather excitement, his vocabulary changed: 'thousand' became 'grand' and would probably soon shrink to being a K. Mark thought that there was no doubt that more slang would follow.

"So, I'm putting together an offer for four people to join me in the deal. Each'll have to put up fifty-five grand so we've got a ten per cent contingency for any problems or cost overruns. I'll manage the whole project and take a normal share plus five per cent of the sale price on completion – so you should be able to turn your fifty into ninety-five."

"I know you've got that fifty K sitting in your US bank account doing nothing 'cos you were bitching about it last time we spoke," Ziegler continued with a smile. "What do you say?"

Mark had indeed got fifty thousand dollars in a bank account in the USA and had confided this to Ziegler when they had a few beers together at the last trade show. He'd also let him know of his frustration that the money was not earning any interest. In fact, Ziegler was the only person who did know about it. Charlotte knew there was an account – they had an almighty row when he first set it up, so she was bound to remember, but even she did not know how much was in it.

-

Opening the account, and the row immediately after he had done it, had happened two years previously, when he and Charlotte had been on holiday in Florida. They had booked a villa, together with Mark's sister Susan and her husband, Hugh, for a two-week stay. It had been a really good holiday during which they had made friends with the couple who managed the agency that rented the property.

Sean and Lorraine were ex-pat Brits who had left the UK and found themselves this ideal job. Mark had a long conversation with Sean one afternoon over a couple of beers by the side of the pool at their villa. Apart from realising that Sean and Lorraine had a pretty good lifestyle, he was able to put in motion one of his ideas. He asked Sean if he could use the address of the property agency as a correspondence address in the USA, and Sean said "Sure, no problem".

The following day Mark had used a card-printing machine outside an office supplies store in the local shopping mall to print some business cards with his name, and the address of Florida Homes Network – or FHN as it showed on the card so that it might stand for anything he chose.

A few days later when he took Charlotte and Susan on yet another shopping trip (how these women could spend so much time shopping, he never understood) he called into a local Florida bank to see if he could set up a personal account. It was ridiculously easy (way easier than it would be for an American tourist to set up a bank account in the UK certainly) and half an hour later after depositing a hundred dollars, he had an account, a temporary chequebook and the promise that a VISA debit card would be in the mail. The card even arrived before the end of their holiday.

He told Charlotte that his idea was to use the account as a way of saving up money to buy a few gadgets when he came over – because everything from laptops to phones was way cheaper in America. But when he added that he was going to ask his employers to pay his quarterly bonus into the account, she had accused him of trying to hide money from her, defraud the taxman, launder money and just about everything else she could think of.

But he now had the account, and the success he had achieved since working for American Power had resulted in his bonus of ten thousand dollars landing in his account every quarter. Even Mark could not buy that many gadgets, and apart from using it for spending money on one subsequent US holiday with Charlotte, it was all sitting there and annoying him by not earning any interest – which was the fact he had let slip to Ziegler.

They discussed the business proposal for the next hour. Ziegler had an answer for everything and let him know that Steve (one of their fellow salesmen at AP) was going to be one of the investors, with two of Ziegler's local friends. He thought the whole project would take a maximum of six months to complete – Mark was not surprised. A project of this nature would take longer in the UK but planning restrictions were much less stringent in the USA.

"Seeing as there are three of us from the company in the deal, have you told Martin?" he asked. He respected Martin's opinion and would ideally like his input on the proposition before deciding – but obviously, if Ziegler did not want Martin to know then this would not be possible.

"Sure, of course he knows," said Ziegler.

Mark realised they would have to join their colleagues for dinner at seven, so he would have to finish the discussion now to have a chance to freshen up. "Can I have until the end of the week to think on it?" he asked, and Ziegler was happy to leave it there.

He knew he could never tell Ziegler one of the things he was thinking, which was something like 'Since I found a certain briefcase, I've now got enough money that I've stopped worrying about this sum in the US account not working.'

Dragan

August 2005

James had once asked his father how much he knew about Dragan, with whom he had now been working for so many years. The answer he received was evasive, as James would later understand, once he was dealing with the man. Dragan was a very private person.

Dragan Zawadski had a major problem throughout his childhood. He could never remember the names of all his relatives. Both his parents were children of wartime immigrants. His Polish father and his Serbian mother both came from large families, and the proliferation of aunties and uncles – not just the real ones that were siblings of one or other of his parents, but the inverted comma aunts and uncles (more distant relatives or close family friends), seemed to be endless. And when it came to his cousins – it was impossible to remember them all. This was not just a problem of their sheer numbers, but when you added in the complexities of two different sets of languages spoken within the family, in addition to the English language he was determined to master to fit in with the other kids at school, life was challenging for a young boy.

He spoke all three languages well enough – and worked hard to speak English just like the English kids and not with the immigrant accent that his brothers and sisters had. He found it easy to get on with everyone – but didn't always want to get on with them and longed for some time to himself. But with so many others always around, seldom got it.

The continued presence of the innumerable family members was a burden he just had to live with. So, when he left school – a typical product of that time, when too few resources had been focused on the development of this new generation – he was unencumbered by too many qualifications. His employment hopes had a ceiling of skilled manual labour.

Turning down several offers to work with members of the enlarged family, Dragan tried his hand at many different jobs without ever settling to any particular one. The family presence was also hard to escape. When he worked at a local garage, he noticed that several family members began bringing their cars to him for repair. Getting bored there, he moved to a less physically demanding job in a burger bar, and once again gave his employers a short-term boost in business as members of his family began to pop in from time to time. He escaped the problem for a while, working in one of the factories on the booming Slough Trading Estate. He would work his shift, take advantage of whatever overtime was available – and there was always plenty available), go home, pay his rent loyally to his parents and look forward to some future unspecified escape. But boredom eventually overtook him again and he moved on.

He reached his first goal of independence when he passed his driving test and invested his savings into his first car. His next aim was to get a place of his own and to achieve this he took on a job as an evening taxi driver. Again, his family connections helped his income level – as from that point onwards nobody in his family ever called for a taxi – they called for Dragan. He continued this role while he continued to frequently change his daytime job.

His spell at a local building company was probably his favourite job. It also meant that all those little building jobs that were needed in the properties of family members came his way too. He enjoyed the time spent in the open air, the physical exercise, and the variety of tasks to be tackled. A friend on the building site also introduced him to one of the first pursuits to engage him when he took him along to the local gym. Dragan loved the challenge of the weights and the bodybuilding machines. He found comfort in building his strength and bulking his muscles and started spending some of his spare cash on the protein powders and such that meant his physique grew to be noticeably powerful.

Over the years another activity began to fill his time. He was often asked by members of his extended family to help sort out various problems. He was just one of those people who seemed approachable. His ability to converse in different languages was useful – and having held so many different jobs gave him an appearance of worldliness that many others didn't seem to have. And for some of the problems he helped with, his growing physical presence was an additional benefit too. Dragan was not averse to accepting the gestures of thanks he received – varying from the baking of a cake to a brown envelope of cash, depending on the size of the problem that had been fixed and the family member whose problem it was.

He was soon able to break loose from the immediate family and get his own flat – which was becoming more necessary as the flow of visitors seeking his assistance showed no signs of diminishing. In fact, the arrival of so many new east Europeans into the UK after the easing of immigration controls meant that Dragan was constantly being asked to help one or another of his distant cousins to find a job or a place to stay.

The emphasis also began to change as he connected so many newcomers with employers and landlords. Now it was more often the landlord and the employer rather than the family member who was paying for his expertise and his connections. The size and frequency of the commissions meant that in no time at all it became his full-time method of earning a living. He had done his last shift of manual labour. And the family helped again – his younger brother Tomasz became his loyal lieutenant.

Dragan sometimes connected directly with the employer, at other times through a go-between. He was very happy with the business that Harry Lavinsky put his way in the South-East, and the same was repeated in various areas around London in that area so quaintly referred to as the 'Home Counties'.

He never got involved in any work in London itself – there were bigger fish swimming in those waters (and many of them being the types of fish you would not want in your aquarium). If he kept away from their territory, he was free to reap the rewards outside the metropolis. And the rewards were both plentiful and growing.

Sam's – A Great Place for Steak

August 2005

The dinner with Martin, the President and Co-Founder of American Power, always formed the perfect ending to Mark's visits to the USA and had become a ritual they both enjoyed. They shared a liking for steak, and his boss had a knack for finding out the latest contender for the best steak in the area.

"Sam's – A Great Place for Steak" was situated on a highway frontage road a short drive from the office. In urban America, the land of the automobile, highways are roaring four-lane or six-lane roads carrying heavy traffic loads. Unlike freeways, which mostly run from one city to another, these urban highways have interchanges every few miles – often in the form of traffic lights - where local traffic transfers onto the frontage roads, which ran either side of the main highway and allow local access. One side of the frontage road faces the highway, the other side is built up with homes, shops, and restaurants.

Like most buildings in the area, Sam's was a wooden building. The difference was that it had no pretence to be anything else. It just pretended to be a lot older than it was. Outside it looked like a transplanted log cabin. Inside it was one hundred per cent fake wild west. Wooden floors with real sawdust on them (the sawdust being the only thing in the place that was real). There were wooden tables and chairs, minimal cutlery and condiments on the tables. The walls were covered in a random collection of 'wild west' paraphernalia: monochrome photographs of late nineteenth century western USA, reproductions of wanted posters, advertisements for cattle auctions, horseshoes, you get the idea. The waiters and waitresses were all attired in smart jeans, check shirts, neckerchiefs and what Mark would call 'cowboy boots' – but they probably just called 'boots'.

They were shown to their table by a waitress with Marylou on her nametag. Mark wondered if they had to change their names to fit in with the décor. Could they permit a cowgirl called Skylar or Brittney, or a cowboy named Carlos or Mohammed, he wondered? She took their order for drinks – two beers – and left them with the menu.

Ordering the meal took longer than it needed to – but this was entirely Mark's fault. Right from the first time he had visited America he had found out that the popular meme of American women saying to an English guy "Oh I love your accent" had more than a grain of truth in it. Whenever he had the opportunity, such as when discussing the various menu options with Marylou, he would exaggerate his British accent (which he normally dialled down as far as possible to improve communication with his business colleagues). It worked. Marylou asked him where he was from, told him how much she loved the English accent and how she would love to visit England one day. Mark spun out the conversation by reassuring her that London was just the same as it looked in the movies, enjoying the flirtation just as much as he always did.

It wasn't quite the success of the British guy in 'Love Actually', but it would do.

Marylou eventually left them.

"Don't worry," said Martin, as he watched Mark taking in the surroundings and trying very hard not to react adversely. "The steaks are really, really good."

And they were. Mark enjoyed a prime rib, a cut that he never saw in the UK, which was marbled with more fat than most other cuts of the meat and was, in his humble opinion, all the tastier for it. He was sure that the piece of meat on his plate, which was a normal US-sized portion, in different circumstances would have been a Sunday joint for a family of four in the UK. Martin enjoyed a similarly huge porterhouse.

The discussion between them was energetic and friendly, moving easily from personal to business topics and back again. The two men were of similar age but quite different backgrounds, and there were many shared ambitions and plenty of mutual respect.

Mark knew the key parts of his boss's history. He had been brought up in New Jersey and had gone to university (or college as Americans always referred to it) in Midwest USA, got a degree in Business Studies, returned to his home state, and then had a series of jobs in New York. He had worked for an advertising agency, and a Wall Street firm as well as two or three other companies, in marketing or administrative jobs, none of them lasting more than eighteen months. His 'life-changing moment' had occurred when he attended his college's five-year reunion, and met his ex-roommate Andrej, for the first time since their degree ceremony.

Their different personalities were the key to their successful relationship - each having entered college with a different agenda.

Martin planned to achieve a degree, but to do so with the absolute minimum of work – and to maximise his social life and entertainment. Andrej, on the other hand, intended to get the very best degree he could, to progress to an academic or research position in his chosen field of electrical engineering, and to enjoy the opportunity of sharing the intellectual and physical resources that were available.

Martin was thus able to open the door for Andrej to have a social life. Although Andrej did not go through this door too often, he nonetheless appreciated the occasional relief it gave him. In return, Andrej, by a combination of example, persuasion and guilt, made sure that his roommate did do some work from time to time, and eventually managed to negotiate three years of partying whilst staying the right side of the authorities and emerging with a degree at the end.

When they met at the reunion, Andrej was able to update Martin with his progress. He had indeed secured a job befitting his intellect at a leading research establishment. Luckily, Martin was able to steer the conversation away from the topic of his job history and to explore the other news that Andrej had, which was the progress he had made with his hobby.

He had been working in his home lab on developing a new electric motor. As befitted a true boffin he was quite modest that he had developed one that was substantially lighter and more powerful than anything on the market, and that he had also built a couple of prototype hand tools to use it – specifically an electric drill and a hand sander.

Martin was able to steer the conversation into the commercial possibilities of such an idea and they agreed to meet up a couple of weeks later to discuss it. He was so interested in the idea, he not only invested some of his time and money into travelling to Andrej's home – but also made the huge sacrifice of travelling on a Greyhound bus.

He described the year after their meeting as a year from hell, and Mark introduced him to the phrase annus horribilis, which he enjoyed. He'd continued working in his latest dead-end job, but also worked with Andrej in taking his idea forward; organised the building of a few prototypes, paid for them to be electrically tested and safety certified, and raised a loan from the bank. His biggest challenge was to persuade Andrej to leave his job and start a company with him because he had suddenly discovered what he most wanted to be – his own boss. Andrej had eventually agreed to give it a couple of years, matched Martin's investment, and American Power had come into being.

Now, five years downstream the pair of them were beginning to reap the rewards of the hard work and were looking forward to moving their company onto the next stage.

The conversation over the steaks and beers ranged from business plans to personal stuff. In the business section, they talked about the main development in the US market – the pilot project with Home Depot – the largest chain of home improvement stores in the USA – which was test marketing the AP tools in a small number of their outlets. Martin was optimistic of the full take up of their products within the next year – something that would have a drastic impact on his company.

Mark was pleased about this, having gotten over the disappointment he had felt when hearing about it at the sales meeting. He had hoped to impress his colleagues with his big project, but the news that this deal was not only much bigger but had also progressed one stage further had rather gazumped him.

He was pleased to hear that the deal was being run by Jeff Dupont and looked forward to comparing notes with him as they both progressed their separate deals. But he also realised that if the company succeeded in landing a deal of this size it would change things substantially, and this might not be a totally good thing for him – he was quite happy with how they were right now.

He tried to remind Martin about the possibility of growing the European operation of AP but quickly realised that with his big domestic deal front and centre of this thinking, now was not the time to progress this issue.

In the private section of their conversation, Mark gave an update on his change of domestic arrangements and accepted commiserations. Martin then let him know what very few others knew - that his wife, Ankhara, was expecting their first child. He asked him not to pass this information on as he was being selective as to who knew right now. Mark appreciated the confidence. Mark was one of a few people who knew that Martin's wife's name was Ankhara. It came from her parents' previous hippy lifestyle – Ankhara being the name of some minor Egyptian deity. Most Americans assumed that her name was a joining together of the names Anne and Kara. A reasonable assumption since Americans had been joining two names together for their female children for years - since before Peggy Sue got married or anyone even said goodnight to Mary Ellen Walton.

Mark took the opportunity to ask about Ziegler.

"He's told you about his latest scheme, has he?" Martin asked.

"You say his *latest* scheme – does he have many of them?"

"Oh yes. I've known Ziegler for years, and he has *always* been coming up with schemes. I sometimes wonder if his job at AP is just useful to help fill in his time – he seems to make more money outside the company than he does inside."

"So, these schemes are successful, then?"

"You bet. If he offers you the chance to join in one, I'd certainly give it some serious consideration. If my money wasn't all tied up in AP, I certainly would. He's a successful young man. You know he drives a caddy, don't you?"

Mark had a strange image leap into his mind of Ziegler arriving at a customer's place driving a golf cart.

"A *caddy*?" he asked.

"Yeah, a caddy. A Cadillac"

"But aren't Cadillacs really expensive cars?"

"Well, his is not the top of the range, and it's not a new model, but yeah. It's a caddy and they're pricey."

"And what do his customers think when they see him arriving in it?"

"Oh, they love it. Nothing like being a bit of a character and showing that you're successful".

Mark considered briefly what he thought his customers would think if he arrived driving a classic Bentley or Rolls Royce. You could pick one up for reasonable prices - an eccentric friend of his in Norfolk had a vintage roller. But the cost of servicing and repairs, and the amount of petrol you would need to do any serious mileage were ridiculous. Maybe it was a lot easier for an American, knowing how much cheaper their gas was than British petrol.

He was pretty sure of one thing. If he turned up at a customer's driving one, the reaction would not be that they 'love it'. Yet another difference between the Brits and the Yanks' he thought. There are two very different reactions on the two sides of the Atlantic to people being successful.

However, Martin's attitude did give Mark the confidence to talk a little about his private property deals in the UK. "I'm only doing it to increase building activity and sell more power tools, of course," he joked. Martin showed some interest and wished him well. He also learned that this type of activity was also common in the USA where it was called 'flipping'. A new piece of colloquial American was thus added to his vocabulary, but he could not dare tell his boss how the deals were funded.

A few things were decided in the steakhouse meeting that evening – mostly to do with routine matters of sales plans for American Power in the UK. The significant discovery for Mark was that his boss had no problem whatsoever with his employees working on deals outside the company. 'Yet again, could there be more difference between American and British attitudes?' Mark thought. With any potential restrictions caused by Martin's feelings having been removed, he would shortly be signing a partnership agreement with Ziegler and writing him a cheque (or maybe a check) for fifty-five thousand dollars.

Raheem

August 2005

It was just after nine o'clock in the morning and James was having a eureka moment. Defined in the dictionary as 'a moment of sudden, triumphant discovery, inspiration, or insight' the phrase is believed to originate from Archimedes, a Greek mathematician living more than 200 years BC. He was trying to figure out a way to measure the exact volume of an object and, so the story goes, he realised that when he placed his body into a bath, a volume of water was displaced, so if he could measure the volume of this displaced water, he would automatically know the volume of the object. He is then said to have rushed out shouting "Eureka!" - which roughly translates to "I've found it".

If it was not surprising enough that James was having a Eureka moment, sitting in his office in Chatham on a Monday morning, then it would be even more surprising to know that the cause of his excitement was a story in the local newspaper.

In his previous life, the only published work that James would regularly read was the Financial Times, or occasionally, articles from The Economist for light relief. But now his role determined that he needed much less global news input and far more knowledge of local matters. So, he made sure that the main local paper was delivered to each of his business premises and found time to read them every week.

He called Ron Webster, and after exchanging pleasantries and reassuring him that he wasn't chasing up for non-existent and unexpected progress on the lost briefcase, told him the reason for the call.

"I'm just reading a story in the local paper about a young man by the name of Raheem DaCosta,"

James referred to the article to check the details.

"He was in the local court last week, charged with some form of credit card scam," he continued.

He might have been more specific about the scam if he had been able to glean this information from the newspaper report but had a distinct impression that the reporter was not able to fully understand or explain it.

"I'd like to know a bit more about this young man and get the chance to meet him. Do you think you can help?"

"What sentence was he given?" Ron asked.

James checked back with the paper and replied, "looks like he had to do some community service in addition to a suspended sentence."

"He'll be under the Probation Service then," replied Ron, "so I'll be able to get the information from one of my old contacts there. But can I ask why on earth are you interested in him? "

"I want to offer him a job"

Ron promised to get the information to James the next morning.

-

"Fairly typical story," he said, handing over the report.

"Broken home. Quite a bright kid, no criminal record. Went on from school to do an IT diploma at college, couple of low-level jobs in IT, neither of which lasted long, and then this bungled attempt to make a quick buck. Probation has housed him in a local HMO. If you want to meet him, I'd suggest we go together, it's not the nicest of locations."

It took only a couple of minutes for James to read the report and to agree with Ron's summary.

"How far away is the address where he's staying?" asked James. Discovering that it was five minutes' walk, he asked if Ron was able to go with him immediately. Five minutes later they were knocking on the door of Raheem's allotted room in a run-down Victorian pile. Raheem came to the door in a dishevelled state that suggested he had just thrown on the white T-shirt and black jeans, and had very recently left the unmade bed which was immediately to the right of the door. The rest of the room matched, being untidy, disorganised, and scruffy.

"Who are you?" he asked.

"I'm ex Detective Inspector Jenkins."

James noticed that the 'ex' was spoken a lot more softly than the rest of Ron's title "and this is my colleague, James. We'd like a word with you."

James stepped into the 'good cop' role and suggested that they could go to the nearest burger bar to have their chat. Raheem was naturally suspicious but, having been processed through the criminal system so recently, he was also somewhat cowed by an ex-Detective Inspector (assuming he had even heard the 'ex' part). Plus, he was hungry, and a burger sounded very enticing. He put some shoes on and followed them out of the room.

Raheem ordered the largest burger on the menu, large fries, and a large coke. Ron wanted only a cup of coffee. James chose chicken nuggets. He wanted to show empathy by eating something – but also needed to be able to talk freely and not be encumbered by a large burger dripping sauce everywhere.

Once seated, James began his pitch,

"Raheem, it seems to me that you know a bit about IT." A non-committal grunt and small nod was all the response he expected. And it was all he got.

"You see I've got a problem. I've just taken over my dad's business, and it needs some IT installing. I need someone like you to help, so I'd like to offer you a job."

Raheem was suspicious of the offer. "Why me?" he asked.

"Good question. I could hire anyone – the job is not that complicated. I need some wireless networking installed, some websites set up, that sort of thing. You could handle that couldn't you?" This elicited a slightly more positive nod and a 'Yeah' instead of a grunt.

"The thing is, I can't afford the kind of money that IT firms would want to charge me. And I want some things done in my special way, which they might not agree to. I reckon if I paid you four hundred quid a week, you would do it my way. Am I right?"

James thought the level was set just right. Four hundred a week was a lot less than an IT consultancy would charge, even for the lowest level of IT, but it would probably seem extremely appealing to someone whose only alternative was a Social Security cheque.

Raheem was still suspicious. "What's he got to do with it?" he asked James while pointing at Ron.

"He's just here to make sure you realise this is completely legit and to make sure that I was safe going into that place you are living. So - do you want to give it a go?"

Although he was not entirely convinced that he had heard the full story, by the time the meal was all done, Raheem had decided that there was not much to lose. "When do you want me to start?"

"Tomorrow. Nine o'clock. Let's take a walk and I'll show you where the office is." And then to Ron, "Think I can manage now, thanks. Send me a bill for your work."

"Nah, a free round of drinks next time's all I need".

James and Raheem walked back to the club. James talked a little about the business, explaining that what he was about to show him was one of the four clubs that he owned. He explained that his first two jobs would be to install a database of the club members and to put a wireless network in each club.

"You see most of my customers are quite old. Not many of them use the internet all that much, but I'll be trying to get some younger customers, maybe younger members of their families. I'd rather they sat in my club drinking coffee and browsing the web than sit in McDonald's."

They reached the club and Raheem was given a brief tour.

"Not much in the way of office space, I'm afraid. You'll have to work on one of the tables in the bar – or in my office if I'm not there and you want some privacy. I'll get a portable computer for you to work on and order a wireless router to be delivered as soon as possible – you can tell me what else you need when I've given you a full list of what I want to get done. That OK?"

Raheem had not yet progressed much beyond grunts of assent and gave another.

"Couple of other things. You'll need to smarten up a bit. No particular dress code here – but something a bit better than that," he said, indicating Raheem's current attire.

"I'll advance you some of your first week's wages so you can get kitted out."

He handed his new employee two fifty-pound notes.

"You can pay me back when you've had a few paycheques, I'll make sure of that. Now, one last thing I want to show you – five more minutes' walk."

It actually took them ten minutes to walk to their next destination, a small block of flats with builders' rubble outside that testified to its status of being under renovation. James took a set of keys from his pocket and used one of them to open the front door. He led them up a flight of stairs without explaining anything and used a second key to open the door to a studio flat. It was small, plain, minimally furnished, and had obviously not been occupied since its very recent renovation.

"It's just a room and shower," he explained. "Shared kitchen with the three other studios on this floor. One of my club members owns it. It's a hundred a week – but if you want it, I'll take the rent straight out of your wages."

Raheem was aware this was a good offer. The place where he was currently living was a hole – and he would not have the best set of references to offer any other landlord. He was still having difficulty believing this was all happening - and was beginning to wonder what the catch would be – but what the hell. In for a penny, in for a pound and with nothing to lose, he said yes.

"Right – you'll have to pick the keys up from me tomorrow. You've got some clothes to buy, and I've got to get some kit for you to work on." He escorted Raheem to the door. Anything else?"

"Yeah – I like to be called Ray, not Raheem."

"OK then Ray – I'll see you at nine tomorrow morning. Don't be late."

When he showed up the next morning, still wearing his battered leather jacket James noted that he was now sporting a new T-shirt, new casual trousers, and new trainers. James recapped what needed to be done. He pulled the box containing the card index of the members out of his desk drawer and placed it in front of Ray.

"This is the list of members, and I want you to put all their details into a database. Everything that's on the front of the card. And I'd like you to create some extra data fields for each of them that we can use later. I want to know what they do for a living – if I want a plumber, I'd rather he was a club member so I might get a discount. And their date of birth and the date of birth of their wife or partner."

114

He thought Raheem was looking a little puzzled, so he continued

"This is supposed to be a club. We'll be sending them a card to let them know they can come into the club on their birthday and get a free drink. I'm betting that if they do come in, they'll bring their other half and stay for three or four more. So, I'll want to find out if we've got any members in the greetings card business, for starters."

He looked up and confirmed that Raheem was following him, even if not yet smiling at his humour.

"Later I'll want to know their email address and mobile phone numbers. I know that they may not have email addresses yet, but they all will sooner or later, you'll see. You'll probably get sick of me saying this – but I cannot stress too much how important it is for a business to get as much information about its customers as it possibly can."

He waited to get a nod from Ray – he was learning to expect no more than this to signify agreement. 'Maybe verbal communication might come later,' he thought.

"There's a copy of Microsoft Office on the laptop – you OK to use that?"

His face bore an expression that said "Can I do that? Is the pope Catholic?" He conveyed his answer without saying a word.

"Don't worry about the figures on the back of the card, I'll go through that with you later. And then maybe you'll start to understand why I want to have my own in-house IT man rather than have some outsiders involved, OK?"

Although he had not yet fully explained anything, he felt that Raheem was somewhat reassured that there was a genuine reason for his employment.

"Then I want each of them to know they can log on to the internet using the wireless link you'll be putting in place, but we'll talk a bit more about that when you've set it up – the equipment should be arriving in the next couple of days."

James took him into the back room where was a laptop computer on the corner table, and a pad and a pen in case he needed some more old-fashioned work tools. James returned with the box of membership cards.

"Make sure nobody else can see these, and when you've finished with them, make sure they're still in the same order and get Ben to lock them back in my desk drawer.

"I'll be leaving you alone now, you just call me if you need anything - Ben'll know where I am– otherwise just get on and do it and show me when it's up and running. There'll be other stuff – but let's get this bit working, then you'll set up the same system in the other places. We'll also be setting up a few websites on the server, but I'll tell you more about that later. Any questions?"

Ray shook his head. He had either a hundred questions or none at all, so he went for the second option. He shook his head, took off his jacket, hung it over the back of the chair, opened the portable computer and started work.

James spoke with Raheem at least once a day for the next few days to check on his progress. He had allowed him a whole week to complete two basic tasks and was pleased to hear from him on Monday afternoon that all the work was finished. James would need to change his routine to see what had been accomplished. The next stages of work he intended to assign him were ones which he needed to discuss carefully with him – and this was not a task to be conducted over the phone. He made the necessary changes to his plans and was in the Chatham club at nine the next morning.

Ray showed him what he'd achieved so far, and James was pleased to see that everything was how he hoped it would be. There was a simple database on the laptop which could be quickly accessed and interrogated. The wireless network was installed, and James was able to connect his PC and verify the internet connection.

"Good work, Ray. We'll need to get a regular PC installed as well, so you can transfer everything off your laptop. But I'll put that off for a little while, so you'll have a better picture of what's needed."

Ray nodded. The praise from James seemed to have softened his expression ever so slightly, and James hoped he was beginning to appreciate the responsibility he was gradually being given.

"Let's move on to those mysterious numbers on the back of some of the customer cards. Have you worked out what they're for?"

116

"No. I reckoned you'd tell me when you were ready"

"They record loans that have been made to club members."

James picked up a card and put it on the desk between them.

"The first number is the amount they borrowed, with the date next to it. After that, there's a list of the dates and amounts they've repaid. All the loans are supposed to be repaid within the year, so I need a record of every loan and a reminder when each payment is due to be made. I'd also like to know how much money is out on loan, how much to expect in repayments, and when."

Ray seemed to instantly understand what was needed, and asked his first question,

"Are you allowed to do that – lending money?"

"Good question. Let's just say that if I hired a very good lawyer, I could hopefully persuade a judge that this was part of the club's membership terms, but I hope I don't have to do that."

Ray still looked a little puzzled, but when James continued "Maybe you can now see why I want you as my IT man and not an outside company," the penny dropped, and his expression changed.

"OK got it," was his reply – as brief as ever.

"How long do you think it'll take you to do this?" Mark asked

"It's a bit more complex than the other stuff - I'll show you something in a couple of days, then maybe another day or so to make sure it's OK."

"That's fine – let's see where you are at the end of tomorrow."

Ray nodded – he was already working out how to do it.

The following week, James and Ray had another IT consultation. James was pleased with what he saw – it was a little rough and ready, but since he was the only person that would use this part of the system, it only needed to be good enough for him. He wanted one other output from the system that he had forgotten to tell Raheem – he wanted it to produce an initial letter confirming the loan - one copy for the customer, one for the files and one for Zlatan. Raheem said he would finish it all off the next day.

James now moved on to the next part of his plan.

"You've set up the wireless network so that it can only be accessed by someone with a password, yes?"

"That's right"

"And we can allocate each member a password and allow them to change it if they want?"

"Yeah. The system has a full password management module."

"Good. We'll send a letter to every member of this club and get it running before we roll it out to the other clubs. But here's what I want you to *not* tell the members. Remember how I told you how important it is to know as much as you can about your customers?"

Ray gave the tired nod of someone who expected to hear this mantra many times.

"Well, I want to know what they do when they're using this system to go on the internet, what websites they visit, and so on. As much information as possible. Understood?" Ray understood. He also got his first inkling of why James was not using professional IT consultants. He even wondered, very briefly, if it was even legal. But he didn't care and didn't ask.

"I can install some basic packet capture software easily enough. I guess you won't want anyone else to have access to this info though, will you?" he asked.

"I knew you'd be smart enough to understand. That's why I hired you," James smiled.

"Well, it won't be as easy to read as all the other stuff, but I should be able to give you a table showing who went where."

"Great. Before I lend any money to someone in the future, I'd like to know just how often they visit gambling websites," was James's justifying explanation.

Ray wondered if this was the only reason James was going to acquire this information. He suspected not. In truth, James was not sure what he was going to do with all the information gathered in this way – but he was sure it could have value.

Too Many Whirlpools
August 2005

The downside of the biannual trip to the USA was the journey home.

The last day of Mark's visit was spent in AP's head office, having meetings with the various company personnel with whom he wanted to discuss issues, and making sure that the list of action points from Pat and Cheryl were raised, and hopefully answered. Then it was a taxi ride, or occasionally a lift from Martin or one of the company's employees, to Newark airport and the early evening flight back to the UK. After four and a bit days in America, he was just about adjusted to the time difference so it was obviously time to go home!

The flight took off in the early evening. There was no work for him to do, and Mark took time to go over the events of the previous few days. He spent very little time thinking about the deal with Ziegler. That had all been agreed – he would send him a cheque when he got back and then there was nothing he could do. It would be successful (hopefully) or it would not.

He spent more time thinking about the deal with Home Depot that was in the pipeline for the US office. Having seen one or two of their stores in his trips to the US he looked online at the company information and was amazed at their size. Over three hundred thousand employees in nearly two thousand stores. A deal with this company would change American Power in a big way.

This would also be the first time he had returned from the USA to an empty home. Coming so soon after meeting Ziegler's family and then Martin's private announcement of his impending baby, it all combined to unsettle Mark in a way he did not quite understand. He was scheduled to have lunch with his parents on Sunday and knew he would get a subtle interrogation from his mother concerning the departure of Charlotte and his resulting solitude. His mother had also told him that they had some news for him – and he feared that this might not be good news.

The journey was all that you would expect of a 'red-eye special'. It took off from Newark at 7:45 in the evening – Mark having arrived at the airport two hours before this to make sure there were no problems with check-in, luggage, passport control or security.

By the time the evening meal had been served, eaten, and cleared away it was around 10 pm in the USA. Even with his serendipitous ability to sleep almost anywhere, he was lucky to get three hours of sleep before hey presto! It was six in the morning in the UK, breakfast was being served, and preparations were underway for landing.

He was sure to spend the rest of the day – as he usually did when he came back from the USA – feeling like death warmed up. His visit to the office would be perfunctory before he went home to an early (and lonely) night.

After catching up on domestic chores on Saturday, Mark drove to Brentwood for Sunday lunch with his mum and dad. He had not been there for months – justified because he had been so busy – and wondered what the news was that his mum had promised. He realised that something was up when he turned the corner and saw the 'House Sold' sign outside his parents' home. Obviously, there was no need to tiptoe around wondering what their news was. After presenting his mum with the obligatory bunch of flowers and receiving a hug and kiss, he was able to come right out with it. "So, you've sold the house, then?"

His dad explained that he had decided it was time to pack it in. He would be sixty-five next birthday, which was, after all, the official pension age, and he was starting to have difficulty with some of the physical demands of being a builder.

"Jeremy has agreed to buy the business," said his mum.

It took him a few seconds to unpack this statement until he remembered that his mum was the only person, apart from Jeremy's own mother, who called him Jeremy. To everyone else, he was Jem (and if you don't know why Jeremy made sure that everyone just knew the shortened version of his name, then you don't know much about builders).

Jem, the guy who had worked with Mark's father for nigh on twenty years since he started as an apprentice. Mark realised he had never known – because he had never asked – if Jem was an employee or a partner in the business. It was clearly worth something to him to take over the business name after Mark's dad retired. It all added up. And the way his dad had told him a few months ago that he would not be able to help him on his house conversion project made sense too. He was presumably already starting to wind down his involvement in the business at that point.

"Yes, we're selling up. I think they call it downsizing, is that right?" his mum continued.

"How far are you moving?" he asked and was a little surprised by their response.

"We're going to move to the coast. Clacton, we think".

Mark was wise enough not to question this decision, despite his immediate misgivings. He had heard of many retired couples facing problems when they moved away from their hometown to a different location – even if, as in this case it was only about fifty miles away. Ties with friends, family and social life became fractured and there could be a huge problem when one of the couple died and left the other alone. Hopefully, by them taking the step (relatively) early, the possibility of this happening too soon should be minimised, but he would try, where he could, in the next few weeks to make sure they were confident in this life-changing move before they made any irreversible decisions.

His parents had often holidayed in Clacton, so it was understandable that this might be their chosen destination, and the benefits of sea air were alleged to be life-enhancing. But he was still a little uneasy. He assumed his sister would already know about their parents' plans, and he made a mental note to speak with her on the subject as soon as possible.

"We'll buy a house that needs a bit of work doing on it, so I can keep myself occupied," his dad continued. "We were hoping that with your new-found property expertise you might come and have a look at a couple of places with us."

Mark wondered whether this offer was genuine. Did they really want his input into their decision? Or were they simply making sure that he did not feel left out? Either way, he resolved to do his best to go property viewing with them.

"Have you got anything in mind?"

"Yes, we've seen details of quite a few, and we think that a couple of them look very suitable".

He realised this project was well underway. Yes, the sign outside had said 'House Sold' not 'House for Sale' hadn't it?

"Now we've also got something for you" his mum continued, and walked over to the bureau, opened the drawer, took out an envelope and handed it to him. The envelope was full, the flap tucked in, unsealed, and it had his name written on the front in his mother's unmistakable handwriting. Only she formed a capital M with three separate downstrokes and a cross-stroke. Mark immediately knew what was in the envelope without opening it. He had some recent experience of similar envelopes, and it was unmistakable. It was money. Peering inside the envelope and seeing the familiar pink-red colour he knew that it contained fifty-pound notes, and although he couldn't say so – he immediately knew that it must be five thousand pounds.

"Now don't say anything – we wanted to give you and your sister something when we retired. We've sold the house and the business so there's five thousand in there for you. Susan has already had hers – she's going to use it to put a conservatory on her house."

Mark thought that was typical of his sister. so organised and practical. No chance of squandering it on a family holiday or a new car. She would, no doubt, already have had a plan for a conservatory to be the next big-ticket item she and Hugh were going to buy. She would have conducted an initial investigation of likely suppliers and costs, calculated the date by which she and Hugh would be able to save enough money for it, deducted six weeks to allow for delivery and time to pay off the credit card, and pencilled in a date for provisional purchase to be made.

That was what he was thinking. What he said was "Mum, Dad, you didn't need to do this. It's very generous. Are you sure?"

"We thought you should have something and not have to wait until we're gone. You can do whatever you want with it. We had thought it might be a wedding present, but we won't talk about that."

'Yeah, not much,' he thought but didn't say anything. He just thanked them very much for their generosity.

"Buy another one of your houses or whatever," were his mum's last words on it.

"Well, I'll be sure to make good use of it, thanks again."

'Sometimes you don't know when to laugh or cry,' he thought to himself. 'Just when you've got all this cash that you're trying to get rid of, the last thing you expect is your parents to add to your problems – but in a good way, of course.'

His mum smiled and went into the kitchen to finalise lunch. Dad poured two beers. An important question sprang to Mark's mind concerning their regular Saturday outing to watch football.

"What about the Hammers? You won't be able to get there from Clacton, will you Dad?"

"Well to be honest it's all getting a bit much for me anyway. The winter weather is no friend as you get older, you know. I haven't renewed my ticket for next season."

Mark had to make sure that the immensity of the impact that this part of their announcement had on him was not visible to his father. In his world, where everything was changing just a little bit quicker than he liked, the potential loss of this ritual played on his mind way more than it should.

The trip to football alternate Saturdays throughout autumn and winter was surprisingly important to him. It had been a constant for literally as long as he could remember. He would leave home with his dad at lunchtime on Saturday for the short drive to the tube station, where they would board the District Line train for its forty-five-minute journey to Upton Park station, talking football all the way. His dad always seemed to find some excuse to include something in their conversation about the glory days of the nineteen sixties when West Ham had 'won the World Cup'.

As every football fan knew, the World Cup was contested by national teams, not club teams. But West Ham had provided three of the eleven players in the England team that had won the World Cup in 1966 – the only year that England had ever won it. And all four goals in the final against West Germany had been score by West Ham players - three of them by Geoff Hurst who was revered by his father in the way that many men would only honour a religious figure.

Then there was the walk from Upton Park tube station to the Boleyn Ground, stopping on the way to buy a hot dog or burger from a street vendor and a match programme, every word of which Mark would devour on the tube journey home before it was filed away in his collection.

When he left home the ritual changed very little. He would now meet his father at the station, and he no longer bothered to buy a match programme. Everything else remained unchanged, and the loss of this cornerstone of his life was not something he welcomed.

But Sunday lunch was everything he could have hoped for. Roast beef cooked by his mum and carved by his dad, served with hot horseradish sauce, plentiful helpings of fresh veg, and his mum's homemade Yorkshire puddings and gravy. Followed by homemade rhubarb crumble and lashings of custard. All the hallmarks of a mum cooking for her now single adult son. Her guess that he was not eating this kind of good food too often was uncannily accurate. He had seldom had such fare when Charlotte was still there. Since she had left, he had to rely on his own cooking – of which the less said the better.

Over lunch, the impending house move was the main topic of conversation. Mark was pleased to see that they both seemed very positive, even excited, about it. He made sure that they knew what days were not already booked in his diary in the next couple of weeks, and his parents said they would speak to the estate agents in Clacton and get back to him with a date when they could go and look at some houses together.

They eventually moved on to other topics. His father asked about his business, and his mum asked about his trip to America. He knew from the tone in her voice that she was going to be relating all that he told her to her coffee circle at the earliest opportunity, and he was pleased to give her this chance to boast.

He told his dad that things were going well with Howard and thanked him again for the introduction. He also told him some of the things he had learned in America. His father was amazed that there could be builders' merchants with two thousand branches and three hundred thousand employees.

Eventually, he digested the lunch and declined the offer of even more calories for ''tea' as his mum called it. He was just beginning to feel a little lingering jet lag and wanted to get home.

He spent the hour it took to drive home to his empty house going over the events of the day. 'At least she didn't nag me about splitting up with Charlotte' he thought. 'And I must call Susan tomorrow.' But as his mind turned to his sister, another thought struck him. 'Of course, a conservatory! If I added a conservatory onto my own house, I could pay for it in cash, and it would add to the value of the property – and then I could sell it and not even have to pay capital gains tax on the profit. Then, if I bought a house that needed some work done on it, I could pocket the profit tax-free. I could even pay part of the deposit in cash as well. Why didn't I think of that before?'

He resolved to speak to Howard at the first opportunity. The fact that he would be forcing himself into an even more rootless existence for the next few months, and the problems that might cause, never crossed his mind for a moment. That was not what kept him awake that night. The reason he found it so difficult to sleep – despite the jetlag – were more personal.

His dad was retiring. He had completely forgotten that this year his dad would be sixty-five. He would have to speak to Susan about getting something special for his birthday. He was still disturbed at the loss of his company at West Ham games. He had been planning to discuss their chances for the upcoming season – the standard talk that every football fan would have at this time of year. 'This is a rite of passage,' he thought. 'Your parents becoming pensioners. I've not been prepared for this.' When he stopped thinking about that, what kept him awake was how he had felt at returning to an empty house.

There were just too many whirlpools in the stream of his life right now.

Maybe his mum had sensed his discomfort because there had been no inquest on Charlotte's departure. He really should do something about it. His only relationship with a woman right now was the one with Gina, and that was distinctly unhealthy. Not in the physical aspect – they were both scrupulous on that front – but mentally. He knew it was not good that his only intimacy was paid for by the hour. He needed to do something to fix it. He went to sleep with a resolution to register for online dating and by trying (and failing) to remember the names of some dating agencies.

Clacton-on-Sea
August 2005

The town of Clacton in the county of Essex (or Clacton-on-Sea to give it its full holiday brochure title and official town name) held a special place in Mark's memory. It was always a magical place to visit in his childhood, and the family went several times every summer. A whole day of escape. Hours spent playing on the beach and in the sea. A picnic lunch served from an array of Tupperware containers neatly packed into his mother's wicker picnic hamper and served on pale green plastic plates to be eaten with matching pale green plastic knives and forks. All washed down with cold orange squash for the children and hot milky tea for the grown-ups, served from trusty Thermos flasks. And his dad's awful jokes.

"Kids, did you know that the Thermos flask is the most incredible invention in the entire history of the whole universe? Do you know why? Because you can put a cold drink in one flask and it keeps it cold, and you can put a hot drink in the other flask -and it keeps it hot. How does it know which is which?

Lunch was usually followed by games on the pinball and penny push machines in the amusement arcades, an ice cream, or a massive sticky candy floss, then maybe a trip onto the pier to ride the Dodgems, the Waltzers and the 'Stell Stella' rollercoaster. And the day was invariably finished off with a massive portion of chips from Reg Brown's chip shop. Eaten directly from paper folded into a cone; the chips served piping hot with lashings of salt and vinegar.

But now, a trip to Clacton meant an hour crawling along with holiday traffic to a town that time had begun to forget. A town desperately clinging on to its faded former glory. Many of the attractions had closed - and those that remained were trying, but failing, to cover up the crumbling brickwork and rusting metalwork with a fresh lick of paint every summer season. The large chain stores had long since given up hope of turning a profit from their seaside branches and had departed years ago. The major holiday park had been replaced by a housing estate, the classic old hotels had been converted into, or replaced by, faceless blocks of apartments, and although there were still a few souvenir outlets and gift emporia in the town centre trying to make a living, most had been replaced by the retail acne of pound stores, low-price minimarts, and charity shops.

Mark drove through the town centre for old times' sake, and promptly wished he'd left his childhood memories undisturbed. If the town was in transition (as he had heard some say), then although it was obvious where it had come from, it was less clear what it was transitioning into.

His parents were planning to move to an area immediately along the coast from the main tourist (or ex-tourist) town - Holland-On-Sea, an area populated by pensioners to the point where it had almost become a large retirement community. Road after road of small bungalows, interspersed with the occasional two-storey house or business premises, standing out like random teeth in the mouth of a gnarled old third world peasant. This area didn't have the air of something that had faded from previous brightness - it had always been dull.

At least his parents were looking to buy a proper house – the collapse of their life into bungaloid existence was the next step thought Mark. And then he told himself to snap out of this depression before he met them. His parents wanted to do this, and he should be as positive as possible.

He accompanied them as they viewed their two shortlisted houses. One was occupied by a young family and needed nothing more than a coat of paint to make good the wear and tear. The second property, although depressing in its appearance, with obvious signs of non-use for many years, and non-maintenance for even more years before, had plenty of scope for improvement – and was much closer to matching his father's plans. Mark agreed that there seemed to be no signs of any serious problems, and it was the better choice and felt confident that this was his first visit to what would become his parents' future home.

After viewing the two properties, they adjourned to a local pub for lunch. A pleasant old-fashioned English pub serving real ales and proper home-cooked simple fare. Mark had the unusual experience of being by far the youngest person in the bar – something he had not known since he was a teenager. And this had to be the only place on earth where the spaces in the pub car park closest to the pub door were marked out half-size for the regulars to park their mobility scooters. He left his parents to continue their scouting mission and made his way back down the A12. 'Welcome to retirement', he thought.

Just as he was leaving Clacton, Mark received a phone call from a number that neither he nor his phone recognised. It was a landline with a dialling code belonging to Colchester, a town fifteen miles away, where his sister lived. He took the call, immediately recognising the voice of his brother-in-law Hugh.

"I believe you're dropping in on us today," he stated.

"That's right," Mark replied, "I should be there in about half an hour, why?"

"I wanted to pick your brain if that's OK. Is there any chance you could drop by my office on your way?"

Mark was surprised by the concept of Hugh picking his brain – he had always thought of him as having a brain the size of a planet and was not even close to understanding what it was he did for a living – letting it just rest as 'something to do with computers'. He was intrigued and happily agreed to drop in on his brother-in-law.

"You're on the University campus, aren't you?"

"Yes, you know where it is? If you follow the signs for the Student Union Building, you'll find some visitor parking spaces and I'll treat you to a coffee."

Hugh was obligingly waiting when he parked twenty minutes later and led him through reception to the coffee bar. Mark scanned the clientele - a more varied cross-section of humanity it was hard to imagine. Students, members of the teaching staff, office workers, the more mature scientists like Hugh, and even the occasional visiting salesman all seemed to be represented.

Hugh returned from the counter with their two coffees and after the briefest of introductions, not being one for small talk, he verbally changed gear and started into the topic he wanted to talk to Mark about.

"I want your input on a matter concerning both family and finance – and I believe you're the best person to ask." He checked and got an "OK" from Mark.

"I don't know if you know what we do here," continued Hugh, and realising that Mark did not know, went on to explain. "Put simply, we've been working on a new data communications protocol that will allow data to be transferred across the public phone network quicker and more securely than any method currently available."

Mark recognised a vast simplification when it was given to him - and realised that he had just received one.

"I expect that's quite valuable if it works," he replied.

"Exactly," Hugh continued. "We've had considerable interest from banks and telephone companies, and we've demonstrated it working in the lab – but now we need to move on to the next phase and test it in a real-world environment."

Mark was enjoying the simplified insight into his brother-in-law's world, and could feel some of the excitement being transmitted, but wondered exactly how this was relevant to him or the family. Hugh would get round to it in his own scientific manner, sooner or later.

"So, to raise the funds, the company has decided to sell shares – I believe the correct term is an AIM listing" Hugh continued, and Mark nodded, having something of an understanding of the Alternative Investment Market.

"Well, each employee will receive a small number of shares in appreciation of the work we've done – but many of my colleagues are talking of investing their own money. They're talking about the shares doubling in value in a year, and some of them are even taking out bank loans so they can join in."

Mark was now beginning to see where his advice might be sought but waited for Hugh to eventually get to his point.

It took a few more minutes to talk through his difficulties. Was this an opportunity that comes along once in a lifetime that he would be foolish to miss? Could he realistically take the risk of taking on some personal debt to speculate? With the same company being his source of a regular income as well as the speculative vehicle would he not be putting too many important eggs all in the same basket? How would he be viewed by his colleagues if he did not join in? Would it show a lack of commitment if he didn't make the extra investment that so many of them seemed prepared to do? And then there was Susan to consider – she was the most cautious of people and would be unhappy if he took too much risk, and he couldn't dare invest without telling her, could he?

Eventually, Hugh finished – somewhat petering out, rather than reaching a conclusion. Mark, realising that he was being asked to fill the role of adviser on both family and financial matters was unsure where to begin. He was also feeling a little guilty that his role as financial adviser was only partially justified. He had some commercial acumen, certainly more than Hugh, who had not really left the academic world. But Mark's more visible financial success was partly based on a lucky find, a stroke of fortune – or even a fortuitous mistake. But this was now irrelevant. He was being appointed as an unofficial financial adviser and could not escape the role. What was that song he heard from time to time " ... *and it won't make one bit of difference if I answer right or wrong. When you're rich they think you really know.*"

He thought it best to start from the family angle.

"Hugh, I agree that Susan would not be happy if you borrowed money from a bank to speculate – no matter how good the prospects for the investment are. I'm sure you know this – and that the only thing you could do to make her more unhappy than this would be to conceal the borrowing from her."

Hugh nodded in silent and complete agreement.

"I can't speak for how your colleagues think of you – but my guess is that you will not be the only one who lets this cup pass by. There may well be some who are great at talking the talk but I'm sure that some of them will stop short of walking the walk." Another nod.

"But I think there is a way you might be able to minimise the risk and escape any brickbats from Susan", Mark continued.

An idea that had been forming as he listened to his ramble was taking shape as he spoke. "Put simply, you could blame me".

Hugh understandably looked puzzled.

Mark outlined his idea. "You could tell her that you've talked to me about it – man to man we might say – and I've asked you if we can do something together. I'll put up the money for you to buy the shares. We'll agree that after a year, you'll pay me back half of the money and give me half the shares. That way you've minimised your risk."

Hugh pondered the idea, and over their second cup of coffee, the conspiracy took shape. He rehearsed some of the things he would say to Susan, and they agreed that he would float the idea this very evening – and let it lie for a few days to see what happened.

As they parted, soon to be reunited for dinner as pre-arranged, Mark realised one important question had not been touched on.

"How much were you thinking of investing?" he asked.

"Well, I thought that ten thousand would be enough to show a nice profit if it worked out, and not too much to cause me real problems if it didn't work out."

So, the plan was hatched – Mark assured Hugh that he could put his hands on the money at a few days' notice. Ten thousand for Hugh and the same for himself.

His sister's house was unusually in a state of disarray when he arrived. Building work was in progress at the rear of the property, and the contents of the living room had been redistributed around the house.

"Wow, you don't waste any time – I only just heard from Mum that you were having a conservatory built" Mark exclaimed, wanting to make sure, subtly, that she understood that he has heard about the way she was planning to spend the windfall.

"Oh, we were doing that anyway," said Susan, "but that money from mum and dad means that we can get it done to a much higher spec. We'll have automatic blinds, proper flooring, the works – so it really will be an extra room on the house. Which reminds me, I've got to speak to you about Graeme."

"Who's Graeme?" Mark asked, trying to hang on to his sister's verbal coat tails.

"He's Naomi's husband and he's had some real problems, but I'm sure you can help him." Mark was familiar with his sister's scattergun method of talking. He had no idea who Naomi was, and he could not begin to understand how he was going to be able to help someone he had never met or even heard of before now – but he was sure it would all become clear, eventually.

131

"He had a terrible time with his last employer, so he's gone out on his own and has been simply marvellous," Susan continued, trying to extricate something from one of those handy display boards that are found in so many family kitchens. Months of post-it notes, flyers, business cards, school circulars and the like had been tucked into each of the many pockets on the wall-mounted reminder system. He feared that by trying to retrieve a document she might cause the entire thing to collapse, but luckily the required card was close to the surface and the system appeared to have survived disgorging this vital piece of information.

She handed Mark the business card.

Graeme Porter, Professional Builder.

No job too big or too small - Mobile number xxxxx xxxxx.

"He's been really good – and I told him that you were buying houses and doing them up. He needs some work to get going, so I told him you'll give him a ring."

She paused briefly in her stream of speech.

'My sister has only one speech impediment', thought Mark, 'she sometimes needs to draw breath!'

"I'll be sure to give him a ring," he said.

No further words were needed. Twenty-something years of siblinghood meant that he knew he had to make that call – and she knew that he would not dare to not make the call. He also knew that he would probably soon have a new business partner for house development in the North Essex area.

He suddenly noticed something he felt he should have noticed earlier. The house was quiet.

"Where are the twins?" he asked and was reassured by his sister that they were attending their first-ever sleep-over. And she and Hugh were looking forward to having a proper grown-up dinner party with him that evening.

Susan was no mean cook, and the dinner was thoroughly enjoyable. Mark's need to drive home afterwards curtailed his alcohol consumption, but she and Hugh took the opportunity of freedom from children to enjoy wine and after-dinner drinks.

The conversation was mostly concerned with their parents move – about which they both had mixed views. Hoping that they were making the right move, and, at the same time, feeling powerless to do anything much about it anyway. He reported on his day, and gave them an update on his latest venture in the property market.

A lull in the conversation gave Mark the chance to say, "You know Hugh, I've never really understood what you do for a living." Hugh responded by giving an overview of his company's developments.

"We're working on a new communication protocol that will allow data to be transferred much more quickly between computers," was his sufficiently simplified starting point.

"How much more quickly?" was Mark's first thought, and he spoke it out loud.

"At least ten times faster. The banks are very interested because it not only means that they get the info more quickly – so they can buy or sell shares, and so on – but it also means that it makes the information more secure because they can scramble it and make it more difficult for hackers to break into. You know it's particularly interesting because the very first developments of computers were in World War Two to combat the Germans replacing the Enigma coding machines that you've all heard of with the much faster Lorenz Geheimschreiber machines that worked so much faster."

Mark interrupted before he went off on one his favourite tangents about the fascinating history of the development of computers. He rerouted him to the more mundane details about his specific opportunity.

"How close is it to being available?" was his unsubtle redirection. Hugh took the hint.

"Well, we've proved the system in the lab," he continued, "but now we have to verify it in the real world."

"How difficult is that?" came the next prompt from Mark.

"It's actually not all that difficult, but it takes time and money. We're going to have to buy a lot of kit – to make sure it works with all the leading manufacturers, Cisco, Siemens, and so on – and we'll have to rent some circuits from providers like BT – and the providers in other countries too. It's an expensive business."

They talked a bit more about this until Mark felt sure that the point had been made – and he finished the conversation by saying "That sounds really interesting. I'd like to know how it goes. Sounds like a chance to make some money, and you know I'm always interested in that." He felt he'd achieved his (and Hugh's) objective and did not want to say any more in case it seemed a bit heavy-handed. So shortly afterwards he began the process of saying farewell and making his journey home.

-

The phone lines between Benfleet and Colchester were buzzing for the next few days.

First Mark telephoned Graeme the builder, who explained that he had become fed up with being stiffed by his previous employer and had set out on his own. He stressed that he was an experienced builder with all-around skills – but would call in specialist colleagues if needed for jobs like detailed electrics, complex plumbing, or large-scale plastering tasks, and was very keen to work on any house makeover.

Mark realised that the business relationship with Graeme would be straightforward – he would pay for the work done but there would be no partnership involved. Graeme gave Mark the details of the main auction house that sold properties in north Essex and Suffolk, and the date of their next sale. This amount of preparation by Graeme impressed Mark and he had already decided that they should work together as soon as possible.

Finding out that the next auction was in two weeks, he called the auction house and made sure that they would send him a catalogue. 'More time off work to look at properties,' he thought – but relished the opportunity to move some more of his cash mountain.

The third call was to Hugh to remind him to let Susan know how interested Mark was in investing in his company. Hugh promised to bring it up at dinner that evening.

The next day Mark called her, ostensibly to let her know that he had spoken to Graeme and there was every possibility of him being able to put some work his way. Susan was delighted.

"I hear you're also interested in investing in my husband's company" she continued. "Do you think it's a good idea?"

"I wouldn't be interested if I didn't think it was," he replied.

"But aren't you breaking the rules if you get him to buy shares on your behalf?" she continued.

"Not breaking – maybe just bending a little. I'll send you both an email to make sure that everyone knows I instigated it, just in case something goes wrong." Then casually, "Is he thinking of investing himself?"

"That's up to him".

'Well, there's a first time for everything,' Mark thought but left the thought unsaid.

"You'll have to ask him if he's going to," were her final words on the subject.

'I fully intend to,' thought Mark.

He immediately called Hugh, to hear the outcome of his financial pow-wow with his wife. "Has she given you the green light?" he asked.

"I think so," was the reply.

Mark said he would visit Hugh's office to deliver the funds in the next few days on his way from the property auction and suggested that Hugh open a separate bank account for this transaction but left the decision to him.

"Perhaps we could go out to lunch when you drop by," said Hugh in a rare attempt at fraternal bonding.

"On condition that you don't take me to some University refectory," replied Mark – not entirely in jest.

"Oh no, there are some lovely waterside pubs just down the road in Wivenhoe. Maybe we could try one of them."

Ten days later, having exchanged a couple of emails that clarified the financial arrangements between them, they sat together in a pub garden overlooking idyllic riverside scenery, enjoying a ploughman's lunch and a pint of the local brew on a sunny afternoon. Mark handed over a cheque for £10,000 and a brown envelope containing an identical amount in cash for Hugh to deposit. Mark had taken another bite out of the mountain – and having viewed a very suitable property earlier that day, he was confident that Graeme would be helping him onwards to his goal very soon.

Debbie

August 2005

People react differently to milestone birthdays. Not the legal milestone dates like eighteen or sixty-five. Nor the sentimental or traditional milestones such as the twenty-first birthday. The ones that make people reassess their position in the cosmos are usually the round number ones. - three-oh, four-oh and so on. It's often the thirtieth birthday that causes people to have a few minutes of reflection on where they are and where they would like to be or had planned to be. This was how it was with Detective Sergeant Deborah Coulson, known to everyone as just Debbie.

Two significant events had shaped Debbie's adult life. The first when she was twenty and the second at twenty-five.

By the time she had reached twenty, Debbie had already undertaken several roles. Problem child, rebel, difficult person, and job-hopper were just some of them. Twenty was a crucial point in her development. She had tried a few jobs. None of them lasted any length of time and all of them failed to engage her in any way.

She could have been a model – she certainly had the looks for it – but that would have required an element of focus, dedication, and direction - all of which were then lacking in Debbie's psychological make-up. She was at that time enjoying making an 'easy living' – being what her mother called a 'kept woman.' But, having changed from one keeper to another, several times in a few months, nobody referred to her as 'kept'. Many referred to her by other four-letter words, mostly starting with the letters 'sl' and none of them complimentary.

What changed her life was a brush with the law when she was one of several people arrested in a well-known London nightclub. Once identities were verified, she was one of a small number of women in the group who were released. None of the men were.

Debbie stayed the right side of the law – if only just – and this event allowed her to see herself in a harsh but true light, and to experience, at first hand and at close quarters, some of the aspects of the role of a policewoman in the London Metropolitan Police. She was immediately (and to everyone who knew her, somewhat surprisingly) sure that this was the job for her. She was under no illusion that it was easy but could see it was varied and interesting. It would give her a place in the world for the first time in her life, and she was sure that in the job, she could make a real difference (as all the good recruiting slogans said).

Debbie began immediately to clean up her act, cutting ties with most of her acquaintances. With a promise of good behaviour – which she kept - she moved back in with her parents, got a 'real job' on the cosmetic counter of a local shop, and applied to the Metropolitan Police. After due process, several months later, shortly after her twenty-first birthday she was accepted and began the training.

The seventeen weeks of training at the Police College in Hendon completed her transformation. The college was less than two miles away from the place where she had spent her whole life, but it might as well have been on another planet. Debbie emerged a changed woman. Her parents were proud and surprised in equal measure when they attended her passing out parade, and the photograph of her in uniform was the last photo that her sole surviving grandmother saw before passing away soon after.

Debbie used a small legacy from her grandmother to put a deposit on a tiny studio flat and began a new life.

The second event that changed the direction of Debbie's life occurred four years later. If she were to tell the tale, which she could not, she would have said it was an undercover operation. The truth of it was that a police operation required several attractive young women to 'decorate the set' of a London nightclub. It was a role that Debbie had already performed a couple of times, and on this occasion, she was able to take a leading part, tapping into her earlier self as it were. However, during a successful operation, Debbie saw something that she should not have. To be more precise she saw a very important someone doing something that he should not have been doing in a place where he should not have been doing it.

Only Debbie and two senior officers were witnesses, and this resulted in her attending a meeting with the two officers the following day. They reminded her in a measured and friendly way of her obligations to keep confidential any information gained in the course of her duties, and she reassured them that she had no intention of breaking this rule. The discussion then moved on to her career, and it was suggested that having spent some four years in the same spot, she should consider how her career should progress. Perhaps a move would be beneficial to her.

Debbie had the wit to state how much she would like a move into the world of CID, and, when asked if she would be willing to relocate to achieve this, quickly confirmed that a move would not be a problem to her – so long as it was not too far. A posting in the Home Counties would suit her fine.

A few days later Debbie was informed that if she were to apply for a position with the CID in Essex, the job would be hers. She was also told that her service records would be amended to show that she had worked in a different place to where she had really been for the last twelve months. She understood that this would therefore mean that the record would show that she could not possibly have taken part in a certain recent operation, but she had no problem in agreeing.

She transferred to Chelmsford in the county of Essex and was very happy with the posting. Less than fifty miles east of London, there was a mixture of 'urban' crime, and with Essex countryside on the doorstep, plenty of rural crime to add to the mix. The posting was a good opportunity and one that she enjoyed. Moving out of London also meant that she could swap her very small studio flat for a larger flat – one that might even be big enough one day for two people to live in.

And this, years later, was part of her problem. In five years, her career had moved on nicely and she was still enjoying her job. But she was still the only person living in the flat. In fact, the number of days (and nights) when there had been two people in the flat was ridiculously small. Far too small. And she had to do something about it. Much as she would slap anyone who said anything to her about her body clock ticking, she hated the thought of being officially a spinster (she had always thought it a revolting word) and just longed for some non-police company from time to time.

So, on her thirtieth birthday, she decided to take the huge risk of registering with an online dating agency. Even though she knew that some of her male colleagues had already used online dating, and, knowing that there could certainly not be any discrimination between men and women in the police service, she had still checked very privately with her boss that it would be OK before taking the plunge. He assured her that so long as she was not doing anything that could be perceived to put the impartiality of her office at risk and was not behaving in any manner which had the potential to bring the service into disrepute (quoting from the oath that all police officers swear) she was completely at liberty to go ahead.

She knew she would take some flak for it from colleagues when they inevitably discovered what she was doing, but that was a one-time pain barrier, and she was prepared to go through it. She would put her real first name and age on the page, and since she still retained enough of her good looks, she had no worries about her photograph – anything would do. But she was not going to show her real occupation. Her job would repel most blokes, and she knew from bitter experience of some of her fellow female officers, stating it would attract some of the entirely wrong sorts of prospective partners. If this led to any success in the relationship stakes, she would let the lucky man know the truth soon enough – but not immediately.

She had a clear plan for her disguise, having amassed a very good knowledge of IT and had worked on several cases where this expertise had proved useful. In the course of this work, she had interfaced with an outside organisation that the police used for detailed IT forensics and had visited their premises when trying to obtain information held on a suspect's computer hard drive. She had been impressed with both the firm's expertise and its security processes. Knowing what was to be seen on some of the hard drives she took to them, a high level of security was needed.

She knew exactly what they would be going through when working on a case whose newspaper headline would say something like *'23,000 Images Found On Suspect's PC'*. They would have to view most, if not all, of the twenty-three thousand.

She decided she would tell any dates that her job was with an IT security company. This would help her to justify unusual working hours – overtime on urgent cases – and would eliminate any possibility of talking about her job in any detail.

And those dates would only happen after her careful screening process. Several emails would have to be exchanged, and she would read each one very carefully. And of course, she would follow all the rules she preached to others – arrange the first meeting in a public place, ideally just for a coffee or possibly a couple of drinks – before going even as far as having a meal together.

Meanwhile, she had a thirtieth birthday to celebrate – alone again. She had not told anyone at work, so they had not even had group drinks at the end of their shift.

Both her sisters had called her at different times earlier in the evening. They were not terribly close, just birthday cards and a call to pass on best wishes and do a brief catch-up, but no presents.

The calls that day were even shorter than usual – they had caught up a couple of months earlier when the terrorist attacks in London had prompted them, like so many other families in the country to check up on their loved ones who were, or could have been, in London on the day. Debbie remembered she had had to remind her mother that she now worked in Essex and was no longer in London, and despite the man on television saying that they were calling in police from all over the country, there was no word of her having to be involved.

She had known her older sister was almost certainly safe as she travelled only a few hundred yards from her home in Hendon to the local school where she worked but the family had been very concerned about her younger sister. She worked in London, and it turned out that neither her mother nor her older sister had an office contact number for her, and with all the mobile networks being shut down on the day, they had not been able to verify that she was OK for several hours. She was surprised that they did not even have a name or address for her employers and had always relied on contact by mobile phone.

Debbie remembered the hours of concern and the strange way her elder sister had reacted when she asked why she did not have an office contact number for her younger sister, despite taking responsibility for her children every day after school.

But now, she sat on her sofa and took a call from her mother. She had already opened the present which her mother had sent – which, unusually, was something useful – a special bottle stopper to keep the fizz in an opened bottle of sparkling wine - and the obligatory twenty-pound note in her card telling her to buy herself something nice. She put the present to immediate use by taking a bottle of cava out of the refrigerator, opening it, and pouring herself a large glass.

After thanking her mum for the present and chatting with her for a few minutes she said goodnight, put the phone down and said aloud "Happy Birthday Debbie! Let's hope it's the last one you have to celebrate alone!"

She took a gulp of wine for the last ounce of Dutch courage, opened the dating agency web page on her computer, and started to enter her details.

Not Quite up to Las Vegas Standards
September 2005

James continued the process of gradual change at the clubs. All four clubs were benefiting from the additional revenue from the gaming machines, and customers were beginning to trickle in a little earlier to enjoy a cup of coffee and to access the internet on their phones.

Ray had also been kept busy with the introduction of more technology – some obvious to the members, and some not so obvious.

The obvious change, appreciated by some customers, was the ability to use credit cards. The club stewards also much appreciated this change once they realised that the amount of cash left in the till at the end of the day was often much less – so there were fewer days which had to end with that awful trip to the bank to deposit the cash in the night safe.

James hoped that he was not causing Harry to turn in his grave as his business, once so focussed on the accumulation of cash was moving into a world of immediate bank account credits.

The reduction in cash left in the till was accelerated by the additional facility offered to members – the ability to take cash advances on their card accounts. (James had implemented a house rule that such advances would carry a flat five-pound fee – but would be recorded as purchases on the card avoiding the necessity to pass this additional five pounds on to the bank).

He had also implemented another change with the assistance of Ray, having once again stressed to him the importance of knowing what was going on with members. He felt he had to continue the practice which Harry had offered since the very start – the ability for any member to use the office in any club free of charge. James had always believed that Harry knew what the meeting would be about, even if the member had not told him – Harry was just like that. James had achieved the same status but by use of modern technology. A voice-activated recording system was now hidden under his desk in every club office, and only he was able to activate it and access the resultant recordings.

But now, James needed to make a show of the way he intended to make the clubs more attractive.

The idea came to him one sleepless night, sat in his lounge, flicking through the late-night TV schedule and marvelling at what passed for entertainment in the small hours. He came across a programme covering a poker championship from Las Vegas.

'We could do that,' he thought. His clubs were not up to Las Vegas standards, but they had an active and growing number of poker players, and he was sure that a tournament would capture their imagination. Fetching pen and paper from his study, he sketched out his thoughts: a knockout round in each club to select two winners, leading to a table of eight players in the final. He was confident that fifteen to twenty would enter from each club and if each entrant paid twenty pounds, there would be a prize fund of around fifteen hundred pounds - a thousand for the winner, two hundred for the runner up and fifty for each of the other finalists.

The tournament would not make money – it would be a loss leader because there would be expenses, but it should generate extra revenue and interest from the customers.

The next day he checked whether there were any legal problems and was pleased to discover that recent changes in betting legislation meant that such an event would be entirely legal. He put the idea of a tournament to each of the club stewards by phone and was both surprised and pleased to find that he got their complete agreement.

A month later he was nervously awaiting the start of the first heat. The indomitable Peter, a big poker fan in addition to his known organisational skills, appointed himself organiser and referee. Three large tables and suitable coverings had been purchased and arrangements made for one of the club members to transport them from venue to venue – the tournament rounds taking place on four consecutive nights in the different clubs.

Peter selected three members of the Medway club to act as dealers for Old Kent Road and Dartford rounds, and three members of the Dartford club to deal at Bexleyheath and Medway.

The tournament started at 6.15 pm prompt and all fifteen participants were seated in the Old Kent Road Club and ready for play. By the time of the first break at 8.00 pm, four players had been eliminated. The second break saw a reduction to one table (it also saw an impromptu game begin, for much higher stakes, amongst the eliminated players.) At eleven forty-five, Ian Harris became the unlucky thirteenth player to be eliminated and the first two finalists had been chosen.

The night was a great success. The highest takings the club had ever experienced, as many of the players brought family with them, and they sat drinking in the main club room until the winners were known.

From a staff point of view, it had been all hands to the pump; the club steward offering table service of drinks to all the players, and a temporary bartender hired for the main room. Zlatan was present to ensure security and even Ray and James had rolled up their sleeves. James had made sure that the club had been spruced up for the occasion – and several members, especially the newer ones, were delighted to find that there was excellent internet connectivity.

The results were similarly encouraging at the other three evenings that week, with the Medway Club having to close the entry list when the number of participants reached the maximum of twenty-four.

The Bexleyheath club had been chosen as the venue for the final because it had the largest backroom – and James realised additional income when he found that so many people wanted to watch the game that he was able to charge five pounds for a seat in a cordoned off spectator section of the card room.

The success of the event as far as he was concerned was not only the one-time boost to takings but also the lasting effect of increased attendance and increased awareness of the new facilities at the clubs, which was much more important. Everyone wanted his assurance that the tournament would become an annual event.

He could now turn his mind to the next phase of his recovery plan - the final area of his father's business activities that had been neglected before he took over and had been ignored since. But James had also been turning his fertile mind to this area and had a plan that he was sure could be implemented to generate more revenue. But once again, Raheem would be vital to this new business venture and James knew this one might be quite challenging.

144

Football
September 2005

The choice of which football team a person supports is something peculiarly British. For example, Mark remembered hearing a story on the radio of a young man who had left Ireland to find work in London. Living alone in digs with nothing particular to do at weekends, he wanted to find out more about this peculiar British obsession and was beginning to fear that he might never be able to hold a conversation with his workmates unless he became a supporter of one club or another.

His ignorance of football was only matched by his ignorance of the geography of the vast area that comprises London. So, one Saturday afternoon he had walked from his digs to the nearest bus depot, found a friendly bus inspector and asked if any buses left from this depot to a football stadium.

The inspector told him that if he waited at 'that stop over there', there would soon be a bus that travelled to The Valley (home of Charlton Athletic) and one to Selhurst Park (home of Crystal Palace). Both of those teams were playing at home that day, and, depending on how the buses were running to schedule, either bus could be here first.

The Selhurst Park bus had arrived, he had boarded it and gone to the game. Twenty years later he was still a loyal Crystal Palace fan, but if the other bus had arrived first, he would have had a completely different club allegiance for his whole life.

Mark had become a devoted West Ham fan by the more normal method of having a father who was a passionate supporter and had been taken to the home games every Saturday in the football season for as long as he could remember.

-

The start of a new season is a special day for all fans - a whole new season and a blank sheet. The one day of the year on which all the teams are level - with the promise of better things to come. New signings probably, and new hopes – certainly. At least that is how it should be. But Mark was having mixed feelings. For as long as he could remember the one thing that was fixed rock-solid in his life was that alternate Saturday afternoons in late autumn, winter, and early spring would be spent with his dad. Today he was on his own.

The journey to the game was as it always had been – leaving his car in the station car park at Upminster, riding the tube to Upton Park Station, the half-mile walk along Green Street to the stadium, pausing only to buy a quarter-pounder with onions from a street vendor. There were just two adjustments to the normal pattern of the season's opener. This was not actually the first game of the season – he had missed that two weeks ago when he was in the USA. But in many ways, it was even better. West Ham had won their first game and drawn their second – so hopes were already high. But he was on his own – and that just did not feel right.

He made his way to his usual seat and exchanged pleasantries with Nigel, the VAT inspector who had occupied the seat next to him for the last ten years. But the seat on the other side was empty and remained that way throughout the game. It was a permanent and unhappy reminder of his father's absence, and on his way home after the game, Mark decided he needed to make a change.

So, on the following Monday morning, he called the football club to find out if there were any seats available in a more expensive part of the ground. He figured he could treat himself – he was after all earning plenty of money – and a change of viewpoint would not only give him a better experience of the game but would also help dispel some of the discomfort he was experiencing in the absence of his dad.

He was pleased to find out that there was a vacant seat in a much better area of the ground – in the middle tier of the main stand, almost on the halfway line. A near-perfect view of the game. And the club was more than happy for him to trade in his existing seat and simply pay the price difference. Within a few minutes it was all dealt with – his new ticket would be posted to him within forty-eight hours.

-

Two weeks later was Mark's first chance to experience his new, improved seating arrangement and to make the acquaintance of his new neighbours with whom he expected to share the joys and frustrations (mostly frustrations in the case of West Ham) of following the team for years to come.

It was the first Monday night game of the season and his journey did not quite go to plan. Years of experience meant that he knew exactly what time he needed to leave his house or, for evening matches, his office, to arrive at the ground in time for kick-off. But on this occasion, he was a few minutes late in setting off. And, of course, on that day there was a set of temporary traffic lights guarding the non-existent workmen on a nearby water main repair. So, he was even later arriving at the tube station, managing to just miss the train pulling out from the platform.

The train he caught was also the victim of signal delays, and as a result, he arrived even later at his destination. Despite saving a few moments by skipping his usual pre-match hamburger, he eventually got to his new seat just in time for kick-off, making it impossible to say a brief hello to his new neighbours. The half time interval would normally have offered a second opportunity for an introductory chat, but his rumbling, unfed stomach gave him a different priority and he spent the break queuing for, buying and consuming a burger; getting back to his seat just in time for the start of the second half.

He noted that one of his new neighbours was a fellow middle-years man, quite large in build and possibly just slightly over-dressed. On the other side of him sat a father and son, the son being about twelve years old and occupying the seat next to Mark. 'I'll make sure to get here on time for the next game, and they'll realise I'm not just a one-time ticket purchaser, so we'll start to talk then,' he thought to himself. 'After all, we are hopefully going to be spending a couple of hours in each other's company twice a month for years to come.'

Two weeks later Mark was able to make the acquaintance of both Don, his slightly overweight and over-dressed left-hand-side neighbour, and his twelve-year-old neighbour on the other side. He didn't catch the name of the boy or his dad, but he was able to have frequent conversations with both his immediate neighbours, so it didn't matter.

The youngster was a typical twelve-year-old football fan who knew everything there was to know about his team and most other things relating to the Premier League of the day. Mark enjoyed chatting with him, and the youngster enjoyed the chance to show off his knowledge.

"It's like having a personal expert summariser alongside you" was how he described it later to one of his friends. "I can ask him anything about how many appearances a player has had, what was the result when we last played a particular team, who their stars are, just about anything. I swear if I asked him their shoe size and inside leg measurement, he'd know that too!"

Mark had his first conversation with Don, his other new neighbour, in the halftime interval. Discovering that Mark had not just bought the ticket on a one-off basis and was going to be there for the foreseeable future, he was happy to get to know him.

"What business are you in?" was an obvious early question for the newcomer to be asked. Mark had already decided that if he was asked this – in the new, up-market circle of seats and of society he was now moving in - he would not say that he was a salesman for a building supplies company.

"I'm in the property business," was the prepared answer he gave.

"Snap!" was Don's unexpected reply. "What developments are you involved in?"

"Oh, I'm not involved with any particular development," Mark replied "I just buy and sell – trying to make a living where I can. How about you?"

"I'm currently working on a development in Beckton – lots of investment opportunities if you're interested," came the slightly too pushy reply. But by now, the teams were coming out for the second half and no further conversation was possible.

At the end of the game, a goalless draw to London rivals, Arsenal, Mark delayed a few minutes before leaving. With a full stadium, and most home and away supporters travelling to local destinations, the crush would be unpleasant. Don presumably had similar feelings as he hung around for a while. After exchanging brief comments about the match, Don made the unusual offer of sending details about the development he was working on (in a sales capacity, Mark correctly assumed). Mark was happy to give him his email address and thought no more about it as they shook hands and made their separate ways home.

The Premier League had a break to allow for international matches to take place, so it was almost a month later that West Ham had their next home match, where Mark renewed his acquaintance with the junior football expert and the slightly pushy property developer. Sure enough, during the half time interval, Don tried as casually as he could to ask if he had received the information that he had emailed. Mark tried to make sure that his "Yes, thanks" was expressed in such a way that it would be pleasant enough, but would close down the discussion, and he was pleased that Don went no further than saying "Good, let me know if you are interested" before moving on to the much more important discussion of how well the game against Middlesbrough was progressing.

In Mark's opinion, a friend or acquaintance offering you information on the product or service they are selling was perfectly acceptable. Offering you a small discount in acknowledgement of your relationship is also fine. But pushing too hard just is not acceptable. He had read the information that Don had sent him – and would even be open to a discussion, but if Don was too salesy, he would have the opposite effect to the one he desired. He was pleased that the pushing had stopped and felt that he would be prepared to talk to him about it later.

At the end of the game, Mark allowed the crowds to thin a little before leaving – he did not enjoy the crush at the local station and on the train, and he was quite prepared to waste a few minutes to ensure the journey home was a little less uncomfortable. Once again, he noted that Don was also delaying his departure.

"Got far to go?" Don asked (they had not, in their brief snatches of conversation, ever discussed where either of them called home).

"I take the tube to Upminster", Mark replied. "You?"

"I live quite close, so I drive," said Don – interestingly neither of them yet letting the other know where they actually lived. "I usually hang about for a while to let the traffic clear. Do you fancy a drink?" Although not a frequent drinker, an afternoon of shouting encouragement at his team had given Mark a thirst, so he accepted Don's offer and allowed him to lead the way.

Don's regular drinking hole was a nearby pub, which had a street-level bar crammed with fans after each game. But the pub's regular customers knew that it also had an upstairs bar that the casual visitors never noticed. It was here that they went. When they entered the bar, it was immediately obvious that Don was known to the staff, as his pint was delivered in his personal glass – which bore a picture of a Godfather caricature and the name Don on it. Mark settled for a regular glass for his pint.

When they took their seats at a corner table, it was not long before the subject of property development came up.

"The last thing I want to be is a pushy salesman," was Don's opening gambit, "but when I hear someone's in the same line of business, I can't help letting them know what I'm working on. Hope you don't mind."

"Not at all" was Mark's obligatory white lie in response. "How's it going?"

"Well, to be honest, we do have our challenges. You've probably heard about some of the issues with people buying 'off plan'" Mark nodded his agreement. He'd read about some of these 'issues' in the property section of his weekend newspaper, a recent edition of which carried a report about some of the excesses of this section of the market. Some investors were making significant profits when the final price of apartments exceeded the original estimate, but many others were losing out heavily when the final asking prices failed to match the price at which they had bought.

"Well, we've had to come up with some innovative ways to get around the bad publicity – and thankfully, it looks like the new idea we've just launched is going to be successful. Just as well, because we need that initial investment from the buyers to fully fund the development," he confided. Mark encouraged him to continue – even if it was not going to be profitable, it was going to be educational.

"So, we're offering a new idea which we're calling a 'Right to Buy'. Basically, an investor purchases an option to buy at a certain price. He pays a quarter of that price upfront. When we sign off the property as complete, he's got a month to decide whether to continue with the purchase at the fixed price. If he doesn't want to and decides to bail, we refund his money less an admin fee. So, he's kept his chance of making a profit, but also minimised his chance of making a loss. And we have the money for the duration of the development without paying any interest to borrow it."

"Interesting," Mark said. "How big's the admin fee?"

"Good question. I get a bit of discretion on that – I try to make it a couple of thousand – but it can be reduced to five hundred if I need to. It's very early days, but I think it'll catch on. If everyone else starts to do something similar, then we'll know it's a good idea."

Their discussion did not go much further; the second pint was accompanied by more football talk and they both had plans for their evening. But Mark kept the idea in his head and told Don he would give it some serious thoughts and perhaps they could set aside a bit more time for a deeper discussion after the next game.

"Sure," said Don. "If you're interested you can even come and have a look at the place – and I might even buy you lunch!"

They left it there.

The Rules for a First Date
September 2005

So far, the dating game had not been going well. Mark had contacted three women, each chosen with three essential credentials: firstly, they had to be really pretty. If this made him a shallow person, then so be it, but he only ever dated women he found to be very attractive. Not just attractive, but very attractive. And when you considered that he was looking at a photo they had chosen as the best representation of themselves, it needed to stand out. Secondly, they had to live close by. His life was challenging enough with business demanding a lot of his time, frequent travel, and the commitments resulting from his newfound wealth. And lastly, there had to be that certain something about them.

So, he had dated Heather. She was tall - almost as tall as Mark himself - slim and elegant, shoulder-length dark brown straight hair, wearing very little make-up (he liked that) and to his untrained eye, clothes that looked stylish and expensive. She worked for a PR Agency that had relocated its offices from central London to St. Albans, and she was pondering the decision to move home because the commute was now quite awkward. They talked a lot about work and very little about family or interests. Although the evening had been enjoyable and the time had flown by, they both knew that there was not that certain spark, and they would not be repeating the experience. The truth of the matter was that she was just a bit too posh for him. Or, to put it another way, he was just a bit too common for her.

Sandra was different. Very pretty, bright and bubbly with some of her good looks being a result of good presentation. Her make-up was very skilfully applied, but there was quite a lot of it. And she made the best of her assets by wearing a skirt that was perhaps a little too short and a blouse whose neckline was maybe a little low. As Heather had done, she specified the pub where they should meet, but in her case, it was obvious that she was known to some of the regulars. They had talked a lot about friends and family (she was well endowed with both of these - as well as being well endowed) and she had not wanted to talk about her boring job in administration in the council. They had an enjoyable evening together, but both knew that it would be their only date.

The consolation when dating in your thirties is that even if you do not know what it was you are looking for, you know enough to know when it is not there. And you accept that sometimes it just does not work out. That does not make you a bad person or give you cause for self-doubt. At least not after a couple of dates. Whether you still felt the same after a long run of one-date-wonders, Mark hoped he would not discover.

And then there was the elusive Debbie – the third of his choices. She had warned him that she wanted some email dialogue before going on a date. She felt strongly that knowing a bit more about each other would make it more likely that the date would be successful, and he had agreed to be patient.

She had asked him about his family and where he had grown up, and he was happy to tell her. In return, he found out that she had been born and brought up in Hendon, north London. She was the middle one of three sisters. The other two still lived there, and although she was close to them in age, she was not close to them in other ways. They exchanged Christmas and birthday cards, she sent presents to her two nieces and two nephews (one of each from each sister), and they met at occasional family parties, weddings, and christenings. She was closer to her mum, they spoke every week on the phone, but her dad was 'no longer on the scene'.

She asked him if his first name really was Mark or whether he was one of those people who was known by his middle name. He explained that in his family it was traditional for the oldest son, or in his case the only son, to be given his mother's maiden name as a middle name. So, he was Mark Milton Reynolds and surely nobody in their right mind would call himself Milton.

He learned that she was Deborah Jayne, possibly because they were the two poshest names her mum could think of. She hated being called Deborah – only the doctor's receptionist and her mother ever called her that - it had to be Debbie for everyone else. He had responded to this by letting her know he was disappointed as he had planned to play her 'Deborah' by T Rex at the first opportunity and took this as an opening to let her know that his musical taste was all the fault of his father playing him endless rock music of the late sixties and early seventies when he was a child. She responded by saying that she would forgive him this major failing, if he would forgive her for having posters of New Kids on The Block on her bedroom wall – back then, not now! Music was not all that important to her - but if she played anything it was likely to be from one of the CDs she'd bought with her first pay-checks back in the day. Depeche Mode, The Happy Mondays, stuff like that.

His profile had told her he was a salesman, so she asked what he sold for a living, posing the question humorously by stating that if he turned out to be a lousy date there was always a chance of getting some useful or interesting free samples. Not wanting to disappoint, as he had phrased his answer, he told her who he worked for and that he was sure he could get her a great deal on electric drills if she had any sudden urges to create a lot of holes. She apologised for not being able to give him more information about her job in computers for security reasons.

She told him she lived on her own in a small flat close to the centre of Chelmsford, where she worked. She owned it - or would do in twenty years if she kept up the mortgage payments - and he was happy to let her know he lived in a modern box on a small estate in Benfleet that was once a nest for two but was no longer, and that he had been sentenced to the same twenty-year term of payments as she had.

Just when he was beginning to think this email dialogue would go on forever, she agreed to go on a date and asked his suggestion for a venue. He suggested TGI Friday's restaurant and bar - the most neutral venue he could think of. Not too posh, nor too cheap, and lively enough to provide a positive background and a clientele that might provide topics for conversation if all else failed. She agreed to meet at eight pm the following Friday.

Mark arrived fifteen minutes before the appointed time and found a seat at the bar which gave him a good chance to see everyone as they entered. He ordered a pint and mentally crossed his fingers. She was going to show up, wasn't she? He mentally uncrossed them ten minutes later when Debbie arrived. She surveyed the room, recognised him, and waved as she made her way across.

He ordered her a glass of Prosecco and they chatted briefly. During their email dialogue they had built up a kind of standing joke about the rules of first dates, so after fifteen minutes he felt able to ask her "Am I right that after fifteen minutes we can decide whether to move from the bar to have a meal together?"

154

"Well, my book says twenty minutes," she smiled," but I'm OK to settle for fifteen – yes, let's eat."

Mark had booked a table, just in case. As a salesman, he was an optimist, after all.

Sitting down at the table and perusing the menu he continued the running joke by asking, "My copy of first date rules doesn't have any more in it after the first fifteen minutes, does yours?"

"Oh yes, just one more rule," Debbie replied. "At the end of the date, we have to say goodbye in the car-park and not contact each other again for twenty-four hours, so that we can be sure that the response is well thought out." She was smiling, but Mark also realised she meant it, and it seemed like a good rule, so he said so.

Having crossed the awkward fifteen-minute barrier, their conversation flowed from then on. He had a glass of red wine with his steak and Debbie risked a second glass of Prosecco with her Jack Daniels chicken. Neither wanted a dessert - but both ordered coffee, seemingly happy to spin the occasion out to its maximum duration.

They duly parted in the car park and Mark risked a brief kiss before leaving. Was it a kiss? Maybe a peck would be a more accurate description.

Debbie drove home happy and relieved. If she were to provide a written statement, how would it sound she wondered? He matched his profile photo – which was a good start. He was well-dressed, the clothes had quality, and he presumably knew that the shades of cream and brown suited him. His shoes were shiny, and he was completely at ease with himself. He was used to looking his best. As was to be expected of a salesman, he was a good talker, confident and amusing. He seemed to enjoy his job and was probably successful at it – he certainly had a very nice car, which was never a bad thing.

She liked the way that he had made sure to tell her that he travelled, regularly, staying away one night per week and getting home late on other occasions. She thought it showed that he was thinking of the difficulties of arranging dates. At least she hoped that was what it was, he could of course be making excuses for not making another date, but she thought that was unlikely.

He had not complimented her on her looks – which was completely fine. She knew how good she looked - and most men were clumsy about complimenting her anyway. And on the downside? He was five years older than her; his hair was just beginning to recede and there was the tiniest hint of grey. But at least that meant that he probably didn't dye it. Everything about him seemed straightforward – and there were no contradictions from the very limited amount of information on his profile and the rather more significant information she had gathered from her careful background research and the exchange of emails in the pre-amble.

She had, of course, checked him on the police database – that's why she had verified that he did not have an alternate first name. Neither he nor any of his immediate family had any criminal record, nor any financial irregularities, CCJ's, or anything similar. His whole family would appear to be a contender for the most boring family in South Essex, which was just perfect as far as she was concerned.

One of her other matches on the website had fallen at this hurdle, another to which she had been attracted did not have the patience to carry out an email conversation with her – which eliminated him from her consideration, and the one man she had dated so far had turned out to be so desperately dull that she even briefly reconsidered the whole idea of dating.

She thought Mark was a little old-fashioned but in a good way. He had insisted on paying for the meal – she had not resisted too much, and he had further reinforced his old-fashioned image by paying for the meal with cash rather than a credit card. Her professional instincts told her that there was perhaps one small area of doubt that she could not quite put her finger on – but there should be a little mystery surely, she reasoned.

And then there had been that kiss. Unexpected, certainly. Perhaps it was even 'against the rules.' But it had felt very nice all the same. A little bit of spontaneity was good, wasn't it? Yes, she decided, if he asked, she was sure she would not hesitate to go for another date, and hopefully even more, with him.

-

Mark got into his car and hoped he had not blown his chance with that last kiss. He would never forgive himself if he had. This had been a really good evening. She was very pretty. Surprisingly even better than her profile photo. She wore very little make-up – she did not need much, but she had made an effort to look her best. She knew she looked good and had probably dressed very carefully – the red sweater, black trousers, and black jacket was a good look. And she was pleasant and easy to talk to as well as to look at.

The fact that her job was in security meant that job talk was a no-go area, which was not a problem. It meant that she talked about herself a little more. She had also told him that her job entailed some non-standard hours, which meant she had to plan her personal time around it. He thought this was a good sign. Hopefully, it meant she was thinking about dating again. He hoped so. Just so long as he hadn't blown it with that kiss. 'Well, I guess I'll know in the next twenty-four hours' he thought.

At exactly eight o'clock the next evening he sent an email:

Your explanation of the rules did not specify from which point the twenty-four-hour period of non-contact commences. Is it from the commencement or termination of the first date? Or from the time at which I was apprised of the existence of the rule? I trust that you will forgive me if I am sending this email too early, but can we go for a meal together in a better restaurant next time?

An immediate reply came back:

The twenty-four-hour period commences from the termination of the first date. Please wait a further two and a half hours for a reply to your email.

He smiled and thought this was a good sign. Two and a half hours later Debbie sent him an email agreeing to a second date, with a list of the days when she could be available. He replied with a suggested date and the details of a gastropub that he had been to a couple of times previously. A second date was duly agreed upon.

157

Big Deals
October 2005

Mark's crowded business life continued apace. He made every effort to ensure that neither his dealings in property nor his other new ventures had any impact on his ability to do his day job. He knew that his life plan would only be achieved if his new money formed the basis of an additional income – it was not intended to replace his existing one.

So, he burned his holiday allowance one or two days at a time, visiting auctions and properties, so that his nine-to-five was not affected. 'I don't have anyone to go on holiday with, anyway' he reasoned.

And one phone call received a few days later meant that his working life would shortly become a lot busier. Darren Palmer, his contact on his major deal, opened the conversation by saying "Mark, I've got some good news and some bad news for you." This chatty behaviour from Darren was unusual - he had always acted rather formally so far - so Mark was optimistic that the good news would outweigh the bad.

"We've decided to go ahead with a test purchase of your company's products," he announced. Mark realised that the script called for him to ask what the bad news was.

"I'm afraid that we don't run test campaigns during the last quarter of the year, so we won't be able to go ahead with it until next quarter."

Mark, ever the glass-half-full guy, replied that it would give them more of a chance to prepare and help make sure they could work together to make the test a success. He didn't voice his private concern that if the USA test, which was just about to begin, was successful, then his company could be receiving some very big orders just as the UK test was due to start – but he knew he would have to make sure that this did not cause a problem.

Darren promised to send a list of the stores that would take part in the pilot, and, having made sure that there was nothing else needed right now,

Mark expressed his thanks for the confidence they had placed in him and his company, and ended the call.

As soon as the USA came on stream, he called Martin to give him the good news. He asked how things were going with the US deal, and, at Martin's suggestion, called Jeff for a more detailed update.

-

Jeff Dupont was Canadian by birth but had married an American and moved to Minnesota in the USA. Mark and he had bonded at the end of the first evening with the US sales team. Returning to their hotel after a team meal, they were the only two who felt the need to adjourn to the hotel bar for a nightcap. No surprise there – the Canadian and the Brit being last at the bar!

Although they only met twice a year, they spoke on the phone from time to time and exchanged frequent emails, both work-related and, since they had a distinctly non-PC sense of humour in common, often very non-work-related. Being the only two non-Americans in the company, they often shared light-hearted disparaging remarks about colleagues – "Those damned Yankees" was a popular phrase between them.

Soon after they had first met, Mark had asked Jeff to help him with a subject that always fascinated him. He knew that nothing offended a Canadian more than being mistaken for an American, so he asked Jeff how to tell a Canadian from an American by his accent. Mark could recognise some regional US accents – New York, Deep South, and Texas for example. And thanks to film and TV he had added recognition of a Boston accent (thanks to re-runs of Cheers! and the occasional snippet of JFK in a newsreel) and the Minnesotan accent from one of his favourite films, Fargo – but how to identify a Canadian escaped him.

"Well first off, don't bother asking an American," Jeff said. "They're useless at recognising accents."

Mark did not need to be told this – he had often been asked by Americans if he was Australian.

"They just think we all say 'eh?' at the end of every sentence. Some Canadians do this – but not many. Your best bet is to wait until they say the word 'about'. If it sounds more like 'aboot' than 'about', he's Canadian for sure. But the only sure way to know for sure is to get him to say, "I'll be really merry when I marry my Mary. If all three of those words beginning with m sound the same, then you're hearing a true Canuck!

For the second time in a day, Mark received good and bad news in a call. Jeff told him that the test in the USA had run into some problems. Jeff had not been able to get as much support from his fellow salesmen as he needed. Pilot sites for the deal were scattered across the length and breadth of the USA, and Martin had asked the local salespeople to help on the deal by visiting the stores to help them get their early sales. This lack of co-operation seemed to surprise Jeff more than it did Mark.

"You mean they are not helping you do a deal that will be good for you, but very bad for them when their local customers will lose business to the big chain?" he asked.

"Yeah, something like that," Jeff replied.

"Well thankfully that will not be a problem on my deal – all the sites will be on my territory – I'm just going to have to spend more time on the road," Mark replied.

Having talked some more about Jeff's problem, Mark promised to add his weight to Jeff's request to Martin for an increased travel budget so that he could visit the stores himself. 'After all,' he thought, 'if he's helped me by delaying his deal and not impairing mine, it's the least I can do.'

Into the Twenty-First Century
October 2005

James called Ray into his office first thing to share a coffee and to discuss the next steps in his rescue plan for his father's business.

"I'm very pleased with what you've done so far," he began, "how do you think it's going?"

"Mostly OK" was the less than enthusiastic reply he received.

"So, tell me what's not OK," was James's immediate reply. He needed Ray more than Ray probably knew, so he wanted to make sure any problems were resolved as quickly as possible."

"Well, the stuff we're doing on the computer and the wireless network's fine. Enjoying that. But I'm getting fed up having to explain everything to the customers all the time."

Mark appreciated his honest reply and the way he had moderated his language. He probably wanted to use a stronger term than fed up, and he knew that Ray would often refer to the older members of the club with a much more derogatory term than customers.

"What sort of things are you having to explain to them?" James asked, confronting a problem he was completely unaware of, but not surprised by.

"Well, they're getting these smartphones and it starts by me helping them log on to the wireless, but then they're asking me about how to use email, and how to browse the internet. Really basic stuff."

James smiled at the frustration of this Olympic sprinter of the computer world having to teach grown adults how to take their first steps. But his antenna recognised an opportunity.

"How about we offer a computer class once a week – charge a tenner for an hour of basic computer skills, with you as the teacher," he suggested.

"I guess that would cut it down, but I'd still have to do it," he replied, not completely won over to the idea.

"How about if we put half of that tenner into club funds and you have the other half," James responded.

"OK. Yeah, that would work, sure," Ray replied – and James knew he was suppressing a smile. This could give Ray a significant increase in income – especially if it was repeated at each club and ran for a few weeks. He was fine with that – Ray deserved it and he was vital to the next stages of James's business plan. And anyway, the club would be taking a fiver off each attendee – and they would probably buy a coffee or a beer while they attended the course too. It always felt good to solve a problem profitably. Now he could move on to the reason he'd asked Ray to join him.

"I've got another new task for you too. How are you at creating websites?"

Ray shrugged, which James recognised as his normal self-deprecating way of saying 'Yes I can.'

"You wanna do some websites for the clubs?" he asked.

"No, not for the clubs. There's another part of my father's old business that you probably haven't heard anything about."

James explained some of his father's chequered history. How he had a fringe involvement in the sex business, trying hard to paint it in terms of a man facilitating a business transaction between two willing partners. So much of what Ray might have heard about prostitution would have been in terms of pimps, coercion, human trafficking, and a whole host of extremely unsavoury practices that he knew his father would never have been part of.

Ray listened attentively, and if he was surprised by what he was hearing, he showed no reaction.

"What I'm left with is a full list of his contacts - women in the business who knew and respected him, but there's no money coming in from it. What I want to do is to assist these women to move their businesses into the twenty-first century. I've done some research and I don't think any of them has a website. And I'm pretty sure that their business, just like every other one on the planet, will all be going online more and more in the

162

future. I think we can help them get there – and help them move to the 'cashless society' everyone is always talking about."

Ray looked a little puzzled but continued to stay silent.

"I reckon that if we can give each of them a website, and enable them to take card payments, we'll deserve a slice of the business. OK?"

He was quite surprised that Ray still looked uncomfortable, but he carried on anyway.

"You think you could do a website like that?"

"Yeah, but what do I put on it? I don't know anything about that stuff."

James couldn't help but smile at Ray's understandable uncomfortable reaction.

"Don't worry about that – all they need is a couple of pictures in scanty underwear and a paragraph about their er … attributes and the services they offer. I'm sure they'll help with that – and if in doubt, copy it off another site. All the girls in London have started to have websites. They're hardly going to go to court if you copy them!" He smiled, but Ray had not relaxed.

"I'll give you a couple of web addresses or you can use a search engine. Just type in 'escort', and then look at the pages which are not selling Ford Motor cars. And then all we'll need is someone to take the photos."

"I've got a mate who does photos" was Ray's first contribution.

"Why don't you give him a call? See if he can help." James asked.

Ray left the office to make the call and returned a few minutes later.

"He says he can do it. If it's over a lunchtime, he'll charge a hundred quid."

"OK," said James, "for our first couple of customers for this new line of business, we'll throw the photos in for free. After that, we should be able to charge. Oh, and not to forget, there'll need to be a line of code that makes sure that when they take a card payment, ten per cent goes into our account – you can do that I assume."

"Yeah. Easiest way is to set it up so that when they receive a card payment it calculates ten per cent and raises a payment into our account."

"Yes, that works. We'll just have to make sure that it gets updated when their card expires and that they don't go over their limit or else we won't get paid. Otherwise, you OK?"

This time the shrug was accompanied by "Yeah, s'pose so."

'Nothing like enthusiastic support', thought James.

"Good, because the first one is going to be here to meet us in five minutes. Her name's Estelle," he said.

The Egg Cannot be Unscrambled
October 2005

The biggest problem with telling a lie is that it can never be untold. The egg cannot be unscrambled, the potato cannot be un-mashed. This was Debbie's problem and she desperately wanted to unscramble her particular egg.

She had recently read an article in a celebrity magazine while waiting in the doctor's surgery. It was the story of some female soap star's wonderful whirlwind romance with a young football star. Even though he was also a celebrity, he was as anonymous to the soap star as she had been to him. The relevant point that she took from the article was that when the pair had first met, she had concealed from him the fact that she was a well-known TV actress. Uncannily, he had also concealed his true profession from her.

He thought he was dating a hairdresser, while she thought she was going out with a car salesman. When they had revealed their true identities to each other it had catapulted their relationship onto new heights of ecstasy or something. The doctor had become free at that point, so the full excitement was never completely revealed to her.

'Wouldn't it be nice,' she thought, 'if something similar would happen when I tell Mark this evening what my real job is.'

She had decided now was the right time. Two months had passed since they first met, and they had managed to meet almost every week since, despite both having busy schedules.

For their second date, he had taken her out for a meal at his favourite gastropub (and insisted on paying – she loved that aspect of his old-fashioned manner). Their conversation had flowed easily – often a problem on a second date when all the easy conversation starters have been used in the first date.

Like everyone else in the UK, they could not avoid talking about the recent terrorist incidents in the capital city. Mark had told how his

165

peaceful drive around the East Anglian countryside visiting his customers had been interrupted by frantic calls from his mother and his ex-girlfriend. All because he sometimes went into London.

Debbie told him about the panicky calls caused by her younger sister not letting anyone in the family have a work phone number to call her. They both agreed that millions of people would have had similar experiences, and many would have had much worse outcomes to their calls.

He had told her how instead of putting money into a pension, he was investing in properties and using his contacts in the building trade to do them up and sell them. He was quite proud of the progress and hoped one day to own a property outright (without a mortgage).

The evening had ended with a very enjoyable kiss in the car park. At that point, she had informed him of one more additional rule. Before a third date, both had to agree that they were not dating anyone else. He had immediately agreed to this condition, and they fixed the day, but not the venue, for the third date. It was her turn to choose where they would meet, and she promised to get back to him.

She had decided to relax her caution a little. For their third date, she would cook for him at her flat. She was not the world's best cook – much the opposite. 'If that's going to be a problem,' she thought, 'best to get it out of the way immediately.'

He had brought flowers and had even noted her previous comment that she liked flowers to have a lot of colour, to offset the plain décor of her flat. More than that, he bought her a belated birthday present, having found out that she had signed up with the dating agency on her thirtieth birthday. He made a corny remark about how her thirtieth birthday had brought him a present, so he had to do something in return. She loved the diamond earrings he gave her – she wore very little jewellery for very practical reasons, and these were just perfect – so much that she wore them every day. (If she had known how much he had spent on them, she might not have done).

He had stayed at her flat that night, and the sex had been surprisingly good. She blushed slightly, remembering just how much she had let herself go that night (and the following morning). She had allowed far too many months to pass without, and he seemed to have the knack of unlocking her self-imposed restraints.

Every time they slept together, he continued to take great pleasure in her enjoyment – so much so that it was almost unbelievable. She kept planning to take some time to see to his pleasure – but somehow, he never got around to letting her be unselfish. 'Maybe tonight I'll have to be – if he doesn't throw me out before I get the chance,' she thought.

Tonight was to be a first – she was going to see his place. He had told her that he was having work done in his house and it was too messy to allow a visitor. But it was now complete, so they were going to have a takeaway and she was to get the guided tour. And then, she resolved to tell him what she did for a living. 'Best to tell him when he's on home turf. That way he can't storm out. And if he's going to react strongly, or there's going to be a scene, then it's best not to be anywhere public. If he wants to end it, then I can leave quietly – or storm out if I feel like it.'

They finished the Chinese meal. The empty containers were still on the table, remnants of noodles and rice still there on their plates, and the last of the champagne – necessary for any successful launch he had joked – was in their glasses.

"Mark, I've got something I need to tell you. And now seems like the best time." It was a little abrupt, but then she felt sure that this was not something you could just casually drop into a conversation.

"When we first met, there was just one thing that I told you about myself that wasn't true, and I need to put that right."

Mark was paying complete attention and she had to plough on quickly.

"I don't work for a computer security firm. I work for the Police."

There were a few seconds of silence. 'At least he hasn't gone crazy. That's good', she thought, knowing from her training that when something important like this is revealed, a few seconds of silence is a good way to make sure that the information has sunk in.

"What exactly is your job?" Mark asked.

"I'm a Detective Sergeant."

Mark digested this information carefully. He mentally ran through a checklist of their previous conversations. Was there anything he had said that he wouldn't have, or shouldn't have if he knew he was speaking to a police sergeant? He couldn't think of anything significant. And if he had, he reasoned, then their relationship would not even have lasted this long.

The silence was starting to press down on them. He thought he ought to say something.

"That's a surprise", was all he could manage. It was easy to understand why she had hidden this information. Would he have made contact if he had known she was a copper? Probably not. Did it make any difference now they had become as close as they had in the last couple of months? Not really. He wanted to know if this was the beginning and the end of any secrets - but thought it was best to wait a while before asking that.

"Is this a problem?" Debbie asked.

"No. I just need a few seconds to gather my thoughts."

"You can understand why I didn't tell you right away, can't you?"

"Yes. I'm just making sure I've not said anything that I might later rely on in court", he said with a smile.

She returned his smile. "And you're not going to throw me out?"

"No. I'm not going to throw you out. Maybe it would be easiest if you told me as much as you can about your real job, and then we can take it from there."

"Well, I do actually work with that security firm – but I sit the other side of the table," she began, before going on to give him a summary of her career to date. He did not interrupt – but occasionally gave an uh-huh or hmmm to show that he was paying attention.

What she did not, and could not, know was that he was also thinking, 'Well there's no chance I'm going to be able to tell her about the quarter of a million quid sitting ten feet above her. Not right now, and probably not ever.'

At the end of the story, she felt quite drained. A lot of nervous tension had evaporated. And it looked like they were going to be able to move on from this.

"You checked me out, didn't you?" he asked.

She knew she had to be completely honest and nodded. "I have to do a CRB check. You understand that don't you?"

"Yes. Helps explain the delay before you agreed to meet. Did anyone else pass the checks?"

She wasn't sure this was any of his business, but also knew that she had to be as open as possible to make up for being less than honest before.

"There were three others. One had a record, so he was eliminated. One was too impatient and wanted to date immediately, so that was no good and the third one passed the check but couldn't match up to the competition." She indicated that he was 'the competition' and tried to change the subject by asking what had happened to his matches on the dating database.

He told her about his unsuccessful hook-ups, but she knew that the discussion of her job was not finished. He had abandoned his glass of champagne and moved to the cupboard in the kitchen that he always referred to as his drinks cabinet. He was concentrating on pouring himself a whisky and extracting ice-cubes from the freezer to put in it.

Although a little worried about him drinking more – he rarely had even a couple of drinks in the same evening - she knew he needed time and activity to allow him to think things through.

"Why tell me now?" he asked.

"It's not easy," she began. "I had to be sure there was a chance we were going to be something to each other before I let you know. And I think there's a good chance we are going to be. And Christmas is coming up, and I'd like to spend some time with you then, so I couldn't wait any longer."

He took a sip from his drink. She could tell there was still something on his mind. Most of his reactions had been pretty much what she had expected. But she felt there was something still lurking in the shadows. She was prepared to either let it die or surface when it would.

"No more secrets?" he asked, his voice attempting to signify it was a closing question.

"I can promise you there are no more secrets", she said.

He got up from his chair, came round to her side of the table and put his arms around her.

"And I can promise you that I'll have no problems making love with a copper," he replied – and very soon afterwards proved it.

A Right to Buy
October 2005

Mark had examined the details about the Beckton development that Don had given him. It seemed like an opportunity that could make money, something that was always close to Mark's heart, and he was confident that Don would want to do his best to offer him a good deal. After all, he would not want to spend alternate Saturday afternoons sat next to an unhappy investor, would he?

With the added impetus of recent events encouraging Mark to speed up his consumption of the briefcase contents, he also wanted to find out if there was a chance to move some of it in Don's direction, so he arranged to meet Don at his office later that week.

The office turned out to be the corner of a portacabin on the edge of a busy building site. Every spare inch of space was crammed with paperwork and the occasional building tool or implement – most of them being objects of complete mystery to Don and some of them were only vaguely familiar to Mark from his years in the building supply trade.

Don was into full sales mode, describing the glories of the apartments they were in process of building. He tried his best to make Mark see a vista of open grass spaces, trees sheltering children happily playing while mothers sat chatting on nearby park benches, flanked by tall, elegant apartment blocks. Mark was more interested in the financial aspects but allowed Don to complete his spiel.

Once they got down to the nitty-gritty, Mark said he would want to minimise his risk as he had never yet bought 'off plan' and asked Don to focus on the single bedroom apartments – also believing from his research that the smaller apartments were usually the fastest to sell on this type of development.

"The expected sale price of one of these units, when complete, is ninety-nine thousand five hundred pounds," Don said.

"OK," replied Mark, "for the rest of our discussion, let's just call it a hundred, that'll make things easier." Don agreed. "What is one of your Right to Buys going to cost me?"

"Round figures – which is what you seem to prefer", he smiled, "twenty-five thousand."

"And the admin fee, if I decide not to go ahead?"

"Five hundred pounds. And that's a favour - because it's the absolute lowest I'm allowed to charge.

"Appreciate that. Now here's a question you might not have had before. Some of my other investments bring me an income in cash, which I don't always want to deposit in my account for one reason or another. Could I make at least some part of my investment in the form of cash?"

"You're right, I haven't been asked that before. I'd like to call my boss on that one, is that OK?"

Mark shrugged a sign of agreement and was a little surprised that Don got up from his seat and stepped outside the office to call his boss, but patiently waited while he completed the call.

"I've had a word with him," Don said, returning to his chair a few minutes later.

He moved closer and dropped his voice to a conspiratorial level.

"He's told me that the absolute maximum I can take in cash on one deal is five thousand." His voice now almost became a whisper "But I'm ninety-nine per cent sure I'm signing another deal with one of my regular investors this afternoon. He'll happily work a deal with me, and I'll present it to my boss as two separate cash purchases – so you can make ten thousand of your deposit in cash. How does that sound?"

It sounded good to Mark. It would eat up almost all his current reserve of 'real' money, but it would take another ten thousand out of the devil's box as he was beginning to think of it. They shook hands.

The paperwork was complex and took several hours to complete, but he had another part of his property investment portfolio in place, and progress towards a particular zero target – a lighter loft - was being made.

There was also a small, but potentially important postscript to their first business transaction. When they went for what was to become their regular post-match couple of pints together, Don drew his chair close to Mark and once again adopted his conspirator persona.

"I told my boss about your challenge of dealing with cash that you don't want to immediately put into the bank. Seems he's quite familiar with this problem. He's given me a name to pass on to you." He handed Mark his business card, drawing attention to the hand-written details on the reverse side. The name was David Stone, and it was accompanied by an address in Baker Street, London W1 and a contact telephone number.

Estelle
October 2005

Estelle (which James thought was highly unlikely to be her real name), was still an attractive woman – though not quite as attractive as she once had been. Showing a little too much leg and wearing just a little too much makeup, she settled into the more comfortable of the two visitors' chairs in James's office.

She obviously believed that gentlemen prefer blondes, as she had invested some money in making her hair appear much blonder than it really was, and some considerable time into making it appear that there was a whole lot more of it than there really was.

After the introductions and initial pleasantries had been completed, James turned to the reason he had asked her to come to the club. He reminded her that she had done business with (or rather via) his father in the past, and that in common with others, that business had dwindled over the years.

"So, now I've taken over from my father I'd like to see if we can help you do some more business in the future", he started.

After she had given her condolences over Harry's death, he thought it important to lighten the mood and said to her with a smile, "Estelle, this young man is going to do you a big favour."

"That'll make a pleasant change," she replied. "I'm more used to dealing with old men than young men, and it's always me doing them a favour." James smiled as she laughed at her joke.

"Young Ray here is going to create a wonderful website, just for you, so you can advertise your charms," he continued.

"Oh. Why would I want to do that? And what's that going to cost me?"

If Estelle's life experience had taught her anything, it had taught her not to trust anyone offering her something for nothing.

"Estelle – I'm sure you've heard of this thing called the internet." She smiled at his feeble joke. "Well, when men are looking for the kind of services that you provide, they're going to look more and more towards the internet. They'll not be looking in the private ads of the local paper or the newsagent's window anymore."

Estelle shuffled in her seat. James had just described the two places she currently got her business.

"Yeah, but you're not going to do nothing for nothing are you?" she asked

"It won't cost you a penny." James tried to reassure her. "It'll be your very own website with lots of sexy photos of you on it. And a full list of all the wonderful services you offer, stunning reviews from some of your previous clients and all the details of how to contact you. What's more, your customers will be able to pay you by credit card – I bet lots of them ask for that, don't they" he continued.

"Yeah, but I tell them they have to pay cash"

"Wouldn't you like to be able to let them pay you by credit card if they wanted to? The money will go straight into your account, there'll be no chance of them grabbing it back or you having it stolen."

"Yeah, that would be good sometimes. I'd like that." She had experienced several attempts by customers to grab their money back when the business had been completed – and one or two had occasionally been successful.

"Well, that's what you'll be able to do once Ray is finished. Of course, when the money goes into your account, a ten per cent deduction will go into our account, but with your brand new website and the chance to pay by credit card you could probably increase your charges."

Strangely enough, this little catch at the end of James's sales pitch did not deter her. Once she knew that there was something in it for him, she was much less suspicious of the whole idea. She also knew that ten per cent was not very much. A fiver off a blowjob, a tenner off full sex. She could give that much up.

After several questions had been asked and answered, the deal was done. He was certain that the service he was offering would bring extra ease of business for all the local Estelles, and a healthy flow of money into his business.

"Have you got loads of sexy photos to put on the website?" he asked. And when Estelle said that she only had a couple he offered, "If not, I'm sure Ray could help you. Now you go with him and start work on putting that website together."

-

A few days later, Ray was able to show James his finished work and it looked as good as he had hoped.

"Just a couple of things," said James, "Put your contact details on the front page in small print so that when Estelle's colleagues see this and want to know how to get it done, they'll know how to contact you. Call yourself RDC Web Design or something. And when I introduce the rest of the girls to you – tell them it's a hundred and twenty cash to have the photos done."

A month later James had contacted all the girls local to the Medway area that were in his father's book and there were now eight more websites up and running. The first time Ray brought him the twenty pounds excess from the photoshoot, James handed him back ten pounds. "Your first commission", he explained. He knew that this would encourage him to make sure the websites included professional photos – after all, if a job is worth doing it's worth doing well.

"He looks at women in a different way"
October 2005

Dragan was quite content with his life and his lifestyle. His business – arranging work for immigrants from Eastern Europe filled his time and filled his bank account. He was doing well and keeping very busy. He was very aware that his line of work was not considered entirely reputable by many people, but he was earning an honest living, working hard, and matching the needs of parts of the UK economy with those of many incoming eastern Europeans.

Their wish was to work hard for six months, spend very little, and then return home with a small pot of money to keep them and their family for the rest of the year. The rates of pay were so low that they were unacceptable to large parts of the domestic UK workforce yet were well above what could be earned in eastern Europe. He did not believe it was right, but this was how things were, and it allowed entrepreneurs like him to match supply with demand and make a good living in the process. The very model of successful capitalism.

The reputation issue he could handle. It was the inevitable result of some of the more unscrupulous operators in his line of business. Middlemen who exposed workers to unhealthy living conditions and even to dangerous work practices. And those who were, in Dragan's opinion, the lowest of the low; exploiting women who were led to expect proper jobs when they arrived in the UK only to find themselves forced into prostitution in one of the growing numbers of illegal brothels. He would not speak out against them, of course. Partly out of self-preservation – these people did not respond well to any criticism. And they provided a service that he knew some of his workers used occasionally - they were, after all, away from home for six months at a time.

He could make a good living – in fact, a very good living, by matching buyers and sellers, and working very hard. Anyone who thought he didn't earn his money was mistaken. He had to work by word of mouth to find potential employers and then match their needs with contacts back in the 'old countries'.

The workers would arrive – usually either at Luton or Stansted Airport, the two suburban airports close to London where the cheap flights from east Europe terminated, or at Victoria Coach Station in the heart of London. They had limited, sometimes zero, language skills, and, as a minimum, he had to find them a job and arrange accommodation and transport to and from their place of work. He handled the financial details, collecting cash from the employer, paying the rent, and arranging them into teams, with one member of each team as team leader made responsible for housekeeping. And the inevitable problems that needed his assistance; medical or legal emergencies in the UK, family problems back home, and so on – and on.

But at the end of the day, each financial transaction meant a slice for him – and many slices added up to a substantial cake. A cake that he was pleased to be able to share with his young brother, Tomasz.

Tomasz was special. His most noticeable trait was that he spoke very little. He had been that way ever since childhood. He was not stupid. Quite the opposite, he had a remarkably good memory and significant ability with numbers, but he found it very difficult to communicate with other people.

A typical example from his early childhood was when his mother said to him one day "We're going to see grandma. Isn't that good news". When he told his mum that he did not think it was good news, she asked him why.

"Because she's old and ugly and she smells bad," he replied, and could not understand why his mum was so angry at him. He was not lying – he knew it was wrong to lie. His grandma was old and ugly – and she did smell bad.

Incidents like this led him to believe that it was probably best if he said as little as possible – and that is what he did. The only person to whom he spoke regularly was his older brother, Dragan – who always looked after him both at home and school.

Dragan would speak to him when they were alone and would listen to what he said. And his older brother called him Tom, not little Tommy, which everyone else in the family did – even when he was as tall as the rest of them. Dragan was often surprised at some of the things his younger brother knew.

177

On one occasion, their uncle Ryszard, always the life and soul of the party and the centre of attention at any family gathering, had been visiting. Dragan had asked Tom, "What do you think of Uncle Rick?" and Tomasz had replied, "His wife is very unhappy."

"Why do you say that?"

"He looks at women in a different way to other men. All men look at one or two women differently – their wife, their girlfriend, maybe one other woman. But Uncle Rick looks at all women this way. His wife notices this and she is very unhappy about it. She will soon divorce him."

Divorce in their mainly catholic community was extremely rare, and when in due course it happened, Dragan had to act as surprised as anyone else. He never found out all the details, but the way his parents talked about it, or rather the way they didn't talk about it in front of him and his brothers and sisters, made him realise that there was more that he would never be told.

"There is a problem with another woman," Tomasz told him. "Only it is not another woman exactly, they talk about a girl, not a woman."

Dragan guessed that because Tom was so quiet all the time, adults would say things in front of him in the mistaken belief that he would not understand. But this only went halfway to explaining Tom's unique abilities. As soon as Dragan had enough work to need another pair of hands, he had no hesitation in taking Tom as his assistant. He was pleased to be able to share some of his good fortune with Tom – who would find it difficult to get a well-paid job anywhere else. And Dragan was happy to pay him well, as he often learned valuable information from him about the people with whom he was doing business.

Dragan was comfortable in his apartment, enjoying frequent visits to the gym and their effects on his physique. His place would always be the focal point for friends and family when there was a big fight on TV – there was a huge fridge full of beer and a plentiful supply of snacks, a giant TV, and a subscription to all the channels necessary to catch the top boxing and UFC bouts from all over the world – and the party would be long and loud.

There was no special woman in his life. There were women, sure. There were always some who were attracted by his physique, and his ability and propensity to spend well. But they never seemed to stay long, and he had long since resigned himself to this being his way of life. He was not unhappy to be alone and was certainly never lonely.

If Dragan did have a concern, it was that his business felt so flimsy. There was no substance to it. No assets, nothing tangible, not even any business premises – the meetings he held were either at the workplace of one of his customers or at convenient locations, which were mostly motorway service stations or cheap cafes.

He was concerned that it could not continue this way forever. There was no legislation or control on the whole business sector in which he operated – which made it so much easier for the cowboys to occupy – and Dragan felt sure that this could not last for much longer.

There was growing concern in the general community about the high numbers of East Europeans in the country. He would scoff at their complaints of foreigners "taking our jobs" as he knew that it was only because so many of the English preferred the generosity of the state machinery to the harsh realities of the marketplace for unskilled labour. And he was quite pleased that the person who served his meal – whether in a cheap café or an expensive restaurant – was so often of east European origin. But he knew that this opposition in the community might make it more difficult to do business in the future. He wanted to diversify into something a lot more *real*.

Life Choices
November 2005

James had expected some difficulties in his latest business venture. But they came from a quarter he had not expected. There was remarkably little resistance from the ladies. It seems he had judged very correctly and at the right time, that they were concerned about losing customers to the agencies which had moved out from London and were capturing the business as the modern punter turned to search engines and databases to source his carnal pleasures. And they were all getting requests from customers who wanted to pay by plastic and had no idea how to achieve this.

What he had not anticipated were the difficulties that Ray brought to him. Up until now, he had been impressed with the way that Ray had set about the tasks he'd been asked to do. He got on with whatever he was asked to do and found ways of solving any problems he encountered. But this was different. Things were not progressing as quickly as James had hoped and he asked Ray what the problem was.

At first, he told James that he was not happy meeting the ladies – the term 'the ladies' had first been coined by his father. James had picked up on the term and now everyone used it.

"It's alright for you," he said. "You meet them in your office. You are the boss, and they treat you like the boss. I have to meet them in the bar, with other people looking on, and it is obvious I am not the boss - so they do not show me any respect."

James wanted to make sure there were no problems, so he readily agreed that Ray could use his office if he wanted.

"Will that solve the problem?" he asked.

It was obvious from Ray's expression and manifest discomfort that it would not solve the problem.

"Maybe there's something else you are not happy about?" he asked. And the real problem started to become clear.

"These women. They're erm, it's not right what they do and it's not right that we should make it easier for them."

'Ah. Now we're getting to the real issue,' James thought. This was going to be more difficult to deal with. He knew very little about Ray, his upbringing and the values that it had instilled in him. Maybe his mother had fought long and hard not to take the 'easy' route of earning money this way? Who knows? Whatever it was, he knew he needed to overcome the problem – or one of his four key plans for revitalising the business would be dead in the water. James looked at his watch – it was coming up to lunchtime.

"How about I buy you a burger?" he asked Ray, knowing that Ray would find it impossible to refuse.

Over lunch, he tried to tease out from a reticent Ray what it was that he was finding difficult. Without fully getting the answer, he was able to understand that somewhere in his upbringing Ray had received a very strong message that what these women did was wrong.

He did his best to overcome it.

"Ray, the way I look at things is that it's all about life choices." He saw Ray's eyes begin to glaze over at this vague term that he probably had heard before from social workers and the like, so James moved on quickly.

"You know about these things Ray. Have you ever thought of selling your body for sex?" He got the expected strong negative reaction.

"Of course not. It's something you would hate to do – and you've got other choices. Now let me ask you another question. Would you do something right now to break the law and risk going to prison?"

This time Ray merely shook his head.

"That's right you wouldn't. But a few months ago, you did. And the difference is now that you have got more choices. You had an opportunity, and you took it. So now you could go to a Job Centre and say 'I've got a work record. I can apply for a real job,' and you would stand a chance of getting it. Last year you couldn't do that – you didn't have that choice."

He paused to take a bite of his burger and to give Ray a chance to respond. He had some points he wanted to get over, but he didn't want this to become too long a lecture.

"Now, these women – the ladies – they have choices too. They could find work as cleaners – or maybe as checkout operators at the supermarket. But they have chosen not to. Why? Because they want more money? Possibly? I'm no expert, but I reckon it's because they think that having sex with a stranger for half an hour and making fifty quid is easier than sitting behind a cash register and scanning groceries for five hours to make the same money. Maybe they prefer having sex with an old man for an hour rather than spending the whole day cleaning up after several old men to get the same money. It's all about choices"

James was pleased to see that Ray was still attentive and was processing this train of thought.

"You wouldn't do it. Nor would I! Nor would my wife or my mother or your girlfriend. But they've all got other choices. But that doesn't make these ladies any worse. They just make different choices."

James returned to his burger and coke and waited for Ray's response.

"But they show me no respect," he said, returning to his earlier complaint.

James thought for a moment and replied, "Do you think it might be because you don't show them any respect?" This caused Ray to stop and think.

"Why don't you try this. When you talk to the next one, invite her to go out and have a burger or a coffee with you. You'll be showing her that you are friendly – and you'll also be showing her that you are important enough that you can get your boss to pay for burgers and coffees – as long as you bring me a receipt. But more importantly, you'll be showing her that she is important enough for you to spend some time and money on with no strings attached because we want her to do business with us. How do you think that might work?"

Ray said he would give it a try, and so he did. The next time James checked with him, things were moving forward at a better pace, but Ray now confronted him with another problem.

"They want me to come back and do some more work on their websites," was the answer he got when he next asked Ray how it was going.

"So, what's the problem?" he asked.

"Is it OK for me to do some more work when they want to add stuff? And not charge them for this?"

"I guess if it doesn't take too much time, that's OK. We want them to do as much business as possible – and if they update their pages it should help."

"But I don't need to go and visit them to do it do I?"

"No reason to – surely they can tell you what they want, and you can make the changes without even leaving our office, can't you?"

"Yes, but they keep asking me to go and see them."

The penny dropped. "So now you are being nice to them – showing some respect like I suggested, buying them a coffee and a burger – they want you to come and visit them."

Ray said nothing, and James thought he could detect the signs of embarrassment.

"Don't worry Ray – it's completely natural. So often, they have to have sex with old and ugly guys. Then along comes this fit young guy who is nice to them. Why wouldn't they want you to come and see them." He couldn't resist a smile.

"It's up to you. Every job has its perks Ray, and you will have to decide. If they are offering you something for free that every other man on the planet has to pay for, I'm not able to advise you. You'll have to make your own decisions about that!"

Farmer Ryan

February 2006

Ryan Docherty was facing even more challenges than he had imagined in taking over his father Ken's farm. Ken had built the business over many years from its original status as an all-purpose fruit farm into a more modern specialised farming business. He had started the process many years earlier, by reducing the number of different fruits that they grew to build specialisation and expertise in soft fruits, mainly strawberries. By building the expertise, he had also built something of a brand – and benefitted from getting premium prices from retail outlets as well as developing a healthy local direct sales business.

His son was trying to build on this by investing in specialised equipment (having sold some land to fund the investment), intending to make the business an all-year-round entity – using modern greenhouse technology, solar heating and so forth.

But there were still many challenges to be faced. As the business moved away from doing all its fruit picking in the summer months (when casual workers were easily available), he was becoming exasperated at the difficulties of hiring more permanent labour. Sure, the pay rates he could afford to offer were low – it was unskilled agricultural work after all. But even though he heard every week of the high levels of unemployment in the local area, he continued to be dogged by difficulty recruiting workers.

He aired the problem on the online chat group formed by his class at Writtle College when they graduated. One of his colleagues came back with the suggestion of using eastern European labour – and gave him the contact details for Dragan Zawadski, and a recommendation for his ability to provide good honest labourers at a reasonable rate.

Ryan contacted Dragan and, learning that he preferred to do business face to face, invited him to the farm.

Dragan was very impressed by all the investment – he had visited many British farms and generally found them to be not much more developed than ones back in Eastern Europe. Bigger, yes, but not exactly brimming with new technology. Ryan's farm was different. But it still needed labour to make it work.

He learned that twelve people were needed to keep everything ticking over – and because of labour shortages, the farm was often operating at reduced capacity. He was quick to make sure that Ryan understood that the labourers Dragan supplied would work seven am to seven pm, six days a week. He would probably only need seven or eight to replace his current staff.

They negotiated while Ryan showed him around. Dragan insisted that his workers were paid a fair rate and checked if accommodation would be available (which it was not) and if Ryan could offer transport to the relatively difficult working location (which he could, using a dilapidated but functional minibus).

Ryan asked for a little time to make up his mind – but promised not to take too long as he was losing business every minute that he was understaffed. He needed to check exactly how many of his present staff would remain if they became the minority.

Dragan did not let on – but this would be an excellent contract for him. Most of his farmworkers worked only six months of the year – which suited both the farmers and the workers. To have a whole year contract was very attractive.

Dragan could also see another interesting possibility in this contract. If the workers would be needed all year round, they would need some permanent accommodation. Normally he would rent accommodation, where it was not being provided by the farmer. But here was the chance for him to increase his profit. He could buy a nearby house and receive the rent money that normally he had to pass to a third-party landlord – and this would not only make the deal even more profitable for him, but it would also satisfy another need – the need for something permanent in his business.

He was happily making plenty of money – but the whole business was transient. There was nothing to show for it, and he liked the idea of owning a house – not forgetting that this was an asset that would grow in value every year.

-

He eagerly awaited the call from Ryan – and started looking online at local property auctions. As luck would have it, there was an auction due in a few days, so he telephoned and asked for a catalogue.

When it arrived, he spent the evening with a local map open alongside the catalogue and worked out which properties would be within 'commuting distance' of Ryan's farm and marked three that seemed to be the right size and price. Knowing that he would not be sure of committing to buying the property until hearing back from Ryan, he decided to send his brother Tomasz to the auction.

The call came from Ryan on the day of the sale. He wanted to hire seven people – and, of course, wanted them to start yesterday! Dragan would have to make a few calls to get the people in place as soon as possible and asked Tomasz to bid at the auction – having given him a top price for each property.

He was jumping between calls on the afternoon of the sale but made sure to take the call from Tomasz when it came. The news was not good. All three properties had sold above the top price that they had agreed to bid.

"The last one was only five thousand above what we said," Tomasz said. Dragan was disappointed, he had been making excellent progress with recruiting people and would be able to start the contract (and start making good money) very quickly.

He had an idea. "The man who bought the last property. Has he gone to the office to complete the purchase?"

"No, I think he is interested in what price other properties fetch. He is still sitting in the auction room."

'Good,' thought Dragan, 'probably a professional buyer, not someone buying for personal reasons'

"Here's what I want you to do, Tomasz. Go to the boot of my car and open the section where the spare tyre is stored. You'll see a brown padded envelope. Take it out and go and speak to the guy who bought that last property – show him the envelope and tell him he can have the five thousand pounds in the envelope if he lets you buy the property – then you can go together to the office and let them know it was a misunderstanding. See what he says."

A short while later he got a call back. Tomasz had succeeded. The guy had been able to buy another property and was delighted to have five thousand pounds for doing nothing. 'Well.' thought Dragan, 'I had to spend ten thousand more than I had planned, but I just got my first solid business asset.'

Apples Only Fall in Orchards

February 2006

Mark was familiar with the phrase 'Apples only fall in orchards' and had often heard his father use it. Another similar phrase he had heard used to describe the same phenomenon was "The river flows to the sea". A less prosaic, but more direct phrase was "Money goes to money". All of them describe the fact that people who have money are often able to use it to make more money. It is a fundamental fact of capitalism – the very thing that gives capitalism its name - the use of capital (i.e. money) as a method of earning income as opposed to using the sweat of your brow (labour) to acquire funds.

What tends to cause some of the above phrases to be trotted out are occasions when people with money seem to get more money for no apparent reason. Fair enough if you use your capital to buy something and then rent it or sell it at a profit. That would appear to be OK. But getting money just because you already have some? That seems unfair. At least it always had seemed unfair to Mark until it happened to him.

He had been sitting in the saleroom, having successfully bid for the first property on a list that had interested him. Sure, he'd paid a few thousand over the auctioneer's assessment, but knowing the local area and local market conditions, it was still a very good price in his opinion. He would certainly have gone higher.

Having made his purchase, he decided to hang around – it was always useful to see what price some of the other properties achieved in the auction. Having travelled to north Essex, gathering market data like this was the most productive use of his time. And then along came a stranger offering him five grand to not go through with his bid. He immediately bid on another property and got it, and happily accompanied Tom (for that turned out to be the name of his benefactor) to the auction office to allow him to take over the earlier bid. He had even made sure to give Tom the contact details for Graeme the builder for the work that needed doing on the house.

And now, a few months later, sitting in the same saleroom with a marked catalogue in his hands, who should he see but Tom.

Mark made his way across the floor and they school hands.

"Maybe we can make sure we don't bid for the same properties and drive up the price for each other," he said. Tom smiled politely.

"Yes, that would be very sensible for both of us" he replied.

They kept each other company and exchanged a few remarks as the sale proceeded – and, by the end, each had bought a property at a price they were happy with. Mark asked Tom some casual questions to try to understand the nature of his business, learning that Tom's brother was the real decision-maker, who was interested in buying property from time to time and was also involved often in renting property to his contract workers.

Mark was intrigued. He had not forgotten that this was a businessman who sent out his deputy with five thousand in cash to complete a transaction, and so he asked Tom if there was a chance to meet his brother.

"Sure, he will happily meet you – but you will have to pay for a big breakfast," he laughed and promised to get his brother to call Mark as soon as possible, before shaking hands and saying goodbye.

A Bad Habit
April 2006

The friendship that developed between James and Karim Shenwari was, on one level, surprising. But on another level, not surprising at all. James had developed a bad habit since taking over his father's business – he was smoking two or three cigars per day. Sometimes he found it a good way to pause and think over the multitude of minor issues he faced. Sometimes he smoked to pause and think of his one overriding issue – how to get rid of the millstone that his father's business had become. And sometimes he did it just because he enjoyed it.

Every couple of days he would cross the road from his office to buy a pack of cigars at the small shop which appeared to be, in the words of the old phrase, open all hours. Whether it was at the early hour he sometimes arrived at the office – he had never got out of the habit of rising very early, and still had to on his two days a week in the London office anyway – or the evening when he sometimes stayed late to meet a customer, the shop always seemed to be open, and the same young man, Karim, was behind the counter.

From polite exchanges, and remarks about how they seemed to both work the same unsociable hours, their conversations grew longer each time. Apart from their mutual liking or necessity for working long hours, they found they shared many other aspects of their lives.

It was obvious that Karim had very few outlets for conversation, and when James showed some interest in him and accepted his invitation to share a coffee and a lunchtime sandwich in the back room of the shop, the floodgates opened, and James got to hear his story.

Karim's parents had emigrated from Afghanistan when they were young. If Karim knew the full details of why they left, they did not come out in the first telling of the story, but there must have been a reason they were so summarily despatched by their parents to a foreign land. They must also have had some money, as they had bought a small shop in south London and spent their lives making it a success.

190

Karim, their only child, had grown up helping in the shop. At first unpacking cases of produce, then filling in for absentee paperboys and finally serving behind the counter. He was destined for a life in retail but, hoping for better things than a suburban corner shop, he persuaded his parents to let him go away to university. They put two conditions on giving him their full moral and financial support – he had to follow a business-related course and he had to agree that on completion of his degree he would take over the family business for a short period to enable his parents to take a trip back to their homeland.

He was not happy with the second of these conditions, not being as convinced as his parents were about the safety of their homeland, which was currently in a state of virtual occupation by the armies of the USA and other western nations. But they persuaded him that this was probably the only chance they would ever have to see the country of their birth and to meet their long-lost family members.

When he returned from college and confirmed he would do as he'd promised, they made the arrangements for their trip. The difficulties of getting visas were far more significant than they had expected, and they were not able to set off until the following January. At least this gave him time to fully understand the business and made sure he did not have to face the Christmas rush with only part-time staff to help him. 'I'll just look on this as a highly unusual gap year,' he thought.

His parents had planned to spend a month in their home province and a few days in Kabul, but the trip had an unexpected, tragic outcome. On their way from Herat to Kabul their flight, which had taken off during a winter snowstorm, crashed into mountainous terrain on its approach to Kabul airport, killing all ninety-six passengers and eight crew.

Karim continued to run the shop for a while but soon realised that surrounding himself with permanent reminders of their absence both at home and at work was not helping him recover. He sold the shop and decided he wanted to prove himself by taking on a challenge of another shop. Hence, he had bought the one he was now in. James had never seen it in its original run-down status but took Karim's word for it. He certainly bore witness to how Karim was throwing himself into it.

Hard work had been accompanied by some brainpower too. Karim had decided that to succeed he needed not only to spruce up the premises and make sure the stock levels of all the items expected to be found in a corner newsagent and tobacconist were there, but a specialisation was also required.

So, he had latched on to the fact that even though smoking was diminishing in society, there was still a huge number of smokers and they needed somewhere to buy their smoking requisites. Not just the everyday brands of cigarettes that were still easy to source, but the more obscure items – the rarer packs of cigarettes, the small cigars such as James purchased, and the myriad of other items for those who still rolled their own. These items he stocked and profited from; and as their availability in other shops waned, so the price he could charge for them increased.

Thus, they found their common ground. Despite the immense difference in their backgrounds, they were both familiar with the advantages and disadvantages of inheriting a parental business. James was more and more coming to think of Harry's business as a burden. It was consuming three days a week of his time – seemingly all spent on minor tasks that he could not delegate – and was going nowhere. Worse than that it provided an income for half a dozen people, including his mother, none of whom could take it over, but was not profitable enough for him to take a salary for himself nor to be able to find a reason why someone else would buy it.

Originally, he had thought of the monthly payment to his mother as a type of insurance. She was, at first, not spending it and he knew it had begun to pile up in her account. But that had recently stopped. He was quite pleased that she had begun to shake off her widow's weeds and regain a life. She had begun to join some of her friends on holiday excursions via Saga and gain additional joy through telling her son all about the different parts of the UK she was visiting. Coach tours were certainly not extravagant, but accommodation for a single traveller was always more expensive – and his mother now needed the income she had been receiving from the business.

-

James reciprocated Karim's invite, persuading him to join him at ten one evening (the closing time of the shop) for a drink in the club. This allowed him to tell Karim his story and receive sympathetic sounds in return.

What James did not expect was a serious enquiry at their next tête-à-tête. Karim asked if James would let him know some of the financial aspects of the business. Having completed the turn-round of the shop, he wanted a new and different challenge. He had plenty still in his bank account from the sale of his parents' business and was confident of getting a good price for the flourishing business he could now sell.

And this was where James's depression deepened. He showed Karim around the club and gave him as much detail as he thought necessary about this part of his business empire – he thought that the loan business and the escorts' website part of the business was best kept separate – and asked his opinion. Thankfully their friendship was well enough founded that he was able to bear the reply he received from Karim – which was wrapped in as polite a way as was humanly possible – but was clearly enough stated. Karim just could not think of a way in which he could develop the business, and sadly thought that it was not really worth anything at all.

This prompted James to realise that he had never cross-fertilized his knowledge from his main job into this side-line. After receiving this assessment from Karim, he took off his club owner's hat and put on his financial analyst hat. He ran the figures through the standard spreadsheets used at Libera – and it confirmed the finding. The business was worthless.

Reluctantly James realised he had no choice. He would contact Dragan and get him to buy out the stream of revenue in return for a one-off payment. Zlatan would probably offer him something in return for the loan portfolio, and he would give the website business to Ray, instead of a redundancy payment. And the rest of the staff would have to be paid what they were due, and he would probably have to tell his mother a small white lie and pay her pension himself.

He did not enjoy the cigar that accompanied this period of reflection.

Annual Review
May 2006

Mark had put the date in his diary, to insure against the unlikely event that he might forget it. He had always planned to do a review one year after the find that had impacted his life so significantly. Not being prone to self-analysis, he thought that this would be a useful exercise in other ways. It might help him review his situation and think about where he was heading.

To keep track of his complex financial life, he had adopted a system - of sorts. Ever fearful that somebody might find out about the source of his funds, he had resisted the temptation to keep a journal or spreadsheet with all the financial information in one place. Instead, he had kept the three different bank accounts he had opened when he had started – one for his property dealings with Howard, one for those with Graeme, and the third for the rental properties acquired from Johnny.

He had added a fourth account – in yet another different bank – for all other dealings such as the 'Right to Buy' with his football buddy, Don, and the share purchase with his brother-in-law, Hugh.

He entered each transaction into his diary on the day it occurred. Each house (or project) had a letter allocated, and every expense was coded accordingly. 'I've got as far as F,' he thought. 'I wonder how far down the alphabet I'll eventually get?' It was easy for him to then find these transactions because they were the only ones written in orange ink.

One of American Power's competitors seemed to be obsessed with the colour orange. Not only were almost all their products bright orange, but so was all their packaging and promotional material – including pens which wrote in bright orange ink.

Everywhere that their products were available seemed to have the pens in abundance – Mark assumed it was because only six-year-old children would want to write in this ghastly colour. But he could not resist pocketing a few of the pens and had at last found a use for them.

194

He had a pad of ruled paper on the table in front of him, together with copies of his bank statements, and his trusty diary. He had now bought three houses in collaboration with Howard. Each had taken about four months to process - one month to buy, two to develop and one to sell. Two houses had been completed and sold, the third was under offer. In each case, he had paid Howard ten thousand in cash for work done. Each sale had netted him a clear profit of about ten thousand after all his expenses. He had also achieved similar results on the first house in Suffolk with Graeme. Their second joint property had just been sold and he had successfully bid on a third property the week before. His deposit cheque had not yet been presented.

To keep it simple, he used the first sheet for his workings, transferring notes from his diary and bank statement and then headed the next sheet *"Cash I've Spent"*

For the development costs of the five houses, he wrote fifty thousand pounds. This was followed by another five entries of ten thousand each on his list. Pay-off to Charlotte, Loan to Hugh, Investment in Hugh's company, 'Right to Buy' with Don, and the work Howard had done on Mark's own house.

This caused his first pause for thought. Originally, he had planned to sell his own house once the work had been completed, intending to buy and develop another house to sell without incurring capital gains tax. Why had he not done that? He had to admit it was because of Debbie. If he had let her know that he was selling his house, first he would have had to explain why. That would be easy – feigning feelings that the house would always remind him of Charlotte and that the redevelopment work that he hoped would change it had not worked. If not a white lie, it was at least pale grey.

What might have been more difficult would have been her involvement in him choosing a new place. If he was to look for a new house, this would be bound to bring up the subject of them moving in together. They had now been together for almost nine months, and the subject of cohabitation had been in both their thoughts He was ready to commit but knew he could not do this with over a hundred grand still in his loft. Put simply, he could not move in with Debbie until the briefcase was empty. Not for the first time, he resolved to try even harder to get rid of it as soon as possible.

Back to the orange ink. The cash he had spent on his day to day expenses amounted to only five thousand, spent during the first six months – since then he had been moving cash received from his parents' gift, his windfall from Dragan, the rent payments from Gina, and loan repayments from his two loan customers. (In addition to his original loan of nine thousand to Craig, he had been introduced to one of Craig's mates who also had money troubles and Mark had loaned him six thousand on the same terms.)

He made a mental check as to how he had lived up to his promise of sharing the money with the less fortunate. He continued his weekly donation to the foodbank and had topped it up with a couple of envelopes of cash labelled 'Foodbank' stuffed into the letterbox of the local vicarage (not too much, to avoid any unwelcome publicity). He had also taken out a couple of direct debits for homeless charities and given substantial credit card donations to two television fundraisers. It was enough to ease his conscience.

Mark returned to the task in hand and noted fifteen thousand as 'loans made' on his list. Lastly, there were the four bank accounts, each with ten thousand, and the twenty-five thousand for the purchase of the 'fixtures and fittings' on the property bought from Johnny.

The total was a hundred and eighty-five thousand – roughly two-thirds of the original amount.

On another sheet, he made a brief list of where the money had gone. This sheet was headed *"What I Own"*. Noting the numbers in thousands his list read: Increase in own home equity 20, Outstanding Amount on Loans (3, including Hugh) 20, equity in London flat 50, house under offer 20, Beckton flat equity 50, Hugh shares 10, Total 170. He had a total of another seventy thousand in his various bank accounts – which meant the 185 had grown into 240.

It took longer than expected to piece together even this rough approximation of what he had done over the last year, and it was getting late by the time he had finished. He decided to call it a day, tore up and binned the pieces of paper, filed the bank statements, put his diary back into his briefcase, and went to bed.

No plans for tomorrow – just some shopping and a date with Debbie in the evening. A great end to a good week.

"We'll all have to like the colour orange"
August 2006

Almost before he knew it, it was time to go to the States again. Mark had been so busy that he had not been able to devote any time to research how to spend his free day in New York. He settled for a plan to visit the two main art museums in the city. Aware of his under-education in the arts, and his philistine attitude to modern art, he decided to give it a chance to convert him by visiting the museum of modern art, and then continue to the main museum of art where he was sure the more conventional art would be more interesting.

He carried out his usual planning on the flight from London to Newark and prepared the presentation he had to give as a result of his recent successful pilot installation with the major UK DIY chain. He also planned the various aspects that needed to be discussed with department heads to ensure that the successful pilot developed into an even more successful major customer relationship.

The meeting went well – there was plenty of team spirit and self-congratulation after the success with their major deals on both sides of the Atlantic.

The steak bar Martin had chosen for their annual dinner on the evening after the sales conference could not have been more different from the cowboy bar where they had dined together a year earlier. The decor was an imitation of an old-fashioned English gentlemen's club – at least that was what Mark assumed, never having set foot in such an establishment. Heavy oak tables were surrounded by heavy oak chairs with dark green leather seats. The walls were covered floor to ceiling with bookshelves, crammed with books – which had to have been bought by the yard (or by the foot seeing as how this was America). Books for decoration, not for consumption. The prices were expensive, and Mark had high hopes of an excellent steak.

Their conversation meandered as usual from work to home and back again. Martin was pleased to be a father, and possibly even more pleased to have an excuse to have an evening out of the house. Mark spoke about Debbie, and then suffered the banter he expected when letting his boss know that he was 'dating a cop'. Eventually, they settled down to steady business talk and Martin made his announcement.

"Mark, I need to let you know some important information, and to ask you to keep this to yourself for a short while."

He paused to make sure of Mark's full attention and to help emphasise the importance of what he was about to say.

"Andrej and I have decided that we have taken the business as far as we can without external investment, so we've accepted an offer to buy the company."

"Who have you sold to?" asked Mark, even though he knew who it must be. There was only one name in the business.

"Smith and Raiter" Martin answered as expected.

Mark briefly mused to himself how strange it was that so many large, well known global companies had such unassuming names – he presumed this one was named after the founders some time back in history – while young upstarts such as the company he presently worked for searched out such grand names as American Power.

Martin continued, "We plan to let all the employees know early next week. We're just finalising the detail and making sure that someone sufficiently senior from S&R - that's how they always refer to themselves by the way – will be able to visit our offices and take part in the announcement."

Mark offered his congratulations and Martin accepted them.

"Part of the deal is that every one of our employees will be offered a job equivalent to their present position – they'll be keeping our offices here open for the foreseeable future, but I don't know exactly what they will do in the UK – but you will all get something offered to you. Is that going to be practical? I've no idea where they're located in the UK."

"Their office is quite close to us – or at least it used to be. I went for an interview there once – many years ago. It was somewhere near Gallows Corner, I believe – sorry, that probably doesn't mean much to you."

"You guys have such quaint addresses – did you really say Gallows Corner?"

"Yes – it's a major road junction not far from our offices – I'd never thought how odd the name sounds. Can you check on the internet to see what their address is in the UK?" Mark asked – indicating Martin's phone, which was lying on the table, and which he had learned earlier that evening was the latest technology with in-built internet access.

Martin turned the screen so he could see it. "That looks like their UK HQ address. Is that what you thought?"

Mark recognised the Romford postcode and nodded

"Yes – it's about ten miles from our current office, so that won't be a problem for us. Pat and Cheryl will be able to get there too."

He wondered how his colleagues back home would react to this latest news. 'Probably quite positively,' he thought, 'they'll get lots of social benefit from it. And the chance to move up in the company one day maybe. The sort of things they would never have got from working for a small company like AP.'

"And there'll be a special bonus in everyone's pay packet as soon as the deal is finalised" Martin went on. "In fact, you guys will get extra from it – so don't tell anyone over here."

"Why's that?" Mark asked. It was not usual for the UK employees to get a better deal than the USA ones, so he was understandably intrigued.

"We'll do an extra payroll run for everyone – so you'll all get an extra month's pay. In the USA we do payroll twice a month, so they won't get as much, but it's the easiest way to deal with it."

There ensued a brief discussion during which Mark learned for the first time in his life that most US companies paid their employees twice a month. 'Every day's a school day,' he thought, not for the first time.

"Will you and Andrej stay on?" Mark asked.

"No choice. They insist on us staying a minimum of a year. After that – well we'll see."

"And how do you think you'll fit in?" asked Mark, knowing that it was often difficult for entrepreneurs to adapt to large company culture.

"I guess we will all have to get to like the colour orange," was the slightly enigmatic reply that Martin gave to this question.

"Nobody else in the sales team knows about this right now so don't say anything. We'll make sure the meeting takes place at nine in the morning, and we'll set up a conference call so you can take part from the UK."

They continued chatting for the rest of the meal. Mark got around to asking how much money they had sold for, but Martin said that had to be kept confidential. He also wondered to himself if this would be the last time that they would enjoy a meal together. He thought it probably was – but said nothing. It was a little sad.

After they parted, he sat alone in the hotel bar with a large scotch and let the many thoughts about how this might change his life pass through his head. There was very little planning that could be done. He would have to see exactly what was offered by his new masters, and then make his decisions based on that. There would be plus points. Big company benefits like private health insurance and pensions, but there would be drawbacks too. He would almost certainly be much less his own boss. There was only one certainty - things would never quite be the same again.

If it Rains, Buy an Umbrella
September 2006

Julie Medcraft placed the file labelled *American Power* into the filing cabinet. She was pleased to have successfully completed the induction programme for the employees of the latest acquisition. All the complexities of pay and conditions, pensions, and so forth had been completed, the employees had all had their onboarding programs completed and they would now be able to be treated just as any other company employee. Another small task completed. On to the next.

She had received word from 'on high' that this intake – just four people who formed the entire staff of a company that the US parent had acquired, were to be given jobs within Smith and Raiter. Although small, AP's products were of considerable interest, and the new employees should be given a good welcome.

So, she had met them on Monday morning, had introduced them to John, one of her staff who conducted the induction training for the first half of their first day. Full company presentation, history, including the founding by S. Duncan Smith and Alonzo G. Raiter back in 1910 and the origins of their famous hexagon bolt logo.

John was always an enthusiastic presenter of this session no matter how many times he did it. It was also important for them to learn how different product ranges had developed from their resources or other acquisitions as it helped understand the different procedures in place throughout the organisation. The range was vast and took some time to cover.

She then took them through the company procedures, the pension scheme, contracts, benefits such as health insurance and pensions, and the staff purchase scheme for all the products of the company (with the normal warning to shop early for Christmas because just about everyone had someone who would receive some piece of electric hardware as a present every year).

For their second day, they had been provided with rail tickets to Manchester and taken to the factory – the company made a point of

201

producing some part of its product range in each of the major markets it served, although the vast majority was still made in the USA, and a growing amount produced in China to take advantage of the lower costs. They received a full guided tour of the factory from one of her northern-based colleagues, overnight accommodation, and her colleague made sure to take them out for a steak dinner.

Returning to base on Wednesday, they had been introduced to their line managers whose responsibility it was to integrate them into their respective departments. Julie would check back on their progress intermittently to ensure everything ran as smoothly as possible.

She was sure that the two office-based staff would settle in well – their commute to work was only marginally longer than it had been, and they seemed very pleased to learn about all the big company benefits they would soon be receiving.

She was less sure about the manager, Mark. Not that he wasn't talented. All four of them were well above average in qualifications and seemed to have a good attitude. But he was a bit of a maverick. Pleasant enough, but her experience gave her a good instinct for who would fit in and who would not, and she had mentally placed him in the second of these categories. But this was not her problem, this one was Geoff's responsibility. As Managing Director, he would have the challenge of finding the right shaped hole for this peg. No doubt she would hear all about it from Malcolm.

Julie was conscientious, proud of her job and the way she carried it out and was convinced that the Human Resources department – any Human Resources department, but particularly the one she headed – was a vital part of any organisation.

She was not an unattractive woman – quite the contrary. Anyone taking the time to look at her for a few moments would realise that she had quite a pretty face. And a very good figure – especially for a woman in her mid-thirties. She verified this early every morning when she caught sight of herself in the changing room mirror at the swimming pool. But nobody did take the time to look at her, that was the problem. She kept her hair cut short for convenience (it certainly made things a lot easier after her daily swim), dressed always in a business-like manner that she thought befitted her senior managerial role, and wore minimal amounts of makeup and little or no jewellery.

She was single. Not by deliberate choice, but by circumstance. She had been part of a couple for most of her twenties – never actually married, but as good as. And she had enjoyed it. She tried her very best to keep Terry and to keep him happy and was devastated when she learned of his serial infidelities.

They had split up immediately. What was worse was that it had come at the same time as the loss of her father. Being an only daughter, she was very close to her dad and his premature death had hit both her and her mother badly. The only consolation of the two losses – father and partner - happening within the same month (apart from the possible benefits of a combined mourning period) was that she had been able to move into her mother's home and they had been able to help each other through a difficult period.

Her mother had refused to accept any rent from her – the mortgage had been settled by her father's life insurance, and she made it clear that if Julie tried to pay her rent, then she would demand to pay Julie as a full-time companion. They got on well – and even holidayed together at least once a year. An annual holiday that was exotic, exclusive and expensive was one of the keystones of Julie's life. Not just the holiday itself, but the research, and planning for complex travel arrangements to remote parts of the world, made sure that the event filled many parts of the year for her.

Another keystone of her life, and one that helped fund the holiday extravaganzas, was Julie's other obsession – stocks and shares. Ever since childhood she had been fascinated by the whole concept. A small legacy from a deceased great uncle, received while still at university, enabled her to start her investment activities. She had also put a small amount aside throughout her time with Terry (she wondered if the fact that she had never told him about it was some deep-seated acknowledgement of the fact that she never really trusted him). But since moving back in with mum, she had decided to invest the sum of money that would have been monthly rent (or, more optimistically her contribution to a monthly joint mortgage with a new partner).

As with all things in her life, if she did it, she did it well. She was a voracious reader, and when not reading a book about some aspect of Personnel Management, Employment Relations or some other tome relating to her job, she was reading about investment strategies.

One of the few perks of her job was that Geoff, her direct superior, had given her approval that any book concerning business matters could be purchased on company money but remain as her possession. He was more than happy to take on board this additional expense as he knew it kept a very valuable employee – one that he relied on to provide him with the latest information in legislation and best practice in employee relations, an area that was always changing and growing more complex all too quickly for him.

When asked about her investment strategy she would just say "When it's raining you should buy an umbrella". A more accurate representation of her success might well have been: 'When you have a really good way of telling what the weather is going to be, and you strongly believe that there is going to be a prolonged period of rain, then you should search out the name of the leading supplier of umbrellas - because they are likely to have a period of sustained success. Then, when a lot of people realise that this umbrella company is being successful, they will want to buy shares and the price of these shares will increase. At this point, you should decide whether to sell your shares or, if you believe that the company will wisely use the additional revenues it has accrued, you should continue to hold some or all of the shares you now own'.

But she decided that just saying "When it's raining you should buy an umbrella" was more concise and therefore probably better.

Although her success in this endeavour brought her some happiness, it also was beginning to raise some concerns in her mind. What was originally meant to be a means to an end, had become an end in itself. She spent a couple of hours on her computer almost every night, checking on prices, reinvesting dividends, buying and selling. It had become a job not a joy.

She had started to concern herself with what would happen if she ever did find a new man. Would her nest egg be a cause for concern? Would she worry that he was only marrying her for her money? If she carried on with it, she would not be able to hide it from him, and it could become a source of contention. And then lastly, she hated the way she was beginning to think of this nest egg; she was beginning to see it less as a possible deposit on a new home and a new life, and more as a supplement to her pension. And she was only in her mid-thirties.

Such thoughts were being stirred by the possibility of there being a new man in her life. She had never deliberately avoided men – it just seemed that for the last few years very few had crossed her path. And those who had must have been put off for one reason or another. But there was a very good possibility that things might be moving forward with Malcolm.

Malcolm Bettridge had been in the company almost as long as Julie and they had worked in the same office block for several years. His face was familiar to her, but they had never actually spoken more than a casual greeting until they were placed on the same team in a recent cross-department training exercise.

They worked on a couple of assignments together, and he had subsequently, very carefully asked her out for a meal. She knew he was in the sales department, and that he had a steady but not spectacular record in his time there. Closer examination, or a review of his record by a more sales-oriented individual would have let her know that he was that type of salesperson known to all other salespeople as the guy who always does enough – just enough. It makes for career longevity, but not popularity with sales management. But his career progression was not her concern. It might have been if she had been wearing her HR hat – but she was presently thinking of him as a potential partner – not an element of the business's human resource.

He was pleasant enough looking and possessed what was becoming thought of as old-fashioned good manners. He was of average height, and, when she thought about it, he was pretty average in all respects. Not particularly good looking, she'd even checked his test scores from when he joined the company – they were all about average. And he had stayed in an average job. He didn't seem to have any strong characteristics or affiliations either. Some slight interest in politics – his views being to the right of centre, as were hers, and seemingly his main reason for getting involved with the party he belonged to were social rather than political. In many ways, he was a bit of a blank page – but one that she could write on, given the chance.

She was not desperate. But she was aware that while she had an exceptionally good mother-daughter relationship, it would not be such a good situation if it morphed into a patient-carer relationship, and there was every danger of that happening as her mother grew older, unless she made some changes in her life, and made them very soon.

Smith & Raiter
October 2006

Mark looked around at the décor of the office of his new manager. He liked it. All four walls carried half a dozen photos, each tastefully framed and connected to the company in one way or another. They included an enlarged photo of the two founders, S. Duncan Smith and Alonzo G. Raiter, taken in the early years of the twentieth century; an enlargement of a garish advertisement for the company's products, probably from the 1950s when tastes were very different; a group photo of the entire company's headquarters staff, taken on the company picnic on the occasion of the firm's seventy-fifth anniversary; and a modern aerial photo of the UK production facility shortly after its construction.

The overall effect was both to give the office a pleasant aspect as well as imbuing the visitor with an impression of the company's size and longevity.

The current occupier of the office stood up and walked towards Mark with an outstretched right hand. "Welcome, Mark, I'm Geoff Ambrose, Managing Director. But then you probably knew that already." His whole attitude conveyed a man at ease and a genuinely warm welcome.

"Have you enjoyed your last couple of days of indoctrination?"

"Yes, thanks – everyone's been very welcoming, and your set-up is as impressive as I'd expected."

They chatted briefly about what Mark had experienced over the last couple of days. Geoff praised American Power's products and complimented his achievements.

"Getting your products into a major UK chain single-handed, that's pretty impressive. I hope we get the chance to put your skills to good use here. You might even be able to teach us a thing or two."

Mark was pleased with the praise and thanked him for it, allowing Geoff to move on to his next topic.

"I don't know how much you've heard about our sales organisation," Mark signified that he knew almost nothing, so Geoff continued. "I'm responsible for the whole of the UK operation, and I'm acting as Sales Manager until we fill that vacancy. We have a Marketing manager, Margaret, who handles everything to do with product promotion. She decides which of the promotional stuff that comes from the USA we can use, what needs modifying, and what we need to create for ourselves. She's first-rate, and I'll introduce you to her when we've finished. On the sales side, we focus heavily on the major chains.

We have four people covering two major multiples in the UK - a senior account manager and a junior account manager for each of them. The senior account manager deals with everything corporate at the client and then we split all their branches on a north and south basis between him and the junior AM, who also can fill in for the senior AM if needed."

"OK if I take notes?" Mark interrupted, sensing, quite correctly, that the explanation might become lengthy and complex.

"Sure," Geoff continued, "The other five retail chains each have one account manager. Then we have two other salesmen – one covering the north and one in the south – they look after all the independents. Eleven in all – a good number of players for a good team as I like to put it. And, as you might have guessed, some of the team work out of this office, and some out of the Manchester office. There should be a sales manager in position, but we had to part company with the gentleman that was in that position recently, and I haven't had the chance to replace him – so everyone reports directly to me at present."

"That must put a load on you," Mark commented, hoping to align himself with Geoff, and to achieve his aim as being thought of as a potential team leader, rather than just a team member.

"The truth is it's going to have to stay that way for a while yet. We're just entering a crucial quarter and I'll have to wait until it's over before I can spare the time to fill the role – it's vital to get the right person."

Mark nodded sagely in agreement.

"Now, we come round to you. I see a potential problem, but also an opportunity here. Let me share them with you. The problem? Well, I could find you a job in one of the team roles – do a slight reorganisation, or just wait until someone leaves – there's always some turnover in a sales team as I'm sure you know. And you would be making as much money as you did in your previous job, with a few additional benefits on the side. But I suspect that this might not give you the erm" he hesitated as if reaching for the right words, but Mark was confident that he knew exactly which words he was going to use and was only pausing for effect, " ... the independence that you previously experienced. Am I right?"

Mark considered his response carefully. "It's hard to say exactly – not knowing how much independence I would get here, but you are addressing one of my concerns. I like to believe I'm a good team player, and always welcome a new challenge, but yes I have been my own boss for quite a while."

"Good answer. Let's put that problem aside for a while and look at the opportunity. I've been told that we're not going to change American Power's products for the next three months at least. They'll have the same names, prices, everything. They'll just be available via Smith and Raiter.

So, here's what I'd like to propose. You help us get the absolute maximum we can out of those products for the next three months. Work with every one of my team to make sure that they and their customers know all they need to know about these products, go on sales calls with them, work with the retailers' staff, whatever it takes, and let's see if we can get some real numbers out of them. You'll have the job title of sales specialist, and a commission plan that rewards you on sales until the end of the quarter."

Geoff took a two-page document out of a folder on his desk and passed it over to Mark. "How about you have a look at this and give me your immediate thoughts. Meanwhile, I'll use one of my perks and get someone to bring us a pot of coffee. What do you say?"

"Fine" Mark replied.

He had expected that Geoff might make him an offer like this. The devil might well be in the detail, so he was keen to read the document and see what the bottom line was. And, as he was sure Geoff knew, the opportunity to put his products in front of just about every potential retailer in the UK, on the back of an existing relationship and with terms and conditions all in place was something he had always longed for.

He started to read the document while Geoff picked up his phone and asked for coffee and biscuits to be brought in.

Mark read the document carefully. It was laid out in the form of an addendum to the employment contract he had signed as requested during his induction. He quickly scanned the legalese that defined what was covered in terms of territory and products, the period it covered (the next three months) and – the vital part – the target sales amount and rate of commission that would be paid. Mark had always believed in the mantra that if something looked too good to be true then it probably was (too good to be true) and this appeared dangerously close to falling into that category.

The pot of coffee, two cups and saucers and plate of biscuits (even including some chocolate ones) arrived – Mark wondered idly when he had last drunk coffee out of a cup and saucer that was not in a restaurant.

He put the agreement on the desk between him and Geoff, pointed at the relevant section and asked, "I have to reach this target?"

He paused, and Geoff nodded

"And from that point onwards I get paid this much," pointing to the relevant figure on the agreement, "on every sale made in the UK?"

Another nod.

"And I devote my whole time to selling the AP products - nothing else?"

"Yep."

Mark paused to think where the catch might be, which gave Geoff a chance to fill in.

"Yes, you stand to make a lot of money. I can't promise that this will carry on after this quarter – if you agree to this role, we've just kicked that problem down the road by three months. I'd like you to help me make my number, and if that means that you rake it in at the same time, then enjoy it while you can."

Mark agreed and signed on the dotted line. Turning down such a potential money-spinning opportunity would have been tantamount to an act of criminal neglect in Mark's way of thinking. Having finished the coffee, Geoff took him to meet Margaret.

"Can you let our new American Power Product Sales Specialist know how we go about marketing around here?"

"Of course," she replied – she was expecting the visit and had set the time aside.

"Let me know if you finish before close of play and I'll take Mark to meet the others in the team."

As it turned out, the range of activities that Margaret covered, the range of questions Mark wanted to have answered, and one or two interruptions, took them way past five o'clock and he had to wait until the following morning to meet the others in the sales office.

Only four of the six salesmen based in the office were there the next morning, and Geoff called an impromptu meeting – apologising for the lack of notice but explaining that he could not be sure the meeting was needed until he'd spoken to Mark the day before. He outlined Mark's new role and asked if they had any questions. One or two minor points were raised – the main issues, entirely good news to the team, were that they could now sell the new products, their sales targets would not be increased, they could call on Mark's help, and they would get paid their normal commission.

Geoff left him with the team to get on with it.

Just Like the Old Country
October 2006

James had continued the monthly meetings with Dragan, even going so far as to partake of the same breakfast, sacrificing his health and his taste buds in the service of good business relations.

Now he wanted to have a deeper discussion and had asked Dragan if they could meet at one of the clubs. As part of his plan to implement an exit strategy (as his Libera colleagues would no doubt express it), he wanted to discuss the possibility of introducing him directly to the contacts.

'A direct connection to the people who hire his labourers must surely be worth something to him,' was James's line of thinking.

He knew how to perform a relatively straightforward calculation of Net Present Worth – it was one of the calculations he did several times a week in his real job - to determine the current value of all future cash flows generated by a project. It was even a standard formula included on spreadsheet programs. But James also knew that something was only ever worth what someone was willing to pay for it.

Dragan would not use a spreadsheet to work out a figure, but he would know that if James wanted to sell this piece of business, then only Dragan (or one of his direct competitors) would be a potential buyer. It would be an interesting discussion.

He was also distracted by events that had occurred the previous day and he was still trying to deal with the consequences. Bob Harvey, the longest-serving club steward of the four, had told James that he had some major family problems and would have to quit. James had talked sympathetically with him –making sure not only that everything that a long-term employer could expect to do was being done, but also that Bob was not quitting unnecessarily. His loss would be a difficulty for the business, and he would be hard to replace. His request to leave immediately made it all the more difficult.

The reasons James did not enjoy running the business were crystalised in this one event. One person quitting – a quite reasonable occurrence – was going to cause chaos for weeks to come. Finding a replacement was difficult, and the interim period would need reshuffling of everyone's rota, and even when the replacement had been found and had started work, it would take more time until everything was back to normal. There was just no slack to cover instances like this – and there was no prospect of this ever-changing. James found it immensely unsatisfactory.

-

Dragan arrived at the appointed time, and James gave him a brief guided tour of the club offered him a drink as they sat down in his office. Surprisingly, Dragan asked for a beer.

He was not what people call 'a drinking man'. He shared the occasional beer with friends, the occasional glass of wine with a meal - and, of course, most family get-togethers involved the sharing of strong drink between the men as they solved the problems of the world together. Dragan did not regularly frequent bars or pubs, but one thing struck him immediately about this place – it was very similar to the bars he had visited back in Poland. He'd been back to the old country a few times – tracing his ancestry on a couple of holidays and making a few visits to maintain his connections – and noticed differences between the bars there and the pubs in England. But this place was just like the old country and so it seemed oddly appropriate to ask for a beer.

James started the discussion by apologising to Dragan that there was a recent problem in the business, and he might receive some interruptions – something he would normally never permit in a meeting as important as this. Dragan was sympathetic and immediately said it was not a problem – "I understand – when you are running a business you must master the act of doing many things at the same time, of course."

He then asked James. "You have more than one bar, I understand?"

"They are actually clubs, not bars – it's a different license – but yes there are four of them."

"And now that Harry has gone, you are now running them, yourself? This must be quite a change from a job in the financial district."

James smiled and nodded. 'So, he's done a bit of a background check on me,' he thought. 'I like that. I think I might be able to work with him.'

They then got down to the main discussion. James said that he wanted to simplify his father's business. His father had been involved in so many different activities – this brought forth a knowing nod from Dragan – and so he thought that if he allowed him to conduct all future transactions directly with the customers, there would be less expense and his business would be more profitable for the future.

They were both conducting a form of ritual dance, and they knew it. Dragan knew who the customers were. He had never approached them directly in the past as it would not only have been discourteous to Harry but would also have cut off the supply of future customers. With Harry no longer in the picture, the loss he would suffer from a direct approach would be much less. But it would be worth something to him.

James gave his opinion of what it might be worth to Dragan not to have to pay the regular 'royalty' and put a figure on it. Dragan naturally had a different figure in mind, but eventually, they settled on a figure and proceeded to draw up a list of tasks that each would have to perform to smooth the transition.

James was expecting Dragan to start to leave, and he was a little surprised when he asked him what was the problem that he had had that caused the interruptions to the business meeting.

"One of my managers has a family problem and has asked to leave immediately. I have to reshuffle people and find a replacement as quickly as possible so that the club can stay open."

Dragan asked if the other clubs were the same as this one.

"Yes, very similar, why do you ask?"

"I know someone who might be interested in buying them. Would you be interested in such a transaction?"

"Dragan, we are businessmen, aren't we? So, we know that everything is always for sale if the price is right."

He smiled and nodded. "Is it possible that I could visit the others?" he asked.

James arranged to take Dragan to the other three the following week, at which time they might be able to conclude the first piece of business. Dragan offered further "If you want a reliable person to help out for a short time, I am able to help."

James was surprised and interested in equal measures. Anything that bought him some time could be very useful to him right now.

"I might take you up on that. Do you have someone specific in mind?"

"Yes, I would only offer someone I was certain you could completely rely upon – so I would offer my brother. He helps me with my business, but I can manage without him for a short time, and since we have done so much together, I would like to help if I can."

Having established that Tomasz would be paid the same as he would pay a newly-started employee in the position and that he was immediately available, James asked if Dragan could bring him to the meeting next week to seal the deal.

"Of course," said Dragan. "You will see that Tom is not the most chatty of men – but he is a very quick learner and totally reliable. He will help you out of your short-term problem, I'm sure."

James felt the meeting had gone extremely well – the original plan to cash in the ongoing commission on employment would relieve him of one drag on his time, the possibility of selling the business which he was otherwise going to have to close down was intriguing and the short-term help for a reliable person was a bonus. He shook Dragan's hand warmly as they parted.

Dragan walked away delighted and intrigued. He would have to find the money to buy James out of the employment commission – that was no problem. But the possibility of buying the whole thing was almost a dream come true. To have a real business with premises and everything – to replace his nomadic lifestyle. And, of course, having Tomasz work there for a brief period would be very useful to him. Knowing Tomasz's unique capabilities of finding out what was going on, Dragan felt sure he would be very well prepared indeed when it came to discussing a price. He would probably have to give James an unpleasant surprise when they came to negotiate, but this was truly an amazing opportunity.

-

After James had shown Dragan around the other clubs and Tom had started work, another month passed before Dragan called him and asked for another meeting.

James continued to be amazed at how quickly time seemed to pass. It was not all that surprising when you consider that he was doing two jobs – going from one club to another, supervising Raheem and the delicate tasks he was performing, and tackling the endless minor issues involved in running a diverse business inherited from his father. Most days he felt like a hamster on a wheel. And then there were the two days of his normal job at Libera that had to be completed every week.

Thankfully Tomasz had been a godsend. He had quickly mastered the litany of tasks required of a club steward and was diligent in performing them. True, he was not one of life's great conversationalists, but more than made up for this by hard work, often staying later than needed to make sure everything was perfect before leaving for the day. Just as well in many ways because James had not been able to make any progress on finding a permanent replacement.

Not surprisingly he was under-prepared for the meeting with Dragan, and this made him distinctly uneasy. He had intended to conduct a background check on Dragan as a minimum, but time had slipped by, and it was now too late.

They met in James's office, and he thanked Dragan for lending him Tomasz and complimented him on his hard work. Dragan pulled a piece of paper from his jacket pocket and opened it on his lap. James assumed it was a cross between a prompt list and an agenda for the meeting.

"If you will permit, I would like to sum up what I know about your business," Dragan began.

James nodded, "Go ahead."

"Apart from the business which Harry and I conducted, which we have already closed to our mutual agreement, there are four other aspects: the bars, the card rooms, the lending of money, and the erm 'ladies' I think you call it, is this right?"

James was not sure if the question referred to the whole statement or just the last bit – but he gave a yes, to cover both.

"There is interest in the first three parts of the business – the proposed purchaser has no objection to the other part, but I hope you can understand that as a member of the East European community it would not currently be ahh …. appropriate for him to enter into this type of activity, do you understand?"

James agreed. The current news stories of trafficking of women from eastern Europe to the UK for prostitution would make a move into this line of business rather stupid for someone from that part of the world.

"My brother has been able to tell me a little about the business, how it functions, how well it is doing and so on," Dragan lied. His brother had been able to tell him much more than a little – with his uncanny ability to find out information, he had delivered a thoroughly forensic account of the business.

"This has helped me to inform the proposed purchaser and to assess the true worth," Dragan continued. "If we look first at the bars, it is obvious that there is no profit in this part of the business. It might even be running at a loss, subsidised only by the money which comes in from the weekly card games. I trust you will agree with me."

James was neither willing nor able to disagree with this painful summary. He nodded once more.

"The business of lending money has some profit in it – that is true, but there is the question of how legal it is, which I do not wish to go into, but I think you will understand that this affects the value and the price my client is willing to pay."

Again, James found it hard to disagree. The only good thing so far was the phrase 'the price my client is willing to pay.' At least this signified that his client was considering a price.

"I assume your client sees some value in the opportunity to develop the business, to build on the improvements that have been made in the last few months." James thought it wise to inject some positivity into what had, so far, been a rather negative summary.

"Oh yes, of course. There is value in the business and my client has plans to develop it. He appreciates how valuable it is to have good customers, and even more how important it is to have good information about those customers."

James wondered how to take this last remark, not being aware of how much Dragan knew. Was he just referring to the membership system that James had shown him, or had he somehow been able to find out about the computer-generated information that James had not shown him? He wondered about Tom's diligence and his willingness to put in those extra hours but could not say anything.

"You understand that it has been necessary for me to make certain estimates about the total amount of loans that are currently outstanding and their value. Would you be able to provide this information to my client?"

"So long as this information remained confidential, of course. I have records of all the loans and the amounts outstanding, but you understand the delicacy of this data."

"Of course – we must be careful of customer data at all times. This information is, of course, crucial to the valuation of the business. But we can leave it aside for now. I would like to come on to one last point. I understand that the only money which currently leaves the business is the income from the loans, and a small salary paid out to one member of your family. You do not draw any payment yourself is that correct?"

James was becoming more surprised about the diligence that Dragan had undergone, and so decided that he might as well play an open hand. This would be the best chance he had of getting anything for the business in the near term.

"A small salary is paid to my mother, and the income from the loans does not get entered into the accounts, that is true."

Dragan paused, looking at the piece of paper in his lap and finally spoke, having seemed to reach some decision.

"James, I am a man who likes to be open and honest in my dealings. I appreciate how honest you have been with me and so I will tell you now three things. One, the person who is interested in buying this business is me. Two, the only real financial value that I truly see in the business is the value of that loan book. Three, I will make you a clear offer.

I will guarantee to you that the clubs will keep going. All the clubs will remain open, I will keep all employees on the payroll at their current rates of pay and will continue to do so as long as they keep to their contracts. I will also continue to pay a salary, at whatever level it is currently set, to your mother for as long as both she and I are alive. But the only amount of money I will pay to you to purchase the business is the total you can prove to me is outstanding from loans."

He took the sheet of paper from his lap and passed it to James. It was a written offer to buy the business and confirmed all that he had just said.

James was somewhat taken aback. He had expected the meeting to involve much more questioning about the business, but it seemed that Tomasz had gathered enough data for Dragan to make his decision – and he was obviously a man who did not let the grass grow beneath his feet.

"Dragan, I appreciate your directness and will do my best to respond in like fashion. This business involves my family, and it would not be right and proper for me to give you an answer without consulting them. Also, the importance of such a decision means that it should not be made too hastily. Will you give me one week to answer your proposal?"

Dragan was more than happy and suggested they meet again the following week.

"The same day, the same time, and the same place, yes?" was his final comment before shaking hands and leaving

Having grown up hearing the story of how his father had started the business, James was able, much later, to appreciate the irony of what had just happened. The business, which his father had acquired by paying a pension to the widow of its previous owner, had just been sold. In return for the payment of a pension to Harry's own widow.

As soon as Dragan left, James moved swiftly to catch up with some of the actions he should have taken earlier. He called Ron Jenkins and asked him to do as thorough a background check on Dragan as he could do in the next seven days. He gave Ron as much information as he had managed to gather from their meetings over the last few months, but acknowledged it was not much. Ron promised to do what he could.

James then examined the loan book to establish its current value, and whether any issues might need attending to before making a sale. He was instantly grateful for the database that Ray had created (and his own decision to hire Ray in the first place).

James discussed Dragan's offer with his wife that evening. She asked a few relevant questions, which James appreciated – he needed another pair of eyes to look at the deal, and she was uniquely able to do this from both a professional and family viewpoint. They agreed that all things considered it was a fair offer and would provide Rose with more than enough security for the rest of her life. They also agreed that subject to a satisfactory result from Ron's work, they would accept the offer and book a table at their favourite restaurant to celebrate a return to their former normal life.

One week later, James was able to finalise the deal. The background check had thrown up very little of a negative nature, and Dragan had agreed to James' request that the payment to be made to Rose would increase in line with inflation each year. And the meal with his wife, at a suitably expensive small restaurant in Sevenoaks, was as good as expected. James granted himself a week off – well, three days actually – before booking a meeting with his boss, Alex Cameron, to discuss his return to full-time work at Libera.

Background Checks
October 2006

Up until that point, it had been a good day for Debbie. She had organised and run a straightforward surveillance operation, based on information received, to a successful conclusion. Danny Mason had been caught in the act of selling red diesel illegally – caught 'red handed' you might say. Debbie had arrested him - and he was currently in custody, meeting his solicitor, Claire Dunmore, before being interviewed and charged.

Danny was a farmer, or more correctly, a farm manager, and thus a permitted user of red diesel, able to buy it at substantially below the price of normal diesel. Whilst almost everyone in agricultural circles would admit that not every drop of red diesel is used in agricultural vehicles and a certain amount of sharing with employees, suppliers, friends and family does go on, Danny had turned the operation into a larger scale, and therefore criminal, enterprise. A considerable amount of cash had been seized at the time of his arrest.

What Debbie didn't know is that her luck was about to change. Claire Dunmore, Danny's appointed solicitor, was walking him through the events of the day, at least that portion of the events that had entailed several police officers entering his premises and finding him in conversation with Paul Wilson, whose SUV just happened to have a full tank of diesel, which the police would no doubt be able to prove by forensic analysis was identical to the red diesel supplied to Danny under terms of restricted use. Paul had already admitted that he had purchased the fuel from Danny. She was also confirming that several hundred pounds had been found in Danny's office.

"Yeah, well it would've been more if she hadn't nicked some," said Danny.

"Are you saying that one of the officers took some of the money from your office?" the solicitor asked.

"Yeah, that bitch stuffed some in her pocket. She's too pretty to be a fucking copper anyway."

Having established that the alleged theft had taken place in the brief period when Danny, the female detective, and the money, had all been in Danny's office with nobody else present, she suggested to him that it was probably not worth him trying to push his claim since there were no witnesses, and it would come down to his word against hers. She also suggested to him that if he owned up to even more money than the police had found, it might make his crime look more serious, but he would not budge. He insisted that Debbie had stolen some of his money.

Claire carried the unfortunate tidings to Debbie. She could only rationalise Danny's claims by believing that he thought by accusing the police officer who arrested him of wrongdoing, it would either throw doubt on his conviction or persuade them to drop the charges, either of which she had assured him would be highly unlikely. She also added, off the record, that in her opinion, "If brains were dynamite, Danny wouldn't have enough to blow his nose."

Danny had to be interviewed and charged by another officer, and, with him sticking to his claim, Debbie knew she would have to face an interview with the Professional Standards Department. Although she knew herself to be innocent, she was also painfully aware that the slip she had made by allowing herself to be alone with the accused and a pile of cash could cost her dearly.

The PSD, referred to by many police officers as 'the rubber heel brigade' and by many other more colourful, derogatory, and profane terms, upholds the standards of police behaviour in the UK and is part of the apparatus for investigating complaints against serving officers.

They say that bad luck often comes in threes, and two further pieces of bad luck duly befell Debbie. Firstly, her case was allocated to Detective Sergeant Peter Crawford, and secondly, it was allocated at a time when his workload was relatively light, and so he had plenty of time to investigate.

Peter was an experienced PSD member. He would not go as far as to say he enjoyed his job, but he did take satisfaction in executing it thoroughly. He was renowned for his attention to detail and accordingly was either hated or admired, depending on which side of the court you sat.

He took possession of Debbie's file and checked it thoroughly. The first thing he noted was that she had transferred from the Metropolitan Police to Essex Police. Such transfers are not unusual, but they are infrequent and the 'Distrust Thermostat' of a member of PSD is set one degree higher than that of anyone else. 'Infrequent' is reset to 'Unusual'; 'Unusual' is reset to 'Suspicious'; 'Suspicious' is reset to 'Bloody Suspicious'; and 'Bloody Suspicious' is reset to 'Guilty But Not Yet Proven'.

Peter examined the file carefully and noted some discrepancies concerning her time in the Met. Certain entries to the file seemed to have been made in the wrong sequence. To anyone else, this level of imprecise record-keeping would have passed without comment. Cockup comes ahead of conspiracy in the likelihood stakes, especially when dealing with information entered into police personnel records. But this was not anyone else, this was Peter Crawford. He cross-checked the information with the records of officers serving at various Met police stations, and it was obvious that something was wrong.

With his suspicions thus aroused, Peter checked on Debbie amongst her colleagues and found that she was both liked and respected. In checking whether there had been any recent changes in her demeanour or behaviour, the best he could come up with was that she was making more of her appearance recently, wearing more makeup and sporting some expensive jewellery. There was a strong suspicion amongst her fellow female officers that there was a new man on the scene, but Debbie was always careful not to reveal anything about her private life. Peter paid particular attention to these recent changes.

She was called in for interview, under caution and in the presence of her federation representative. She expected the interview to cover the allegations made by Danny Mason and was ready to strongly refute them. When asked about the discrepancies on her service record, she was surprised and, knowing what they were and why they were there, made sure to limit her answers to 'No Comment'. When she was asked about her current personal life, her federation rep made sure that this line of questions was brought to a very swift conclusion as it was outside the scope of the investigation.

Later that same day she checked the police database to find out if the two senior officers who would know about her real service record and the incident that had propelled her transfer to Essex, were still serving as she had had no contact with them since moving to Chelmsford. She found that one of them had retired, but the other was now an even more senior officer than he had been when their paths had crossed. She noted his phone number and called it that evening. After completing the brief call, she was confident that this aspect of the investigation by PSD would be rapidly closed down.

Peter presented his findings to his immediate superior, highlighting the discrepancy in her service record and his suspicion that there might be something behind the recent arrival of a new man in her life. His boss told him that the discrepancy in her record with the Met had been perfectly explained to him and could not be further examined for security reasons. The trust that Peter had for his boss was such that he did not question this at all. But he asked for permission to look into Debbie's boyfriend.

"He's bought her a few items of jewellery that seem rather expensive, and she's been unnaturally secretive about him. Something is not quite right there, gaffer, I can just sense it", was all the justification he could offer. Trust between Peter and his boss was a two-way street, and Peter did seem to have a knack for uncovering matters by turning over the right stones, so he was permitted to carry out further investigations.

He set to it with a will. Cross-referencing Debbie's phone records allowed him to establish Mark Reynolds as the man in her life and he gathered all the information he could. Over the next few days, he also used some of his spare time to check out Mark's home and work addresses and to examine his financial records. His suspicions grew. There seemed to be much more going on than there should be, and the books just did not balance. He was certain that young Mr Reynolds had another source of income that he was not disclosing, and to an investigative officer of the Professional Standards Division, that could only mean one thing. Criminality.

He checked back in with his boss and asked for permission to investigate further but was refused. As his boss put it, "Peter, this guy may well be bent -but he is not a copper, is he? Which means it's not our job to deal with him. If you're sure that there's something there, what you need to do is to gather all the information you have on him, and then pass it over. We can't give it to the CID because it concerns one of their own, so it'll have to go to Major Investigation, they'll have to investigate him."

Peter was disappointed but could not fault his boss's logic. Besides, he was confident that a recommendation from PSD would mean that someone would follow up – and he'd make sure to keep in touch with whoever that turned out to be (unofficially of course) until there was a result.

So it was that a file on Mark Reynolds landed on the desk of Russell Burcombe in the Financial Investigation Unit of the Major Investigation Department of Essex Police. He read it and instantly realised that it was not straightforward. 'Ideal for Dawn,' he thought, and, having checked that she was not currently assigned to any major investigation, called her into his office.

Dawn Mepham knew that she was nicknamed 'The Terrier' – even though she had never heard anyone use the name in her hearing. She was small, Scottish, and extremely thorough in all her work. It was her habit of never letting go of a case until it was absolutely and completely finalised that had earned her the nickname. That and the fact that, like all other Scots who had emigrated from their country of birth, her strong Scottish accent remained undiluted by the passage of time.

Not known for his concise briefings, Russell addressed her. "Dawn, I need you to handle this case. It's an awkward one that's been passed to us by PSD, so we must be seen to thoroughly investigate it – even if there's - nothing in it. And, knowing that it came from PSD and in my opinion, none of those buggers would know a major criminal if he jumped up and bit them on the arse (but of course, I never said anything like that) there probably isn't anything in it. But we've got to show that we've looked into it."

He handed her the file.

"I don't recognise the name, sir. Who is this Mark Reynolds?" she asked.

"Strictly between you and I, he is, erm, shall we say romantically linked to a member of the force."

Dawn realised he was having trouble spitting it out but stayed silent to give him the chance to get his words right.

"He's Debbie Coulson's boyfriend. But I don't want that information to get out, and it must not colour our judgement in any way whatsoever, do I make myself clear?"

"Perfectly sir, I'll put it out of my mind. And I assume that I'm not to say anything to DS Coulson?"

"Correct."

Dawn knew Debbie. As two women in the male-dominated environment of the police, they had spoken from time to time. 'This is going to be bad for her, no matter what the outcome,' she thought to herself. 'Bloody men!'

"Now don't waste too much time – I'd certainly want to have this cleared by the end of the month. And use whatever reasonable resources you deem necessary – but get it done. Any questions?"

"I'll let you know if I have any after I've read the file, sir," she said on her way out of the office.

Once Dawn had looked at Mark Reynold's financial information, she understood why he had been flagged for further investigation.

"How many bank accounts does one guy need?" she asked aloud. She spent an afternoon going through them and isolated a few issues that needed answering. She was encouraged enough to want to proceed but realised there was no way that a request for police surveillance could be justified. An off the record chat with her boss was needed.

"There's definitely something there, sir," she reported, "but we'd need surveillance reports before we can go any further, though."

"I'm sure you know there's no way we could justify that," he answered, as she'd expected, "is there any other way you can move forward?"

"Well. I would need to call in a big favour if I did, and I was wondering.."

"OK, spit it out, what's it going to cost me?"

"Well, you know that I've requested a transfer, sir. I think that a move now would be best for my career,"

"And you think I'm holding on to it?"

"It would be much appreciated if you would approve the request, sir."

"And you would be able to come up with a way of getting rid of this mess in a satisfactory manner?"

"Certainly, sir"

"Consider it done"

"Thank you, sir, I'll have a full action plan on your desk in a couple of days."

Now she had to call in her favour.

Dawn had been part of Richard Boulton's mid-life crisis. She was never sure whether she had played a leading role in it, or whether she was just part of the supporting cast, but she had been there for several months while his marriage and career had crashed around him. That had been a couple of years back, and she was sure that he still owed her for the way she had supported him while he needed it, and then bowed out of his life when it was the right thing for him – regardless of whether it was the right thing or the right time for her. She had no qualms about calling him for a favour now and knew that even after making this withdrawal from the favour bank, her account with him would still be in substantial credit.

Having established over the 'phone that he was well and that his private detective business was keeping him busy, she got to the point as soon as she could. "I need to have somebody watched for a few days, and there's no chance of getting it done officially," she told him.

She provided him with all the necessary contact details and let him know that all she wanted was as much information as possible on who he met, where, when, and for how long.

"When do you want it done?" he asked.

"Now would be good," she replied.

"Your lucky day," he replied, "I've had something postponed at the last minute so I can do it next week. Is it a 24-hour one?"

"No, if he gets up to any mischief, I'm sure it'll be during the working day, so seven till seven should be more than enough."

Mark's details were passed over and Dawn awaited the report.

-

In all walks of life, timing has an important part to play in determining the success or failure of a venture. For example, Mark could have told Dawn how important timing was in the world of sales. Calling a customer one week might produce no positive response whatsoever, whereas a call the following week could be ideally timed for the customer to do whatever it was you wanted him to do.

It was the same in the field of police investigation. If she had chosen a different week for the surveillance, she would have had possibly the most boring surveillance report in history. 'He went to his office and stayed there all day, returned home, and did not go out again. Repeated four times.' But the week she had chosen was the one that Mark took off work to conduct several of his private business activities.

Score One Point for Every Yes

October 2006

One of the reasons that Julie Medcraft enjoyed her job was the variety of challenges it posed her. Like any job, there were many routine and mundane tasks that had to be completed. And then there were weeks like the one she was currently experiencing. Weeks when you needed to remind yourself that facing new challenges is a good thing – even if the challenges themselves might be particularly, well..., challenging.

An ex-employee of S & R had recently been convicted of some unpleasant charges relating to child pornography. And the reason he was an ex and not a current employee was his arrest. The day that happened and the disclosures were made was the day his employment ceased.

As head of Human Resources, Julie had been metaphorically holding her breath from that day onwards. She was waiting for the solids to hit the air conditioning, fearing that the press would uncover the fact that one of this ex-employee's roles was to supervise the company's apprentices. It was possible that if the press got hold of this nugget of information, they could create some very bad publicity for Smith and Raiter. However, as today's newspapers were rapidly heading for their next stage - being tomorrow's fish and chip wrapping – it seemed that the company was going to escape this potentially damaging revelation.

However, she was implementing changes to make sure that not only were lessons learned, but that the company could never again find itself in a similar situation. Whilst the company could not be legally held responsible for the fact that one of its employees had deliberately concealed his criminal record when joining – a criminal offence in its own right – it might be criticised for placing such a person in a position of responsibility for employees under the age of eighteen. Her recommendation to the board had been that the company employ a third-party vetting service for all employees that were placed in a position of authority over others. The recommendation had been accepted and it was now her task to implement it.

She had received proposals from two organisations offering such a service and planned to run a test to decide which would get the contract. There were currently two management vacancies open – and both were likely to be filled from within the company. So, she decided that all applicants for both roles would be vetted. Although this would involve an additional expense of vetting some employees who would not immediately be taking responsibility for others, it would provide a test of the two competing companies – and any information they elicited about employees would also be of value.

She had checked and re-checked her thinking on this to ensure her personal situation did not influence her thinking. The reason for her dichotomy was that one of the positions being filled was that of Sales Manager, and one of the applicants was her boyfriend (how she hated that term, it seemed so juvenile at her time of life, but there seemed no adequate alternative since he had not yet transitioned to being her partner). She would treat any information professionally and just hope against hope that no metaphorical skeletons emerged from his particular cupboard.

Accordingly, she passed details of Malcolm Bettridge and Mark Reynolds to the first contender, PSVS (Personnel Screening and Vetting Services) and the details of the two applicants for the job of Production Supervisor (the position which had been only temporarily filled since the previous holder of the role had so suddenly departed) to Staff Security Limited. Both companies promised full reports within seven days.

The email from PSVS arrived on Friday evening, just as Julie was preparing to leave the office. It had two attachments, one for each employee. Rather than delay her departure – already she was almost certain to be amongst the last to leave the building, she decided to print the two reports and take them home to read. Her evening plans easily lent themselves to this – her mother was going to the cinema with a friend, and she had decided to pick up a takeaway from the local Chinese restaurant and to enjoy it with a bottle of New Zealand Sauvignon Blanc which was sitting in her fridge.

-

She scooped the noodles and meat onto her plate, sipped her first glass of wine, opened the envelope, and began to read the reports.

She decided to look first at the report on Malcolm. It contained confirmation of all that she knew about him in her official capacity; the dates of his previous employments and his educational qualifications – such as they were – were exactly as he had stated them. But there was one surprise for her. At the age of eighteen Malcolm had been found guilty of causing an affray – a quaint old English term if ever there was one – and had been fined.

The absence of this information from his personnel record was not a problem. She knew that under the terms of the 1974 Rehabilitation of Offenders Act, by the time he had joined Smith and Raiter, the offence had occurred more than two and a half years earlier and was considered as spent. Malcolm was under no obligation to inform his employer of its existence.

The surprise was personal. He had not only concealed this event from her – he had actually lied.

The reason she was sure of this originated from a silly internet questionnaire that she had seen when they had first started dating. The quiz had had a title such as "How bad are you really? Score One Point for Every Yes." Followed by a list of twenty questions.

She thought that this might be a good way of discovering each other's past – because when you start your relationship in your thirties, it's reasonable to expect there is something of a past. So, she had shown him the list of questions of the 'Have You Ever' variety which had included things like:

Been Arrested?   *Taken Illegal Drugs?*

Had a One Night Stand?   *Committed a crime?*

Lied on a Job Application Form?   *Had sex in the open air?*

Cheated on a partner?   *Broken Something Valuable?*

She had introduced the list to him and said something about how boring she must be because she only scored one – and then asked him what he scored.

After reading it, he had said "two". Definitely only two because they had then gone on to confess the details behind the answers to each other. He had admitted to taking illegal drugs once – and had said that it was after going drinking with a couple of mates and winding up back at their place, whereupon they had rolled joints. He told them that he'd never smoked marijuana and they had said "Want to try?" He'd agreed, they'd shown him how to roll a joint, which he proceeded to smoke. His significant

230

memory was that while his friends started to talk rubbish and giggle a lot, he felt no effect at all. And that had been that – he had seen no need to repeat the experience.

She told him that her one point was also scored for the same offence – but, if it was possible, her involvement had been even more boring than his. At the end of her first year at university, she had got into a bit of a mess when revising for her exams. One evening she found herself raiding the vending machine at her hall of residence, trying to keep herself going for a few more hours. She had an exam the next morning for which she had done absolutely no revision. Having confessed as much to a girl called Jenny, not a close friend but a fellow machine raider at the time. Jenny had told her that she could help her – one tablet of amphetamine would be sure to keep her awake for the next twenty-four hours, and she could get a lot of revision done before the test the next morning.

"You'll fall asleep when it wears off, and probably feel pretty shitty for the next day or so – but you'll have a chance of passing the exam" was how Jenny had put it. Julie had agreed to the offer, and bought one tablet – if it didn't work, she thought, she would be no worse off.

The tablet had worked as promised, and she had revised right through the night, then showered and changed at eight the next morning, and gone on to do (at least in her own opinion) pretty well in the test.

She had never repeated the experience – partly because it was illegal (and costly) but also because of something that happened right at the start of the exam. The invigilator had instructed everyone to turn over their papers and begin, and she had started to write her name and candidate number at the top of the paper as instructed. For a brief moment, she could not remember her own name. The problem had to be caused by the drug. The feelings of amnesia and panic lasted for a few seconds (it had seemed much longer inside her head at the time) but it had been so intensely frightening that she had found it very easy to vow never to touch drugs ever again. And she had kept that vow.

Malcolm's second confession was that he had had a one-night stand. He was a good storyteller, and he had told the story in full, doing his best to make it as amusing as possible.

Many years earlier he had gone to a party, but once there, he had discovered that he knew almost nobody at the event. The only exception was a girl called Jill whom he knew only slightly. She was in similar circumstances to him – knowing almost no one else there. They had had a few drinks (obviously a few too many) and had ended up back at his flat, where they spent the night together.

The sex had been unmemorable, partly because of the excess of alcohol limiting both performance and memory, and partly because it was just plain unmemorable.

What he did clearly remember was waking long before his partner the next morning – that was not hard to believe, she thought since Malcolm seemed to need less sleep than anyone she had ever known. He had lain there realising that not only did he not really like Jill very much – but in the cold light of day he didn't even find her all that attractive either.

He carefully extricated himself from the bed, took some clothes into the bathroom, showered and dressed. Then he had sat in the kitchen with a cup of coffee and a couple of slices of toast, waiting for Jill to wake up, and dreading what might come next.

Eventually, she had woken, and after a brief stay in the bathroom, had appeared in the kitchen and sat at the table opposite him. At least she hadn't come and thrown her arms around him – it looked like he was getting the indifference he had wished for. But the silence was almost unbearable.

"How are you this morning?" he ventured to ask.

"Surprised," she had replied after a lengthy pause.

He let it hang for a couple of seconds before asking "Surprised?"

"I don't usually," she raised her left hand and sort of wiggled it horizontally, "do this."

He left another few seconds of dead air before saying – "I don't usually do this (and here he mimicked her hand gesture) either," but only got a "hmmm" in response. He offered breakfast.

"Tea and toast would be fine," she said.

He was reinforced in his feelings of disconnection with her. 'Who on earth drinks tea for breakfast?' he thought to himself.

He made the tea and put a mug of it in front of her. Milk and sugar were on the table, and she helped herself. While he waited for the toast he ventured "But we can still be friends, can't we?" No response.

"Nobody needs to know anything about this" (he re-ran the hand gesture).

She perked up a bit at the 'Nobody needs to know' comment and replied "And nobody will know? Can I be sure of that?"

"You can be sure," he said. "I don't need anyone to know that I completely failed to overwhelm you with either my charm or my er performance. OK?"

She seemed to understand his point. He called a taxi for her – she would certainly not want to walk home on a Saturday morning wearing Friday-night-out clothes. She left in the taxi a few minutes later, nobody ever found out about their night together, and they never met again.

And that was the last of Malcolm's confessions. Only two points. No mention of being arrested. And now she knew that he had not only been arrested - he had been charged and convicted at a court hearing. There was no way he could have forgotten about it.

Julie was left to wonder if this had been his only omission. Had he been too ashamed about the conviction – she doubted it – there was always an element of bravado in this type of offence. Was he worried that with her having only scored one point on the stupid test (she was now seriously regretting ever having suggested it) it would have been a problem if his score had been any higher?

She knew that complete disclosure was a lot to ask for. She had not told him absolutely everything about herself – there hadn't been time yet – and some things would wait a long time before being revealed (her considerable nest egg in stocks and shares being one example). But she had not lied, and he had specifically been untruthful. And because she had only discovered the lie by looking at his records in her official capacity, she could not let him know about it.

After some thought, she decided that if it was the only omission, she would never mention it. No, she would just file this little nugget of information away and hope never to need to use it.

She put another scoop of noodles on her plate, refilled her wineglass and turned to the second printout. The one for the new employee, Mark Reynolds.

Everything seemed in order – his academic record was even more meagre than Malcolm's and his list of previous positions was clear and concise, and completely in agreement with the information he had given when joining. She turned to the second page and there it was. A couple of lines of text that would completely scupper not only his chance of promotion – but would end his career with Smith and Raiter.

Julie re-read it and wondered how best to use the information. The best course of action would be to allow Geoff to go ahead with the interviews, which she knew from Malcolm were scheduled for Monday (Mark in the morning, Malcolm in the afternoon) and she could then confront Geoff with this new information.

She cleared the table, put the remains of the meal in the bin, put her plate and cutlery in the dishwasher, and permitted herself another glass of wine - and a smile.

Interviews for the Position of Sales Manager
November 2006

The interview went well in Mark's opinion. The first few minutes were spent by Geoff verifying Mark's background, early jobs and so forth. Geoff then went on to cover Mark's time with American Power – what he had achieved and how he had achieved it. Mark was keen to establish that he had been successful in building a business as something of a loner, whilst leaving room for him to establish his credentials as a team player.

Even though Mark was not one hundred per cent sure that the job on offer was exactly what he was looking for as his next role – nonetheless it was an interview, and the objective of the interviewee was always to get offered the job. There would be time afterwards to make sure that it was what he wanted. He could always say no, after all.

Mark anticipated the biggest challenge would come in the final section – which could be titled "What will you do if you get the job". He knew that he would have to show that he had some new ideas but would have to be aware that Geoff might not want too much change. He would also have to be very careful that some of the things he might want to change could well be things that Geoff had either agreed to or even instigated himself.

But he decided not to err on the side of caution. In response to the dreaded "What changes would you plan to make if you got the job, Mark" he ploughed on.

"I believe there are improvements that could be made in the incentivising of the sales team and their ability to follow through and achieve what they are being asked to achieve," he replied. As expected, this rather vague statement drew Geoff to ask for more detail.

"You want to achieve sales targets in all the five different product groups, correct?" Mark asked.

Geoff nodded. He was constantly trying to juggle his resources to meet the company's goals. If he overachieved in four of the five areas in any given quarter, he knew that his boss in the USA would spend most of their quarterly review asking why the fifth was not doing as well as it should.

Mark continued, "I understand that, and like a good boss you pass the problem down." He paused and exchanged smiles with Geoff. 'Good,' he thought, 'rapport established.'

"You give each salesman a target for all five product areas and a bonus when they achieve it if I understand correctly."

Geoff nodded.

"And then you increase their commission rates when they get the target – that's right isn't it?"

"Actually, we increase the commission rate in two stages – one when the individual product group target is achieved, and once again when they've hit their targets in all five groups".

'Good grief,' thought Mark, 'it's even more complicated than I thought.' Hopefully, it would reinforce what he was going to suggest.

"What I see is how this affects the guys' performance. On the good side, they'll know if they need to up the sales of one product to make that bonus, and they'll try to do that. But on the bad side, they don't know how much they make on any individual order, so they focus totally on that bonus. If they have no chance of getting it, they'll try to hold back business until the next quarter. And if they do hit the target and get the bonus, then they'll do the same thing and delay whatever they can to the following quarter to get the bonus then."

"Do you have any proof of this?" Geoff asked – the smile was no longer there, Mark noticed.

"Look Geoff, no names no pack drill. Maybe it's because I've been lucky enough to be an insider and an outsider at the same time for the last three months - but that's what's happening, and I've been able to spot it."

"So, what do you suggest in its place? Asked Geoff – still without the normal friendly interview smile on his face.

"I'd suggest a simpler system that started with all products getting one rate of commission. Let everyone know just how much they make on each order. And with the ability of each one being able to sell what he feels best at selling – it should produce a better overall figure. When we reach the end of the second month of the quarter, we can assess where we stand as a team – after all, what matters is that the whole team reaches the target in all five product groups, right?" This got an enthusiastic nod from Geoff.

"So – with the knowledge of which group or groups need to be boosted for the last month to get that target, a bonus can be introduced just for that part of the product range. Every team member is motivated to bring in all business – no point in delaying if there's no particular figure to aim at next quarter – and for the last month you've got everyone putting their effort where it needs to go – on the items which earn the salesman the most – which just happen to be the ones you and I need to achieve the overall target."

Geoff's reaction confirmed that his idea was 'gaining traction. He knew that more detail would need to be filled in – but he was pretty sure he'd scored a point.

"Anything else you'd change?" Geoff asked – Mark was not surprised that his preamble of stating that he had two changes had been forgotten after he had exploded the bombshell of changing the commission structure.

"I would like to see more training for the sales team. Don't worry – it won't cost much. A lot of stuff that can be done internally."

He guessed that Geoff would have the usual prejudice against taking salespeople away from their territory for training and then paying for it. He was right.

"I think I've found that the team are – how can I put this", he was treading on eggshells here, "a little sleepy in the way they go about things. I'd like to get them thinking more about what the customer's wants and needs are. Even when they're dealing with a branch manager in a large chain – he'll have problems that are specific to his store – local issues, local competitors, and so on. If we can focus more on these issues – see if we can help him in any way with training for his staff, running a promotion or providing marketing materials, we've got a lot of tricks up our sleeves that we don't use."

He had a list from his meeting with Margaret to pull out if necessary – but it wasn't necessary. Implying that he thought the salespeople could work harder and make more sales was a message that any General Manager would want to hear.

After probing Mark's idea with a couple of questions, Geoff asked "Do you think you can do this?"

"With help from others in the company – yourself, Margaret, maybe one or two of the product management staff – yes, I believe I can," was Mark's ready answer.

Geoff was impressed with Mark's enthusiasm for the tasks ahead – it reminded him very much of his own enthusiasm when first joining the company. He was becoming very tempted to appoint Mark to the sales manager role, despite the inevitable flak he would receive from longer serving people in the company. He would have to give this some serious thought.

The main points having been covered, the interview continued through to the normal winding down phase, ("any questions you would like to ask me?") and was completed about fifteen minutes later. Geoff promised Mark the decision would be made the next day.

A Busy Week
October 2006

Mark had hoped by now that he would be coming to the end of the money in the suitcase and could devote more of his time and energy to normal work and pleasure. But a few setbacks had slowed his progress to a snail's pace.

Asbestos had been discovered in the latest property that Howard was working on, and this had not only cost him some of the profit on that deal but had also chewed up several months in locating the specialised company, finding time in their full diary to deal with it, and then getting the necessary paperwork completed.

He had also had problems selling a property in Suffolk. The cash coming in from the loans to Craig and his mate coupled with the rent from Gina was more than he could spend. On top of that, his brother-in-law had profitably sold some of his shares and had redeemed his loan by proudly presenting Mark with ten thousand pounds in cash, not realising that Mark was expecting a cheque.

He was going backwards and needed to discover other ways to speed up the process, and so dug out the card with the details of the man who could make cash disappear that Don had given him months ago. He had taken an opportunity to have a whole week off work and decided to add a visit to this magic man to his string of appointments.

His first meeting of the week was with his personal bank manager at one of the banks where he held an account.

There was a strong sense of irony that he was meeting the bank manager to talk about borrowing money. He had never needed to borrow (with the sole exception of the mortgage on his home, and that did not really count) when he did not have any money. But now he had plenty, he was going to discuss borrowing more. 'I guess that's capitalism,' he thought.

What he wanted to discuss was that every time he bought a property to re-develop, he had to get a mortgage. There was no difficulty in getting the money, the banks were only too pleased to gain the custom, but it was not the most cost-effective way of doing it. The interest rates were low, but because he had to pay all the start-up costs and then the early redemption penalty when he paid off the borrowing in months rather than years, he ended up paying a much higher rate than was necessary. And there was all the paperwork involved in getting the mortgage and then closing it down.

Dennis Barnes, the bank manager was very pleasant - and far too young in Mark's mind to be a real bank manager. He was also a Charlton supporter, and this enabled them to bond over the subject of football. Mark outlined his problems and had to spend more time than he thought would be necessary to explain what he was looking for. He had to overcome the bank's restricted way of thinking which was 'You buy a house – that is financed by a mortgage.' He needed something that was anathema to banks – creativity.

Eventually, he thought that Dennis understood what he was looking for - a single loan that could roll over from one property to the next. This was clearly outside the norm, and all he could hope for at the end of the meeting was that when Dennis proposed it to his boss, as he had promised to do, the outcome would be positive. But Mark would certainly not be holding his breath waiting for an answer.

He left the meeting and headed for his lunch with Johnny. Despite only having met him twice, Mark was looking forward to meeting again. He enjoyed Johnny's company and although they came from totally different backgrounds – Johnny was a personification of the phrase 'born with a silver spoon in the mouth', which Mark certainly was not – they seemed to think in such a similar fashion that their time together was enjoyable for both parties. He liked to think that the speed with which Johnny had accepted his invitation to another lunch showed that the feeling was mutual.

They met once again in Dirty Dick's and repeated their order of burgers and beers. They chatted at length about each other's business lives and had almost finished the food before a pause occurred and Johnny said, "So you'd like to buy another property from me?"

"Yes," said Mark. The first one has gone pretty well, so I wondered if you've got another one that you'd like to turn into spending money for your retirement."

"And you'd want to work with the same structure as our previous deal?"

"A carbon copy would be perfect" Mark confirmed.

"Well, I do have another one just south of Marylebone Road, which would probably fit the bill. It's a basement flat that I've had for some time - for the last few months, it's been rented to a young lady called Gemma. When would you be looking to buy?"

"As soon as you'd be ready to sell," Mark replied, knowing that it would take a couple of months to complete the transaction, by which time a couple of his deals would have closed and he should have enough capital for a significant deposit.

Johnny, never wanting to stand on ceremony, took out his mobile phone. "I'll give Gemma a call and arrange for you to look at the place – I assume you want to do that." Mark nodded.

Johnny's call was quickly answered and after exchanging brief pleasantries, Johnny explained that he was planning to sell the flat, reassuring Gemma that it would make absolutely no difference to her, but that the new landlord would like to look at the flat as soon as it was convenient. Mark asked if Friday would be possible – knowing that he had already planned a visit to London on that day – and an appointment for eleven o clock was set.

Johnny finished by saying "It's OK, Gemma, I'm sure young Mark is a man of the world. I believe he has a cousin in the same line of business as yourself, so you don't need to hide anything."

Johnny passed on Gemma's request that he get there as close to the agreed time as possible because she would be making specific arrangements to be available then.

They finalised their plans for the transaction – Johnny promised to send all the relevant details by email as soon as Mark confirmed the visit was successful. This allowed them to return to putting the world to rights over a second pint. 'Shame I can't get to buy a property from him more often,' Mark thought, 'this is a most enjoyable lunch'.

-

Mark's next appointment could have been even more pleasurable in another set of circumstances, but this visit to Gina was business only. He told her that from now on he would no longer collect the rent in person and needed her to pay it into his bank account.

She made a play of disappointment that he would no longer be enjoying her services. He had been "too busy to stay" on his two most recent visits to collect rent, so she was not surprised and guessed that he must have a new relationship; that, or a sudden decrease in available funds, were the usual reasons for her customers losing interest.

He gave her the bank details and confirmed that she would only have to pay the same as she had paid him every month. Her experience of men made her sure of one thing. 'You'll be back,' she thought - but said nothing.

-

Wednesday began with his meeting with Dragan. Mark had agreed, acting on advice from Dragan's brother Tomasz, that their meeting would be at eight a.m. at the motorway service station on the M25 just north of the Dartford Tunnel which crossed the River Thames just east of London. Tomasz had told him that Dragan had no office – he worked from his home and was constantly on the move. Meeting at a motorway service station was not only convenient but also allowed him to indulge himself in his love of big English breakfasts.

Already they had something in common. Like many people, Mark would never think of cooking various meats, eggs, and vegetables for breakfast. Toast or cereal was more than enough. But, given the opportunity when travelling, for someone else to cook and present breakfast in front of you, well that was completely different.

When setting out on the long drives to customers that were not far enough away to justify an overnight stay but needed the journey to start in the early hours of the morning, it was the thought of a full fried breakfast that got him going. He even knew which were the better service stations for this culinary treat. The one where he was meeting Dragan was too close to home for him to have ever visited, so he was looking forward to checking it out.

As agreed, Mark called Dragan's mobile number when he arrived at the services, five minutes before their agreed meeting time.

"Good morning, Mister Mark Reynolds. You have arrived at the services, yes?"

"Yes, I'm just walking across the parking area now."

"Then you will recognise me very easily. I am outside the services enjoying my first cigarette of the day. I am the tallest man you will meet today." The call was ended with a hearty laugh.

Mark was immediately able to identify him, walked up and shook hands. Yes, Dragan would certainly be the tallest man he would meet - not just today, but probably for a long time to come. Mark was five-eleven and slim. Dragan was more than six inches taller and well built. A walking brick outhouse was how Mark would later describe him. A shock of black hair, a neatly trimmed moustache and a pointed beard were all just beginning to show flecks of grey.

Dragan's voice was hearty and loud. "So, we will share an English breakfast, Mr Reynolds?"

"Please call me Mark – mister Reynolds is my father," he responded, maintaining the tone of amusement in the dialogue.

"And you will call me Dragan. Of course you will, you are not able to properly pronounce my other name anyway" Another hearty laugh and they headed into the service station.

They purchased a standard breakfast that contained one of everything available and both bought black coffees. Once they were seated and tucking in, Mark explained his property activities – leaving it reasonably vague as buying and selling and occasionally renting.

Dragan asked "When you buy these properties to develop. How do you raise the capital?"

Mark had no problem in simply stating that he took out mortgages to raise enough money.

Dragan showed interest "This is where you have the advantage – I am not in a position where the banks will lend me money."

"When I met Tomasz for the second time and spoke briefly with him, I thought there might be some ways we could co-operate," Mark continued, "what exactly is your interest in property?"

Dragan gave a brief explanation of his business focussing on how and why he often needed to use rented houses.

"My business is now expanding into some farms which are further from London, and it is more difficult to find properties to rent for my workers. Maybe when you buy one of these houses to develop you might be able to rent it to me for a few months. My workers do not care if it is not in the best condition – so long as it is clean and safe; they wish to keep the rent as low as possible so that they have more money to take back home with them when they finish their work period."

Mark nodded his understanding.

"I could certainly do that – so long as it was profitable. If you told me where you need housing, it might help me to decide which property to buy."

He was thinking that the rental would more than cover the mortgage cost, and if it spread the costs of setting up the mortgage over a longer period, that would not be bad for him either.

They talked some more about shared business interests and then finally shook hands – another thing which Dragan did very heartily, Mark noticed – his hand hurt for several minutes afterwards – and they went their separate ways. There were not any immediate prospects of doing business, but they were both optimistic that opportunities for co-operation would come.

-

Mark met Graeme for lunch – they were celebrating the delayed sale of their second property. Meeting in a rural Suffolk pub they enjoyed a superb ploughman's lunch with locally baked bread, local cheese, and, best of all, beer that was locally brewed and superbly kept. In the afternoon they went together to look at a couple of properties, which were coming up for auction the next day. Either would fit well within their budget and Graeme left it to Mark to see how the auction went the next day.

He purchased one of them at the auction and cleared all the paperwork with the auction house in time to join Hugh for lunch. Mark was interested to hear how Hugh's company, and hence how his investment was progressing. He was pleased to hear it was going well and enjoyed the opportunity to chat with Hugh. He had originally thought him a bit of a boffin and found him hard to engage with, but the more they spoke the more he enjoyed Hugh's company – so long as he could keep him away from his in-depth knowledge of, and fascination with, the history of computing. It might enthral his colleagues, but it bored Mark to tears.

He made a flying visit to his parents in the afternoon. All was well, the house was looking neater every time, but he explained he had a lot on his plate and had to get back, so he could not stay for dinner.

Thursday was spent with Howard, reviewing their third property. Howard was getting better attuned to what Mark expected from their partnership.

There had been a problem with the first house because Howard's definition of job completion did not agree with Mark's. The actual building work was complete, but Mark had to explain that he wanted to sell the house – not live in it. He had to make sure that the house was saleable – and a few seemingly cosmetic and insignificant changes had to be made to achieve this. If floorboards were to be left bare, they had to be sanded and polished. If this was not possible, due to their age, or mismatching in a house that was too old or had been altered during its lifetime, then carpet had to be fitted. The carpet could be as cheap as chips, it didn't matter.

People made buying decisions on houses in ridiculously quick time and on the back of immediate impressions received when looking around. The merest detail that said 'work needs to be done on this' would put a buyer off.

Howard was now getting to understand Mark's strange ways, and very little had to be done to the latest development. Howard agreed that another week would see it all done, and Mark went on to the estate agent to arrange for them to visit, take photographs and put the property on the market.

-

Friday's diary had two meetings in it – a viewing of Johnny's flat with Gemma and a meeting with David Stone, the accountant recommended by Don's boss.

Mark looked at the building on Cheltenham Place whose address Johnny had given him. It was in good repair and somewhat strangely was marked with a Blue Plaque denoting that it was once the residence of some famous Uruguayan poet that Mark (in common he was sure with most other people) had never heard of.

He opened the wrought iron gate at the end of the railings in front of the building and descended the steep, narrow, curving set of steps that led down to the front door of the basement flat. The concrete floor of the well which formed the front space of the flat was clean and free from debris, and, more importantly, any signs of water accumulation from the previous day's heavy rain. Someone had even brightened up the space with a couple of large potted plants which seemed to be flourishing despite the lack of light. 'That's a good sign', he thought, 'someone is taking care of the look of the place'.

He rang the doorbell, and it was quickly answered by an attractive woman in her early thirties. She had shoulder-length brown hair, a darkish complexion and was dressed in a multi-coloured full skirt and a bright red blouse. She instantly made Mark think 'Gypsy – that's the look she's aiming for'.

How to describe her figure? Buxom? Curvaceous? Voluptuous? All of the above? Yes, all of the above – and all was certainly above! Her blouse had one more button undone than might be thought normal, and it offered the viewer an enticing sample of her two biggest assets (along with her winsome smile and great personality, of course).

'That bra of hers is a miracle of modern engineering,' thought Mark. 'It's amazing she can stand upright.'

"You must be Mark, "she said, quickly looking him up and down and giving him a smile that showed a set of large, straight white teeth. "Hmmm. Distinct improvement. Come in".

She led him through an entrance porch into a large, combined living space and kitchen area. "You're taking over from Johnny, I understand."

"That's right. I'm planning to buy the place from him. You must be Gemma." She confirmed. "I wanted to have a quick look at the place beforehand if that's OK"

"It costs nothing to look…" she smiled, and then added, after a very brief pause "at the flat".

He refused her offer of tea or coffee but asked for a glass of water. Crossing to the kitchen area, she opened the fridge which he noticed contained several bottles of mineral water, a bottle of white wine and very little food.

He took a sip from the glass of water and started to look around the living area. It contained a small TV on a table, a cabinet, a sofa, an armchair, and a lot of space. The furniture was all presentable but none of it matched. The floor was covered in a plain fitted carpet, typical of a rented property, and the large front window was obscured by closed venetian blinds.

"About ten meters by six or seven I guess," he said aloud and received no response. He noted the dimensions on the notes page of his mobile phone and then did his potential landlord thing examining the corners, one by one, checking for any cracks or signs of damp.

"Have you been here long?" he asked, automatically using the word 'been' instead of 'lived' as it seemed much more appropriate.

"About nine months," she replied.

"You have a tenancy agreement with Johnny?" he asked, and she told him that there had been one, but it had elapsed after six months, and she and Johnny had agreed to roll over the contract on a month-by-month basis. When asked, she confirmed she was happy to agree to sign a new six-month agreement with Mark if his mortgage provider demanded it.

"So, you plan to stay?" he asked.

"It's convenient – and the price is right, so yeah" she replied.

Moving back into the kitchen space he noted, and said aloud, "Cooker, washing machine, fridge and microwave."

"The microwave is mine," Gemma said, "but everything else came with the place."

The cooker was both quite old and very clean – he doubted whether it received much use but decided not to comment. At the corner of the room opposite the front door, a small passage led towards the back of the property. Mark pointed there and said, "May I?"

"Of course."

She followed him down the passage. Halfway down a door on the right-hand side opened into a small bathroom. He opened the door, pulled the cord for the light switch, and was pleased to hear the ventilation system whirr into life. He checked the room for any cracks in plaster, dripping taps or other issues and saw none.

Returning to the passage, in front of him was another door; he looked at Gemma and she nodded. This room would normally be a single bedroom – but currently contained no bed – only a wardrobe, a chest of drawers and two free-standing clothes rails, each of which was fully loaded with dresses of various colours. Mark also thought he could see a few uniforms – police, nurse, flight attendant, schoolgirl. It was pretty obvious how Gemma made her living.

The room had a window looking towards the rear of the property, but it was covered with a closed blind and was not easily accessible, so he chose not to try to look through it. Again, he made a note of the approximate room size and went to the next door, which was at right angles to the one he had just closed behind him. This opened into the main bedroom.

Mark had, from time to time heard various places compared to a tart's bedroom. Now he was able to see the real thing. Everything in the room was as soft and as pink as it could possibly be. The pale pink walls blended into the curtains which were lightly patterned and pink. The bedspread was pink, surmounted by several pillows encased in pink, lacy pillowcases. Even the white furniture had pink areas painted in.

Again, he noted the approximate room size, checked its condition, and moved to the window which looked out at the back of the property. Parting the curtains gave him a view of a small, concreted rear space that was totally empty. "No access to the rear?" he asked, and immediately regretted it.

"No" came the reply. "No access to the rear," and, after the briefest of pauses, "of the property that is," Mark did not dare make eye contact as he knew he was being played with.

Instead, he carried on in a business-like fashion, "Where is the rubbish collected from?"

"Outside the front, up the stairs, every Thursday".

He completed his inspection. "Everything looks OK to me," he said, closing the notes section on his phone. "I guess I should ask if you have any problems with the place?"

"Had a couple of small problems but Johnny was very good and sorted them out straight away. I hope you'll be just as good to me."

"Of course," Mark replied. "Always like to keep my tenants happy – helps make sure they pay the rent on time", smiling broadly to make sure Gemma understood it was a partly humorous remark. It enabled him to quickly add "You pay your rent to Johnny by direct debit?"

"Yes," she replied, "I guess you'll want the same? Unless you want to collect it in person, that is?" Again, accompanied by a flirtatious smile.

"No, direct debit's fine," he countered.

"Shame," she said, "No chance to offer to pay part of the rent in kind."

Mark smiled, trying to respond pleasantly to her flirtation without taking it any further. 'Thankfully', he thought to himself, 'you are definitely not my type.'

He thanked her for her time, and she showed him out. 'Looks like I've got myself a second rental property,' he thought to himself.

A Man Who Did Not Waste Time

October 2006

Mark arrived a few minutes early for his meeting with David "Solly" Stone. He was not sure what he had expected, but the office location was a little strange, situated on Baker Street, a few yards south of the junction with Marylebone Road above retail premises that contained the unlikely combination of a mobile phone shop and a currency exchange office. Next door was one of the many English language schools that populated this part of London.

There was a lengthy queue in the currency exchange office, which added further to the unusual aspect of the place.

Mark looked at the list of company names, each engraved on a brass plaque next to the robust-looking blue entry door. In addition to a plaque which simply stated David Stone, Accountant there were several other companies, all seeming to bear generic titles like General Trading Ltd. or Associated Communications Inc.

Mark was reminded of some of the early spy novels he had read, where a whole cluster of companies would be registered at one address to cover up the presence of an MI5 or CIA office. There would always be a communications company to explain the satellite aerials on the roof, and an international trading company to explain the foreign visitors.

He smiled to himself and rang the doorbell. He was not surprised that it was connected to a camera system, nor was he surprised to be asked to stand still for a moment so that his identity could be verified before being allowed in. It was entirely possible that the office might contain a plentiful amount of cash and of an even higher value currency, secrets.

Once admitted, he climbed the stairs and opened a second security-protected door to David Stone's company. A mature, efficient, but friendly, receptionist welcomed him, escorted him to a comfortable furnished small meeting room and brought him a cup of freshly brewed coffee.

He was joined moments later by an immaculately dressed and coiffured man. He looked to be a little older than Mark with short grey hair and a lean and hungry look.

"Good morning, Mr Reynolds. My name is David Stone - but you may well have been told that my name is Solly. I'm happy to respond to either," he said with a smile that conveyed professional courtesy but not any warmth.

"I'm happier using David, and please call me Mark," said Mark.

"Then David it is. Tell me, how can I help you?"

Mark got a distinct impression that this was a man who does not waste time. And as he explained his current range of business activities, and that previous unspecified activities had left him with a substantial amount of cash, Mark was impressed by how David only ever interrupted where further explanation was needed. He made no comments, nor showed any interest in any aspect of his story that was not immediately pertinent to the financial situation. He made occasional notes, and when Mark completed his explanation, gave his response.

"We offer two types of service, Mark. We're more than happy to provide a straightforward accountancy service, presenting your information to the revenue services clearly and accurately, making sure that you receive the full benefits of all allowances to which you are entitled, and advising you where possible of actions you might take which would have benefits to you in minimising your tax exposure. Our fees for providing this service are roughly in line with any other firm of accountants.

But, as you have presumably been informed, we also offer a more advanced service. Many of our clients find themselves in a situation where they have accumulated cash resources that are not covered by their records. In those cases, we can provide activities which will withstand an independent audit, and which will show a transaction history that justifies the presence of the cash." This produced another smile from David – professionally friendly and conspiratorial at the same time.

"In other words, we convert an amount of cash which a client is unable to deposit into his bank without questions being raised, into a series of deposits into his account which appear totally legitimate." Mark noted his use of the word 'appear'.

"I'm sure you realise that this is a more difficult exercise and that it is essential that all due taxes are paid. So, it may not be possible for the whole sum to finally arrive in the account". He paused, and Mark assumed it was for the obvious question to be asked.

"What proportion of the money would you expect to end up in the account?" he asked, as this was what he most needed to know and was also, he expected, what David was expecting to be asked.

"We normally find that taxes have to be paid amounting to about ten to fifteen per cent of the money – depending on how quickly you need it to arrive in the account – and then there are our fees which normally amount to five per cent of the sum concerned."

"And would I be right to assume that the lower the urgency of transferring the money into the account, the lower the cost would be?" Mark asked, finding himself slipping into the vaguely technical and obfuscating language that David had been using. David confirmed that this was indeed the case.

"So, from what you have told me about your situation, either of our services may suit your needs. With regard to the sum of money which you currently hold, would this be five figures, six figures…?" asked David.

"Six figures" Mark replied.

"And would that be one hundred, two…?"

Mark cut across him and said, "Assume exactly two hundred".

David made a note, giving a 'no problem' nod.

"As for the basic tax work, it appears that you have taken all the necessary steps with Mister," he checked his notes, "Rogerson. I doubt that there is much more we could achieve. Possibly one or two allowances he may not be aware of. However, as regards the other sum, that is something that needs addressing. This money is sitting there, and it is not working. Money, like people, should not sit idle, it should be made to work, do you not agree?"

Mark wondered if David would be familiar with the phrase 'singing off the same hymn sheet' because it certainly would describe how he felt about what was being said. He nodded.

"Tell me, would you regard yourself as a patient man, Mr Reynolds?"

"I suppose I can be, it depends," was the best Mark could come up with in answer to this unexpected question.

"Let me make a suggestion," David resumed. "Your sister could open a hairdressing salon. She would have some four or five stylists working for her – each of them being self-employed and renting a chair from her as I believe they call it. Of course, you realise all of this," he waved his left hand loosely in the air, "is only happening on paper, so to speak." Mark nodded his understanding.

"She would rent the property from your company, of course, purchase some general supplies from one of our companies, possibly employ a junior on minimum wage, pay herself a small salary, probably into a joint account with you and automatically transferred to an account you control, these details are not important right now."

'For someone who doesn't believe the details are important, you sure seem to have thought of a lot of them very quickly,' thought Mark but said nothing.

"What is important," continued David, "is that this business would pay you a sum of say one thousand pounds per week for erm …just short of four years… yes, four years – two hundred and eight. At the end of four years, you would close down the business because sadly it had not been profitable." He focussed his sharp eyes on Mark to check he was following. The man was talking money – of course, Mark was following.

"In that circumstance, Mister Reynolds, the total amount would reach your account, and what is more, you would not be liable for any tax on the money."

Mark took a few seconds to take this in. "I hope you don't mind me being direct, but where's the catch?"

"I don't believe there is one. There is a reward for patience. I would be happy to commit to these figures, as my costs and the tax liabilities would all be met from using the money in the interim."

Mark thought about it. He did not want to ponder too much about how this man might use the money in the interim, that was not his problem. What he was thinking was that the burden would be taken off his shoulders and he would be free to talk about buying somewhere with Debbie – assuming that was what they both wanted. With more than four grand going into his account every month. Add in the rental income from three properties and the loan repayments he was receiving, it would quickly mount up, and he could probably still add to his property empire every few months. It was very appealing.

"Of course, you understand that much of what I've explained would rely very heavily on trust as so little could be put in writing – but I would be more than happy to let you contact some of my other clients who would attest to the fact that I keep my promises."

Mark was pleased to feel that no pressure was being put on him to take any immediate decision, and after a few more minutes of conversation, David was quite happy to allow him to think it over and get back to him when he was ready. They shook hands and Mark was escorted to the internal security door and buzzed out.

He walked a few steps down Baker Street, mulling over what he had just heard and wondering whether to take the tube to Liverpool Street to connect with his train home, or to treat himself to a taxi ride. It was a hot day, and the midday street heat of the capital was not pleasant. He did not fancy the idea of spending even the necessary half an hour underground, so decided to hail one of the many taxis driving south on Baker Street at that time of day.

His mind wandered to the last time he had taken a taxi – a couple of hundred yards south of where he now stood, having walked a similar distance from Gina's flat. It was then that the thought struck him.

-

There are many ways in which the human thought process has been described over the years. Authors speak of an idea 'coming to someone' or 'being born'. More vivid descriptions include someone being 'struck by an idea'. In the case of Mark and the events that followed him leaving Solly's office, the description of being struck by an idea is by far and away the most accurate.

The last time he had stood on this spot was the day he had found the briefcase. He had found it in a taxi that had probably dropped its previous passenger very close by. A briefcase full of money, yards away from the offices of an accountant who specialised in 'normalising' large sums of cash. Could it possibly be that the briefcase's real owner, who would always in Mark's mind be a criminal mastermind, had been on his way to visit Solly to deposit the sum? And there Mark was, possibly having walked right into the lion's den!

Mark's memory of the events that happened next would always remain patchy. He could remember a group of people around him, faces looking down on him; remember being lifted, a mask being put on his face, a series of bright lights and movement, and then a stranger removing his clothes. Nothing was really clear until he gradually came around to find himself lying in bed, with a tube stuck to the back of his hand and his sister sitting next to him with a look of concern on her face.

"Can you hear me now?" she asked.

"Yes, where the hell am I, and why are you here?" was his abrupt answer. She explained that he was in hospital, having been picked up by ambulance after collapsing in the street.

"Did I bang my head?" he asked – noticing for the first time a throbbing pain emanating from the back of his head.

"You probably banged it when you passed out, or whatever it is you did" she explained.

From the mist of clouded thoughts, he slowly remembered being on Baker Street, having come out of Solly's office. It would be some time before he recalled the reasons that had brought on the panic attack that had laid him low. His current concern was how and why his sister had come to be with him.

"You have my details as your emergency contact in your diary, I guess," she said.

-

Mark's diary was something of a running gag with his friends and family. Not for him the use of a loose-leaf system or an electronic organiser. He had always insisted on using a good old fashioned pocket diary. He felt that when he made a return appointment at a customer visit, it lent the next meeting a greater air of importance if his customer saw him take the trouble of inking it into his diary. He always bought the same make and when the year was done and the essential information had been transferred to the new diary, he kept the old one in his desk drawer – not one of them had been thrown out since his sales career had begun.

There were also three important sections for him at the back of the book. The first was a map of the London Underground. Like most non-Londoners, and even many of the capital's inhabitants, the tube map was not merely a set of linked underground stations and lines. It was *the* map of London and was invaluable for both business meetings and social engagements.

The second important section was the series of maps of the UK. His knowledge of the geography of his own country – especially anything north of Watford - was poor, and he needed to refer to this section when planning his business trips. He knew, for example, that Sheffield and Carlisle were both 'up North' but needed the map to tell him they were a hundred and sixty miles apart and to help him avoid making impossible commitments for meeting times.

And lastly, there was that invaluable section that listed the conversion factors between imperial and metric measurements. In his line of work, problems concerning metric and imperial systems arose quite frequently. The older generation (and all Americans) thought in terms of feet, gallons, and pounds, but the younger generation (and all Europeans) thought in terms of meters, litres, and kilograms. The conversion charts solved problems on an almost weekly basis, and if a dispute ever arose, which it did from time to time, about which system of measurement was better, Mark would always dispel it with the same little story.

'There are these two guys. One is an imperial measurement guy. He's got a fish tank which is one foot by one foot by one foot (moving his hand in the air to show length, width, and depth). Now he knows that it has a volume of one cubic foot, but he needs to know how many gallons of water is needed to fill it, and how much it will weigh. Can anyone help him?' Mark would pause for a few seconds of silence – and silence always followed because nobody knows how many gallons are in a cubic foot or how much a cubic foot of water weighs. 'So,' he would continue 'The other guy is a metric guy – his tank measures thirty centimetres by thirty centimetres by thirty centimetres (using the same hand movements as before). Now, he can work out that thirty times thirty times thirty is twenty-seven with three noughts after it, so he knows the volume of his tank is twenty-seven thousand cc's. And he also knows that a thousand cc's is the same as a litre, so twenty-seven litres are needed to fill his tank. And a litre of water weighs exactly a kilogram, so it will weigh

256

twenty-seven kilos. I'll leave it to you to decide which system is better.'

But today the diary had proved its worth in one other way. He had indeed entered his sister's name and mobile number as his emergency contact.

"Luckily, I was on my way to a conference in London today," she said. "A conference which I will not actually get to see. They called me to say you had collapsed in the street and that I'd find you here."

Mark was very relieved to see a friendly face after his brief but worrying event, and, having realised how rude he must have seemed when he first came to, tried to make sure his sister understood how grateful he was.

Eventually, Mark was seen by a white-coated doctor who informed him in a roundabout way that they could not find anything really wrong with him. They would do a few more tests, and unless something surprising showed up, after keeping him in overnight for observation just to be sure, he would be discharged the next day.

By this time, he had started to remember what had triggered his fall. He was not happy to hear it described as a panic attack – that seemed such a wimpy, new-age, thing to have knocked him out – but was not able to come up with a better description. Of course, he was not able to give even this description and explanation to his sister, who had to remain mystified. But having assured herself that he was OK, he was able to persuade her to go home and, more importantly, to extract a promise that she would not tell their parents about his little escapade.

His business plans had to be modified slightly because of this event – he was certainly never going to step anywhere near Solly again. He would have to stick with his more normal, boring accountant. And he vowed to himself once again to try to speed up his disposal of the money sitting in his attic.

It was beginning to be a bit of a pain in one or more areas of his body.

And one last thing. He remembered that moment in Solly's office when it seemed possible that the briefcase and its contents could be magicked away and the possibility of Debbie moving in with him had been real. He liked that feeling - and decided to float the idea of getting a place together on their next date. It would take a few months to find and buy a house, and this would give him the final incentive to get the money gone.

That same afternoon, Detective Sergeant Dawn Mepham received a call from Richard Boulton, updating her on the progress of the surveillance.

"He's in Bart's Hospital, and they'll be keeping him in overnight," she was informed. Having established the details of his sudden 'event' in the middle of Baker Street, and that it had been Richard himself who had been the first person to Mark's assistance, loosening his tie, checking his vital signs, and putting him in the recovery position until the ambulance came, she confirmed his opinion that there was no point in them staying with him.

"I never forget a face"
October 2006

One of the resources Dawn used in her search for information on Mark's activities was a friend she had made on one of the police training courses she had attended. She could not remember if it had been training for diversity or inclusivity or one of the many other 'ivities' that the police deemed essential to twenty-first-century policing. But she was sure that Donna would remember which course it was. That was Donna's speciality, remembering things.

They had hit it off immediately – not just because they were both women accustomed to being permanently outnumbered by men – on the course it was ten to two – but also because their personalities seemed to click.

Donna Beaumont was tall and gawky with large facial features and long hair that was dead straight and dead black. She accentuated her looks by wearing the largest glasses with the darkest frames possible. She and Dawn were absolute opposites – tall and short, posh southerner and working-class Glaswegian, near recluse and outgoing extrovert – but they got on like a house on fire and they stayed friends after the course. Dawn was sure that Donna must have shortened or changed her real name - parents as posh as hers would never call a child by such a simple name as Donna, surely. (She was right about this. Donna's mother had studied the Italian Renaissance at university and had named her daughter Donatella in honour of the great sculptor.)

Donna's life had been forever changed in her late teens when she saw Dominic O'Brien appear on a TV show. He carried the unusual title of World Memory Champion and was using the chat show appearance to demonstrate some of his feats and to promote his latest in a string of books on how to improve your memory. She already had a good memory but was inspired by what she saw and vowed to work her memory into the advanced state that Dominic had shown to be possible.

259

Her prodigious memory helped her pass all the exams the British education system could put in front of her, and to pass them with flying colours, finally achieving a first-class honours degree in History.

Armed with this, she decided to see if the police could put her unique skills to good use, joining via the graduate entry scheme – much to the disappointment of her parents who did not want to replace their dinner party boasting of her excellent academic progress by telling people she now was a policewoman.

She had, not surprisingly, ended up in the records division where her skills were legion. She truly never forgot a face, or seemingly, anything else. In any discussions about the plans to use the recent developments in computer-based facial recognition, someone was always bound to say sooner or later – it may be good, but is it as good as Donna?

Dawn called her and asked for her help. "I've got a set of photos of someone, but no idea who he is, and address details of a company that is mentioned in the database but with no really useful information there," she told her. "And a boss that wants an answer yesterday," she added.

" They always do, don't they," said Donna. "Email me what you've got, and I'll see what I can do."

Even though she knew her friend's skills were remarkable, Dawn was surprised to get a call back only fifteen minutes later. "The guy's name is Quentin Johnstone – although he understandably prefers to be known as Johnny. Vice have investigated him a couple of times because he owns quite a few flats that are used for prostitution – but they've not found him guilty of anything other than financial opportunism. Seems that the toms pay good rent so as not to be bothered, and he don't bother them."

Dawn was always amused at Donna's ready use of police slang and bad English to hide her inherent poshness.

"How did you find that so quickly?" she had to ask.

"I recognised his face and remembered his name," Donna replied. A smile crept across her face. The memory method she had mastered involved the superimposition of an image on a face – an image to help you remember the name. The recommendation was to use as ridiculous an image as possible to plant it more firmly in your memory, so her mental picture of Johnny would always have his long nose covered with a condom –

because condoms were always referred to as 'johnnies' at boarding school.

"Then I just looked him up and filled in the rest. Oh, and that company in Baker Street you sent me information on – now that is really interesting." Dawn prompted her for more. "It's an accountancy firm run by a guy called David Stone – who everyone calls Solly for some unknown reason. We've never been able to pin anything on him – he appears to be as clean as a whistle – but he deals with some of the best-known criminals that you'll ever see outside of an episode of Crimewatch. His speciality is laundering money, and he is an absolute ace at it. We treat his name as something like a royal warrant, but in reverse. If your man is dealing with him, he is certainly up to no good."

Donna promised to send over full information – including a photo of Mr Stone that Dawn had asked for, and their call was prolonged for a few minutes as Dawn fixed a date to buy Donna at least a couple of drinks as a reward.

Dawn added this information to the information she had already acquired on Dragan – Richard had been sharp enough to capture a shot of his car registration, so it had been very easy to get a full set of gen on him, and it was also an interesting little story. This, and the other bits and pieces that came from the surveillance, completed the draft of her report.

That afternoon she was back in Russel's office. She knew he would want a verbal report before a written one.

"What's your take on him?" he asked.

"I think he's ducking and diving, trying to make a fast buck, and mixing with some distinctly dodgy people," Dawn replied. "And I don't know why - since he has a decent job and everything."

"You know you can take the boy out of the East End but you can't always….." Russell interrupted her, and she, in turn, cut him off by saying "Yes, I know. But there's nothing criminal there."

"Are you sure? I can't afford to let anything slip. If something goes wrong and PSD get involved, it could blow up in all our faces."

He was obviously still concerned. Nobody could have risen to his rank without a decent awareness of the damage a bad report from PSD could do to their career.

"I'm as sure as I can be," Dawn did her best to reassure him.

"Alright – but we need to show we did our best. Bring him in for questioning, scare as much shit out of him as you can and then we'll write him up as a person of interest. Agreed?"

Dawn would have suggested the same plan if given a chance. "Seems like a plan. I'll take DC Leech with me for an early morning call tomorrow, and we'll wrap everything up by close of play tomorrow."

Helping with Inquiries

November 2006

Surprise was not a sufficiently strong enough term to describe Mark's reaction to the knock on his door and the presence of two plain-clothes police, one male and one female - the shorter, female officer being clearly the one in charge.

They told him that they would like to interview him at Chelmsford station concerning a number of issues, making sure that he understood that his attendance would be completely voluntary – but he read between the lines that a refusal on his part would not be a good idea.

Mark went up to his bedroom and got dressed – his mind racing all the time. What to wear? Why do they want to see me? Should I contact a solicitor? Hundreds of unanswered questions. Choosing casual clothes – best to feel as comfortable as possible for what is likely to be an ordeal, he made himself calm down and think as rationally as possible.

First, overcome the sense of guilt that everyone feels when confronted by the police. The equivalent of slowing down when you see a police car on the road, even if you are already below the speed limit. Then think! What could it be about? He really could not come up with anything. Just make sure to co-operate as fully as possible. The last thing we want is them getting a search warrant and finding a briefcase in his loft containing over a hundred thousand in cash. That would take some explaining – and that was something he would rather not attempt.

He accompanied them in the back of their car for the half-hour journey to Chelmsford Police Station. He made one attempt to ask what it was all about – but, as expected, was only told that it would all be explained when they got to the station.

At the station, he was shown into an interview room – the dullest, emptiest room imaginable, attractively painted in plain grey and scuffed wherever scuffing was humanly possible. Offered a cup of tea or coffee he wanted to avoid the potentially cruel and unusual punishment of a police station brew and asked for a glass of water. It arrived ten minutes later. A further ten minutes elapsed with no sign of anyone coming to talk to him. He supposed it was all part of the plan – which it was. Eventually, the two people who had earlier turned up on his doorstep entered, the woman carrying a file with an inch of paperwork in it – a file, which he noticed had his name on it.

He was as ready as he could be for any questions, but was still surprised when, having reiterated that he was here voluntarily, cleverly morphing the statement into a statutory reading of his rights, that she began the interview by saying "Mr Reynolds, you are the owner of Flat 13B Mansfield Court London W1U 5EN, am I correct?"

"I'm the leaseholder of that flat, yes"

"We have good reason to believe that this flat is used in the provision of sexual services – are you aware of that?"

"No, I'm not aware of that – but I am not surprised."

"That's interesting, why do you say you are not surprised?"

"Well, I've visited the flat, met the tenant, and seen how it is furnished – so no, I'm not surprised."

"Are you aware that under Section 30 of the Sexual Offences Act of 1956 it is an offence for a man knowingly to live wholly or in part on the earnings of prostitution?"

"No, I'm not aware of that."

"What would you say if I told you that we are considering prosecuting you for this offence?"

"I would be surprised. I've got no influence or control over the actions of the tenant of the property, and while I do make a profit from the rent, after expenses, I would not say that I am really living off the proceeds. "

"Yes, well we'll possibly return to that later".

Mark felt that he had dealt with this issue so far and expected a change of tack – which is what happened. He was shown a photograph and asked, "Do you recognise the person in this photograph?" He recognised it as Johnny Johnstone and told them so.

"And what is your relationship with Mr Johnstone? "

"I bought the flat at Nottingham Court from him."

"And have you had other business dealings with Mr Johnstone?"

"I've discussed buying another flat from him. He owns more than one".

Mark noticed the other policeman write something in his notebook for the first time.

'I guess they didn't know that,' he thought. 'Best if I try not to tell them anything else they don't already know.'

"Yes, Mr Johnstone does indeed have quite the property empire, doesn't he? Will this other flat you are considering buying from him also be used for the provision of prostitution Mr Reynolds"

"I can't answer that."

"But it is another flat in the same part of the city, correct?" she fished.

"Yes."

"Perhaps you might understand that if you were to be the owner of two flats, both of which were used for the provision of sexual services for profit that we might well reconsider the charge of living off immoral earnings." Dawn was hoping to score a significant point with this statement and was surprised that Mark had a comeback.

"I guess that if you charged me as the leaseholder, you would have to charge the freeholder as well?" Mark asked.

Dawn was not ever going to answer a question like that, so she responded by saying "I do not believe that is of any relevance."

"Well, I thought I'd better say it because you said something about me not mentioning something I might later bring up in court. And if you were to charge me, I think I'd certainly bring up the name of the freeholder of the properties. Suggesting that you were charging them with living off immoral earnings should get both of us on the front pages of all the tabloids."

-

When reading the paperwork for his proposed purchase of the second flat from Johnny, Mark had been intrigued to notice that the freeholder of the property was the same anonymous sounding company that also held the freehold for his first property – even though they were two streets away from each other. An internet search had revealed that the company was a management company for one of the major members of the aristocracy. Not surprising since much of central London was owned by various dukedoms and royalty who had owned it for centuries.

He did not know whether the police had also discovered this – possibly not – and he hoped to deflect her by bringing it up, which he succeeded in doing.

She changed tack again – Mark was certain that this constant changing of direction was planned – he needed to be prepared for them to examine many different aspects of his life and had to stay focussed.

Another photo was brought out from the folder, and when he was once again asked, he identified as Dragan, telling them that he remembered the guy's first name, but his last name was rather long and Polish sounding, and he couldn't recall it exactly. (He was risking a lie here. Mark had always had a faultless memory for names, partly it was a natural skill, but it was also a skill that he had actively worked on all his career. Customers are always impressed when you remember their name.)

He wanted to know if the police knew the guy's name – and since he knew next to nothing about Dragan, having only met him the one time, hoped to learn more.

"Would it be Dragan Zawadski by any chance?"

"Yes, I think that was the name."

"And what is your relationship with this man?"

"We co-operated on a property deal a few months ago, and I have met him once since."

He cursed himself inwardly when he noticed that the male policeman wrote something in his notebook for only the second time in the interview. I guess they probably didn't know about that property deal – no reason to suppose they do,' he thought.

He continued trying to multi-task his thought processes – wondering where this information was coming from and what direction they were heading in.

He was asked if he knew anything about Dragan's business interests and kept his replies as brief as possible – saying only that he seemed to be involved in buying and renting property, which is why they had met and briefly talked.

"Would it surprise you to know that Mr Zawadski is heavily involved in the supply of immigrant labour, and is involved in many dubious practices concerning matters of property law and the payment of income taxes?"

"Like I said, I've only met him once and know very little about him."

Another photo emerged from the folder and was placed in front of him. This one he took a few moments to identify, having only met the person once – it was David Stone - and it took a few seconds for the name to come to him. Again, the same questions followed, "What is your relationship with Mister Stone?"

"I don't have one. I met him because I was looking for an accountant to help me with my tax returns, but the services he offers did not match my needs."

"Are you sure that you have no dealings with him?"

"No, none," he answered emphatically and felt a brief pause in the questions – and thought 'So far so good.'

Dawn placed the photos back into her file. "I'd like to talk some more about the property that you own in Nottingham Court."

'Well, I guess that's what we're going to do then' Mark thought to himself but said nothing.

"You stated that you receive rent for this property is that correct?"

"Yes"

"And how often is this rent paid? "

"Monthly"

Dawn had noticed that one of his bank accounts seemed to be dedicated to receipts and payments for the Nottingham Court property, which included a repeated cash deposit of the same amount, but at irregular intervals. So, she continued her line of questioning by asking, "How is the payment made?" Mark was a lot less happy with this line of questioning. He gave a quizzical look to buy some time.

"Is it paid by cheque, by standing order....", she asked by way of a prompt. He wondered if this was heading down the line of them looking for him to own up to having other bank accounts, so he had to answer

"In cash."

"In cash. Hmmm. And how does the tenant deliver the cash to you?"

"I collect it from her."

"You collect it from her – once a month?"

He nodded.

"Now that surprises me. You're a very busy man aren't you Mr Reynolds – and yet you find time to call in every month to collect the money in cash?"

"I'm in London pretty often on business – so it's not a problem to arrange a time for the collection." He began to realise how bad this could be made to look.

"So, you call in on your way to or from a business meeting to collect the rent." She paused for effect.

"And I guess that would normally be during the working day?"

He tried to make his "Yes" sound disinterested but probably failed.

"And the tenant is always at home during the day to pay you. Doesn't that strike you as odd? "

"I guess she fits it around her work – or works from home."

"Works from home – yes, indeed" Dawn managed to convey something between contempt and disgust into this statement.

'No solidarity in the sisterhood, there' thought Mark, but she certainly had managed to make him feel distinctly uncomfortable – which was exactly her aim.

She moved on again – "I'd like to return to the meeting you had with Mr Stone. How did this meeting come about?"

"His details were given to me by someone who knew I was looking for an accountant – and he told me that the guy was really good – so I arranged to meet him, but.." Dawn cut across him

"Yes, you decided not to do business with him. Who was it that gave you his name?"

Mark thought that an answer of 'the guy I sit next to at West Ham home games,' although completely honest, would not sound right, so instead said,

"I'm not sure – must have been someone I bought a house from, I guess".

Mark was skilled in interviewing – in sales situations, not suspected criminal ones - but thought he could usually spot when someone was lying (which customers sometimes did). He was confident that Dawn would be able to spot his own deficiencies in telling the truth. She pushed him a little further with some questions, trying to tie him more closely to David Stone, or to whoever had introduced them but was getting nowhere.

"Returning to the matter of your bank accounts," she changed tack once again and noticed Mark's discomfort.

"Exactly how many bank accounts do you have, Mister Reynolds?" She had seen four and wondered if there were more.

He disappointed her by saying "Four."

"Why do you need so many?"

"I have one for my personal financial matters, one for the houses I buy and sell with Howard Turnbull, one for the houses I buy and sell with Graeme Porter, and one for the rental property in London."

All this she had already worked out, but she moved on to the questions she hoped would turn up something. "I noticed that you opened three of these accounts at about the same time, is that correct?"

"Yes, about a year ago"

"And each of them with a cash deposit of ..." pausing to ostensibly look up the amount in her notes, but really for effect. She knew how much it was, "nine thousand eight hundred pounds. Is that correct?"

"Yes"

"So, you suddenly found yourself with almost thirty thousand pounds of spare cash is that correct?"

"I received a cash sum from a family member and at around the same time, I was also given some information that made me decide to use my windfall as a bet. The odds were five to one and I turned five thousand into thirty thousand." He had rehearsed this lie from the very beginning of the saga, just in case it was ever needed. It came out smoothly and had the desired effect of halting Dawn's line of questioning.

"Is there any possibility that you would be able to confirm who that family member was? Or any details of the bet you placed?"

"I'd rather not," he answered.

She suggested that they have a break for lunch – for indeed it was that time - and she asked her colleague if he could go and get Mark a sandwich from the canteen. Having established that he would accept anything except egg or prawn in his sandwich, DC Leech returned with what was probably the least inspiring cheese sandwich Mark had ever seen in his life. He was left alone for half an hour to eat it and drink the accompanying can of lemonade.

He welcomed the time to think over the unusual events of the morning and to try to analyse where he currently stood in the interview. Some of his sales interview skills were relevant, some not. He tried to keep personal feelings out of it but found it nigh on impossible to do so.

Normally there were three attributes that he found particularly attractive in a woman. Thinness, red hair, and a Scottish accent – but he was granting Detective Sergeant Dawn Mepham a special exemption on all three counts. She was not thin or slim. She was wiry. And the Scottish accent was not a pleasing gentle brogue from the highlands or islands – it was a harsh Glasgow accent that seemed to convert even the most benign of statements into a threat. And she did not have red hair – it was ginger. He didn't like her and was sure the feeling was mutual.

Putting that aside, he had mixed feelings about how the last couple of hours had progressed. He was still unsure of any specific direction the questioning was taking. He was delighted and relieved that there had been no connection to the briefcase or its contents - but felt that he was suspected of involvement in some illicit financial dealings. He also realised that he was on shaky grounds with any questions about Gina and her flat – nothing criminal, but some embarrassing behaviour he was not proud of. He also noted that his decision to no longer deal with David Stone – taken for reasons that could never be divulged - had been a good one. Although nothing had been said about him – that very fact, coupled with his knowledge about David's ability to clean unwanted cash surpluses for his clients meant that he was not surprised that this would be a man in whom law enforcement might be very interested.

Two floors above the room where Mark was eating his sandwich, Dawn and DC Leech were also going over the morning's proceedings. To give herself a break from talking and a chance to eat her lunch, Dawn asked him for his thoughts.

"Hard to see anything criminal going on," was his opening remark. "He's obviously done some dodgy deals. And he's not telling the truth about where the money came from. If he really did place a bet, he'd be happy to boast about which bookie he'd done, and how he did it. That thirty grand came from somewhere he ain't gonna tell us about, that's for sure. But let's remember, he's in the building trade after all – it would almost be more suspicious if he wasn't pocketing some cash somewhere."

Dawn had to agree with his summary.

"And there's certainly something off about that flat in London - and he certainly seems to mix with some very iffy individuals. But I'm not sure if he's much more than just a jack the lad", he finished his summary.

"Or perhaps only an aspiring Jack the lad," Dawn added. "I mean he's got a proper job and everything – what on earth is he doing with all these low-lifes?"

"I guess you can take the boy out of the East End, but …"

"Yeh, yeh, yeh" Dawn interrupted. She did not feel able to fully confide in him that the real reason Mark had consumed so much of their time was something of a political issue for her boss to be seen to be doing something. "Any potential lines of enquiry you think we could usefully pursue after lunch?" she asked him.

"I can see how he has dealings with Johnny Johnstone. Those hookers probably pay top dollar for their apartments for a landlord who's prepared to keep schtum – and cash is always king as they say. Just wondered how he came to know him in the first place – and what does he do with that cash."

"Good thoughts," she said. "Let's chase them down with him, and then we can send him home and get on with some real work – what do you say?"

Half an hour later they were back with Mark and questioned him for a further hour. Dawn summed up what they had learned, managing to use language that portrayed everything in the worst possible light. She asked him a few more questions about his dealings – past, present, and future – and left him feeling that he was generally under suspicion for living off immoral earnings and failing to disclose his income fully to the authorities.

By mid-afternoon, they told him that they had no further questions and would arrange for a car to take him home. He politely refused their offer – inventing a wish to do some shopping in Chelmsford and volunteering to take a taxi home. 'Better not to have the neighbours see me being deposited from a police car', he thought, 'and I could do with a bit of fresh air - or the closest thing possible in the middle of Chelmsford - to clear my head.'

It was on his way home that he first thought about Debbie. Initially, there was a rush of guilt that she had not entered his thoughts for the whole day – but he let himself off that hook when he considered all the things he had had to think about and answer. But what would she think? He would have to tell her – she would be certain to find out anyway, and best if it came first from him. Of one thing he was certain – telling her was not going to be a pleasant experience.

One Mill – Tops
November 2006

James knew he should have guessed something was wrong when his boss, Alex, invited him to lunch to discuss his plans. Alex never did lunch unless it was at the request of a client, and a pretty important one at that. If someone else hadn't already coined the phrase 'lunch is for wimps', there's every chance that Alex would have done.

Nonetheless, he enjoyed a very pleasant meal, telling Alex as much as he thought sensible about what he had been up to whilst sorting out his father's business, and of course, how much he was looking forward to getting back to full-time employment at Libera.

This last part was not totally true. James did have a desire to climb one more rung up the ladder if he could. The next level was what some private equity firms called Vice President and others referred to as Partner. In Libera, the term used was Associate.

An Associate was given overall responsibility for one or more deals. He was 'the lead' as it was termed. He would still work on a small number of other deals where he would be a team member, but he would carry ultimate responsibility and be the main client interface for his deals. On those deals, he would be able to take a larger share of the profits made, and they could be substantial.

Being the lead on a successful deal would provide a bonus that would be enough to secure his lifestyle forever. A second successful deal would create the possibility of buying a new home. One with a swimming pool perhaps, or a bit of land – maybe a couple of horses for Bethany and her friends, and maybe even her mother, to ride. A third successful deal – well maybe a holiday home somewhere? But that was a long way off. First, he had to get back to work, and then…

But a part of James also knew that he had enjoyed some aspects of the last few months. The two days working for Libera gave him enough money for his current lifestyle, and the unique hands-on experience he had

273

enjoyed while running his father's business had given him a taste for running his own business. 'Wouldn't it be nice to see if I could run a real business – and make decisions that would have an impact on real people,' he thought.

"You know I must confess that I was not sure that this arrangement we made between us last year was going to work out," Alex said. "And yet it has done. Surprisingly well, in fact. We had to bring forward a couple of the younger chaps a bit sooner than we might otherwise have done, and I must say they performed rather well".

One thing that James hated about his boss was the way he put on an exaggerated English accent. Alex had the benefit of having been half English and half American both by parentage and upbringing, and he could relate exceptionally well to either nationality. No doubt it had contributed to his success. But when he exaggerated one side too much, it aggravated James. He realised he must not let this influence him – he had to pay attention to where Alex was heading. At present, the direction did not seem too much to his liking.

"You know one thing these younger chaps have is an amazing affinity for new technology. Of course, the rest of us do our best, but they've been brought up with it – so it always seems to come so much more naturally to them, don't you think?"

"Yes," replied James, still wondering where this was going.

"This always has been a young man's game. So difficult when you're nearer fifty than forty, like you and me – so hard to keep up with the pace."

"But there is no substitute for experience is there?" James said, trying to alter the direction of the conversation.

"Exactly," Alex replied, "and that's why it's so valuable to have your input. It would be a real shame to lose that. But I wonder what you would think about a continuation of your current arrangement. It would suit the firm well, but what about you?"

"Well, I had thought that I would get back to my previous role. Pick up the ball and try to run with it, so to speak." Mark knew he had to be careful to speak in tune with his boss, not parody him.

"That could be a little difficult. You see we have brought these new chaps forward – very hard to push them back again. Of course, if you really wanted to get back to a full-time position, I'm sure there are plenty of other firms who would be able to offer it. And we would give you an exceptional recommendation of course."

James understood just how hollow this promise was. Everything that his boss had said was true, but in an incestuous industry like theirs, the word would be out – younger men had passed him by, and he was no longer a first-team player at Libera. He would no longer command top dollar at any other firm.

"I appreciate that" was what he actually said, accurately summing up his thoughts.

He knew that now was his time to negotiate the terms being offered to him as a part-time employee – because that was what was happening, right in front of his face. Later he could compare those terms with the best offer from a rival.

"If I did er… continue with my present arrangement, there would have to be a proper agreement drawn up."

"Of course, after all, you would want to know you had some security, and we would want to know that you weren't going to sell your services to one of our competitors in your ah free time"

"Naturally. If I was to continue the current arrangement, I would want to find something to fill the additional time, and my recent involvement with a much smaller business has opened my eyes to certain possibilities in that area. One thing I do know is that there is a common issue that these small firms face, and it's one that I would need to address if I were to get involved." He paused to check that he was being listened to. Since it appeared that James was talking about accepting his proposal, Alex was all ears.

"One of the issues they all face is a lack of access to capital. It's quite interesting how many of the problems of small businesses can be traced back to this one issue."

Alex nodded wise assent to this summary.

"So, what I believe Libera could do to assist me in this transition would be to make some capital available to me – on a repayment basis of course.

Nothing too huge, certainly one mill - tops. Being able to borrow a sum like that and make repayments at base rate instead of commercial interest rates – well that would enable me to fulfil a very valuable role in any business which I choose to become involved with."

A million pounds was a lot of money to a small business or any normal individual. But James knew that it was the basic unit of counting at an organisation like Libera. Only there could you talk dismissively of 'only a mill' to refer to such a sum. And he could see Alex was showing signs of accepting the bait.

"If we were able to reach a full agreement, I believe something of that nature could be included," was the long-winded way that he got a positive answer to his proposal.

"Of course, I would have to discuss it with my wife before absolutely committing - this would be a bit of a change of lifestyle, you understand."

His boss understood precisely. He thought there was no way that James would be discussing it with his wife, none of them ever truly discussed their business with their wives. But he thought that James deserved a chance to find out what competitors might offer, which is what he expected James to do. They agreed to meet again in two days to finalise the matter.

One Small Parcel Each
November 2006

Of course, the relationship between Mark and Debbie ended that evening.

They had planned an evening out together – their first for a couple of weeks since they had both been so busy recently. But Mark decided that Debbie should be informed of the events of the day – namely his spell in Chelmsford Police Station – as soon as possible. He also thought, quite rightly as it turned out, once she was aware of what had happened, she might not want to spend any more time with him.

He called her and told her as carefully and clearly as he could, just what had happened that day. After overcoming her initial shock, she gave him his second detailed questioning of the day. Who had interviewed him? Did they say why? What did they ask him? Why? What did he tell them? Why? Always why.

He did his best to let her know everything that happened. He tried to make sure she understood that he had done nothing wrong, but was not sure that this was achievable, her being a police officer and everything.

She ended the call by telling him that she would be speaking to Dawn immediately and would phone him back.

Dawn took the call from Debbie – she was expecting it and knew that she couldn't refuse it, despite what her boss had told her about confidentiality. Life for a woman in the police was hard enough – she owed her as much of an explanation as she could give. So, she let Debbie know that as a result of Debbie's original interview with PSD, Mark's name had come up. PSD had recommended that he be looked into, and she had drawn the short straw and been told to investigate him. She had to let Debbie know that there was no further action planned but that owing to some unresolved matters, Mark had been recorded as a person of interest.

"A person of fucking interest?" Debbie exploded. "Despite there being absolutely nothing on him! Why on earth?"

Dawn took one step across the line and told her, "Debbie. Once PSD has flagged him up, nobody is going to give him the all-clear. Just in case anything ever showed up, they'd be crucified if they'd let him off."

Despite her anger, Debbie appreciated that even the little that Dawn had told her was probably more than she should have. She thanked her for her openness and reassured her that 'this call has never happened.' But as they ended the call, they both knew without needing to state it, that there was absolutely no way that a serving police officer could continue a relationship with someone who had been flagged on the system in this way.

Debbie spent the next hour going through a range of emotions. Anger, grief, and self-pity being the chief ones. Her anger was directed at Mark for his pursuit of money and the shady characters he had been drawn into dealing with; at herself for choosing a police career which produced conflicts in her personal life that were so singularly unfair; at the bloody ignorant farmer who'd raised the baseless complaint against her; at the over-zealous PSD swine who'd investigated Mark in the first place; and at life, the universe, and everything in general.

She also went through many of the seven stages of grief in rapid succession. Shock and denial were certainly there, as were pain, guilt, and the start of depression. She thought it highly unlikely that acceptance and hope would show up for a long while yet.

After an hour or so she calmed down a little, called him back, and let him know it was over. Surprisingly, that was easier than expected. He had had more time to process the day's events and was certain that she would be ending their relationship – it was either that or leave the police - and even Mark's self-confidence did not have him placing himself above her career in Debbie's list of priorities.

It was over. As simple as that. No Christmas together. No staying in touch as just friends, nothing. And the way they had been living, dating in the traditional manner and alternating who stayed overnight at who's place, meant that when it came to returning each other's possessions there were so few that they could do it all in one small parcel each.

They agreed that it was a sad end to what had been a bloody good relationship.

The Five Monkeys Experiment
November 2006

Training courses on man-management, books on the same subject, and many an internet chat group have perpetuated a story that illustrates how corporate culture can develop areas of negativity. The story has arisen in many guises and is often named 'The Five Monkeys Experiment,' although it is highly unlikely that the experiment has truly ever been performed. A typical example of the urban myth would go something like this:

A researcher puts five monkeys in a cage. Inside the cage, there is a bunch of bananas hanging from a string, with a ladder leading to the bananas. When the first monkey goes for the bananas, the researcher sprays all five monkeys with freezing water for five minutes.

Sometime later, when a second monkey inevitably tries to go for the bananas, the researcher once again sprays all five monkeys with cold water for five minutes. The researcher then puts the hose away and never touches it again. But, when a third monkey tries to go for the bananas, the other four attack him to prevent him from climbing that ladder. They are afraid of the punishment that may come.

Then, the researcher replaces one of the monkeys with a new monkey who was not part of the original experiment and was never sprayed with water. And, as soon as he touches the ladder to go for the bananas, the other four monkeys attack him to keep him from doing so. If he tries again, they attack him again. Thus, the new monkey learns not to go after the bananas because he will get attacked if he does.

*The researcher replaces a second monkey with another new monkey. When this monkey goes for the bananas, the other four attack him, **including the new monkey who was never sprayed with water**. The researcher then continues to replace all the monkeys one at a time, until all five of the original monkeys have been removed from the cage. Each time the newcomer goes for the bananas, the others attack, even when they, as new monkeys, have never received punishment for going after the* *bananas. And thus, the new monkeys, who have never been sprayed with cold water, learn not to go after the temptation of the bananas.*

The researchers hypothesize that, if they were to ask the monkeys why they do not go for the bananas, they'd answer "because that's the way it's always been done around here".

This behaviour pattern exists in many large organisations. In the case of Smith and Raiter, the strongest evidence of it could be found in restrictions on employee activity embedded in the terms and conditions of employment contracts.

To understand the origin of this instance – the original spraying of freezing water, to follow the analogy – you would have to go back to the late nineteen forties.

Immediately after the second world war, Smith & Raiter, in line with all other American companies, and the whole of society, was undergoing a period of rapid change. The company was transferring from wartime production which was heavily aligned with the needs of the military, to peacetime work, which was consumer-driven. The demands of the military were reduced drastically and suddenly; the economy, overcoming the challenge of thousands of returning GIs looking to resume their roles in the workplace, was booming; and, in more local news, the reins of S&R were being transferred to a new generation. Both the company's founders were retiring and handing over to Edgar and Thomas, their respective oldest sons.

Edgar Smith and Thomas Raiter held very different opinions about the correct way to develop the company. The former thought the best path to steer was towards scientific and engineering excellence – producing high-end tools for the engineering market - while the latter wanted to develop more mass market, consumer-driven products. They tried to compromise for a couple of years, but the division of the company's resources and energies over the two different disciplines held it back. The split finally came in 1947 after a board meeting descended into an acrimonious row between the two men.

Edgar left the company and set up a separate organisation. Its existence and development threatened the very future of S&R, and for a few years, it was touch and go as to whether the original company would survive at all. What made matters even worse was that Edgar had been planning his departure for over eighteen months. He had been working evenings and weekends (and limited days off) establishing his new company, and, upon quitting S&R, was able to hit the floor running.

As S&R got back on its feet, the board of directors wanted to make sure that the situation they had so narrowly survived could never happen again, and so all employee contracts were rewritten to include a clear and concise clause forbidding the employee to take up any form of gainful employment outside the company. All employees were forced to sign the contract and were made aware that infringing this clause would result in instant dismissal.

-

Julie was certainly aware of the existence of this clause, and the importance bestowed upon it by the US parent company, although she was probably not aware of the full reasoning behind it. So, when she discovered that Mark had infringed this most golden of all golden rules, she decided to wait for Geoff to complete the interviews for the Sales Manager role, and to speak to him immediately afterwards to let him know before he had time to fully make his decision or implement any actions resulting from that decision.

Knowing that Malcolm's interview was due to start at three o'clock, she waited until a quarter past before telephoning Geoff. As expected, he had diverted his calls to his secretary, and Julie asked her to pass him a note that she needed to speak to him urgently - as soon as he was available.

The End
November 2006

Mark was surprised when he received the call from Geoff first thing in the morning - and was even more surprised when he entered Geoff's office a few minutes later as requested, to find Julie Medcraft sitting in one of Geoff's visitors' chairs. Geoff gestured for him to sit down, and immediately let him know that there was bad news.

"I guess I wasn't successful in the interview?" Mark asked.

"I'm afraid it's a bit worse than that" Geoff replied. "You signed a contract of employment when you joined, didn't you?"

Mark gave a "Yes" slowly in response.

"Well, that contract strictly forbids you to have gainful or remunerative employment with any organisation or to be a director or officer of any commercial enterprise," he continued – quoting the relevant section of the employment contract.

Mark was puzzled but decided to say nothing yet.

"Well, it has been brought to my attention that you hold a position as director for a company called Ashtrad Ltd. and that that company is a commercial organisation which has filed a set of accounts."

Suddenly the penny dropped.

-

Harold Rogerson of Rogerson and Partners, a firm of accountants based in Rayleigh, Essex had been recommended to him as the ideal person to handle his income tax returns, in the light of the growing complexity of his affairs. The firm's eponymous principle was everything Mark had been looking for in an accountant. Harold was an ex-tax inspector – a gamekeeper turned poacher– and was possibly the last man in England not employed in education to wear a tweed jacket to work every day. On entering his office, you felt the need to set your watch back twenty years.

In their first meeting he firmly established his credentials and let Mark know in no uncertain terms that he saw it as his responsibility that HMRC was paid all the tax for which he was liable - but only the amount for which he was liable – and that he would impose upon Mark a series of tasks aimed solely at minimising his tax burden.

Among the actions listed, Harold had said "We must get you incorporated, young man." Mark remembered his quip of "Does that hurt?" and the complete indifference that had been shown to his joke. He thought that Harold had probably had an operation for a sense of humour bypass, but in all other respects, liked what he saw and heard.

Harold had offered to register a company and, at Mark's request, had purchased an off-the-shelf company (since its name was Ashtrad, Mark had assumed it was on the top of an alphabetic list somewhere.) Harold had gone on to say that there needed to be one other director and Mark had asked his sister to fulfil the role. He had originally suggested Mark named his wife as the other director, but after the raging success of his earlier funny response, Mark had decided to forego the excellent feed for a marital joke and just say, "I'm not married, I'll ask my sister."

Harold had explained that Mark's properties should be owned by the company (Ashtrad) and all costs and incomes deriving from them should go into its accounts. This would allow Mark more flexibility of when to draw his income – in the form of dividends – and thereby reduce his tax liability. And so there it was. They had formed the company and Harold had duly filed the appropriate reports.

Mark had completely forgotten about this – in truth, he didn't realise that the arrangement would affect his employment in any way. He did not know about the five monkeys.

-

"This breach of contract is something that we regard as very serious at Smith and Raiter, and I am afraid that we need to terminate your employment," were Geoff's final words on the matter.

Mark was shocked – but the resolve that Geoff showed, the obvious seriousness with which he dealt with the situation, and the presence of the HR manager in the room made him realise that resistance would be futile.

Julie spoke for the first time, "It's a clear case of breach of contract, and the company has every right to insist on immediate termination of your employment – however, under the circumstances, we will accept your resignation, and allow you one month of gardening leave on full pay – if you are prepared to agree."

Mark knew that this was the best offer he was likely to receive and accepted it. Julie placed two copies of a resignation letter on the desk between them. 'She must have been pretty sure I'd accept her offer' Mark thought.

"If you could sign these, we can bring everything to a close right now," Julie offered.

Of course, he signed. She thanked him and took one copy with her as she left the room. She was now one hundred per cent sure that neither of the men knew anything about her and Malcolm, or she would never have got away with what had just happened.

Geoff expressed his regrets and told Mark that he would need to remove any possessions from his car and hand over the keys – the company would pay for a taxi to take him home. He would have to clear his desk immediately.

Mark went down to the car park and removed the CDs, map books, and tissues from the car. He placed them on his desk, next to a large cardboard box that had mysteriously appeared while he was absent. Ironically. there were also two large boxes beside his desk containing S&R merchandise ordered a couple of weeks previously. He needed the help of the security guard to carry his briefcase and all the boxes to the waiting taxi.

'My own personal security guard - they think of everything, don't they?' Mark thought to himself.

The journey to his home was quickly completed – there being no commuter traffic in mid-morning. The taxi driver helped him carry his boxes into the house and accepted a tip. There had been no time to think about what had happened, much less to plan his next step.

'Plenty of time for that in the next few weeks,' he thought, carrying the boxes to the dining room.

He liked to think of himself as a 'glass-half-full' guy and tried to focus on the opportunity this would give him to think about his future career. To plan that career in the light of his changed financial circumstances and to progress the projects he had embarked on since finding the briefcase.

'After all,' he thought to himself, 'you're a football fan. And what does a football fan always say when his team gets knocked out of the cup? Now we can concentrate on the league! So now I can concentrate on my property business for a short time.'

But first, there was something that he had to do which related to an even older saying. Having just proverbially fallen off his bike, he needed to get back on as soon as possible. He had lost jobs before and knew the importance of starting the search for a new one as quickly as possible, and so went into his dining room to make a few calls.

The first two were to recruitment agencies that he had used in the past. He updated them on his current situation and told them he would send an up-to-date CV the next day. They each promised to get back to him shortly with details of any suitable opportunities.

His third and final call was to his old friend and ex-employer, Eddie. Mark was surprised – and a little disappointed – to hear of Eddie's imminent retirement. That first visit to Reade's and probable first sale, whatever his new role would be, was going to be more difficult. But he was pleasantly surprised when Eddie invited him to lunch the following day and told him that there was a possible opportunity that he would like to discuss.

A time was agreed, and Mark put it in his diary.

Shortly after completing the call with Eddie, he was surprised to hear his front doorbell ring. Not expecting any callers, he headed to the door dreading the inevitable salesman or religious zealot he anticipated meeting.

He opened the front door to be greeted by the taxi driver who had brought him home earlier, standing there holding up Mark's briefcase. "You left this in the back of my car," he said. "The next passenger told me so I thought I'd better bring it to you when I'd dropped him off."

"Oh thanks," said Mark and, after a brief pause, continued, "you know, mate, in the last couple of months I've been in hospital, I've been interviewed by the police, I've lost my girlfriend and I've lost my job. All because I *found* a briefcase. God only knows what string of disasters might befall me if I went and *lost* a fucking briefcase!"

The Other End
December 2006

As she walked into the house, Sarah was surprised to find James singing along to the radio while preparing the evening meal. It was no surprise to find him cooking dinner. Part of their new routine since he sold his father's business was that he would prepare the meal on Monday, Tuesday, and Wednesday when he was at home. And he usually did a pretty good job – concocting some mixture of vegetables, white meat or fish, and pasta to produce a dish that satisfied both adult taste buds and teenage appetites, which was no mean feat. What she found odd was that he was singing. He never did that. This must mean he's had some good news she thought – and hoped.

It was not that she did not enjoy the increased time they were able to spend together now that he was able to start his evening at home at the more reasonable hour that most families enjoyed – which had never been possible during his time of full-time employment with Libera. But for most of their married life, she had grown accustomed to having the house to herself. She couldn't rationalise the way she so hated him asking her where she was going when she went out of the house. But hate it she did.

She had been uneasy from the moment he arrived home to discuss his lunch meeting with his boss and the surprising news that Libera wanted him to continue in a part-time role. She had expected him to resume the old routine, and so she had been more than a little surprised when he told her of his plans to accept the offer and look to buy a business to run on a three-day-week basis.

Of course, he had phrased everything in the right way – letting her be part of the decision-making process, but she could plainly see that he knew what he wanted. Having made sure that there was no need for her to make any changes to her lifestyle – she was prepared to, if necessary, she just wanted to be warned if it was going to be needed - she gave her approval to his plans.

But she had not anticipated the annoyance of him being around the house and asking where she was going when she went out.

"How did your meeting go?" he called out to her.

"Well enough," she replied, knowing full well that he almost certainly had no idea which meeting she had been to. He never would, she knew.

"You're sounding chirpy," she said. "Have you had some good news?"

"As a matter of fact, I have," he replied. "I think I've found the business I want to buy."

"What kind of business is it?" she asked.

"A really interesting one. It's a small company that the owner has built up over the years, and has grown to the point where it has a few outlets. It's the right size, and now he wants to retire. He's got no kids or anyone else to pass it on to, so he wants to sell. And it's just at the right price."

"And you can run it on three days a week?"

"Yes, that's the good bit. He's been preparing for retirement, so he's only been working three days a week – and says the business has run well on that basis for three months now. Of course, I'll be a bit less hands-on than he has been. But there's scope for improvement. He's got no online presence at all, and even builders are starting to use the internet now. And he has a good customer base but doesn't do anything to maximise it. No customer loyalty programme or anything. I think we can make a lot of progress there."

"Who's we?" she asked, fearing for a moment that he was getting her involved.

"Raheem and me. He's not happy where he is, I know. They've kept their side of the bargain and kept him on at the club, but there's not enough for him to do there. He's easily bored and I'm sure he'll join me if I ask."

"Sounds great – but what type of business is it?"

He thought he'd explained everything about the business and gave a quizzical look in response to this question.

"Well," she continued, "first I got used to telling people that you worked in the city, dealing with company takeovers and such. Then I got used to telling everyone that you worked part-time in the city and part-time trying to rescue your parents' business. And if they asked about what line of business it was, I'd say it was hospitality…"

"Yes, there was plenty of hospitality in dad's business, that's for sure," he interrupted with a smile.

"So now I need to know what line of business I tell them you're in."

"Oh, I understand. Yes. It's a builder's merchant and DIY business. Four branches in Essex and Hertfordshire. Name of Reede's. I should be able to finalise everything with the owner, Eddie Reede within the next few days and take over from the first of January.

"But darling..," she replied, and James was immediately wary. Nothing good ever came after she had called him 'darling'.

"You don't know anything about Do-It-Yourself. You have always hired someone to do it for you."

"Yes, of course, I'll have to recruit or promote someone to run the day-to-day business. But Eddie has even told me he might know just the right person. It's someone who used to work for him and has quite a good knowledge of the business. Name's Mark Reynolds. He's even arranged for me to meet him tomorrow for lunch. Should be an interesting meeting."

A word from the author
January 2022

My thanks go to my wife for leaving me alone to write this, to my proof-readers, Cliff Antill and Barbara Primrose (who also helped with promotion), and to my sister, Susan Folkard, for her input on police procedures and terminology.

I will continue the promise of donating half the profits from this book to homeless charities, as I did with my first book, a memoire entitled "An Accidental Salesman".

If you want to know more – please visit my Author Page on Amazon:

https://www.amazon.co.uk/Ian-Cummins/e/B08LSRKY1Z?ref=sr_ntt_srch_lnk_2&qid=1642779504&sr=8-2

You can also reach me on Twitter @Accidental_Ian